Black Rock Bay

Roger Naylor

Writers Club Press
San Jose · New York · Lincoln · Shanghai

Dedication

To all those who could have, perhaps should have quit…but didn't.

Acknowledgements

My sincere gratitude goes to my compadres in the Thursday Night Writers, Don, Dan, Pat, Bud, Jerry, and Marilyn. They saw what I didn't see, heard what I didn't hear, and felt what I didn't feel. And, of course, my two lovers, my Jeanne and my Buffy. Thanks to Jeanne for all her input and patience. Thanks to Buffy for diligently avoiding the keyboard as he checked the monitor and dusted my face with his tail.

Prologue

"All rise," said the small, gray-haired figure, gesturing with both hands from the elevated pulpit.

Hardly a sound threatened the sanctity in the immense hall of the Church of the Rock as one hundred young men rose as one from their pews. Their hardened athletic bodies, their intense self-discipline, and their finely-tuned coordination as a group combined to effect the movement so quietly that only the hushed brushing of their clothing could be heard.

"May the world hear God as He speaks through us," said the religious leader, with cultured resonance. "Amen." He paused and surveyed the group. Not one eye blinked; not one throat coughed; not one body moved. It was as though their very breathing had stopped.

"To you, the members of Company C, I extend my congratulations," he continued. "In a few short months, you have transformed yourselves from the lowest level of the helpless to the exalted position you now hold with Almighty God. You have rejuvenated the bodies of God and passed His physical test. You have revitalized your minds and hearts as you have completed your religious studies. And you have proven your dedication to God through your stellar performance in the work place. You are now poised, prepared, and certified to become loyal members of God's militia, His Christian soldiers—the Minutemen."

The leader paused, as though to gather momentum for the next segment, and then looked up again at his audience. The sound of his turning page nearly echoed through the sanctuary.

"You have been offered the opportunity to lead God's charge against the evil in our world. If you accept the challenge, you will face times of extreme discomfort, pain, and anguish…along with the ultimate joy of bringing God's world closer to Him. If there are any among you who find yourselves unable to make your pledge at this time, please step forward and make your exit through the portal on my right." He scanned the group from front to back. Not one pair of eyes glanced aside in search of movement.

"Gentlemen—your pledge."

One hundred male voices came together in unison, the sheer power of their voices seemingly energized by the depth of their commitment.

"Recognizing that the citizens of the United States of America have voted themselves into a condition of slavery by extending trust to those who are untrustworthy and by permitting those who would lead us to choose the path of self-serving corruption, renouncing by their very actions their commitment to the electorate, I hereby pledge myself to the cause of the Minutemen, of Colony IV, and of the Thirteen Colonies of America.

"Should the deterioration of our once great nation lead to anarchy or armed conflict, I swear that I will uphold this pledge. Further, it is my charge to prepare myself for survival in all circumstances, to stand ready to sacrifice myself for the success of my mission, and to faithfully execute the commands of my leaders. This do I solemnly pledge to my God and to my country in the name of Liberty."

Contents

Chapter 1

Hudson Wade Bryant III rolled his nude, muscular frame over to the edge of the kingsize bed, grabbed the pillow and stuffed it over his head. But the persistent telephone penetrated like the air horn of a semi truck. He squeezed the pillow against his ear.

"Damn it!" He opened his eyes, hurled the pillow at the nearest wall, and reached for the cordless unit on the night stand. Driven by an old habit, determined to face what came with his feet on the floor, he swung out of bed as he pulled the phone to his ear. "Bryant," he mumbled angrily, as he shuffled toward the huge window that overlooked the diamond-studded morning Pacific from his home in Corona del Mar, California.

"Hud, this is Gibby Gunderson. Hope I didn't wake you," a tenor voice said.

Hud frowned and glanced back at the bed. Where there should have been the curvaceous body of…he couldn't recall the name…he saw only a small piece of yellow note paper. Hud angled his six-foot, three-inch, two hundred-pound body around the bed.

"But you did wake me," he grumbled. "What's up?" He snatched up the note and returned to his favorite window.

"They killed him, Hud. They killed our dog!" Gunderson shouted. Then, suddenly subdued, he went on, "Herman's…gone. All this other crap they been pulling…and now…he's gone, Hud." His final words bore the twist of a question.

"Ohhh, Gib, no…." Hud felt a chill run through his body. Then a lump gathered in his throat, and finally, his body went numb, almost like the time when….He glanced at the calendar in the adjacent den. Three years—three years to the day since half of him died, since his Ellie lost her battle with cancer. He felt the tears well up in his eyes, and he recognized the pit he was about to slide into. Taking a deep breath and exhaling slowly, he willed himself past the wall that continually rose up, blocking him from the present as well as the future. But three years to the day? It was almost as though Gibby's tragedy portended something even more ominous.

"What happened, Gib?" Hud asked. "Who's they?" Hud could see the stout old woodsman, his red and black plaid shirt contrasting with the white hair and neatly trimmed beard that wrapped around a weathered, leathery face with squinting eyes. Typically, when old Gibby made calls he sat with his feet propped up on the kitchen table, the phone in one hand and his oversized mug of powerful, black coffee in the other. Gibby Gunderson, always the calm, self-assured old Norskie, more than able to handle his own problems and more than content to let others handle theirs. Over twelve years, their relationship had grown close, but the news, along with the tremor in the older man's voice, told Hud this was a Gibby he didn't know.

"I can't prove it, but it's them Bible Bashers across the bay," Gib said. "Herman heard noises down by the dock last night, so I let him out. They…beat him and then…slit his throat, Hud." The old woodsman's voice cracked. Hud could hear him blowing his nose.

He thought of Herman, Gibby's loyal labrador-shepherd mix, the constant companion who had reluctantly shared his master with a wife, Sarah. Herman had bonded so closely that he could read Gibby's mind. They had fished, hunted...they did everything together. Herman had carried out commands before they were given. A single tear trailed down each side of Hud's nose.

"....and then," Gibby went on, "they stole the depthfinder off your new walleye boat, Hud, and then they punched a big hole in her. Been other things, too....I ain't gonna tell you all of it over the phone. I'll sound like a goddamned crybaby. But I'll tell you this much. I got the Winchester and the shotgun hanging by the kitchen door—and they're loaded."

"Whoa, Gib! Slow down, old Buddy. You've got a right to keep the weapons loaded, and it sounds like you have good cause, too. But you'd better keep cool. If something else happens and you feel pissed, you'd better leave the gun right there on the pegs. You're liable to kill someone without just cause, maybe even kill some innocent person. You got that?"

"Ya, I got that," Gib answered slowly. "Guess that's really why I called. I get along with most all the animals. Shit, the bears and I use first names. But these goddamned two-legged wolves—new game for me, Hud, and I'm scared I'm gonna do something I'll be sorry for."

"I don't know what you're up against," Hud said, "but you're a tough, old dude. The only thing I'm worried about is just that—you might do something foolish. Now listen, give me—"

"Hud, I need your help. Don't guess I've ever asked anybody for help before. How about flying back here early? Get in on the walleye opener." The old Norwegian's voice gained in pitch and tempo until the syllables became rapid-fire bursts, "I'll get your cabin all ready for you, get the water turned on, even lay in a hefty pile of firewood. If you want to fly the Piper in, the airstrip's about dried out now. I can pick you up at International Falls if you don't want to try the strip yet—"

"Gibby! Gibby! Cool it, my friend." Hud said. "Give me a day or so to get the businesses set, and I'll head out. It'll take me two long days to get there. Go run your truck down the strip, will you? Check it for soft spots and gopher holes. I'll call you when I leave, and again when I get to Fargo. Meanwhile, you look after yourself—don't lose it, okay?"

"Thanks, Hud....Wasn't an easy call to make," Gib said. "And Hud? Sorry about what them assholes did to your new boat."

"The boat doesn't matter, Gib. You matter, Sarah matters...and Herman matters. You keep control of yourself, Old Buddy. And give Sarah a hug for me."

As Hud placed the phone back in its cradle, he felt tightness throughout his body. Sorrow and anger pulled at him, as though having a tug-of-war on the one strand of his emotions that he had thought was still intact. He opened a clenched fist, smoothed the crumpled note, and turned his attention to the flawless, feminine handwriting on the yellow paper:

Hud,
   Thanks for a wonderful night. Would like to have stayed but work calls. Today's Friday. Call me and we can continue this— for the whole weekend.

                                                    Your Kristi

Oh yeah...Kristi...he thought, recalling the brunette who might have been attractive sans makeup. *Another* one. Three dates and she'll be suggesting she move in with me. He scrunched his latest attempt at happiness into a ball and tossed it into the wastebasket.

In the bathroom, he splashed cold water on his face, dried himself, and then studied the tanned stranger who looked back at him from the mirror. The face was handsome, they all said, with deep brown eyes and crinkles of character in all the right places, especially around the eyes. His short, wavy black hair seemed to fall in place, looking quite natural when combed and almost as neat when uncombed. But at his best, the gray at the temples gave away his thirty-nine years. And the man who stared at him was not at his best.

"Stupid dummy," he said to the stranger. "Don't know what you're looking for, but you ought to know by now, you're not going to find it in the bottle or the bedroom. If you can't help yourself, go see if you can help someone else." He slipped into his workout clothes, headed down the hallway to his small weight room, and attacked the equipment with a vengeance.

Chapter 2

Brother Vance paused in the doorway of the darkened meeting room, its cedar-paneled walls and its glossy hardwood floor highlighted by the flickering of a smoldering fireplace. As he often did, he had timed his arrival to be early for the upcoming meeting. He needed the dark privacy to think his way through issues to be faced—to crystallize his plan. He could afford no mistakes, no surprises, a lesson his abusive father had taught him well. Pushing the black memories away, he glided through the shadows, with the practice of one whose life had depended upon stealth, to the large picture window that faced southwest overlooking Black Rock Bay. The sun had set and darkness had smothered the details, leaving only the silhouette of the forest on the opposite shore eerily outlined against the nighttime sky.

To his left he saw reflections on the water from the yard lights of the Black Rock Resort and the neighbor beyond, that stubborn old Gunderson fellow. He felt a familiar tension surge through him, constricting his well-toned, athletic body. Though unaccustomed to failure, he had to admit to himself that his efforts at diplomacy had failed. Kimberly Farber, the young woman who owned the Black Rock Resort, and her next door neighbor, Gilbert Gunderson, seemed immovable. "You might call yourselves a church," Gunderson had said, "but you're trying to *steal* our property. We'll both go straight to hell before we'll ever see *that* happen."

Vance propped his right elbow on the left arm that was folded across his midsection, and in his typical posture of contemplation, he cupped his jaw in his right hand, curling the index finger across his thick black mustache. At fifty-one, he sported a thick crop of stringy black hair that curled over his collar in back. His swarthy complexion was unimproved by the cluster of pockmarks on each cheek and the vivid scar that trailed three inches upward from the right corner of his mustache. His eyes were black, intense, and void of expression. He knew they gave others the impression that he could see deep inside them, read their thoughts, and predict their every move. He was comfortable with that.

As he stared at the reflections, he recalled his series of meetings with Kimberly Farber and Gunderson. With the acquisition of their properties, the Church of the Rock would have secured not only the entire two-square-mile peninsula, but also an additional two thousand feet of shoreline on the bay side and the accompanying land out to the road. It would completely isolate the church property and give them total control of the peninsula and the bay.

His attempts to charm the two neighbors into a quick sale had failed for two reasons. He was no charmer, and he had underestimated their perseverance. In a few minutes he would meet with Father Jeranko, and his report would not please his leader. Perhaps Brother Mark's alternative plan would provide Father with at least some satisfaction.

A quick shiver rippled through his sturdy body, reminding him that, while it was the second week of May, winter on the shores of Lake Wasikama near the Minnesota-Canada border was not that far past. He moved to the fireplace and added two logs of well-cured ash. Then he turned to the kidney-shaped, wooden conference table. Nestled against the short, curved side sat a large, luxurious brown leather-covered chair.

Lined against the opposite side were two similar but smaller chairs. Suddenly, the lights snapped on, momentarily blinding him.

"Ah, Brother Vance! I hoped you might be early."

He turned to see the slight figure of Brother Theodore, the chaplain who was up for two days from their headquarters in Minneapolis. Dressed as always in his old brown-plaid sport coat, the diminutive preacher shuffled into the room, his thin, silky gray hair a mess and his wire-rimmed glasses perched askew on his immense beak. It was hard to believe the little man was barely older than he.

"Brother Theodore…unusual for *you* to be early for a meeting," he replied.

"I—I hoped I might have a few words with you, Brother." Theodore glanced back over his shoulder, lowered his voice as he came closer, and continued, "It's Brother Jacob. I'm very concerned about his…his techniques…indeed his *priorities*. Though he's my assistant…well…sometimes I'm not sure his heart is with God. Sometimes it's as though he's more concerned with the cause—" The little man stopped suddenly, his wide eyes suggesting the fear that he had gone too far. He blinked several times and waited.

"Now, Brother, we've been over this before," Vance said. "Perhaps *you* would do well to reconsider priorities. What good is our unswerving dedication to God if we don't manifest it in our actions? You might remember that we're the most dedicated religious faith in America. Certainly the other Christian churches pale next to us. That's because we pray hard and often—and because we *work* hard for the cause of liberty. We should spend *all* of our time in prayer? That might help *us*, but what about the millions of *others*? God is working through us, and if we're to achieve His goals, we can't just sit around on our asses and pray."

The little man flinched. "Bro—ther Vance!"

Amused, Brother Vance went on, "You might remember something else, Brother. You have it pretty cushy. How many other preachers can spend all of their efforts on recruiting and administering to their people spiritually? You have no fundraising problems. The income from our businesses takes care of all your needs. You think about that. Now, let's take our seats," he said, motioning to the two smaller chairs. "Father will be here soon."

They had no sooner seated themselves than Brother Vance glanced at his watch and jerked to his feet. Theodore responded almost instantaneously with surprising agility. They faced ahead, their eyes fixed upward on the modest three-foot cross that hung on the wall above the fireplace.

The rhythmic click of leather heels on the hardwood floor announced the arrival of Father Jeranko. Vance held his focus on the cross as their leader rounded the corner to his place before them, but after twenty years together, he could visualize every detail of Father Jeranko's appearance. While less than average height, the man, dressed impeccably in an expensive navy business suit, a white shirt, and a red tie with white and blue figures, cast an aura of incontestable strength. His medium-length, grayish-blond hair was neatly trimmed around his small, almost unnoticeable ears. Squinting eyes and a perpetual, closemouthed grin drew attention from a nose that swooped downward from a delicate, narrow bridge to a bulbous tip.

"Brother Theodore, the prayer," the leader said in a raspy voice that seemed incongruous with his persona. Their eyes remained fixed on the cross as Father Jeranko turned about to face the wooden symbol.

"Oh, Father of all mortals," Theodore's tenor voice with manufactured resonance began, "we ask once again for the bestowal of your strength, wisdom, and love upon us as we meet to carry on your crusade. You have shown us the way. We pray that you will guide your Christian soldiers as they wage the battle against human greed and selfishness, the battle to finally secure for all mankind the true essence of liberty. We pray that you will credit us for our faith and tolerate our moments of—"

Father Jeranko coughed, almost inaudibly.

"Amen," came a hasty, choked conclusion.

Their leader turned to face them, and as he took his chair they settled crisply but silently into theirs, their eyes now turned to him. He nodded curtly to Theodore.

The diminutive preacher shuffled through his notes, pushed his glasses up on his nose with a middle finger, and began sorting his papers again.

"Brother Theodore...." Vance raised an index finger and moved it in a circular motion. He had little patience with the man, and he knew Father had even less. "You know we have no time for wasted motion and flowery speech. On with it?"

"Oh...yes, yes," Theodore said. "Our membership of patriots in the brotherhood is now up to four hundred and fifty-four, one hundred each in Companies A, B, C, and D, and fifty-five in the new Company E...ah, well...Company B *might* be down to ninety-nine. I'm not sure. It's been months now. Has *anyone* heard from Brother Dan? It's really hard to believe...I mean, I can't believe he'd leave us. Despite his...rough edges...he seemed like a good man."

Vance looked across at Father Jeranko who nodded ever so slightly. "Yes," said Vance, turning to look directly at the little preacher, "we can tell you now, but you must *never* reveal this to anyone. Do you understand?"

"Well...well, of course," Theodore replied. "He didn't *really* abandon us, did he?"

"He's out on a...long-term special assignment. That's all we can tell you, and that information must not leave this room."

"Oh, of course. I'm relieved. I was so worried about him—"

"Go on," Father cut in.

"Yes, of course. Companies A and B have successfully met the work standards, the spiritual requirements, *and* the action commitments. Company C has met the work standards and the spiritual requirements. They're ready for their primary action training here at Black Rock. Company D is looking good on their work standards, but they have yet to finalize their spiritual commitments. The new group...they're working in several of our businesses while being evaluated for perhaps more appropriate job placement. Eleven of them are in our drug rehab program."

Vance studied Brother Theodore. He wondered how much the preacher knew about the primary action program, the physical development training that took place in six-week segments at the Black Rock camp. By appointing young Brother Jacob to a newly created position as assistant chaplain, Vance had constructed a means of keeping the naïve senior chaplain away from the camp. But, he thought, he probably picks up some bits and pieces when the campers return to their church, jobs, and apartments in Minneapolis.

"I am requesting," Theodore continued, "that we look into the condition of the apartments. You know, we purchased old, run-down building complexes, and we've done little to improve them. Many of the units are quite cold during the winter and absolutely stifling during the hot summer months. Such conditions could severely damage the morale of our people."

"To the contrary," said Father Jeranko, irritated. "We gathered these people who were down and out, many of them homeless. We've given them love, support, and self-respect, along with homes and jobs, all adding up to two things: a real reason to keep going and the mental toughness with which to do it. Do you really recommend we turn them back into pampered, soft, and selfish worms, the very scourge that threatens America?"

"Oh, I...of course not, Father. I'm afraid there are...times when my humanitarian instincts cloud my judgment. It was just...a thought," conceded the red-faced Theodore.

"I'm sure," replied Jeranko. "Now, since Brother Craig is waiting to fly you back to your duties in Minneapolis, we'll not take any more of your time. Please tell him to come back for me at two o'clock tomorrow." With but a hint of a nod, he dismissed Theodore, who quickly gathered up his papers and left the room. When the door closed, Jeranko turned to Brother Vance. "He's done an excellent job, you know...."

"Yes—he has," Vance agreed. "He has a knack for finding *our* kind of people, planting the seed of our spirit, and—"

"But you think we've reached the point of development where he no longer fits?"

"I don't see how we can keep the motives and depth of our physical action program from him much longer," Vance said, "and there's no way he'll buy into it. I do think your idea was a good one—as soon as he reaches Minneapolis, the explanation on Brother Dan's whereabouts will become common knowledge. It should satisfy the curious."

"You'd better begin the selection process for a new assistant chaplain, one who can inspire our Christian soldiers and remain perfectly tuned to the cause. Company A's been with us the longest. Start there," directed Father Jeranko. "And since Brother Jacob is the obvious choice as our new head chaplain, let's send him to Minneapolis for a while. It would be good for him to see what Brother Theodore has...or has not accomplished."

"And what will we do about Brother Theodore?"

"When the time comes, I'll conduct a thorough...debriefing...and then decide." Father Jeranko got up from his chair and strolled to the large windows. He stood for a moment in silence, apparently looking out, although Vance knew he could see nothing but reflections of the interior. "Brother Vance, the new facilities?"

"Coming very well, Father," replied Vance. He was eager to address the subject. If his recent failure must come up, he'd like it to follow an unqualified success. "The fourth barracks will be completed this week. The addition to the mess hall is finished. And the blueprints for the new food storage building will be ready by the end of the week. The designers assure us that our theory is sound if we use heavy, sealed insulation to combat moisture. Actual construction should take about three weeks."

"You're convinced your idea will work?" asked Jeranko. "November through March, we shut down the power, open the building vents, and let nature keep our supplies frozen?"

"Absolutely—give or take a week or two in either direction. Days after completion, we can begin transporting from our food division."

"Good, good. When Company B finishes up, we'll move them back to the Cities. Meanwhile, bring Company C in for primary action training. By the way, with the new freezer facility, what's our maximum for independent survival?" the leader asked.

"We can house and feed four full companies for four months, longer if we augment the supplies by hunting and fishing," Vance said, "that is, if we use nets for fishing."

Father nodded. "The seaplane hangar? We really need better security."

"We have all the components ready and waiting. We can construct it, large enough for two planes, and camouflage it in two to three days, once…." Vance hesitated. There was no evading the words to come next. He knew his relationship with Father was beyond jeopardy, but he always felt tense at the prospect of displeasing him. "….once we have the resort owner and Gunderson…ahh…happily relocated. The rest of the land across the bay is national park property…occasional campers, but no full-time residents. We'll have the bay to ourselves."

"What are you telling me, Brother? You've made *some* progress? *Little* progress?" Jeranko turned from the window. The tiny laserlike points burned from behind his squinting eyelids. "Or *no* progress?" He returned to the table and settled into his comfortable chair.

Vance drew a breath, exhaled slowly, and shrugged. "If I've made any progress, it's immeasurable at this point. Ms. Farber and old Gunderson are both *very* stubborn. It would seem," he continued, choosing the words he often used in order to leave room for Father's suggestions, "that we have two options. One, we make an offer far enough above market value that they can't refuse. Two, put some real pressure on. Obviously, since option two would fall to our action group, I've discussed the matter with the commander, Brother Mark."

Without a word, Jeranko reached under the tabletop and pressed a button. A faint buzzing sound reached their ears, and almost immediately the door opened. The husky, well-built six-footer who strode confidently into the room was in his early thirties. He wore military camouflage fatigues, dominated by patches of forest green, and a matching flattop military cover. His rugged, handsome face, with its alert blue eyes, seemed to model a diametric blend of strength and sensitivity. Reaching the table, he clicked his heels lightly, removed his cap, revealing a clean-shaven head, and stood erect.

"Thank you for being available, Brother Mark. Have a seat," Father said. Without waiting for the young man to settle in, he continued, "Your thoughts please on the property acquisition?"

"Yes, Sir. I've done some research," Brother Mark said in a pleasant, soft voice that belied the raw courage and iron will that Vance knew comprised the central strand of his character. "Kimberly Farber is mortgaged to the breaking point. If her recently divorced husband doesn't come through with alimony—and I have a handle on that already—she'll need to run at ninety-five percent of capacity through her four-month season in order to make her payment, maintain the resort, and support herself. She might accomplish that *if* she has happy campers."

"And *if*—" Father cut in, "ten, twenty, or thirty of her bookings left in midweek and refused to pay up?"

"Exactly," Brother Mark said, "exactly. She has a twenty-five thousand dollar annual payment due October first."

Vance looked carefully at his superior. To new acquaintances, Father's fixed smile appeared to be just that, a smile. But after serving him for many years in the Special Forces and then in several unusual commercial endeavors, Brother Vance had come to categorize that countenance as a borderline sneer. Occasionally, as now, there was a slight twist to Father's lips that suggested a genuine smile, not much of a smile, but as much as anyone would ever see.

"Very good, Brother Mark, industrious if not ingenious. Firm up your plan and initiate," said Father Jeranko.

"Yes, Sir. I'll do that."

"However, I want you to keep certain things in mind. First, I want your activities to remain as discreet as possible. We don't want open warfare over this, at least not yet. And perhaps...yes...perhaps you and Brother Vance can befriend Ms. Farber...provide some emotional support."

Oh shit, thought Vance, that's just what I need.

"Second," continued Jeranko, "contact your friend over in the Falls to see what else you can learn about Ms. Farber and her operation. Third, we'll see if we can factor some additional elements into the equation."

"Excellent," Vance said, leaving it at that. After a career as an officer in the Special Forces, Father was extremely sensitive to phony compliments, and that was a line Brother Vance had never violated.

"Now...Gilbert Gunderson," Brother Mark said, "is another story. He's not wealthy, but he's financially secure and his place is long since paid for. He's a pretty tough old man, and it's possible the only way he'll leave that place is in a body bag."

Father Jeranko thought for a moment and then said, "If necessary, that can be arranged."

Chapter 3

David Engstrom snagged the hook with the telephone receiver, turned about in the tiny phone booth, and forced the stubborn folding door open half-way. Sheets of cold, wind-driven early May rain bombarded the rush hour traffic that raced past on Lake Street in south Minneapolis. He needed reassurance that he was still alone, but the clash between his body heat and the cool outside moisture had completely fogged the glass panels of the booth.

He edged part way out, looked quickly around, and popped back inside. In seconds the exposure to the torrents had plastered his medium-length blond hair to his forehead and soaked his black nylon jacket. The quick check proved nothing—he still felt nervous. The adjacent brightly lit service station offered more space and better shelter from the storm, but the seclusion it offered would be comparable to that of a Broadway stage. He glanced at his watch—six o'clock. The clouds and rain had cast the area in a dark gray, but it would still be more than three hours before total darkness set in. Have to be careful, he thought.

A sudden change in the wind blasted the rain into his cubicle, and David slammed the door shut. Leaning his slender frame against a corner of the booth, he tried to relax. Look on the bright side, he thought. In this rain, it's not likely there'll be another idiot wanting this phone. And this is the most privacy you've had in three months—three months with every minute of every day planned for you, with someone watching every move, silently or verbally critiquing everything you do. Three months...without Julie.

What kind of a man, he thought, would leave his beautiful wife alone to fend for herself while he disappeared into never-neverland on what could be a dangerous and possibly a fruitless crusade? Then he recalled the excitement in her voice moments before, and the longing that had built steadily over time suddenly mushroomed within him. His blue eyes watered, and a lump gathered in his throat. Maybe...maybe he should just slide back into society, much the same as he had disappeared from it. No, something inside him said, that's not an option.

When his watch told him it was six-fifteen, he cracked the door open again and peered out and down the street to his left. The wind had slowed and the rain was easing up. Despite his tension, he felt a lift from the fresh smell of the spring rain. He eyed each car in the curbside lane, wishing it to become a red Chevy Blazer. Twice, he almost darted toward the curb, only to be reminded that other people also owned red Blazers. Pulling his handkerchief out, he was mopping the rain from his narrow, nearly handsome Swedish face when he saw approaching headlights flash high-low-high-low.

David timed his dash for the curb. As the Chevy skidded to a stop, he jerked the door open and piled in.

"Go!" he shouted.

"But—" The attractive brunette hesitated, staring at him, reaching for him.

"Hit it, Julie! Hit it!"

She popped the clutch out, spinning the knobby tires on the wet pavement, and quickly accelerated to the speed of the traffic, snapshifting from gear to gear with the ease of a race driver. After two blocks, David directed her to turn off Lake Street and make a series of random turns while he checked behind them. Satisfied, he slumped in his seat, drew a deep breath, and turned his head to take in the profile of his wife of five years.

"It's okay now," he said, reaching over and placing his left hand on her thigh. "You can get us back on Lake now and head for home."

Julie Engstrom said nothing. She stared ahead as she wheeled around the next corner to head west on Lake, manipulating the Blazer like it was part of her. Her usually shiny black hair hung in dull, wet strands around her naturally tan face. She had prominent, high cheekbones and a small nose with a slight upturn at the tip. But her full lips were tightly pursed, and David could tell by the pulsing in her cheek that she was grinding her teeth. It was her pout. It usually upset him to see it, but now it struck him as the most beautiful pout he'd ever seen. The light blue sweatshirt she wore was soaked, and it lay neatly plastered to the high contours of the breasts that tapered to her body nearly at the collar bones. His eyes followed on down the tempting torso to the rounded hips in blue jeans before it registered—she had dashed out to the car, taking no time for raingear or umbrella in her rush to meet him.

She made the split left onto Excelsior Boulevard, and then suddenly she braked hard, throwing David against his seat belt. The Blazer lurched off into a mini-mall parking lot and slid up to a curb. As the front wheels bumped the concrete, she turned off the lights, set the emergency brake, slipped the gearshift to neutral, and unsnapped her seat belt all in one motion. Throwing her upper body across the center console, she grabbed his face in her hands and pulled him toward her until their noses almost touched. She stared at him in silence. The wipers rotated, swap—bap—swap—bap, louder than he had ever heard them.

"David Engstrom," she said, her dark brown eyes flashing, "you scared the hell out of me back there. You go away on this—this *thing* of yours for months, not a word from you. Then you finally call, and I'm

so excited I can hardly drive. And then what? I'm half ready to come—
and you jump in hollering, 'Go!'"

He reached up with both hands and rumpled his fingers through her
damp hair. "Damn! That's my Julie," he said, "feisty and loving, all at the
same time. My God, I've missed you." They kissed, their open lips and
probing tongues frantically searching for everything they had missed,
retracing their path of love so tenderly laid over six years. David slid his
hands down her body. By the time he reached her waist, his erection was
full, throbbing its demands. He hooked his fingers into the waist band
of her jeans and pulled her toward him, dragging her part way across the
console between the seats. Her knees caught against the barrier and she
squirmed to find a way over. She had one leg across when something
thumped loudly on the window.

"Hey, in there! Roll your window down, please. Security!"

Their lips separated. As one, they opened their eyes and looked up at
the window on David's side. They flinched simultaneously when they
saw a large, craggy face with deep set eyes and a huge, burly nose that
nearly touched the glass. Outlining the face was an officer's hat with a
silver badge centered on the crown. David cranked the partially fogged
window down several inches while trying to drape his free hand as casually as he could over his crotch. Julie wormed her way back to the driver's seat. As the security officer looked them over, his eyes focused for a
moment on David's lap.

"I'm sorry, Folks," he said seriously. "You can't do that here. You'll
have to go on home to finish." Then a grin appeared. "Or come back
after ten when we're all closed up. Okay?" One of his large, bulging
brown eyes flicked a wink at David as he turned to leave.

"Uh, yeah, uh," David stammered as he cranked the window up.

"Shhhhit!" Julie hissed as she slammed the gearshift into reverse.
"This is getting worse by the minute." She cut a sharp turn and soon had
them back in the traffic, headed for Hopkins. The rain had stopped, and

far to the west they could see magical beams of sunlight poking their way through silver-gray clouds.

"Maybe…just as well," David ventured after a minute of silence. "I want you in our apartment, our home. You'd have come out of this with two broken legs."

Julie managed a laugh. He leaned her way, put his left hand on her back, and kneaded slowly, firmly with his fingers. His right hand found its way to her upper thigh. It took all of his willpower to stop there.

Minutes later, the familiar, light but pleasant smell that was David and Julie Engstrom greeted him as they entered their small, neat apartment. He kicked the door shut, turned, and took Julie in his arms. A few inches shorter than his five-feet, ten-inches, her body molded into his, and as they alternated between fierce hugs and deep probing kisses, he felt his penis swell again. Then suddenly Julie backed away and held him at arms length. Tears spilled from her eyes.

"My God, David," she gasped, "I'm so glad to have you back! I've been so scared. Couldn't you have called? Or written? You could have given me *your* number. I'd have called *you*. If you only knew—and you acted so weird when I picked you up—"

"Easy, easy," he said, pulling her to him. "I love you, Julie, I love you." Leading her down the hallway toward the bedroom, he said, "I'll explain everything later. Right now…."

By the time they reached the bed, both had nearly disrobed. Julie flopped on the bed, spreading eagerly to take him in. He eased his shaft deep into her moist warmth and held there motionless, afraid to move. His explosion was but a twinge away. With a quick series of contractions, Julie provided that twinge, and their joint climax became a violent, frenzied rolling, tossing, and bouncing, pumping the three-month accumulation of love and frustration from David's slender body into hers. He lay there for some time, supporting his upper body with his elbows, absorbing the love that seemed to flow from Julie's skin through his own. Finally, when he shriveled and slipped out, he rolled off, but she followed along. They held their embrace, kissing lightly and stroking each other, murmuring nothing that made sense.

In minutes his member once again expanded to its hard, demanding state. This time, they embarked more slowly on their journey to recapture the purity, the passion, and the love that had been in their separate hearts for so long. As the long, ecstatic trip up the emotional escalator reached its peak, David felt the ripples from his groin all the way to the top of his head. Totally spent, he tumbled off involuntarily, and they lay side-by-side holding hands, their fingers interlaced, gasping for breath and saying nothing.

"David?" Julie finally murmured, "My saddle?"

David reached over the side of the bed, pulled open a drawer of the night stand, and extracted a large, soft, pink bath towel. Julie grabbed it, stretched it between her legs, and slid out of bed. David smiled as he watched her ritual trip to the bathroom, holding the ends of the towel up in front and behind, the pink saddle contrasting with the light tan of her firm cheeks.

"Do I look loved?" she asked when she returned to the bed, stretching out and nestling one breast on his forearm. "I sure feel loved."

"You *are* loved."

"David, I don't want you to ever be away that long again."

"I won't, Julie. But…I do have to go back—"

"What?"

"I promise—two months, max—maybe only a few weeks," he said, checking his watch. "As a matter of fact, I have to be back at nine-thirty tonight." Her grip on his shoulder stiffened, and he felt Julie's cold tension invading his own body. Damn it, here comes the test, he thought. I'm not sure I can handle it. Got to. Got to be strong—even if I don't feel strong.

"Tonight?" she asked. "Couldn't they even give you twenty-four hours with your wife?"

"Actually, I'm not due in 'til ten o'clock. But they seem to like me. I'm one of the promising brethren, and I want to build on that by being a little early," he said. "And I'm *not* with my wife, I'm with my mother. I told my group leader that my mother needed me."

"Your *mother*! Your mother's been dead for years. Are you ashamed of me?"

"Julie, my angel," he said, turning toward her and taking her face in his hands, "*you* don't exist. If they ever find out about *you*, they find out about *me*. In the Church of the Rock, I'm Brother David, the bum they salvaged from Loring Park three months ago. They don't use last names, but the one I gave them is Lewis. If this is the group Danny hooked up with…and I think it is…they probably know him as Dan Engstrom. If another Engstrom shows up…these people aren't stupid—anything but."

"That's why you were so weird? They were following you?"

"I don't think so, but have no doubt—these people do such things."

"Don't they have any women, other wives in that church?"

"Yes, there are a few wives…and some others, but not Julie Engstrom—out of the question," he said. "Do we have any pizza in the freezer?"

"Da—vid! You're ducking out on me," she said.

"No, I'm not ducking out. As a matter of fact, I have a lot to tell you. You need to know as much as possible, just in case…in case I need someone on the outside. But I've been craving pizza and a beer for a long time now. We can talk in the kitchen," he said. "Come on." David rolled to the edge of the bed and started up, but Julie pulled firmly on his arm. He sat back down, turned, and looked into her brown eyes. He knew what was coming.

"Don't you forget, David…when I finally agreed to this…crazy stunt…we made a deal. If I blow the whistle at any time, you're out of it. And you'd better talk fast, because I'm reaching for the whistle," she said, her eyes taking on a the fierce quality that always told David when he was in for a battle. "Understood?"

"Understood," he echoed. He jumped up, pulling her naked body with him, bent and kissed each nipple, and then, reaching deep within himself for willpower, he began gathering his scattered clothes from the floor.

Soon they were seated at the kitchen table, each with a beer, waiting for the oven to heat up sufficiently for the supreme deluxe pizza. David sat quietly for several moments, looking across the table at Julie, basking in the glow of what he had often called his "special comfort zone." At times like this, he wondered how he had won the gorgeous creature who sat opposite, studying him warmly, her brown eyes pulling at him like powerful magnets, the same magnets that had captured him as a college freshman seven years earlier. Uh, uh, he thought to himself, careful now or you'll find yourself signing off on a job that isn't finished. A quick glance at the clock above the sink told him he had less than two hours.

"Are they…bad people, David?" Julie asked, finally breaking the reverie.

"No, at least not the worker bees like myself. Most of them were down-and-outers, like I set myself up to be. Some made bad mistakes along the way, and some just had bad luck. Thanks to the church, they've turned their lives around," David said.

"You make them sound…almost noble."

"In some ways, they are. But there's a strange atmosphere. They go on and on about brotherhood and the saving of souls. Yet I get the feeling they're watching everything I do, measuring me, judging me, spying on me—even when I wipe myself. And they're into a lot of brainwashing on religion and politics. I really have to fake it on the religion. Supposedly it's a Christian church. In fact, they refer to themselves as Christian soldiers. You ought to hear the men's choir sing 'Onward, Christian Soldiers'," he went on, the enthusiasm mounting in his voice. "They do it in four-part harmony accompanied by a brass group. It's beautiful—absolutely powerful—it sends chills through you."

"They sing it often?"

"It's the exit hymn for every service and weeknight meeting. No kidding, Julie, when you march out to that music, you're ready to take on the world."

"Then, why do you have to fake it?" she asked. "You're a Christian."

"Because of the strange atmosphere, and because they're really militant," David said. When our trainers say Christian soldiers, they really mean the *soldier* part. Most of the dogma comes from the Old Testament, and it's usually taken out of context...loaded with 'eye for an eye' overtones."

"Is it...are they a cult?" Julie asked as she got up and slid the pizza into the oven.

"Awfully close. I'd call them just an Old Testament church...except that...."

"Except what?"

"The commitments each member has to make. In order to be accepted into the fold, we had to turn over all possessions to the church—everything. I'm talking about the business you own, your house, your cars, right down to your wristwatch and your Bic pen. And we had to agree to work hard and faithfully for no compensation other than room, board, medical treatment, and church-sponsored recreation. And...we're allowed no social life outside the group. We don't go shopping, to concerts, to movies...nothing. The only TV we're allowed is on video tapes of carefully selected programs."

"David, you're kidding! They can't expect to keep any members on those terms."

"Would you believe—over four hundred?" he said, getting up for another beer.

"But don't they get *any* recreation?"

"We work six days a week. After two church services and five prayer—that means indoctrination—meetings, we spend the time that's left on calisthenics, boxing, wrestling, and karate. If we're good boys, we're allowed an occasional pick-up game of basketball. I'm in far better shape than when I was on the college swim team. I think the restrictions ease up later, if we pass primary action training."

The oven bell rang, and Julie got up to remove the pizza. A blend of cheese, green pepper, onion, and sausage wafted across the tiny kitchen, stirring David's imagination and taste buds. After rolling the cutter through the delectable disc, she set it before him on the table and took her seat. Holding one hand inches above the tabletop, she grinned at David.

"Ready? Go!" she shouted, slapping the palm of her hand against the table.

"Sixty—fifty-nine—fifty-eight—fifty-seven—fifty-six…" they counted in unison, as fast as they could manage the syllables. By the time David reached twenty, Julie was down to five, and he found himself once again choked up with laughter—and defeated.

"Zero!" Julie shouted, slapping the table once again. "I pick first, and you clean up."

When David's turn came, he pulled out a wedge and gingerly bit through the hot, cheesy pizza. "Mmmm…." he mumbled. "You, the pizza, the beer, our little place…doesn't get any better than this."

"I miss this, David," Julie said, stopping for a small sip of beer. "I miss our stupid games. I miss loving you…but I miss just talking to you, too. No one, not even a dog or cat to talk to in the evenings after work. It's awful. It got so bad I practiced counting backward."

"I thought so," he said with a laugh. "You might not believe this, but I don't have it much better."

"What? With all those people around? Da—vid…."

"I'm serious. Nobody tells anything about themselves, where they came from, what they did, and certainly nothing about what they think. It's as though Big Brother is listening."

"Is he?"

"I—I think so. We talk about what we're doing at work. We talk about politics, strictly from the church's point of view. And we talk about technique when we're working out or fighting. I know I'm certainly not going to challenge the system. If I get in bad with those guys, I'll never find out anything about—"

"They do let you have pizza?" she chided as she reached for another piece.

"Food for the soft worms, the scourge of America," he replied.

"You?" Julie shrieked with a laugh. "That was no soft worm in the bedroom just now."

"Judging by the number of times I've heard that statement about soft worms, I think the real mission of the church is political, not religious. Much of the class time is spent on dissecting and exposing what they call our corrupt political system. According to the brothers, each of the two parties is as rotten as the other. They talk constantly about the unwritten agreement, 'You don't tell on us—we won't tell on you.' And you know what?" he asked.

Trying frantically to lip a long strand of dangling cheese into her mouth, Julie simply gestured the question back to David.

"On the political issues, they're absolutely right," he said. "I agree with them. We need some kind of drastic action to bring our leaders back to the purity the Constitution intended. The thing I'm not sure of....I haven't found out yet what the church intends to do about it. And I have a gut feeling that when I do find out, I won't agree that the end justifies *their* means." He reached for another wedge of pizza.

Julie's face grew serious. She reached across the table and placed a hand on David's. "David," she said, "what about Danny? Have you seen him?"

"No...." David hesitated. He stared at the tabletop, propping his forehead in one hand. "But I'm *sure* I'm on the right track."

"David," Julie said softly, "That big brother of yours has been off again, on again with his drugs and booze for two years now. He's lost job after job, disappeared time after time. I just can't understand why you're so convinced he's in any worse trouble this time, and I don't see any reason for you to lock in on this—this church. He could be anywhere!" Her brown eyes began to show fire, and David sensed she was close to whistling the play dead. "Now, state your case," she concluded.

"I've always been able to—"

"I know," Julie interrupted, "you've always claimed you could sense when Danny was in trouble. You say it's like finding your right shoe on your left foot. You know I have trouble with that, but set it aside for now. You also insist that, since your parents were killed in the accident, Danny has never gone longer than two weeks without calling you, no matter what condition he was in. I admit that the three-month stretch, now almost six months, with no calls is highly unusual. But what else do you have to justify quitting your job, leaving me, and going off on this—this escapade?"

David felt the familiar frustration rise up within him. Her challenge was admittedly very logical, but this wasn't about logic. It was about his brother, Danny, his only sibling. He weighed the situation. This was it. He had to convince Julie there was reason to pursue the search or give way to the promise he had made to her.

"Julie," he began, "my *feelings* about this are stronger than ever. But…set the feelings aside for now. There are facts that say I'm on the right track. You knew when I left that Dan had been seen in the area of Loring Park."

"Yes, the police all but confirmed that."

"He was there, Julie. He definitely was there. I hung out there for a week before the church people saved me." He paused and looked across the table into her eyes. "You any idea how cold February nights are in Loring Park?"

"I think so," she said, wrapping her arms about her body and shivering. "I thought about little else for weeks. I even drove down there…many times…looking for you."

"When lonely, beaten men have to endure something that bitter, they crave warmth in any form, even if it's only conversation with a stranger. I met a couple of older guys—alkies, both of them. They knew Danny by description—and by name. He had helped them survive after someone copped all their gear. They said Dan went with the church guy, the same church guy that approached me—Brother Theodore."

"Really? Then...maybe...you're on the right track? Did you ask this Brother Theodore about Dan?"

"Almost. I was about to ask when I remembered something," David said.

"Remembered what?"

"Remembered how interested Brother Theodore was in saving Danny and then me. But he never once invited those poor, rag-tag, old men to be saved."

Chapter 4

Hudson Bryant banked the gleaming white Piper Archer into final approach to runway Three-Zero at North Platte, Nebraska. Typically he felt a letdown at the end of each flight, for he loved flying his small Piper. Compared to the clumsy, buslike ride of commercial jets, this was real flying. But as he lowered his flaps and lined up with the runway, he was anxious to feel the bump, hear the light screech as his main wheels grabbed the hard surface. After twelve hours of flying, with only brief stops for food and fuel, the growing ache in his hips was taking command of his senses, indeed clouding his judgment. And that, he knew, could be dangerous.

An hour later, after refueling and carefully tying the Piper down, he tossed his small overnight bag on the dresser in his room at a nearby motel and proceeded to change into his running clothes. Tired and stiff as he was, heading out to run held no appeal, but he knew it was what he needed, and he drew from the combination of habit and willpower deep within him. One thing he had done right in three years of wandering through no man's land…he had kept up his workouts. He was in the best physical shape of his life.

Jogging slowly down a blacktop road, he patiently pushed on, waiting for that point when he gained his second wind and the effort became easier. Finally, he increased his stride, relaxed, and began to enjoy the fresh, cool afternoon breeze that drifted over the Nebraska prairies. He resisted the ritual of using his running time for planning and problem solving. Instead, he envisioned himself as a bird, gliding along the country roads, inhaling the clean, invigorating air, listening to the warbling of occasional meadowlarks, aware even of how quiet the staccato exhaust bursts of a nearby farm tractor sounded compared to the rush of traffic in busy Orange County. He wondered if the people who lived out in the boonies recognized and appreciated their freedom. After what he gauged to be two miles, he headed back to the motel where he showered before enjoying a Yankee pot roast dinner at a neighboring restaurant.

Hud returned to his room, content and tired. But he had one more task to cover before hitting the sack. Consulting his address book, he picked up the phone and punched in the local number of attorney Buselli "Boots" Condoli, an old college buddy who had confounded everyone by shunning the large eastern cities and establishing his practice in North Platte.

"Hel-l-l-lo!" came a familiar musical greeting.

"Hi, Boots, it's—"

"Hud—you old son of a bitch! Must be three or four years since you checked in with me. How the hell are you?"

"Fine, fine. You still fleecing little old widows out of their farms?" Hud asked.

"Strange you should ask, Hud. Just today I *saved* a farm for a little old widow. Good feeling—good feeling. You still using that copying service to fleece attorneys so they have to fleece little old widows in order to meet expenses?"

"As a matter of fact, I'm thinking of selling Hudson Professional and concentrating on the other one, Hudson Financial," Hud said.

"Sell it? What's Ellie say about that? Seems to me, *she's* the one who makes it go."

The lump that formed in Hud's throat came as no surprise to him. Even after three years it still happened at the mention of Ellie's name. And each time he wondered how much longer he'd have to struggle with the problem.

"Boots," he said, his voice faltering, "Ellie's...gone. Three years now...cancer."

"Oh, my God...no!" said Boots. "That just can't...be. Hud, you should have called...or written. I didn't know."

"I tried, Boots, I tried...just couldn't tell anybody. Every time I picked up the phone or started a letter...I felt so guilty, so ashamed. Just couldn't do it," Hud said.

"Guilty? Ashamed? What in the hell for? You two probably had the best marriage in these United States, and you were fifty percent of that. Ashamed?"

"Just can't get past the feeling that...there must have been something I could have—should have done." Hud paused. "Ever been there?"

"No—I haven't. But you are, and that just shows what kind of person you are, Hud. Hey—" His friend's voice suddenly raised in pitch and volume. "Where are you? In town?"

"Yeah. I'm out at a motel near the airport."

"You're not staying at any goddamned motel. I'll be right over to get you!"

"Uh, thanks, no, Boots," Hud stammered. "I've been in the saddle for over twelve hours. I'm beat. And there's a front moving in tomorrow morning. I've got to buzz out very early to beat it. Thanks, Boots, but I really need some sleep."

"Okay, Hud, I understand," replied Boots, "so I'll make a deal with you. You promise to stop and stay awhile on your way home...or I'll come over and put sugar in your gas tank. And while I'm doing it, I'll have Mary kick your ass. Okay?"

"Deal," said Hud, visualizing his friend's college girlfriend and eventual wife, a delightful but powerful six-footer. "Not sure when I'll head back, but I'll call before I leave. By the way, know any good lawyers in northern Minnesota?"

"No, but I know a couple of winners in Minneapolis."

Hud scribbled down the names and the conversation drifted to what he often referred to as the Christmas letter format, the catching up on family events. While he listened with interest to the long list of achievements by the Condoli children, the recitation jabbed at him like a sword point. He and Ellie had agreed to put off having children, and now....His conversation with Boots eventually found its way to a comfortable conclusion and Hud hung up the phone. But tired as he was, he wrestled with ghosts for two hours before he finally found a hiding place called sleep.

Early the next morning, with the sun peeking over the eastern horizon and illuminating broken clouds, Hud went through his preflight check. Having filed his flight plan for Mitchell, Fargo, and International Falls, he glanced often at the heavy, dark wall of clouds that rose menacingly between ten and twenty miles to the west. It was moving his way. If he were headed straight east, he would outrun the storm easily, but with the northeasterly course he needed, there could be an eventual convergence. He laid his regional chart on the seat beside him. On it he had circled alternative airports to the east of his course so that, if necessary, he could break and run for one of them.

Minutes later, the sleek Piper with its streamlined wheel pants raced down the runway. Hud felt the thrill he always felt as the wheels lifted from the concrete and the rumbling ceased. It was that magical moment when man, for all his limitations, broke free of his global anchor and became part bird. It was that freedom that added a fourth dimension to travel, that infected pilots and put flying in their blood.

At one thousand feet, he banked to the right and began climbing on a heading of zero-four-seven. At seven thousand, five hundred feet, he leveled off, put the little Archer on autopilot, and ran a scan of his instruments. With the throttle set five percent above normal cruise, he was making one hundred and thirty knots. Good, he thought, I can use that extra ten today. He adjusted the lumbar control of his seat, poured himself a cup of coffee from the stainless steel thermos, and relaxed. At his altitude he could tell that the northern end of the storm line bent back toward the northwest, somewhat reducing the chance of a convergence with his course. As the storm drew closer, he could expect serious crosswinds to develop, but for the moment it was as smooth as sailing a boat in a gentle Pacific breeze.

With the thought, an image popped into his mind—a sparkling new thirty-foot sloop with blue and white sails. Ellie had always longed for a boat, "my airplane," she called it, and Hud had just made a deposit on the craft when her illness was diagnosed. Upon learning that the cancer had metastasized, that her status had been declared terminal, she insisted that he cancel the order for the boat. "You won't even use it when I'm gone. It'd be silly to spend all that money on a toy I can only enjoy for—" Ellie never finished the sentence. She broke into tears, one of the few such episodes in her last months.

Hud's eyes filled as he recalled the scene. If only I could handle my life as well as she handled her death, he thought. To scramble yet again past an impending collapse, he focused on Gibby's unusual call. No doubt about it. Old Gib was in a bind. He could think like any animal in the northern Minnesota woods, and he could track like a bobcat, but dealing with humans, especially human animals, was not one of his strengths. Hud wondered just what his old friend was up against and what he could do to help. A tiny alarm sounded somewhere within his mind. Change course, he told himself. You're heading down dead-end alleys again. You have no control over either of those scenarios.

Ellie's gone and you can't change that. Gib's problem? You don't know enough yet to even speculate on it. Concentrate on things you can control—like flying this plane. He switched off the autopilot. Taking the control yoke in his left hand, he studied the threatening mass to his left. It seemed no closer to him, but the broken clouds beneath him were forming into a solid layer, with the uppermost wisps occasionally brushing past his windows. He quickly switched on his navigation equipment, checked his position on SATNAV, and went on instruments. Decision made, he thought. Definitely going to stop at Mitchell for fuel. Asking for trouble to bop around low on fuel in this weather.

An hour later, he had taxied to the pumps at Mitchell, given his order to the attendant, and headed into the service center for a pit stop and then a telephone call. As he waited through the ringing tones, he glanced at his watch. It was only five-fifteen in Orange County. He could expect Robert Irvin, Manager of Hudson Professional Services since Ellie's death, to be less than warm and fuzzy.

"If this is a wrong number, I'll hunt you down and feed you this phone—backwards," a thundering bass voice declared.

"Good morning, Robert," Hud said cheerily. "This is Hud. Did you have a nice nap?"

"Jesus Christ, Hud, couldn't you have waited another hour? Caught me in the middle of my morning dip."

"Oh...sorry about that." Hud knew well that Robert had no swimming pool. "Can you roll off and talk for a few minutes?" Hud heard a barely audible groan, followed by a couple of grunts and the angry voice of Shawauna, Robert's wife.

"Hudson Bryant, you're gonna be shot by an angry wife one of these days!"

"Better that than by an angry husband," Hud replied. "Sorry, Shawauna, I'll make it up to you."

"Okay, let's start over," Robert said in the rich, deep voice that always tempted Hud to ask for a few bars of "Old Man River." He'd never ask. He knew that many blacks were offended by the association. But God, how he'd love to hear Robert sing it. "What's on your mind, Hud?"

"Did we make the deadline for the Largent firm?" Hud asked.

"Sure did. Due this afternoon. Delivered yesterday about two o'clock. That's fifty-nine straight ahead of schedule. Number sixty's going out this morning. Do I get a raise?" the affable forty-six-year-old, Ellie's prize pupil, asked with a laugh.

"Good job, Robert! I might have something even better," Hud said, warming inwardly at the thought of the portly manager who had proven to be a master at motivating his people. "You're sharp, Robert, sharp enough to know that my heart really isn't in the business anymore, not since...."

"I've been afraid of this, Hud," Robert said. "You going to sell?"

"Depends on you."

"Me? You mean *I* make the decision? I say no—flat out *no*."

"Hold on a minute," Hud demanded. "I want to sell it to *you*."

"Me?" After a long silence, the deep voice returned. "Hud, don't play with me. We grossed almost two-and-a-half mill last year, and we might hit three this year." Then he growled, "Ain't no way I kin 'fohd t'buy dis heah bus'ness!" He paused for a moment and added, "Much as I'd really like to. Damn—would I like to! What you doing to me, Hud?"

"I'm serious. Just tell me this. If you could buy HPS, own it clear in ten years without sacrificing your last pair of shoes, would you do it?" Hud asked.

"Hell, you know that, Hud...I'd even throw in the shoes! Is it possible?"

"I think so. Briefly, here's what I'm thinking. You've got a hundred and forty-three grand in mutual funds with me through the other company. If I remember correctly, you've got a two hundred whole life policy. Let's say, you throw in a chunk...call it commitment money, a down payment. We set up a payment plan. You stick your share of the profits, along with that big raise I'm about to give you and whatever else you can afford, into my bank account, and in something like ten...she's yours." Hud waited for Robert's response. He heard heavy breathing, but nothing more, so he went on, "I'm in Mitchell, South Dakota, be at the cabin in the morning. Might be there awhile, same phone, FAX, and address.

Let's you and I each come up with two figures, total price and your down payment. Then we'll see if we can get together on those two figures. Once past that, we can work out the rest. Still interested?" Hud asked.

"I...excuse me, Hud, I'm having a little trouble handling this. Do you *really* think it's possible? I don't want to get all excited, climb all the way up on your horse, and then find out I'm facing the ass end."

"It's possible, Robert, a *strong* possibility. Will you work on it? I have to cut now. Got some bad weather pushing me. I'll be in touch—"

"Hud?" Robert paused again, then continued in a soft, serious but unsteady voice, "Thanks for the opportunity, Hud, thanks. Can't tell you how much it means to me—even if I find out I *can't* swing it."

"Keep in mind, Robert, I'm not going to just give it to you, but there's nobody I'd rather see have it. You're a natural for the business. And you had a good teacher. She'd want you to have it. Bye now."

Hud smiled, then laughed as he headed for the flight line. "By God...I'm going to *do* it," he muttered. "I'm *really* going to do it—add two choruses of 'Old Man River' to the purchase price. I'll show him what a bad-assed hardnose I can be." A quick check of the western sky told Hud the ugly, gray mass had gained on him. I'd better shag it, he thought, if I'm going to beat that beast to Minnesota.

Chapter 5

Hud examined the thickening gray blanket of clouds above him as he climbed out of Mitchell and headed northeast for Fargo. He estimated his visibility at seven or eight miles, so he elected to fly on Visual Flight Rules. Pointless waste of time and fuel, he thought, to climb up through that soup for a flight of only two hundred miles. He leveled off at twenty-five hundred feet, nearly a thousand feet beneath the cloud mass. But he knew the heavy stuff moving in from the west would bring that mass down on him like a bad dream. If his estimates held up, he might still have a ceiling of a thousand feet for the last leg from Fargo to Lake Wasikama.

As the visibility faded, he found himself scanning the skies more frequently, searching for other aircraft. He called it his healthy habit. It had been firmly, almost fiercely engrained in him by his flight instructor, Jack Ward, who had flown A-6's in Viet Nam. Jack had said repeatedly, "It wasn't God that brought me back to the States alive. It was concentration, sharp eyes, and a head on a swivel. Aircraft are built to fly, not crash—certainly not to crash into each other." Jack had often finished his lecture with the question, "Can you imagine, Hud, how many times you'd shit your pants while you fall two thousand feet after a mid-air?"

Hud made yet another thorough check for traffic and then relaxed, turning his attention to the countryside below. The hills and wasteland had fallen behind him, displaced by a developing patchwork of freshly plowed fields. The reddish-brown South Dakota soil appeared almost black through the gray filter of the hazy sky. Still, despite its somber appearance, the terrain gave Hud a certain warmth; it signaled his entry into his favorite world. He dearly loved the north country with its thick pine forests and thousands of sparkling lakes, its fresh air, clean water, innocent animals, and down-to-earth, honest people.

Reaching to pour himself a cup of coffee, he smiled wryly at the thought. Judging from Gibby's experience, this beautiful pine barrel has a few bad apples in it. He wondered again if perhaps Gibby had overreacted. No, he thought, I don't know what's going on, but what they did to Herman....Sharp gusts of crosswind out of the northwest began bucking the little white aircraft as Hud let down a thousand feet on his approach to Fargo. Calling ATC, he got clearance to enter the downwind leg for Runway Three-Four and turn on final behind an incoming Northwest DC-9. Hud spotted the other aircraft coming his way and extended his downwind leg to increase the gap between them as he did two left turns and fell in behind the white, twin-engine jet. He had developed a healthy respect for the invisible turbulence that spun aft from the wing tips of jet aircraft. The sleek, benign-looking twin jet could flip his little Archer if he got too close.

Despite the crosswinds, Hud's landing was relatively smooth. While the attendant refueled the Archer, he made a hurried phone call to Gibby Gunderson's home. Gibby's wife, Sarah, answered the phone.

"Hello, Hudson," she said in her smooth, low-pitched voice that was tinged with high, happy overtones. "We were expecting your call. Gilbert's down at the dock. Shall I get him?"

"Not really necessary, Sarah. Did he check the strip for me?"

"He surely did, Hudson. He said to tell you it's fine, except there is one soft spot just before you get to that camelsback. He placed a white flag near it. He poured some concrete tiedowns last week, and he put the new wind sock up yesterday for you. You'll like it. It's larger than the old one."

"That's great, Sarah." Hud checked his watch. "Tell Gib I should be there in an hour and forty minutes—about ten forty-five. If I'm more than fifteen minutes late, he should go on home and wait for my call. I'll have landed some place else."

"Hudson...are you having trouble with your airplane? Maybe you shouldn't—"

"Oh, no. Plane's all right. There's a big storm chasing me, and the ceiling's dropping. I'll be fine. What's for lunch?"

"That's a surprise...but you'll like it."

"Good. I'm already hungry just thinking about your cooking. Keep it warm for me. Bye now."

With the decision made to head for the small grass airstrip at the lake instead of International Falls, Hud called FSS to amend his flight plan. Then, after calling for a weather check, he paid for his fuel and headed for the flightline, handing the attendant, a hefty teenage girl, a nice tip. He had watched her meticulous windshield cleaning from the telephone station. She smiled, pointed one hand at the angry western sky, and gave him a thumbs up with the other.

Once clear of the Fargo pattern, Hud climbed to two thousand feet. But the buffeting from the heavy clouds overhead forced him back down to twelve hundred feet. While it was smoother there, it was no place for anyone vulnerable to air sickness. One violation by the storm gods pitched his stomach up to his throat while the next dropped it to his crotch. He wasn't looking forward to an hour and a half of such treatment. Yet, the stubborn part of him found a perverse pleasure in it, like riding an unpredictable roller coaster that would stay right side up only if he kept it that way. He was reminded of how insignificant he and his little white Archer were in the overall scheme of things and what a comparatively small red and white splotch they would make with a stroke of bad luck at the wrong time. He advanced the throttle to the hot side of cruise and concentrated on controlling the craft and maintaining his heading.

Fifty miles past the Red River into Minnesota, the pitching and bucking eased. He had outrun the elements from above. The bumps he would encounter now would be from lake effect, much less violent and much more predictable. He looked over his chart and then located the next set of visual checkpoints. Beneath him were endless forests pockmarked by countless lakes. There were few roads or towns, yet Hud preferred crosscountry VFR navigation over this terrain. Less apt to misidentify what few roads or towns there are, he mused, and there are always the odd-shaped lakes to be used as checkpoints. Of course, there aren't many places to put her down if we have trouble. As always, the thought provoked a period of concentrated listening to the loud hum of the hundred and eighty horsepower Lycoming. It seemed to tell him, "Relax, Hud, everything's fine."

"Damn," he muttered, "how lucky I am to be here, to be able to do this. Most people wear out a life and never experience this." A subtle thrill rippled through him. Since losing Ellie, he had seldom thought of himself as lucky, but here he was, not only lucky but *feeling* lucky. He checked his instruments, rechecked his navigation, poured a cup of coffee, and began tracing the chain of events that had put him "on the high side of the moon," as Ellie had called it.

It was Hudson Professional Services, HPS, that had propelled him from hand-to-mouth to a comfort zone twelve years earlier, the same year he married Ellie. He had arrived in Orange County, California, with a fresh business degree from Columbia. He saw the rapid growth of business in the county accompanied by a parallel proliferation of law firms. As the law firms grew, so did their stacks of legal documents waiting to be copied. Sending the work, most of which was highly sensitive, out to run-of-the-mill copy shops presented uncomfortable risks for law firms.

Hud had borrowed ten thousand dollars, leased two copiers and an office. After a screening by the bonding company, he set out to visit law firms. It was a scary beginning—two small clients from whom the combined revenue failed to pay the rent. But word spread. His service was reliable, and the security and privacy were as he had promised. By the end of the first year, his list of clients included three large firms and twelve small firms. In addition, he had six state of the art copiers and three technicians.

He had doubled his equipment and staff in the second year and hired a petite but feisty office manager, a cute brunette named Ellie. In two months, she had the business in the palm of her hand, and in six months they married. He'd flown into a heavenly relationship and high profits. It was Ellie's management that put them over the top, and he credited her with the secret to their happiness together. She showed him how they could disagree on issues, thus enabling one mate to win the argument without defeating the other. Her penchant for objectivity became his, and it freed them to devote themselves to a love that grew steadily without the threats of peripheral disagreements.

"You know, Hud," Ellie had said after six years, "we've got our house and our toys. We have fifteen good employees. I can run this business blindfolded. Why don't you drain off some of the money and go do what you'd really like to do?"

Astounded at first, he had looked into her warm hazel eyes for the confirmation he needed. Within three months, Hudson Financial Services opened its doors, gaining an immediate jump start from the network he had established through the first business. He had his father's knack for translating corporate reports and his personal investigations of corporate activities into sound stock market decisions. Attorneys trusted him; judges trusted him; and their families and friends therefore trusted him.

Hud smiled at his last thoughts. How ironic. A bull-headed young man in his twenties, he'd refused to join his domineering father's New York firm, a move which probably had cost him an inheritance the poor couldn't imagine and many of the wealthy would have envied. Yet, here I am, he thought, doing well…and in the same business as my father. But we don't do it the same way. That's what's important. I'm doing it my way, and I'm not leaving a trail of bones behind.

He scanned the area once more. Bemidji, an attractive college town he knew well, appeared off to his left. The cloud cover was descending steadily. He dropped down to eight hundred feet and gauged the visibility to be about three miles. With only a hundred miles to go, he knew he should make it all right, but he felt himself tightening up. It was time to fly, not reflect. He picked up U.S. Highway 71 which linked Bemidji with International Falls. He set his course to follow the highway, keeping it several miles to his left. At Big Falls, the highway would angle left, and he would maintain his heading straight to the airstrip. The highway eliminated the need for intense concentration on checkpoints for the next seventy miles.

The threatening mass to the west could no longer be clearly defined. It blended into the clouds above him, turning them to a dark gray with a churning, boiling motion that rolled through the lower portions. By the time he left the highway at Big Falls, an onslaught of contradicting air currents had begun. The rolling forces from above, the vertical pitching over the lakes below, and the strong, gusty northwest crosswinds combined to test Hud's skills as well as the construction of the tiny aircraft. He found himself listening intently once again to the engine. Not the time or place for engine failure, he mused.

Occasional spatters of rain hit the windshield, and his visibility shrank rapidly. But up ahead he could make out the south shoreline of Lake Wasikama. He studied it, searching for the indentation that was Black Rock Bay. Once located, the bay would point him to the small airstrip two miles to the south. There! There it is, he thought, and there's the strip. He banked to the right and began his descent.

Carved out of a stand of tall pine trees, the short east-west runway, barely sixteen hundred feet long, had but one open side, the eastern approach. He checked the new windsock and flew the bucking Piper at only five hundred feet on his downwind leg parallel to the runway. He needed the best look he could get before going in. While there were trees that prohibited a westerly approach, Hud disliked landing from the open east end because of the rolling camelback a third of the way down the runway. If a pilot touched down where he should, it meant two landings, because the hump that crossed the strip would send the plane back into the air like a ski jumper. And that left less than a thousand feet of runway in which to get the aircraft back on the ground and get it stopped.

He spotted Gibby's white flag that marked the soft spot approximately two hundred feet short of the hump. "Hell," he mumbled. "Couldn't be in a worse place—right at touch-down." A figure stood beside a Jeep near a small aircraft parking alcove that had been cut out of the trees on the north side of the strip. The figure waved. Gibby, he thought, good old Gibby. Hud briefly considered making a pass to look things over better and to test what had to be wicked crosswinds. He knew that, at some point when he dropped below the trees, there would occur a sudden wind shear and the aircraft would drop like a rock. But it would be hard to predict. No, he decided, I'll take her in on the first try, but I'll be damned ready to shove that throttle to the firewall and abort the landing.

As he turned on final, Hud felt a quick, flickering of a conflict within himself. He loved challenges such as this, and having never failed one, he had developed a strong confidence in himself and his aircraft. Never failed one—yet, he thought. But my palms are sweaty. Maybe I should head for the Falls. A sudden, short blast of wind-driven rain crashed against the windshield, temporarily blinding him. The decision had been made for him.

Dropping full flaps, but maintaining five knots of airspeed more than he customarily would, he brought the Piper in on a long, low approach, hopefully low enough to avoid serious wind shear. He concentrated on a spot fifty feet past the barbed wire fence that bordered the east end of the landing strip. If he could dump it in on that spot well before the soft area, he should be done bouncing before he reached the soft terrain. Then, if the mush slowed him even more, the camelback would be out of the picture completely.

Crabbing to the right to counter the crosswinds, Hud focused on his spot, refusing even a glance at his instruments. The rain crackled against the windshield in short bursts. He gauged his airspeed by the sound of the engine and the vibrations of the aircraft. Twice, the bottom began to drop out, and he gave the Lycoming a sudden shot of throttle to counteract the loss. It was all happening so fast there was no time for thinking—everything depended on instinctive reactions.

Almost before he expected it, the fence slid beneath him. He chopped the throttle, dropped the nose down slightly, and then eased back smoothly on the control yoke. The usual, long flare in which he felt the ground effect keeping the plane aloft was eliminated. As the nose came up, the white Piper dropped below stall speed and pancaked onto the grass from five feet up. After two mighty bounces it caught the soft turf, slowing so abruptly Hud tilted forward from the inertia. By the time he reached the dreaded camelback, the airspeed indicator read below thirty knots, and the aircraft rolled over the gentle hump with no inclination to return to the air.

As though triggered by his hard, ungraceful impact, the storm exploded, spewing rain in sheets so thick the drops were indistinguishable. Hud applied the brakes and, as the Piper slowed, he breathed a sigh of relief. He turned and taxied slowly back toward the east end of the strip. Blinded in front and on the left by the rain, he was forced to steer the aircraft by gauging the trees off his right wingtip. He felt the wheels cross the hump and the soft spot. The fence was somewhere up ahead, but it had become invisible. Reluctant to push his luck any further, he throttled back to idle and simply sat there trying to relax, grateful for his skills and humbly indebted to whatever mysterious force had granted him such luck. If that rain had hit thirty seconds earlier....He shuddered and then poured a short cup of coffee.

"Gibby," he said aloud, "I need you. Where are you, Gibby?"

Chapter 6

Appearing out of nowhere, a Jeep skidded a sharp turn and stopped ten yards ahead of Hud's left wing, its blinking red taillights barely visible through the rain. A figure in a yellow hooded slicker jumped out and scampered to the right of the Archer. The aircraft shook slightly as a series of bumps announced a visitor on the right wing. The door jerked open.

A hand tossed a rolled-up slicker onto the right seat, and a voice shouted, "Follow me!" The door slammed shut, and he was gone.

"Good old Gib," Hud muttered, "always thinking."

As the Jeep slowly eased away, Hud advanced the throttle and followed the blinking red lights, careful to keep his guide to his left, clear of the propeller. When Gibby made a slow turn to the left, Hud knew they had reached the parking alcove. He followed across the runway and prepared to stop. A yellow arm reached out from the Jeep and waved an up-and-down motion. Hud stopped, revved the engine briefly, then shut it down and tended to his checklist and log.

He struggled into the slicker and stepped out onto the wing, directly into the deluge. Slamming the door too quickly, he caught the slicker and had to reopen the door to free himself. Then he jumped down off the trailing edge of the wing and hurried around to the right side. Gibby had backed the Jeep up close to the aircraft and stood near the rear cargo door of the little vehicle.

"Thanks, Gib, good to see you!" Hud shouted through the downpour. As they exchanged a firm, wet handshake, he felt warmed by the grinning face deep within the yellow hood.

"Toss yer gear out to me and I'll throw it in the Jeep," Gibby said. "Then we kin put this baby to bed."

Minutes later, the transfer had been accomplished and the Piper Archer had been pushed backward into Gibby's alcove and tied down. They scrambled into the Jeep and Gibby aimed the bouncing vehicle down the narrow, rough driveway and out to the gravel road.

"Kind of pushed yer luck a little?" Gibby asked, shifting to two-wheel drive and turning onto the gravel road.

"More than a little, Gib. Should have gone into the Falls. Better have my head examined."

"Not the best landing I ever seen you make," Gibby said with a snort. He flipped the yellow hood back, exposing his weathered face and silver hair and beard. Turning his squinty, mischievous eyes toward Hud, he flashed a toothy grin.

"That was a controlled crash," Hud said.

"But damned smart, putting her down where you did, letting the mud slow you down. Hurt the airplane any?" Gibby asked.

"Don't think so. She's a sturdy bird." Hud replied.

"Been a lot of rain lately. If it don't quit by tomorrow and let the lake settle down, there ain't gonna be many walleyes caught opening weekend." Gibby segued quickly into a monologue that drifted from the weather to recent repairs he had made, the new windsock and tiedowns, and the cyst the doctor had removed from Sarah's ear.

Hud waited for the problems. Finally, as Gibby turned into the long drive that wound its way through the woods to his lakeshore site, Hud's patience gave out.

"What about the problems? Anything more since we talked?" he asked.

"Later. Ain't gonna get you off the plane into all this goddamned rain and then lay all *that* shit on you."

They rounded the last bend in the drive, and Hud felt the anticipation, the soft, warm thrill of homecoming that he always experienced. He smiled to himself, wondering as he always did about the feeling. It didn't make much sense. This wasn't *his* home. He spent only a few weeks a year at the lake, and yet it always did this to him…even more since Ellie. He caught Gibby looking at him.

"Ya, I know, Hud. Still does it to me, and I been living here almost twenty-five years. You know," he said, shifting the Jeep down to second with a jerk, "you ain't really no Californian. You don't fit with all them would-be movie stars, running around in their convertibles, talking on cellular phones, and spending money faster'n they can make it. Well…here we are…in Gibbyville," he announced as they broke into a clearing and approached a circular gravel drive.

The circle was perhaps fifty yards wide, its center covered by thick, green grass. At the foot of the circle rested a well-preserved, white wooden Ole Lind rowboat filled to overflowing with multicolored pansies. A tall, white pole rose from the center of the boat like a mast, and high atop the pole sat an immense birdhouse, a martin condominium. At the hub of the circle stood a gigantic oak tree, its strong, gnarled limbs stretching majestically to claim domination of the loop.

Across the circle at the ten o'clock position sat the small cedar log cottage that would be Hud's domain. A larger home of similar construction faced the circle from the two o'clock position. Gibby and Sarah had lived for five years in the small cottage while they built their dream home. At the four o'clock place, tucked under the thick shade of a cluster of huge oak trees, stood a large, tan all-metal utility building that served as the Gundersons' vehicle garage, workshop, and winter boat storage.

As they circled left toward the small cottage, Hud glanced at the old, traditional rural mailbox that dangled nearly fifteen feet up from a limb of an aged basswood tree. He chuckled as he read the letters painted on its side: AIRMAIL.

Gibby parked close to the door of the cottage. Hud stepped out into the rain and stood, scanning the familiar sight. The dark, gray day and the rampant downpour could only dull, not hide the beauty of the three-acre site. Well-spaced red pines, white pines, oaks, and birches occupied the manicured lawn. Gibby's property extended another five hundred feet beyond the lawn into the woods on Hud's side of the circle and three hundred feet into the woods on his own side. From the structures, the lawn sloped gently down to the shore of Black Rock Bay two hundred feet away.

A wide dock extended out into the bay. Gibby had built the dock himself, connecting raftlike sections, each of which floated on fifty-five gallon plastic barrels, using a heavy log chain to moor the outer end to a sunken automobile engine. Along the left side of the dock stood a covered boat lift that held Hud's sixteen-foot red and silver Lund Walleye boat, while Gibby's larger blue and cream Larson runabout rested in a matching lift along the right side.

"C'mon, my young friend! Don't stand there in the rain like you been memorized," Gibby said.

In minutes they had Hud's gear unloaded and piled in a disorderly heap opposite the fireplace in the small but cozy living room. The crackling fire told him that Sarah must have tended it while Gibby was at the airstrip. That's like her, he thought. She'd trot over here in a downpour to feed that fire. Hud stripped off his slicker and stood before the fire, absorbing the delicate smell of the burning ash logs and feeling the last of his travel tensions go up the chimney.

"Gib," Hud said, turning to his short, chunky friend, "you guys are incredible, the way you spoil me." Hud's emotions, as Ellie had always said, "were cranking," and he was about to set them to words when he saw Gibby turn suddenly and head for the bedroom.

"God...damn! Them mother-fucking Bible Bashers!" Gibby roared.

"What is it?" Hud asked, stepping into the bedroom, a modest room finished like the others in varnished, reddish-brown cedar wood. A set of large windows traversed most of the lakeside wall, and there stood Gibby staring at jagged edges of glass, all that remained of one of the windows. Bursts of rain sporadically charged through the opening, further soaking the bright, multicolored patchwork quilt on the double bed. Scattered about the bed and floor lay shards, slivers, and tiny particles of broken glass.

Gibby grabbed a spare blanket from the tiny closet and tossed one end at Hud. Together they opened the blanket and draped it over the curtain rod to deflect the invading rain. As they worked, Hud stubbed his toe against something. He bent down and picked up a nearly round, smooth stone the size of a softball, and held it out for Gibby to see. The older man's face twisted into a contorted mask, the eyes threatening to pop from their sockets. He snatched the stone from Hud and reared back to throw it against the opposite wall.

"Gibby!" Hud shouted, raising both palms toward his furious friend.

The older man looked at him and blinked, then lowered his throwing arm. His whole body seemed to go limp as he slouched into a posture of defeat, his head down and his hands shaking. Hud took the missile from Gibby's hand and placed one arm around the shorter man's shoulders.

"Don't blame you, Gib," he said softly. "Every reason to be really pissed. But right now, let's take care of the problem and clean up the mess. Okay?"

Gibby grunted, wheeled, and headed for the door. "You're right," he mumbled, then added, "I'll get something to cover that up. You do what you can here."

Hud began gently shaking the glass from the quilt onto the floor. He felt his own anger rising, but when he realized that the saturated quilt was a brand new creation by the talented Sarah, his emotions peaked.

"Damn," he said aloud, "poor Sarah. This is nothing but stupidity! What in the hell is going on here?" But he knew he'd find out only when Gibby was ready to talk about it. He set about cleaning up the glass and water. He heard a ladder bump against the outside wall. A darkening within the room and the thump of Gibby's hammer told him a sheet of plywood was being fastened over the opening. After carefully sweeping the floor several times, Hud stripped off the bedding to be carried to the main house. Then he hoisted the damp mattress up and manhandled it into the living room where he propped it on edge near the fireplace. He glanced at his watch.

Oh, oh, he thought. Quickly, he dialed the FSS and closed his flight plan. Another five minutes and he'd have been over the limit. They'd have begun organizing a search, he thought, and Hudson Wade Bryant III would be in deep doo-doo.

When Gibby returned, Hud looked carefully at his friend's eyes. The intensity was still there, but not the anger.

"Well, you got your work cut out for you," said Gibby with a wave at the mattress and the mound of luggage. "We eat in half-an-hour. Sarah says, 'Don't be late.'" The door closed and he was gone.

Hud toured the kitchen checking each of the cedar cupboards. He absorbed the familiarity of the hodge podge of dishes and noticed that the food sections were well-stocked, including four cans of his favorite chili. The refrigerator offered everything he needed, and the freezer greeted him with his favorites, venison steaks, venison burger, and two packages of walleye.

He returned to the twelve-by-twelve-foot living room and dropped into his favorite rust-colored leather recliner. Over the edge of the upright mattress, he managed his ritual staredown encounter with the regal eight-point buck that occupied the wall above the fireplace. He scanned the rest of the familiar room. He loved the cottage, most of all the living room. The old wood-framed tan and brown plaid couch along the left wall had provided many hours of peaceful naps, and the home-made pine coffee table before him had held many snacks and drinks.

He checked his watch, jumped up, hustled into his yellow slicker, and headed for the main house. Entering, as was the custom, through the kitchen door, he ran smack into the captivating aroma of his favorite, Sarah's venison stew. And as he expected, there was Sarah, her back to him, laboring over the stove. In her early sixties, she was a petite little thing, skinny as a young birch tree, with a glorious head of short, wavy, silver-blue hair. She turned with a start when the door slammed behind Hud.

"Hudson Bryant, my handsome Hollywood hero, you're finally here!" With short, hurried steps she shuffled across the kitchen toward him, her slender face caught up in her best smile, and her blue eyes flashing through her small, round granny glasses. She glided into his hug and stretched up on tiptoes to kiss him on the cheek. Then, at arms length, she looked up seriously and said, "Thanks for coming. Difficult time getting into the strip?"

"Nah—not too bad."

"Oh? You lie, Hudson Bryant. I felt the impact right here in my kitchen. And just look at that mud you splattered all over my kitchen windows." She winked at Gibby, who had just entered from the bedroom hallway. Then she laughed and went back to her stove, chattering over her shoulder as she removed a hot pan of cornbread from the oven. "Hang up your coat, wash up, and sit down," she directed. "We're ready."

"Sure sorry," Hud said, "about the—" He stopped when he saw Gibby frantically waving him off. "….about the mud on your windows," Hud continued, laughing. "I'll practice till I get it right, Sarah."

It seemed that, no matter how high Hud's expectations went, Sarah's cooking exceeded them. He attacked the savory stew and the hot cornbread and honey like a starving animal. On a sudden impulse, he stopped, looked up, and saw Sarah sitting back and grinning, her chin in one hand with the index finger stretched upward over the tip of her nose, shaking her her head slowly. He forced himself to slow down.

"Goddamn," Gibby said soberly.

"Gilbert! Are you saying grace?" she asked. "A little late for it now."

"Yes, Sarah," Gibby said, rolling his eyes upward, "but he still pokes it away, don't he?"

"Not my fault," said Hud. "Haven't had a good meal since I left here last August."

"We'll get you fattened up," Sarah said. "But it's time you find a beautiful woman, Hud, one who can cook."

"Only one in the whole world like that, Sarah, and she chose a good-for-nothing old Norwegian over me," said Hud.

The conversation with Sarah would have been as pleasant as always, but Hud was troubled by the silent undercurrents, the things that weren't being said. Drifting into the catch-up mode, Hud reported on the growth of both businesses and his plan to sell off Professional Services. Sarah recounted her personal projects around home, her activities at church, and some of her experiences while substitute teaching at the area high school. Gibby remained silent.

"You know, Hudson," Sarah went on. "You *do* need a good wife—you deserve one. Have you even *looked*?"

Gibby rolled his eyes again, got up from the table and left the room. Hud found himself staring at the gun rack above the door to the outside. The lever-action Winchester wasn't there. Quickly, he realized that a new gun rack had been mounted on the wall behind the door. The new rack held the Winchester, a twelve-gauge shotgun, Sarah's four-ten-gauge, and a holstered handgun. Ready for anything, he thought.

"I've done some looking," Hud said. "Probably did it all wrong, but I've looked. I think all the women in my age group want the same thing…money. If I can't have a *real* relationship, like—" He felt the lump forming again. "Incredible meal, Sarah, like always. I'm stuffed."

"Thank...you," she said, her gaze fixed on Hud. "I—I'll see that we keep your freezer full."

Gibby strode into the room and reached for his rain gear. "Looks like that rain's letting up. Let's go outside. Got some things to show you, Hud."

Hud carried his dishes to the sink and thanked Sarah again. Donning his slicker, he followed Gibby outside. The older man stepped off quickly into the light rain and headed for the utility building. Once inside, Gibby turned up the gas heater and began hanging up tools that had collected on his workbench. Hud perched nearby on a high stool.

"Okay, Old Friend, what's happening?" Hud asked.

"You saw the latest."

"Why don't you run down the list and give me the approximate times things happened?"

"Started out last fall, little things like dead fish tossed in the boats, fishing gear missing, then flats on the Jeep, a window broke, mailbox out by the road flattened—several times. Then in the winter, the line from the LP gas tank to the shop pinched shut. No heat, froze up the water line and busted it." Anger mounted and the pace quickened with each episode. "Power line to the water pump cut—no water. More broken windows...."

"My God, Gib. Somebody's *really* got it in for you," said Hud.

"And then your boat...and...Herman." Gibby's voice softened, but his intensity was that of molten steel. "Last night, they threw a dead rat through that window." He motioned to a square piece of plywood fastened over a window opening at the rear of the building. "And you saw this morning's action."

Hud shook his head slowly. He had hoped that the slaughter of Gibby's dog would be the last of it. But it looked like they were facing a deliberate, calculated campaign. Who? What did they hope to accomplish?

"Have you ever gone through anything like this before?" Hud asked.

"Nope. Oh, once in a while during the summer, some of them kids staying at the resort next door do something stupid. You know, the kinds of things kids do, not really *to anybody*, more *against everybody*. Ain't never had a long run of things like this."

"Gibby, on the phone you talked about some Bible Bashers? You mean—"

"Yeah, that new church group that bought up the peninsula last year. They call themselves the Church of the Rock," Gibby said.

"You lose me on this, Gibby. I've seen lots of churches I didn't agree with, or even like. But I don't think I've ever heard of a church that would do things like this, for no apparent reason."

"You ain't never seen a church group like this. These guys are more like a goddamn army."

"Guys? All guys, no women?"

"That's right. At least I ain't seen no women…but plenty of big, tough-looking, young guys. Shit, they run down the county road in squad formation, won't move over for nobody, just dare you to do something about it," Gibby said. "Last time we met, I refused to pull over out of their way. I just stopped where I was and made them run around me. When I got home, the gas cap was missing from the Jeep."

"Did you actually *see* any of them do *these* things?"

"No…but it was them all right."

Hud's frustration began to mount. "Gibby, this isn't like you. I've never known you to hold so stubbornly to a point of view with little or no evidence for support. You know something I don't?" Hud asked. "Come on, fill in the blanks for me. Why *these* guys?"

Gibby didn't seem to hear Hud. He ran one thumb gingerly down a hand saw blade as though testing its edge. Suddenly, he raised the saw and then smacked it broadside against the workbench top. *Whack!* He turned to face Hud. His squinty eyes had lost their familiar twinkle. Instead, Hud saw fierce, raw anger there.

"You're right, Hud. I'm jumping to conclusions. I can't prove it's them, and that pisses me off as much as what they done."

"Have you reported this stuff to the sheriff?"

"Yeah. Most the time they get here hours after you call. They just write it down and drive off. The other day, the time they did Herman, Deputy Mertens came out. Good kid, good cop. Known him all his life. His dad and I were good friends till he died couple of years ago. I told Will Mertens what I thought—the church and all." Gibby slammed the hand saw onto its designated hooks in the wallboard.

"Obviously, you didn't like his answer," said Hud.

"He stopped writing his notes when I came to the church, said there's no way Beer Stein, the sheriff, is going after no church, specially no *big* church, and most specially without tons and tons of evidence and with an election coming up this fall—"

"Beer Stein?"

"It's really Robert Stein. Picked up the Beer nickname in high school. Never let it go. Anyway, Will admitted, off the record, that judging from things he's heard, there's a chance I might be right. But for now, he ain't going to mention them church guys, and he said I better not say them things to nobody else, neither."

"But *I'm* not nobody else," Hud said. "Why are you so convinced it's the church?"

"One, I don't like them bastards. Two, the way they chase around the neighborhood imitating people."

Hud translated to himself, *intimidating,* and motioned for Gibby to continue.

"Three, one of the head honchos came by about a month ago, a big mean-looking greaser with a scar on one cheek and eyes like a snake. Name's Brother Vance. Didn't look like no preacher I ever knew. On his own, he went snooping all over the place, just the way they do everything. When I asked what the hell he was doing, he told me he was buying the place. Just like that—*buying* the place! Made an offer right there on the spot. Funny thing, not the kind of ridiculous offer I'd expect from them neither. Only about ten grand under market value. From where he started, I could probably get market price out of them. But I ain't selling to nobody. Sarah loves it here. I love it here. We plan to die here. And what's more, I'd never do a thing like that to my neighbors."

Gibby stripped off his slicker and hung it on a hook beside the door. Suddenly aware of the warmth that had engulfed the shop, Hud followed suit. He returned to the stool and sat quietly pondering Gibby's story. A church? No church would stoop so low, not even a church inflated with the hypocrisy of a TV evangelist. But Gibby had offered some facts that pointed up the unusual character of this particular church...squads of tough, young men...buying the whole peninsula...and then trying for Gibby's place.

"What's Sarah think about all this?" Hud asked.

"Sarah don't know about some of it, this morning's window—broad daylight—and Number Four," Gibby said, pausing. He tossed a crumpled piece of dirty, white paper Hud's way. "*That's* Number Four...came tied around the dead rat's neck."

Hud smoothed the paper and read the brief note:

NO ROOM FOR RATS LIKE YOU AROUND HERE.
CARE ABOUT YOUR WIFE? MOVE OUT.

Chapter 7

"Gilbert, are you there? Gilbert?" The cheap intercom speaker on the wall crackled the nearly incomprehensible sounds.

Gibby leaned over the workbench and pushed a button on the intercom. "Yeah, Sarah, I'm here."

"Kimberly just called."

"What's she want?" Gibby asked.

"She didn't talk. She just said, 'Tell Gibby they're here again.' Then she hung up."

"Got it," said Gibby. Turning to Hud, he said, "Get your coat on, and shine up your brass knuckles. We just got a S.O.S."

Together they stepped out into the light rain, headed up the driveway, and turned on the narrow path that led into the woods on the right. The path, covered with a thick, squishy layer of last year's leaves, led to the Black Rock Resort next door. Hud knew it well. He had carried his bait bucket along the winding trail many times through the years, buying his leeches, crawlers, and minnows at the resort. He knew that new owners, a young couple from Minneapolis, were to have taken over the resort just about the time he left in August.

"What's this all about, Gib?" he asked, twisting through the encroaching hazel brush, hurrying to keep pace with his older friend.

"It's about trouble, I think," said Gibby. "Sounds like those goddamned Bible Bashers are over there again hassling her. I told her to call if they came back."

"Hassling her?" Hud asked. "Why can't her husband step in?"

"Ain't none." Gibby slowed a bit, talking over his shoulder as he walked. "Her name's Kimberly Farber. Her husband and her bought the resort last August. The husband stuck around long enough to help close the place up for the winter. Then he took off for Minneapolis to his old job to make money to carry them through till spring." He brushed a branch aside. When he let go, it whipped back at Hud, nearly catching him in the face.

"And?"

"And it turns out that weren't all he was making in Minneapolis. When Kimberly found out about the other woman, she didn't wait two days. She up and filed for divorce. She's feisty, Hud, one tough gal. Wouldn't be surprised if she beat the shit out of him. She's bound and determined to prove she can run this little resort all by her lonesome, and goddamn if she isn't making a believer out of me," Gibby said. "'Course I been helping her some with the heavy stuff and teaching her about plumbing, electricity, boats, motors, and so on. But she's one tough woman. Wouldn't want her mad at *me*."

Hud visualized Kimberly Farber—a Russian shotputter.

They broke into a clearing and made for the drive that separated two rows of quaint tan Cape Cod cottages. Overlooking the bay on their left stood the front row of four well-spaced units. Three similar cottages in the back row to their right were placed to capture what was left of the view. The seven buildings with traditional horizontal siding closely resembled one another, except for size. Each was tastefully trimmed in chocolate-brown and sported a small deck attached to its front.

Up ahead, the drive led between an old, yellow gas pump and the main building that housed the lodge room and owner's quarters. The recently painted building matched the cottages in style and color. The lodge room, an L-shaped wing, jutted out to the drive. A deck with the entrance door was tucked in the corner of the adjoining sections. On the wall next to the entrance hung a large, brown wooden sign that read in routed letters painted in tan: Black Rock Resort.

Scampering up the wooden steps and across the sturdy deck, Gibby jerked the storm door open. A tiny dangling bell tinkled its welcome. Hud followed Gibby into the knotty pine-paneled lodge room. In addition to several small, brown tables with tan formica tops and matching chairs, there stood a pool table near the center of the large, square room. Three electronic games and an old pinball machine stood in one corner next to the immense picture window that overlooked the property and the bay. In the opposite corner, a black Ben Franklin stove radiated its warmth from a tiny stage, elevated six inches above the floor.

A long counter stretched across the room near the rear wall. Two men sat on stools at the counter with their backs to Hud and Gibby. Hud quickly scanned the room for Kimberly Farber and decided the owner was somewhere back in her quarters. One of the men wore a dark blue business suit and had thick, black hair. He turned as they entered. Spotting Gibby, he stood and took a step to meet him. Brother Vance, Hud thought, recalling Gibby's description. Big, nasty-looking dude. That long scar on his cheek...wonder how a preacher got a scar like that? Scratched by a renegade communion wafer? I don't think I like him very much.

"Ahh, Mr. Gunderson." Brother Vance extended his hand to Gibby, "What a coincidence! May God be with you." His lips formed a smile exposing long, narrow teeth. But no smile lines or crinkles appeared elsewhere on his face, a somber, pitted plaster mask with smiling lips attached to it. Hud looked at his eyes. Gibby was right. All the warmth of an agitated snake.

"Seems like we're having a hell of a lot of coincidences since you built your fort in our neighborhood," Gibby said as he stopped before the taller man and looked up at him, pointedly refusing the handshake.

Seemingly untouched by Gibby's rejection, Brother Vance simply swooped his extended hand gracefully around toward his young associate. "Mr. Gunderson, I believe you remember Brother Mark?"

The younger man with a clean-shaven head rose from the stool. Hud did a quick study. In his early thirties, he was as tall as Hud, but he had even a stronger build. Despite the khaki jacket Brother Mark wore over his white shirt and tie, Hud saw the body of a powerful heavyweight boxer.

"You flatter me," Brother Mark was saying to Brother Vance. "Surely nothing has transpired that should mark me indelibly in Mr. Gunderson's memory." Brother Mark made no lead toward a handshake. He simply stood there broadcasting a confident smile—first at Gibby, then at Hud.

Above the boxer's body, Hud saw a handsome, intelligent face with warm, compassionate blue eyes. What a contrast between the two, thought Hud. No, wait a minute. This guy isn't smiling at us. He's *laughing* at us. On your toes, Hud. Long time since you dealt with anything like this.

"And, of course, I'm only just meeting Mr. Hudson Wade Bryant III. Welcome back to the North Country, Mr. Bryant. I trust the abundance of fresh air will help you to sleep soundly. May God be with you."

Caught by surprise, Hud knew it showed on his face. He'd never met these two before. Only been on the ground two hours, he thought, and they already have me pegged...and what's more, they want us to *know* it.

"With the recent renovations at Mr. Gunderson's," Hud found himself saying, "there is an abundance of fresh air. Unfortunately, fresh air keeps me awake...but then you probably already knew that." Brother Mark's smile was unrelenting. Not one muscle in his face or body betrayed a reaction to Hud's words. And Hud felt Brother Vance's steely eyes measuring him, probing, probing, probing. United and seemingly in complete command of the situation, the two strangers presented a powerful adversary. It was like a sophisticated game of chicken, and Hud found himself inclined to concede the first round. He knew now why Gibby had called for help. But Gibby showed no inclination to surrender. The red cheeks that contrasted so vividly with the white beard reminded Hud of Santa Claus.

"So you're over here again putting the heat on Kimberly to sell?" Gibby asked Brother Vance.

"Oh, to the contrary, Mr. Gunderson," Brother Vance said. "We stopped in to pray with Ms. Farber...and to offer our assistance. With opening weekend approaching she's faced with extraordinary physical challenges. Tasks that would take her hours...we can do in minutes."

"Goddamned right about that," Gibby snapped. "Take her years to wear out them boats out there. But with your cowboys around, they'll be on the bottom in no time. What you doing? Working two shifts now? Send your commandos at night and your sabeetoors in the daytime?"

"Now Gibby," came a woman's velvety voice from the doorway to the small adjoining office. "Don't be unkind to these compassionate servants of God. Why, they were *truly* distressed to hear of all the vandalism we've been having lately. And Brother Mark has graciously offered to meet with the vandals to counsel them...should we ever discover who they are."

At the first words, Hud turned to trace the sounds. That voice, he thought, the sophisticated speech, that *can't* be her. Locating the source, he simply stood there and stared.

Kimberly Farber eased into the lodge room with the elegance and grace of a swan, a tall and slender swan with a beautiful, lightly tanned face. Though she wasn't smiling, a pronounced dimple showed near each corner of her sensuous lips. Her flashing blue eyes projected confidence, and blond highlights radiated from the long, blond hair that was pulled back in a pony tail. Angling for the counter walk-through, she stopped there and leaned against the cash register. She wore a navy blue sweatshirt with blue jeans and white sneakers. The top row of white letters across the sweatshirt said BLACK ROCK while the bottom row spelled RESORT.

Hud was captivated. Emotions he'd long since forgotten coiled up in him producing the vertigo of one caught in a powerful whirlpool, about to go over a gigantic waterfall. He struggled for control, tried to focus on something else. The LA in the word BLACK and the OC in the word ROCK stood out nicely, not obnoxiously, just nicely. He glanced up and felt drenched in embarrassment when he realized that she had been watching him watch her. She looked directly into his eyes for a moment, as though measuring him. Her eyes seemed to say, "Forget it, Bryant. Not available."

Turning to Gibby, Kimberly said, "Would you believe it, Gibby? Brother Vance just offered me ten thousand more than he offered last month. Here I am. I've survived the winter, and in one week I'll be bringing in revenue. They think I should take a loss of *forty* thousand?"

Hud managed to break away. He decided to stay out of things unless needed. He'd learn much more by listening.

"It's *their* game," Gibby said, "but there ain't no reason *you* got to play."

"Please, Mr. Gunderson," Brother Vance said, his toothy smile expanding slightly. "The Church is only interested in Ms. Farber's welfare. We can understand her excitement right now, with the season about to open. But…if circumstances should change, if you should decide…for whatever reasons…" he said, glancing at Brother Mark, "…that you choose not to finish the season, please contact us. We stand ready to help you." He nodded at Brother Mark and moved to leave, the fixed smile unwavering. The two hesitated at the door.

"We never know, Ms. Farber, at which turn of the path we shall find God," Brother Vance said, stepping through the doorway.

"May God be with you," added Brother Mark. He flashed an immense smile and left.

"And may He find out about you, Assholes," Kimberly said as the door closed.

Hud blinked, pondered a moment over the unexpected epithet, and then realized that Kimberly had moved toward him. She extended her hand and he took it, surprised at the strength and the callouses he found in the delicate appearing hand.

"I'm Kimberly," she said with a modest smile. "You must be Hudson. Gibby and Sarah have told me about you."

"I answer to Hud," he replied, smiling, surprised by the electricity in the handshake.

"Good enough," she said. "I answer to Kimberly."

Hud thought he sensed a challenge in the words, a warning to keep his distance despite her overwhelming magnetism. Was this beautiful swan really a female black widow? No, he doubted that black widows gave warnings.

"Well," Gibby said, breaking the momentary tension, "I guess we better head back. Know you got lots to do, Kimberly. Anything we can help you with?"

"No, not really. I finished getting the dock out last night. I'd just hooked the tractor up to the boat trailer to start hauling the boats down to the lake when the *saviors* showed up. Sorry about dragging you over here, but it really helped me get rid of them."

"They...*someone* smashed in a window in my cottage this morning," Hud said. "Any action here?"

"Not last night," she said. "It's tonight."

"Tonight?" Hud asked. "How can you predict *that?*"

"Something *always* happens after they stop in to pray for me."

"Isn't that being a little...obvious?"

"Look, Hud," Kimberly snapped, "that's the point. We *know* they're the ones beating us up. And they know we know, but they also know we can't prove it."

"Unless we catch them," Hud said. "Why don't I come over tonight and hang around—"

"Forget it, I'm not looking for a boyfriend," she cut in. "Get *that* straight right—"

"Outside," Hud finished. Damn, she's touchy, he thought. "I'll just curl up quietly in a dark shadow out there and wait."

"Won't do any good, Hud," Gibby said. "I've tried that. Don't know why, but it's just like they *know* when I'm out there. We *both* tried it. I'm pretty good, but them guys is like ghosts. They always seem to know."

"He's right," Kimberly said. "If we're out there nothing happens, or if it does, it's at the other side of the property. They have a perfect view of both of our places from anywhere on their hill. Right, Gibby?"

Hud moved to the picture window. He scanned the peninsula that bordered the right side of the bay, noticing for the first time the huge, new cedar log building that overlooked the bay from its perch above the bluff at the end of the peninsula. Good point, he thought.

"That's right," Gibby said. "And the church land sits up against Kimberly's property back there," he gestured to their right, "'bout five hundred feet back of the fish cleaning house in them woods there." He looked to Hud for a reaction. Getting none, he continued his chatter with Kimberly. "And they just come down through them woods…perfect cover."

Hud fell out of the conversation. He had a line of thought going. The church vandals had a good view. But something told him they had something else going for them. They seemed to know when anyone stood guard, even when well-hidden. No, he decided, they had other sources of information, like maybe….While Gibby and Kimberly talked, Hud began moving quietly about the lodge room, tilting chairs to check the undersides and peeking under tables. The room grew quiet. He glanced up to find the two staring at him.

"Well," he said, "I suppose you know best. Anyway, it's been a long day and I'm tired. Need a good long nap." He motioned for them to resume their conversation. When they finally caught on, he resumed his search. Then, tilting the third stool, he found it—a bug—a listening device, the key to the Bashers' mindreading skills. Replacing the stool quietly, he made for the door. "You absolutely sure you don't want me to come over tonight?" he asked Kimberly. She nodded her confirmation. "Okay, you win. Come on, Gibby, might as well head for the barn."

Chapter 8

David Engstrom leaned over his tiny desk. His head sank lower and lower until his nose touched the open American History binder. Jerking upright, he blinked his eyes, then rubbed them. He leaned back from his carrel and glanced about the room where the twenty-four other members of Fisher Troop, each at his own learning station, had to be struggling with similar fatigue. But none would ever admit it or even discuss the matter.

Since the hundred Minutemen of C Company arrived at the Black Rock Camp, sixteen of every twenty-four hours had been devoted to physical conditioning, military drill, weapons training, American History class, Economic Geography class, inspirational lectures, and religious services. Of the remaining eight hours each day, two were taken up by meals and personal attendance, such as showers, laundry, cleaning weapons and quarters.

David had never seen such blind devotion, such fierce determination as that demonstrated by the members of C Company. Was each of them afraid to be the first to fail? To a man, they were poring over the day's history lesson, the carefully written, heavily slanted, official Church version of American colonial conditions leading up to the Revolutionary War. He wondered what motivated his company mates, these former *losers*, to endure such abuse and still carry on unswerving? They must, absolutely *must* believe in the cause, he thought. But then, he had yet to see much in the political agenda that he himself disagreed with.

He closed the blue binder, laid it atop the red military binder, and opened the white one titled, *The Minutemen of the Thirteen Colonies—Leaders of the Second American Revolution.* He thought about having become a Minuteman, the incredible impact of the experience on his life. The transition from Church to camp was, in ways, almost amusing.

In Minneapolis, he was Brother David, a studious member of the peace-loving Church of the Rock and a faithful employee of the church-owned Armistern Construction Company. At the northern Minnesota camp sponsored by that same church, he was a Minuteman, a recently promoted Corporal David, of C Company, Fisher Troop, Squad One, Team One.

He flipped to the second page. There was the pledge he had signed. The second paragraph caught his eye.

> Should the deterioration of our once great nation lead to anarchy, chaos, or armed conflict, I swear that I will uphold this pledge. Further, it is my charge to prepare myself for survival in all circumstances, to stand ready to sacrifice myself for the success of my mission, and to faithfully execute the commands of my leaders. This do I solemnly pledge to my God and to my country in the name of liberty.

Man, that's heavy, he mused. But for a chance to find Danny, I'd sign it again. Problem is, this isn't shaping up like it should. I thought, by working hard and fitting in, I'd get to hear things, ask a few questions, and find Danny's trail. I know I'm on the right track. But these guys are all so dedicated—and paranoid—that nobody asks anybody anything.

One question too many or in the wrong place and I'm marked. Did I blow it, Julie? Is this all a big mis—

"Ten-Hut!" bellowed the familiar voice of Sergeant Evans. Instantly, twenty young men turned, jumped to their feet, their combat boots creating a burst of thunder against the hardwood floor, and came to attention facing the center of the study room.

"At ease!" the sergeant ordered. The group responded with two crisp thumps on the hardwood. A short, stocky ex-Marine with a blond crewcut and dressed in camouflage fatigues, he strode to the center of the group. David almost liked Sergeant Evans who, despite his Marine background, preferred to shortcut military protocol, at least many of the commands and responses that David thought were silly. But when there was a job to be done, the sergeant was all business.

It was Sergeant Evans who had lobbied for David's early promotion to corporal. The promotion brought with it the responsibility of leading the twelve other men that comprised Squad One, half of Fisher Troop, a group hand-picked for their experience and skills on and in the water. The sergeant himself had named his troop after the fisher, a fierce but obscure relative of the weasel. David smiled inwardly at the thought. In any other army, they would already have been dubbed *F-Troop*, but not in *this* army.

"We have a mission tonight—not an exercise—a mission. No firearms. Squad One in wetsuits. Squad Two, three in wetsuits and nine in black dress for stealth. Pack your books up. Get some sleep. Meet at the briefing room at zero-one-thirty hours. Dismissed!"

Immediately, the group was engulfed in chatter. "A mission?" "We've only been in training a week-and-a-half!" "Whatever it is, they must think we can do it." David smiled. He had never seen the group react to anything with such normality.

"Okay, Guys," he said. "Don't get yourselves all worked up, or you'll never get to sleep. Is there anyone here who *doesn't* need some sleep?" He checked his black diver's watch. "It's twenty-two hundred hours.

With lights out in ten minutes, we can get about three hours in the sack. Let's go."

Fisher Troop filed out of the Study Center and walked briskly through the rain down the drive toward the frame barracks building that housed Fisher and Wolf Troops. Their boots crunched on the crushed rock, but not a word was spoken. Flashes of lightning in the dark sky were answered by two small, flashing blue lights mounted on ten-foot poles at opposite ends of the compound. Code Blue meant no spoken words out of doors after sundown. The customary evening code was Yellow which allowed soft conversation, but no more than that. Code Red imposed no restrictions. Sergeant Evans had said that the camp would see the red flashers only in the event of a full-scale muster, a fire, or an attack by outsiders on the compound.

Fully aware of how sound travels over water, David had deduced, even before the explanatory announcement, that neighbors for miles around would become restless were they to discover that over two hundred armed men occupied the camp. Even the military exercises of the Minutemen were conducted in relative silence with no verbal encouragement, no yelling, no warhoops. The militia in all thirteen colonies were being trained as guerrillas, whose success and survival would depend upon secrecy, stealth, and surprise. The troopers fired their weapons only at the range, a unique, underground state-of-the-art facility on the east side of the peninsula.

David knew as he burrowed into his bunk that he would have trouble sleeping. The tense anticipation felt by the other twenty-four men was compounded for him. He didn't belong here, certainly shouldn't be part of this group's warfare. While he agreed with the Church's stand against the prevailing politics of the land, the only justification he could find for the military preparation of the Minutemen was for defense in case things deteriorated to anarchy.

But here he was, about to lead his squad on a mission. What possible need could there be for a military mission on peaceful Lake Wasikama?

Was their purpose to destroy property? To hurt people? Or both? He regretted his promotion to corporal. It had seemed that the rank would open doors for him in his search for his missing brother. He had never considered the dilemma he now faced. Cool down, he told himself. Maybe the mission will be canceled....But what if it isn't?

Why the wetsuits? With fifty-five-degree water temperature in early May and nighttime surface temperatures that dropped to forty degrees, the water was not a good place to be—even in a wetsuit. One thing was clear. The sergeant called it "a mission, not an exercise." Those words, along with the wetsuits, indicated they were moving against someone on the lake...but why? David tossed and turned, wrestled with questions, then tossed some more. Every line of thought came back to two short questions for which he had no answers. What? Why?

He felt relieved when his tiny alarm sounded at zero-one hundred hours. He jumped up quickly. After tending to his bathroom chores, he wiggled into his wetsuit and donned his black socks and sneakers. He strapped the sheath containing his combat knife to one calf. Into one pocket of his black, nylon parka he put his small, two-way hand radio. Into the other he jammed a plastic bag of trail mix. Then he set out for the briefing room.

"You're probably aware," Sergeant Evans began, when the last of Fisher Troop had settled in, "that we have a couple of very unfriendly neighbors over on the bay, the resort owner and the next door neighbor. Today, our leaders made another attempt to pray with them and resolve the problems that exist. They were ordered off the property. That, of course, while showing an evil heart, is within the rights of any property owner. But these people went beyond their rights." He paused and surveyed the troop. "They have threatened us, vowed to bring down our church. That—we can't allow."

David listened intently, trying to understand the lines he was hearing and, if possible, read between them. The sooner he understood the mission, the sooner he could search for some way out. Perhaps he could feign illness or injury, or—

"Corporal David, you will take the wetsuits in eight canoes, and hold a position just outside of the bay," the sergeant said.

"Corporal William, you and the others not in wetsuits will proceed through the woods to the clearing at the resort," the sergeant said. "You will scan the property with the infra-red and give the all-clear by radio phone. Then, you will scatter about the upper portion of the resort and take cover. You will be our line of protection against interruption."

"Rules of the mission, Sergeant?" David's counterpart asked.

"Avoid detection if at all possible. I remind you, even in a thunderstorm, sound travels over water. If either of your leaders hears a sound from farther than five feet away during the course of this action, you will all have a sleepless week. We intend to physically harm no one. Under no circumstances will lethal force be used. However…should we be detected, you will take the necessary steps to disarm and disable the enemy. We *should not* be discovered and we *cannot* be captured or identified." Sergeant Evans scanned the group, stopping to stare briefly at each man.

"The objective," he continued, "the resort's eight boats. When you wetsuits get the signal, you will enter the bay, staying close to the peninsula shoreline. Each canoe will pull alongside a boat and rig a quick-release line to tow it. The front man from the last canoe will work the dock, cutting the front and rear bungee cords that hold each boat. Questions so far?"

No one spoke. David felt trapped. There would be little opportunity to injure himself on such a mission. And he was expected to lead the majority of the men. If he bailed out now, he could kiss his personal mission good-bye. On the other hand, a great success on the mission could gain him even more respect…and trust. He needed to hear the rest of the plan.

"You will spread out as you tow the boats to the middle of the bay. Then, the front man from each canoe will board the boat, pull the plug, toss it overboard, and return to your canoe. You will be careful to see that you aren't followed or observed as you return to our harbor on the east side of the peninsula. If you even *suspect* you are being observed, you will continue on past our harbor and lose yourselves in the shallow marshes of Weed Bay. Questions?"

"Sergeant, all boats these days have styrofoam flotation," said one trooper. "They'll sink to the gunwhales, but they won't go down."

"Correct," the sergeant said, a smirk appearing on his face. "But can you imagine how much time and work it's going to take to drag those boats back to shore, bail the water out, and get them ready for the walleye opening day after tomorrow? Now remember…not one word from anyone…and not one canoe bumps the side of a boat. I'll be up on the bluff below headquarters. No unnecessary radio gab, but if you encounter problems, I want to know it. Okay…move out."

As David made for the door, Sergeant Evans stopped him. "Corporal David," he said, holding out a plastic grocery bag, "better take these and hand them out…just in case."

Somehow, the small rolls of duct tape that David saw in the bag brought him a sense of relief. Sergeant Evans was indeed a thoughtful person, and the gesture made it evident that his caution against the use of undue force was sincere. Should they be challenged, they would have quick, sticky means of quieting and binding intruders. David hoped they wouldn't need the duct tape, but he was glad the sergeant had thought of it. He smiled and stepped out into the steady rain. He felt confident. He could do this. There would be no permanent damage to property. Really, it was little more than a high school prank—unless they were caught. That couldn't happen. He would see to it.

Twenty minutes later, eight dark green, unmarked and unlicensed canoes made their way out of the small harbor and headed through the steady rain toward the head of the peninsula. The thunder and lightning had moved its electrical dance far to the east, well past Lake Wasikama. Yes, thought David, as the sleek, lightweight vessels knifed quietly through the rippling dark waters, we can do this. These guys are good. That's why they're Fishers. In ten minutes, the vessels lay quietly snuggled single-file against the shoreline at the head of the peninsula, facing Black Rock. The cone-shaped sentinel stood twenty-five feet high, centered in the entrance to the bay, guarding it like a miniature Gibralter. The rain began to let up. David reached for his radio phone and placed it where he could see its signal light. Almost immediately, the light flashed. He snatched it up.

"Fisher One," he said softly.

"Fisher Two," his counterpart returned. "All clear here."

"Daddy Fisher," came the sergeant's voice. "Go for it."

Chapter 9

"Kimberly," he said into the phone, "this is Hud Bryant. Don't say anything you wouldn't want our friends to hear. Okay? Just answer with yes, no, or uh huh...and maybe throw in some nonsense along the way."

"Look, Mr. Bryant, you're a handsome man, but I'm not interested," she said.

"Oh, that's nice," he said. "You started right out with the nonsense. In case they're listening, you'd better end the same way. Now to why I called—will you listen?"

"I...suppose."

"Do you understand why we should leave the bug right where it is for now?" he asked.

"Yes...I guess so."

"Good. We might find a way to use it against them sometime...*if* you can be convincing. Can you carry on conversations without acting like you know it's there?"

"I...think so," she said.

"Work on it. Now, I'm coming over as soon as it gets dark," he said and then added quickly, "but not to see you. I'm going to spend a few hours somewhere down by your dock watching your navy. I think they'll come tonight. I'd thought I might curl up in one of your boats, but it's starting to rain again. Do you lock that little shed down there?"

"Of course."

"It seems to me, with this rain coming on, that you'd be wise to amble on down there and check the boats. Then, when you put something in the shed, leave it unlocked. Okay?"

"Well…I guess so."

"And if you haven't turned the yard light on down there yet, just leave it off until about ten o'clock. Be quite dark by then," Hud said.

"Uh huh."

"All set, Polar Bear," Hud said with a laugh. "We've got a date."

"Thanks…for calling, but I'm really too busy," came a cold reply. "Good night."

Hud checked the time. Seven forty-five. Because of the northern latitude and daylight savings time, it would be almost two hours before dark, and he had already put in a long day.

After leaving the resort early in the afternoon, he and Gibby had loaded his damaged boat onto its trailer and headed for the dealership at Mallard. He had intended to have the jagged hole in the aluminum hull patched, but at decision time, he weakened. He traded the damaged boat for a new one and had them transfer the seventy-horsepower Evinrude outboard and his personal gear to the new blue and silver Lund boat.

On the way home they had stopped at Kennedy Kerrigan's for one of the owner's famous Bunyan Burgers. Still good, Hud thought, and as big as ever. One was a meal for any normal appetite. But now, after a long day and the big burger washed with a beer, Hud felt toasty and tired. And it could be a long, cold night.

He had just dropped into his comfortable leather recliner for a nap when it occurred to him…the Bashers could be out there watching him. He got up and made the rounds, closing all the curtains and blinds, something he'd never done before. Then he set his tiny, square travel alarm and stretched out. He dropped off to sleep in minutes.

Hud's weightless body drifted off in space until the alarm sounded at nine o'clock. He grabbed the clock and squeezed it into submission, opened his eyes, and adjusted to the darkening room. He could hear the steady rain on the roof, accented by crackling lightning and booming thunder. Then, with a sudden determined effort, he launched himself from the chair and into a series of rushed preparations.

He splashed cold water on his face, loaded the coffee pot, preheated his stainless thermos, unlocked his gun cabinet, and removed his shotgun and a handful of shells. Then he changed into lightweight thermal underwear, warm socks, a lined nylon jogging suit, and his insulated boots. After filling the thermos, he stuffed a plastic bag filled with Sarah's chocolate chip cookies into one pocket, and reached for his heavy black slicker. When he had his camera, which was loaded with fast film, buried in his slicker pocket, he slung the thermos on a belt over one shoulder and tucked the shotgun vertically under the raincoat. Grabbing his heavy duty flashlight, he stepped out into the rain. He paused then for something else he'd never done before. He locked the cottage door.

Hud stopped at Gibby's, rapped three times on the kitchen window, and made for the path to the resort. All set, he thought. Sarah would keep an eye on the house and the dock, and Gibby planned to hole up in his ice fishing house out behind the workshop. Hud wished they had a set of cellular phones or walkie talkies. Something to think about on the next trip to town.

The narrow, winding path proved to be a treacherous challenge in the dark. The rain pelted his face despite the hooded slicker, the footing was slippery and uneven, and his balance was affected by the contorted posture he had to assume in order to carry the shotgun beneath the slicker. The flashlight helped, but it couldn't possibly show what he needed to see. Midway through the woods, he stopped to get a new grip on the weapon with his left hand.

R-r-r-i-i-i-i-p-p baamm! The lightning bolt struck about two hundred yards to his right. His scalp tingled at the sound of the bristling electricity. Hud thought his heart stopped at the cannon shot climax. When he was sure he had survived the phenomenon, he struck out again, much faster and with little concern for traction. He doused the light for the last fifty feet of his tunnel-like passage through the woods and simply barreled ahead, trusting his balance and reactions to keep him upright.

A few feet from the clearing he stopped to listen. Then he moved up to the edge and paused again, studying the acreage for any sign of movement. Cutting to his left, he made his way across the resort between the front row of cottages and the lake. He stopped twice behind trees to watch and listen. The yard light above the shed was dark. What if she left the shed locked? he thought. No way am I climbing into *aluminum* boats with all those fireworks up there. Finally, he trotted the last fifty feet, crossed over the driveway that led down to the concrete boat launch ramp, and made it to the shed.

Fumbling with the hasp, he jerked the door open and piled inside. He located the light switch and flipped it. He wouldn't dare use the overhead lightbulb for long. The light might show outside through cracks in the structure. But he risked it briefly to get his bearings. Except for the small, clear spot where he stood, the four-foot by six-foot shed held a tightly packed accumulation of life jackets, Mae Wests, oars, anchors, coils of rope, depth finders, and marine batteries. Across the end of the building closest to him ran a small workbench.

He quickly unloaded, placing his flashlight, camera, thermos, shotgun shells, and cookies on the workbench. He slid three shells into the magazine of the Browning pump, checked the safety, and stood it carefully against the wall close by. Pulling an empty six-gallon plastic bucket from under the workbench, he turned it over and laid two lifevests across it for padding. As was to be expected in the North Country, he found two candles on a shelf. He lit one and set it in a small tin can. Then he slipped out of his rain gear and hung it on a nail.

Hud surveyed his cramped quarters. "Just as good as the Hilton," he mumbled. "If I had TV, I could watch the Angels game." He flipped off the light and settled himself on the bucket. The spattering of the rain on the roof reminded him of how warm and dry he really was. He poured a cup of coffee and pulled a cookie from the bag. In but minutes, he found himself reaching for another cookie and pouring a refill. Not good, he thought. At this rate my goodies will be gone by ten-thirty, and then what'll I do?

He fell to analyzing his stakeout. The weather had left him little choice. Yet, while he was comfortable, he felt helpless. He could see nothing—he didn't even know if Kimberly had turned the yard light on. With the door closed and the rain striking the roof, he could hear nothing else. Yet here he sat, totally blind and deaf, expecting to catch a couple of vandals.

Just have to chance it, he thought, slowly easing the door open two inches and propping it there with a small cardboard box. Despite the rain, it was obvious that the yardlight above the shed had been turned on. He checked his watch. Ten-fifteen. He thought the Bashers would probably play it safe by waiting until well after midnight. Certainly he would if he were planning trouble. Could he sit on a plastic bucket in the darkness for several hours?

He did his best to make the waiting period productive. He thought for a while about Kimberly Farber. Was she hostile to *all* men? No, she was friendly toward Gibby. Was she hostile to all *young* and *eligible* men? With the sudden implosion that demolished her marriage, probably so. Then too, with her face and figure, she had undoubtedly been the target of male hits for a long time. He decided he could work around her hostility and eventually get past it—unless it really was the deeply imbedded arrogance that it seemed to be.

He chuckled at the irony. In seconds, he had spent more mental energy on Kimberly Farber than on all of the women collectively since Ellie. And for the first time since Ellie, he found himself analyzing, measuring what it might take to get close to a woman. He liked the feeling it gave him, as though the candle burning in the tin can had a counterpart somewhere deep within him. He tried to push his thoughts in other directions, but they rambled out of control.

With the first nice day, he'd fly into the Falls, refuel the Archer, and do some shopping. A number of things he needed. He thought he'd seen a glint of interest in Kimberly's blue eyes that didn't blend with her protective stance. Of course, Saturday was walleye opening, a nearly sacred, annual ritual for millions of Minnesotans. There could be no flying Saturday, only fishing. It had been a long, long time since he had seen a sweatshirt and a pair of jeans look as good as they did on her. He thought, with the storm front that was moving through, he should work that tiny channel through the rocks at Berry Island. He'd try that first. He wondered how much Gibby or Sarah had told Kimberly about him. If Berry Island didn't pay off, there would be a good chance that the storm drove walleyes to school in that long slot on the north side of Sweet's Island.

Unlike all of those women who had paraded through his life recently, Kimberly might be turned off if she knew of his financial status. She's definitely on an independence kick. It might be temporary—might not. He hoped Robert could come up with the money to buy HPS. That's certainly what Ellie would want. Is Kimberly what Ellie would want? Strange, he thought, I never even wondered about that with all those other women. But *now* I'm asking?

Hud seemed to be locked into the strange mental mode. His thoughts, including questions and answers, observations, and decisions, rambled on from fishing to Kimberly, from the Bible Bashers to Kimberly, from his Orange County businesses to Kimberly. But finally, he relaxed, leaned against the plywood wall, and dozed. At one o'clock, the thunder drifted away, its nerve-shattering explosions turning to gentle, distant rumblings. It became easier to ride them out without opening his eyes each time they spoke.

He awoke shortly after two o'clock. Did he hear something? No, he thought, it's what I don't hear. The rain has stopped. He poured the last of his coffee, took a sip, and glanced at his watch, wondering if his effort had been a waste of time. He would have preferred to spend the time up at the house with Kimberly. If nothing else, he'd have some idea by now of what she's really like—

Tzzztttt! The slivver of light allowed in by the partially-open door disappeared. Hud felt the hair on his neck bristle. The moment had arrived. Someone had popped the yard light bulb. They were right outside. He blew out the candle and closed his eyes briefly to speed his adjustment to the darkness. Then he leaned closer to the opening in the doorway, watching and listening.

After a full minute of silence, he began to pick up soft, indefinable sounds. He reached for the flashlight with his left hand and the Browning with his right. By twisting his body around, he changed his line of sight through the partial opening so he could see a portion of the dock. A dark, shadowy figure moved on the dock, stopped, moved, stopped, moved. There's my man, he thought. But I'd better be careful—probably another one out there somewhere.

Slowly he pushed the door open. Stepping out, he gently closed the door. Then he turned to scan the dock, to locate the vandal's helper. There! Hud thought, there he is! In a canoe next to the closest boat sat another dark, shadowy figure. Hud focused again on the vandal who moved about on the dock. He was cutting the boats loose—one by one, he was cutting the lines.

Hud was glad his eyes were adjusting to the darkness, but he didn't like what he saw. He started slowly toward the gangplank that bridged the gap from the shoreline to the dock. Then he saw another movement...and another...and another! Stopping, he held his breath. There were creatures out there, identical creatures swarming around the boats. They were man-sized, but they didn't look like men. They looked like black, leathery aliens from a sci-fi movie.

He jerked the pump action to chamber a shell. The loud *click—click* resonated crisply. Instantly the creatures froze in stop-action. Hud had expected nothing like this. He had no ideas, no plan. But he had betrayed his presence. He released the safety on the weapon and switched on the flashlight. Aiming it with his left hand, which also cradled the barrel of the shotgun, the light focused upon whatever the gun pointed toward. He swept the combination slowly from side to side. What he saw sent icy vibrations from his tailbone to the top of his head.

On each side of the dock floated four of Kimberly's boats, facing outward. Next to each boat was a canoe occupied by two of the intruders. None had so much as twitched. SEALS! They were like Navy SEALS, fifteen to twenty of them, all in black wetsuits with something dark smudged all over their faces. Hud had no idea how to control a group that size. He could only hope they were dreadfully afraid of his shotgun. He kept the light moving from side to side.

"All right, you Bible Bashers," he said in a voice that he hoped was firm and calm. "I'm just a little nervous about this situation, so don't move a muscle until I tell you. I'm fully loaded, the safety's off, and the first quick move'll set *me* off. I probably can't nail all of you, but I can easily get half. Ask yourself *which* half you want to be part of." He paused to see if his brain really was functioning, and if it was, what he should do next.

"Your first move—careful now—raise all hands slowly and turn those white palms toward me," Hud said. "You there—you on the dock! Throw that knife in the water!" The intruder hesitated for a moment, turned, and dropped the knife over the edge of the dock. Then he faced Hud and raised his hands. "Good. Now here's how we're going to handle thi—"

Something sharp suddenly jabbed against Hud's back. He stiffened. At exactly the same time, a pair of quick, agile hands jammed a finger behind the trigger of the Browning, switched the safety on, and wrenched the weapon from him. A strong hand grabbed his collar from behind and pulled, bending him over backwards to a point of helplessness. Yet another firm hand slapped a patch of duct tape over his mouth and another over his eyes. Then the collar hand pulled him down to his back in the sand. He had no sooner landed on his back than he felt his ankles being taped together. He was rolled over to his belly, and his wrists were taped together behind his back. It all occurred in a few seconds, so incredibly fast that Hud had no chance to react, let alone comprehend what was happening to him.

His captors dragged him over to the shed. Throwing him into the small space, they closed the door. Hud could hear the padlock snap shut. He was back in his little world. The outside world from which he had been expelled grew quiet. It was as though the episode never happened, except that here he was, trussed up like a pig destined for the barbecue pit. As he lay there, fitting the pieces together, trying to make sense of the experience, he concluded that he was lucky to be alive. He had carried a loaded gun into a confrontation with occasional vandals only to find himself facing someone's highly trained, professional commando unit.

But from another perspective, his luck couldn't have been worse. The thought prompted him to move, to do what he could for himself. By straining, wiggling, and twisting, he managed to coax the crumpled, embarrassed skeleton of the once great security guard up to his knees and eventually to his feet. Then, after twisting about to feel his way in the tight but now familiar setting, he plopped down on his six-gallon throne and set about preparing himself for the fallout that was sure to come for his pitiful defense of Kimberly Farber's navy.

Chapter 10

Hud alternated between his miserable seat on the bucket and the standing position. It only transferred the aches from one place to another. He couldn't believe at first how difficult a simple movement became with ankles bound together and hands taped behind one's back.

During one of his changes, he inadvertently knocked the lifevests he had used for padding on the plastic bucket onto the floor.

"F-f-fit!" he cursed through taped lips. He felt the pressure mounting inside, expanding rapidly from frustration to bristling, boiling anger. God damn it, Bryant, he thought, it's bad enough you're going to have to face Kimberly. You really screwed up. It's your fault her boats are gone. But are you just going to stand here all night like a helpless whimp? And your bladder's so full your back teeth are floating. You don't look bad enough already—you want her to find you here with wet pants?

In another minute, he had worked himself past the defeat. He considered lying on his side and kicking at the door until he smashed his way out. He could probably accomplish that. But then what? He decided to systematically attack his bonds. They imprisoned him more than the padlock; they denied him the simplest basic movements...like pissing.

First, the eyes. How much of his blindness was due to the tape? Struggling once more to his feet, he leaned into a corner, searching for the light switch with an elbow. After several attempts at brushing an elbow upward against ill-chosen protrusions, he felt as much as heard a delightful *Click!*

"All—ight!" he mumbled, astounded at the rush he felt from the minuscule victory. But the light that sneaked up under the lower edges of his blinder provided a visible trophy. In their haste, his adversaries had slapped the duct tape over his eyes rather carelessly. They had achieved their purpose, but the tape had not bonded to his upper cheeks. By bending over the edge of the workbench and rubbing slowly upward, he loosened the left side to the point where, by tilting his head back, he could identify objects.

He squinted about the small workbench area for items that might prove useful. No use for old fish hooks, or gut leaders, or cheap plastic bobbers. He spotted an old fillet knife stuck in a slot in a small tool shelf. In his present condition, it was useless, but if....There was a rusty, sixteen-penny nail sticking out of a two-by-four stud, about shoulder high. There, he thought, the friend I've been looking for.

He faced the nail, bent over, and by twisting his head back and forth, he worked the head of the nail into the corner of his mouth, behind the duct tape. With a jerk of his head, he felt the tape rip loose from a small portion of skin. It smarted, but the pain was quickly washed away by adrenaline. He remounted the nail. He could taste the rust. The second jerk gained almost an inch of freedom. The progress incited Hud, and he attacked the nail again and again until the silver-gray patch came free, finally remaining stuck to his friend, the nail. As he had worked through phase one of his escape plan, he had already set out the rest.

Hunching far over the workbench, Hud got a good bite on the wooden handle of the fillet knife. But as he tried to lift it upward and out of its slot, it caught and fell back. He thought of the next nine tries as practice. Finally, he lifted the narrow blade out of its slot and dropped it on the bench top. Then, gripping the handle firmly in his teeth, he bent over and carefully dropped the knife near his feet.

It took him several minutes of maneuvering to curl up on the tiny floor in such a position that he could grasp the knife behind him in his hands. Once that was accomplished, he sawed quickly through the duct tape that bound his wrists. Then, trying to save as much of his eyebrow hairs as he could, he used a series of short tugs to remove the blinder. Interesting, he thought, as he slashed the ankle bindings, each step was just that much easier than the previous one. Now, the door.

He studied the construction of the homemade piece. He could certainly break out, but he hated to demolish Kimberly's door in the process. She was going to be upset enough at having her boats stolen. As he searched for the way out, he happened to glance down at the plywood floor. There was an obvious cut there in the wood, a seam that wasn't where it belonged.

Moving the plastic bucket, Hud traced the seam. It formed a rectangle approximately eighteen inches square. After staring at the outline for some time, he felt a tinge of embarrassment when he recognized the phenomenon. The old shed had been someone's ice fishing house. The outline was the standard removable panel in the floor. Remove it and cut a hole in the ice to fish through. "In this case," he said aloud, "if there's room underneath, I'm out of here." Using the knife once more, he pried the panel loose. He shined the light downward. The space was barely adequate, but the ground beneath the shed was one mass of mud because of the recent rains. He checked his watch. Three-thirty. What had seemed like an eternity had been little more than an hour.

Hud eased headfirst down through the hole into the darkness and squished his way on his belly toward the door side of the building. Each movement shook his threatening bladder. When his head protruded from under the shed, he raised it and shined his light at his first glimpse of freedom.

There, inches from his nose, stood a pair of black rubber boots. Oh, no! he thought. They came back? Gradually raising the focus of his light, he tilted his head upward, following the light past the boots to dark-colored jeans, to a navy parka, to the most beautiful face he'd ever seen. If there had been love in those eyes, he'd have been hooked for eternity. But the anger he had expected wasn't there, either.

"I suppose there's some reason you're slithering around under my boathouse?" Kimberly asked.

"Oh man…there must be a song for a situation like this." Suddenly, he cared little for what Kimberly Farber thought or said; he simply wanted to get out from under that shed and find sixty seconds of privacy. He felt his urgency rush beyond that point where one chooses words. "After all that—you show up *now?*" The feet stepped back. Hud wriggled out and scrambled to his feet. "You might unlock the shed," he said, heading around the corner into the darkness. "I'm very late for an appointment."

When he returned, Kimberly was bent over in the shed, replacing the floor panel. Hud stood quietly, captivated by the stimulating shape that peaked out from beneath the parka. She scooped up the remnants of duct tape that were scattered about and turned to face him.

"What's all this?" she asked.

"Uh…before we get into that, I've got to tell you…your boats are gone," Hud said. "I tried, but….I'm sorry, Kimberly. I blew it."

"Are you all right?" she asked. "Did they hurt you?" She waved the scraps of tape again.

"That's all incidental, Kimberly. They stole your boats. Do you understand? Your boats are gone."

"Look," she said, fanning her hands before Hud's face, "we're not communicating. Now, I have a job I have to do right away. Here." She handed him her powerful nine-volt lantern. "Go out to the end of the dock and see what you can see, will you? Now, go—go." She turned from him, pulled an empty half-gallon plastic jug from a box, and began tying a lightweight yellow nylon rope to its handle.

Reluctantly, Hud turned and headed out on the dock. She seems to know exactly what she's doing, he thought, but what is she doing? He pointed the powerful beam out over the water and began sweeping slowly from side to side. He wondered why he was searching the bay. Certainly those commandos are long gone.

"Wait a minute," he said aloud. He thought he saw something out there, slightly to the left and about three hundred yards out. He concentrated his sweep to that area, finally relocating the object. He studied it for a moment, turned and headed quickly for the shed.

"You knew that?" he asked. "You knew one of your boats was out there?"

"I know *two* of them are out there," she said, "and I'm *hoping* they're all out there. I don't think they stole them—I think they scuttled them. You any good in a canoe?"

"I'm okay," he replied. "Let's have a look."

Donning life vests, they grabbed paddles, flashlights, and eight plastic jug markers Kimberly had prepared and circled the shed to the rack that held the canoe. In no time, they had the aluminum craft in the water and loaded with the strange cargo.

"You take the back?" Kimberly asked. "I'm pretty new at this."

Hud saw quickly as they headed out into the foot-high waves that she was indeed new at it. But as they reached the middle of the bay, she was catching on quickly. Kimberly stopped paddling to scan the area with her light.

"There's one!" she said, motioning to her right, "and another one over there!"

With several strong strokes, Hud closed the gap to the first boat. True as advertised, the light-tan aluminum sixteen-footer had sunk only to the gunwhales. The weight of the engine in back tilted the point of the bow up a few inches out of the water. Good, Hud thought, that'll make it easier to find the others. Kimberly tied a marker to the bow, and they moved off to the next. Within a half-hour, they had located and marked all eight boats and were headed back to shore.

"I feel a whole lot better now," Kimberly said. "I was so afraid someone would smash into one of them. The markers might help." With the canoe back on the rack, Kimberly shined her light at Hud's mud-covered belly, shook her head, and chuckled. "Come on up to the house. We'll get you into something clean and dry."

As they climbed the gentle slope, threading their way among the pines, Hud detailed his confrontation with the wet-suited commandos. "Sorry, Kimberly," he said. "They really caught me off guard. I guess my mind had decided from the outset that there would be two of them. Never occurred to me that I'd run into a whole squadron of SEALS. Not too bright."

"Forget it," she said. "I'd have expected more than *two,* but I certainly wouldn't have been prepared for *twenty.* I think your experience—by the way…thank you, Hud," she said, reaching over and giving his sleeve a tug. "We've learned two things: the Bible Bashers do in fact have an army over there, a well-trained army. And they're not ready to get *too* nasty yet."

She led the way through the lodge room, motioning toward the stool that held the listening device. Hud felt so encouraged, almost entranced by her apparent change in attitude, that he had gone several steps before her gesture registered. They passed through a small office into a large farm-style kitchen with old, varnished plywood cabinets and well-worn gray linoleum that had to be at least two decades old.

Kimberly directed him to the bathroom and said, "Jump in the shower. You must be chilled clear through. I've got an extra-large jumpsuit around here somewhere. My dad left it when he visited last winter," she said as she closed the door.

Minutes later, Hud pushed back the shower curtain and reached for a towel. Hanging from a hook on the bathroom door was a khaki jumpsuit. He deliberately squelched the tantalizing thought that Kimberly Farber had been right there in the tiny little room, not four feet away from his nude condition. He doubted that he could have simply hung the garment on the hook and left, had their roles been reversed. Hurriedly drying himself, he dressed, rolled his muddy jogging suit up, and made his way toward the kitchen. As he passed through a corner of the living room, his attention was caught by the hideous brown carpeting, its age evidenced by the threadbare portions. Around the perimeter of the room sat the worst collection of mismatched, cheap, and worn-out furniture he'd ever seen. It had to be leftovers from the cottages. Nobody could deliberately choose a collection like that.

"Feel better?" Kimberly asked as she bent over the stove. The brewing hot chocolate smelled as good as she looked with her red and blue plaid flannel shirt neatly tucked into her jeans. Certainly nothing sexy about her clothing, Hud thought, except that on her....He guessed her height at five-nine, and he couldn't have planned a better distribution. It wasn't a voluptuous figure, just nice—things where they belonged. Her pony tail swished casually as she moved. Hud smiled. Always been a sucker for pony tails and braids, he thought.

"Much better. Thanks for the shower," he said. "That smells terrific. Good idea."

"I thought it would be good to warm us up, calm us—or at least calm me—down after all the excitement, and help us sleep. It is after four o'clock, you know." She smiled as she motioned Hud to a naugahyde-covered chair at an old chrome-legged table. Setting two steaming mugs of hot chocolate on the table, she reached for a small plate of graham crackers and flopped down, with one leg folded beneath her, on the chair to his right.

They sipped from the mugs, took an occasional bite from a cracker, then sipped again. Hud felt an awkward cloud of silence mushrooming. He tried not to look at her, but that seemed to inflate the cloud even faster. Ridiculous, he thought, like a couple of eleven-year-olds. It

seemed like we were doing better. I'm not going to let this, this whatever
it is spoil a good—

"Can we be friends?" she asked, looking at him seriously.

"I thought you'd never ask," he said with a laugh.

"No, I mean friend-friends. Can you handle that?"

"I'm not sure," he said, "but it'd help the odds if I understood."

"Seven months ago, I was a married woman. I'm not sure now if I was
happily married, but I wasn't unhappily married. Then, well I imagine
Gibby and Sarah have told you the story. Since we split, I've been leered
at or propositioned by almost every unmarried man and half of the married ones, within twenty miles."

Hud sipped his hot chocolate and smiled.

"And the way those Bashers undress me," she continued, "I'd much
rather have them scuttle my boats than sit out there in the lodge room
and do things to me."

Hud's smile grew wider.

"Well, after awhile you just get to the point where you look for the
worst in all men. I even took a couple of cheap shots at you." She looked
over her cup for his reaction and suddenly seemed flustered. "You're—
laughing at me?"

"Anything but, Kimberly Farber, anything but." Hud searched the
blue eyes and saw the pain and confusion that had been masked by
anger. Reaching over, he took one of her hands in his. "I'd be proud to
be your friend-friend, Kimberly. You need time…and I've got lots of it."
He gave her hand a squeeze and released it. But the warmth of her touch
stayed with him.

"Thanks, Hud. I hope you understand, right now I need a friend
more than I need a lover."

"Don't particularly like it," he quipped, "but I certainly understand…been there. Now…tomorrow—whoops—this morning, we've
got a navy to retrieve."

"I can do that," she said quickly, her blue eyes flashing. Then her face sobered. "Who am I kidding? I haven't the slightest idea how to do that. I've got eight sunken boats out there, and all I'm left with is the canoe." With her elbows on the table top, she rested her face in her hands. A tear trickled down one side of her small, pointed nose.

"Kimberly, I understand your fierce pride. I really admire it. And I don't want to meddle in your business. But there are going to be times when you *need* help. This is one of them. If I'm a friend...let me help?"

She looked over at Hud through teary eyes and nodded.

"Gibby and I'll have your navy back in action by noon—have to run down to the corner store for new plugs for the boats. Gibby just bought a new water pump, and he's dying to try it out. I'll tow your boats back one at a time and beach them. Gibby'll pump while I go after the next one. Then, when we've got 'em all dried out, we'll give each motor a run around the bay to clear it out good. And for this afternoon and tomorrow, Sarah can help you with the lodge room. I'll do the bait house and the gas pump. Gibby'll take care of the dock, the ramp, and the parking." Hud got up, rinsed his cup, grabbed his bundle of wet, muddy clothes, and started for the door.

"You *do* have it all figured out, don't you? With all that help, what do you need *me* for?" Kimberly asked.

Hud stopped, leaned back into the kitchen, and said, "To count the money...and keep an eye out for the Bible Bashers. With all the pressure on you this weekend, you can bet they'll have *something* cooked up. I think they're just getting started." He smiled and waved. "Get some sleep."

Chapter 11

"At ease, Gentlemen," ordered Brother Vance.

The two young corporals responded crisply. While their bodies matched the template of a soldier at ease, there was nothing about them, from their combat boots to their short haircuts, that was at ease. Brother Vance looked them over, then cast a glance toward Father Jeranko who nodded approvingly. Jeranko stood and stepped close to the pair. He looked Corporal William in the eye for some time, then turned and repeated the treatment with Corporal David.

"I asked for you to be sent over," Jeranko said at last, "to commend you on the fine job you did leading last night's mission. Confronted as you were, you might have panicked and made grievous errors that could have severely compromised our operation. But you handled the situation aggressively and professionally. Corporal David?"

"Sir!" the taller of the enlisted men responded.

"To what do you attribute such impeccable judgment—superior intelligence, training, or dumb luck?"

"Sir, I'd attribute the impeccable judgment to Corporal William. All I did was order my men to hold their positions and cooperate. Corporal

William and two of his squad disarmed and dispatched the man…took him out so fast that I'm sure we were long gone before he figured out what happened."

"Is that right, Corporal William?" Father Jeranko asked.

"Yes…Sir…I guess that's basically what happened."

"Fine job, both of you. It appears that our selection process for promotion has proven sound once more. Keep up the good work, and remember, the example you set will lead to greater victories than the orders you give."

"Ten-Hut!" commanded Brother Vance. "Dis-missed!"

When the door closed behind the corporals, Jeranko turned to Brother Vance. "Check him out…everything."

"Corporal William?"

"No, the other one, Corporal David."

"But—he might be as close as we've ever come to the perfect soldier."

"Exactly…I don't trust anyone *that* good and especially that *honest*. If he is what you think he is, we're all the more fortunate to have a soldier like that and to *know* that's what we really have." Father Jeranko moved to a small table nearby, poured himself a cup of coffee and, after a brief deliberation, selected a frosted French doughnut from the assortment. "When's the last time you had this room swept?" he asked, as he settled into the expensive leather chair.

"Five days ago—no bugs," said Brother Vance. "Do it every two weeks."

"Better make it weekly."

"Weekly it is," said Vance. "Any particular reason?"

"Two reasons…the rapid growth in our manpower…and the extreme sensitivity regarding some of the activities we are about to undertake," said Jeranko.

Brother Vance had waited impatiently through the twenty-four hours since Father Jeranko returned from the Colonial Congress. He resented the fact that the special meeting of the leaders of the Thirteen Colonies had been conducted behind an impenetrable wall of secrecy. Not even he, Father Jeranko's right hand, had been allowed to attend the meeting or even to know its location. Finally, he sensed, he was about to be brought in on at least some of the developments of the Congress.

"You've been a little irked by the secrecy, Brother?" Father Jeranko asked, his perpetual smile showing a hint of compassion.

"Well...yes. Yes, I guess I have."

"Can't say that I blame you," said Jeranko. "You and I have been together a long, long time. I've never forgotten how you covered things when our little operation in Saigon went down. It must be hard, after the trust we've always had between us, to stand by, not knowing what's going on and wondering why I don't trust you."

Brother Vance knew he couldn't have said it better. He simply nodded.

"It might make you feel a little better to know just how far the Colonial leaders went to maintain secrecy for this Congress," Jeranko continued. "It was held in Atlanta. We know the FBI and the Treasury are very interested in us. We don't think they have any idea yet who we are, what we are, or how large we are. But, just in case they had a line on any of the thirteen individuals and were watching major airports, we all flew into various regional airports like Chattanooga, then rented cars and drove to Atlanta."

The leader focused his intense gaze on Brother Vance. "Now, Brother, imagine that a number of you knew in advance of our plans. Somehow, the details slipped out and we were arrested. You would be among those under suspicion. Was your pride worth the risk?"

"I'm...sorry," said Brother Vance. "I should have...known...."

"Brother," Jeranko said, "you have always been more than my trusted assistant, truly, more like a brother. But hear me now. There might again be times when you must be excluded from the loop. If so, you must accept that. Think of it as a means of protecting me. If you can't access certain vital information, that means there are others at your level all around the United States who likewise can't access that information. And that makes travel safer for me."

"I understand, Sir," said Brother Vance.

"The Second American Revolution will rank in history as one of the great endeavors in the name of liberty. It will be compared to the first American Revolution and World War II. But the number of imperialist soldiers who oppose us makes the British army of the seventeen-seventies look like a Boy Scout troop. Therefore, we must, like our compatriots of two hundred-plus years ago, depend on secrecy, stealth, and surprise. We know *who* we are and *where* we are. *They don't.* They only know who they are and where they are—and *we* know that also. Therein lies our advantage. Jeopardize that…and we lose our advantage."

"Of course," said Brother Vance. How many times had he given the same speech?

"From now on, you will be heavily involved in the planning here at Colony IV, and you will be busy," said Father Jeranko. "The Thirteen Colonies have developed a well-conceived, three-phased plan of coordinated activities nationwide. The first phase is to plant the seed of dissent and nurture it, to show the people of the United States, and convince them, that they have become, in fact, the slaves of their elected leaders and that only the Minutemen of the Thirteen Colonies can lead them from this bondage. Our first action of Phase One is scheduled for next week. We'll get into the details in this afternoon's meeting."

Brother Vance felt a familiar surge of excitement and power ripple through him. His leader's briefings had always affected him that way, principally because—Father Jeranko's plans nearly always worked. The only exceptions? In Viet Nam, where Colonel Jeranko had regularly been handcuffed by stupidity and indecision at higher levels.

"Phase Two," continued Father Jeranko, "is a two-pronged effort scheduled to begin on July Fourth. We will continue a series of actions to reinforce Phase One. Along with them, we'll launch a strong political campaign to influence the conventions of the Republicans and Democrats. We know we can't derail their nominations. Obviously, those are already set in stone. But we will inject a virus called uncertainty into their processes. As the campaigns go on into the fall, we have countless well-documented scandals to bring to the public, episodes that will make Clinton's pecker picking look like a Sunday School class. There'll be no need for the prosecutor dog and pony shows. With each exposure, and I do mean exposure, our Minutemen will gain support and momentum."

"Any recent defections from the major parties?" Brother Vance asked, refilling his coffee cup and returning to his chair opposite Father Jeranko.

"I'm told we have four more commitments, three Republicans and one Democrat, all clean enough that we can accept them. They, in turn, are establishing communications with several others, but at least two of the prospects are too messy to touch. At any rate, the four additions bring the total to twenty-two, and this is all before it hits the fan."

"Are these early defectors running scared?"

"No," replied Father Jeranko, "these are the purists, the ones who see what's wrong with our government and have had enough. The others will come running to us when we start turning the lights on about mid-August or so. Then our committee will be working around the clock, sorting out the keepers."

"I take it Phase Three means...?" Brother Vance paused. "Will it come to that—actual war?"

"The leaders feel that if we find ourselves at war—Phase Three—it will be for one of two reasons. The first...we get the worker bees all riled up, but for whatever reasons, don't get them coming to our hive. All hell will break loose. Once they discover that law enforcement can't begin to cope, we'll have a hundred million cannibals in a free-for-all. If it comes to that, the Thirteen will probably have to go into survival mode, protect ourselves, and wait for our opportunity to take control. Realistically, that may never come."

"And the second reason? The government discovers one of the Colonies and moves on them?" Vance asked.

"Right. We hope it won't come to this either, but it would be preferable to the first situation. If government troops move on one of our Colonies, the other twelve will each start thirteen more brushfires—well away from their central location. It will be our hope...." Father Jeranko paused and stared out over the lake for a moment, "our hope that this kind of government action will be the catalyst that will bring citizen support to us in immeasurable droves."

"But, if we must resort to Phase Three, we will provoke the government rather than risk the chaos?" Brother Vance concluded, looking to his leader for confirmation. A long silence followed.

Finally, Father Jeranko nodded. "If we must," he said slowly, "if we must."

He settled back in his luxurious leather chair and gazed once more at the lake. Suddenly he smiled and motioned to Brother Vance. Together they stood at the window, quietly following a strange scenario as it unfolded on the bay below them. A large man in a red jogging suit sat at the steering console of a slow-moving blue and silver Lund.

"Who's that?" Father Jeranko asked.

"Name's Bryant, a friend of the Gundersons. Spends time at their place every summer."

The bow of the boat protruded high out of the water while the large outboard engine at the stern rode so low it was hardly visible. Even from high on the bluff, it was apparent that the boat was mushing along, its outboard laboring heavily. The water behind it churned and boiled, like the contents of a giant cauldron, its light green froth reflecting in the morning sun. Several yards behind the Lund came slogging the object of its labor, a nearly submerged boat, its water-filled hull all but immovable, resisting the towboat like a rocky island.

From their position high above, the spectators could identify the shapes of seven other near-sunken boats scattered about the northwest end of Black Rock Bay. Father Jeranko pointed them out, one by one. Then he chuckled and said softly. "Nice touch, Brother, nice touch." He turned back to his chair. Responding quickly to the cue, Brother Vance took his seat.

"Now, Brother, some movements to arrange—immediately. I want you to transfer the demolition team of Company A up here from Minneapolis. Along with them, we want the intelligence team from Company B and the Company A aircraft maintenance crew from Bendon Airport. Get things moving right away. I'll fill you in this afternoon."

"I'll get right on it," said Brother Vance. Finally, he thought, I'm involved.

"Oh, one more thing," his leader said, drawing two slips of paper from his inside coat pocket. "We have two guests flying into the Falls this afternoon. One is an expert on the kinds of intelligence we need to gather, and the other will work with our demolition team. Here are the flights they'll be on. Send the van to pick them up. When they get here, make sure they have everything they need. We have just three days to finish preparations for the day our nation stood still."

Chapter 12

Hud felt the tension mounting. His headache screamed at him; pain shot upward between his shoulder blades; and there seemed to be no remedy for the agony that carved at his insides. He stood behind the steering console and leaned to his right, out over the water, his taut body trying vainly to lend its strength. He looked beyond the bow to gauge his distance to shore. Behind him, the seventy-horse Evinrude roared like a wounded dragon, hurling thick blue clouds of exhaust that burned at Hud's eyes. But the acrid smoke was only symbolic of the real torment.

For three hours, he had tortured and overheated the engine, and it pained him as surely as sticking a knife into a friend. He was abusing a treasure, a mechanical wonder, and the pain was his reward. No engine should be subjected to such strain, running at full throttle to tug a sunken hulk through the water so slowly that movement was barely discernible. It wasn't the cost of the wear and tear. He could write a check for another new engine and not miss the money. It was the abuse. And he had asked for it; he had glibly volunteered the service. He hadn't considered the power required to horse a sunken sixteen-foot sea anchor through the water for half a mile—or the time it would take to repeat the distressing adventure seven times.

Finally, however, he was on the last trip. A hundred yards more and it was over. During the first two trips, he had glanced up at the monstrous cedar log mansion high on the peninsula. Quite sure he had seen figures watching him from the large window, he had felt the humiliation of defeat. But now, as he saw Gibby motioning for him to disconnect and throw the towrope in, the cloud began to lift. They had done it! He checked his watch. Three hours. Certain the Bashers hadn't anticipated such success, he turned and waved at the huge building. Someday, he thought, I'd like to take my shotgun and blow that window into tiny slivers. Dummy, he scolded himself. You don't even *own* a shotgun any more. Those nice church brethren have yours.

It took Hud and Gibby another hour to finish drying out the last of the boats and give them each a quick shake-down run around the bay. Kimberly's navy had risen from the dead and was once more ready for opening day. But Hud knew that he and Gibby would have to arrange some kind of overnight protection for the boats. As he pondered the problem of how to guard Kimberly's navy, the sharp barb of reality slammed into his brain like a thunderbolt.

Protect the boats *tonight?* he wondered. What about tomorrow night? And the next night? And *every* night? With their commando-like raid, the Bashers had raised the conflict to another level, beyond simple pranks. They had proven how devastating they could be in only an hour. Short of hiring a team of security guards, how could Kimberly possibly protect the resort from sundown to sunrise? Certainly, there was no place in her budget for third-shift security guards. Would she allow him to subsidize the effort? Not likely, he decided.

As he and Gibby climbed the hill to the lodge room, fatigue came crashing down on Hud. The clear identification of the problem combined with his exhausting flight through the storm, the scary landing, the long night and its humiliating defeat, the fact that he had managed only two hours of sleep, and the physical demands of the morning combined to take their toll. He knew he'd not be standing guard that night. Gibby was only slightly better off. He had captured some sleep in his ice fishing house during the night.

The bell tinkled as they opened the door to the lodge room, and Hud's imagination suddenly jingled along with it. His idea would be only a temporary fix, a bandage at best, but it would buy them some time. If nothing else, he might get some sleep for a night or two.

"I agree, Gibby," he said loudly, as they entered the pine-paneled room. "I think with your friends staked out in the woods to the south, and you and I in the north, we can watch the boundaries and the boats at the same time. Only this time, we know it's no use talking to them, right?" He motioned toward the round stool as they passed.

Gibby's eyes narrowed. He nodded. "Probably best get the deer rifles out," he said. "With that much ground to watch, shotguns don't have the range, only sting 'em a little at any distance." They rounded the counter and stepped into the office. Gibby leaned back into the lodge room. "You know, Hud," he continued, "all we really have to do is nail *one* of them goddamned, so-called church people. Just one. I ain't forgot what the Chinese did to me in Korea. We get us one—I'll make him sing—and it won't be no hymn, neither." Gibby led the way on into the kitchen and closed the door behind them.

"Hi," Kimberly greeted them. With the fingers of one hand hooking the handles of three coffee mugs while the other hand carried the coffee pot, she met them at the table. "I can't believe you did it—and did it so fast! Thanks...can I pay you with...coffee? About all I can offer."

"That's exactly what it says in our contract—coffee," Hud said. Her soft voice had the velvety quality he'd always associated with the singer Karen Carpenter. And today, it had a special timbre, a hint of happiness he hadn't previously detected. "You sound pretty frisky for someone who got no sleep last night," he added.

"Look who's talking about no sleep," she said, leaning over Hud to fill his cup. Her light fragrance combined with a slight brush against his arm to bring him to full alert. "You must be ready to drop," she added. "I caught a couple of short naps." Suddenly, she stopped pouring, snatched up his partially filled mug and poured its contents back into the pot. "This is the last thing you need right now...something to keep you awake. You get your butt over on that couch and get some sleep. And Gibby, you flop on the bed in the small bedroom. I'll wake you in a couple of hours. Sarah's bringing lunch over at noon. Now, go," she commanded. A hint of affection in her final command ran contrary to her flashing eyes and the words spoken. But magnetic as it was, that hint was no match for Hud's fatigue.

Hud shed his shoes and stretched out on the sagging couch.

"Kimberly, did you call the sheriff?" he asked.

"Called in about six-thirty, right after you left the house," she said. "They asked if I was in any danger. I told them I wasn't—at the moment. They said someone would be out this morning. Judging from past performance, it'll be about noon. It's really a huge county."

"They sound *terribly* concerned," he said. "It's good...to know...we have such...."

"Hud?" Gibby queried from the next room, "Kimberly's guests'll start pulling in after lunch. Sarah and I should be around, just in case. Maybe, if the sheriff don't show up by then, you oughta run down to the substation and have a talk. I can't get nowhere with Old Beer Stein, but maybe you can. Maybe you can buy him one of them California power lunches. S'pose?"

The words registered with Hud, but his battery was too low for a response.

Chapter 13

"I don't think it's any use. He's really zonked out."

"Poor dear. He needs the sleep."

Hud understood the words, even recognized the voices. The first was that of Kimberly and the second was Sarah's. If they'd just go away. He didn't want to wake up—had no intention of waking up.

"Goose him, goose him big time," barked a male voice. "He'll wake up."

That, Hud knew, was Gibby, and he also knew Gibby would do just as he advised. "Uh, uh, none of that," he said, springing to a sitting position on the old couch, his half-opened eyes taking in the trio that hovered over him, laughing at his sudden lurch back to life.

"Boy, you are a man of action," Kimberly said. "Come on, Sarah's got lunch all ready."

Hud rose to his feet and stumbled into the bathroom where he washed his hands and splashed cold water on his face, and then made his way to the kitchen table. Sarah had laid out a magnificent spread of homemade honey wheat bread, cold cuts, and cheeses to go with her special vegetable soup.

As the two men attacked the food, Sarah delicately spooned the soup to her lips between dainty bites of her sandwich. But Kimberly sat quietly, toying with a half-made sandwich. When Hud had devoured a third of his food, something caused him to stop and look up. His eyes followed from the slender but strong hands to the bare forearms, where the sleeves of her white Black Rock sweatshirt had been pulled up revealing fine golden hairs that contrasted with the deep tan beneath. A bite of smoked turkey sandwich swelled to a lump in his throat as he saw the gentle tears that trickled down Kimberly's cheeks. Hud glanced at the others. Gibby was busy with his food, but Sarah's eyes were fixed on Hud. They seemed to say, "It's about time you noticed."

"What's wrong?" Hud asked, tentatively reaching over and placing his hand lightly on Kimberly's arm.

"Oh, I...." she began in a choked voice, half laughing, half crying. "It's just...you three are about the only friends I have. You've done so much for me...and Sarah brings over this wonderful food, probably the best this kitchen has seen since I moved in." Gibby stopped eating, looked up at each of them and then lowered his eyes. "And...you have to eat off this horrible table...in this grungy houseful of Godawful county dump furniture!" She slapped a hand despondently on the table-top. "I had all those nice things in Minneapolis...and I sold them at garage sale prices...to buy *this?* Something wrong with this picture."

Gibby grasped his edge of the table with both hands, as though testing its stability. "Hmph! Not a Goddamned thing wrong with it that I can tell," he said, "and just where in the hell you gonna find a table with four people as good as these around it?"

Hud laughed at Gibby's pronouncement, but he was surprised at the sympathy he felt for Kimberly. Only one other person had provoked such feelings within him.

"Gracious as always, Gilbert," Sarah said with mock sternness, "but as usual, you're right." A slight smile combined with her flashing blue eyes to take the edge off her crisp, impeccable diction.

Kimberly rose, moved to the kitchen counter, and snapped a paper towel from the wall-mounted roll. Inconspicuously, she blew her nose, dabbed at her tears, and rejoined them.

"You got to understand, Kimberly," Gibby ventured, after the foursome had eaten in silence for some time, "in our neighborhood, nobody's gonna judge you by your furniture."

"I know that, Gibby," she said, "but still...."

The conversation stopped with the sound of tires crunching on the gravel drive just outside the kitchen window.

"Oh my God," Kimberly said, jumping to her feet. "The openers are getting here already? It's nowhere near check-in time!"

As a multicolored bank of lights passed by the window, Gibby said, "Relax, Kimberly. It's just Stein going through his motions." A car door slammed, then another.

"Oh, oh," said Hud, "the bug. They'll expect to talk in the lodge room, logical place."

"So?" quizzed Sarah. "Tell him about it. Perhaps it will touch a spark to his dried up dedication. It could be a good fire."

"But we need that bug, at least for a few days," said Hud. "It gives us nighttime security."

"Let's lead them to the dock," Kimberly said. "I'll head them off. Sarah, will you get a couple of beers from the fridge? And stand by with lemonade?" She disappeared through the door that led to the office and lodge room.

Sarah hustled to the refrigerator and pulled out five cans, handing them to Gibby.

"Uh, no thanks," said Hud. "Not on top of that big lunch."

"Take them," she countered sternly. "If they drink...*you* drink."

"Hello, Sheriff Stein," came Kimberly's voice from the lodge room. "Sorry to drag you back out here so soon. Good to see you, too, Deputy Mertens. I suppose I ought to show you where all the action took place."

Hud and Gibby stalled just around the corner, waiting for their cue.

"Not really necessary, Ms. Farber. We can take your…story about the alleged incident right here," came the reply in a crackling baritone voice.

Haven't yet met the man, Hud thought, and I dislike him already. Gibby looked at Hud, scowled, and rolled his eyes.

"Oh, but you need to see the scene of the…*alleged* incident…*and* the evidence."

"Evidence?"

"Let's go on down to the dock—oh," she added brightly, "would you like some lemonade to take with? Or perhaps a beer?"

Good move, thought Hud, good move.

"Uh, Ms. Farber, *we* don't accept freebies, that is gifts. Never do that. But I'd be glad to *buy* beers for the deputy and myself."

"Oh, for Christ's sake," mumbled Gibby. "What a bunch of bullshit."

"I'm sorry, Sheriff," said Kimberly, "but I won't sell you the beers. I'll get some lemonade instead."

Hud glanced at Gibby. The older man's eyes danced with anticipation.

"You *what?* Won't sell me beer? That's the most preposterous thing I ever heard."

"Somehow I doubt that, Sheriff," she said. "But I don't have a beer license—wouldn't want to get arrested. Shall I get the lemonade?"

Gibby snorted so loudly that Hud was sure it had carried to the other room. He could hear movement suggesting that Kimberly was headed toward the kitchen for the lemonade.

"We'll…take the free beer," the sheriff mumbled.

Kimberly stepped around the corner, took two of the beers that Gibby had been holding, winked at Hud, and returned to the lodge room. Hud heard the cans being popped open.

"Oh, Gibby! Hud!" Kimberly called. "Sheriff Stein's here. Can you come into the lodge room?"

They waited a few seconds and then strolled casually through the office and into the lodge room toward the two visitors, both uniformed in brown and tan, trimmed out with gold trouser stripes, badges, shoulder emblems, and weapons, but no hats. Hud led the way through the counter passage opening toward the officers.

One man, perhaps sixty, was short and wiry, with thinning sandy-gray hair, a hawkish face, and the eyes of a ferret. The other was a heavy six-footer with a belly that hung over his belt, stretching his shirt taut. He appeared to be in his late thirties with tousled red hair over a freckled teddy bear face. That must be Stein, Hud thought, extending his hand.

"Hud Bryant, Sheriff," he said, surprised by the warm, but gentle handshake from the huge man.

"No, Hud," Kimberly cut in. "That's Deputy Mertens. *This* is Sheriff Stein."

"Oh, sorry." He turned to the little man and repeated the self-introduction. The only sign of life in the grim face was the occasional blinking of the eyelids as Hud caught the "looks could kill" glare from the small man's dark eyes. Behind him, he heard Gibby snort again. Forcing a broad smile, Hud said, "Shall we head for the dock? Need another beer to take with?" Oops, he thought, glancing from the stern face to the stool with the Church's bug beneath its seat. Not a good start. Better get them out of here and then back off. Give little Napoleon the stage. He and Gibby led the way to the door. The officers had little choice but to follow. As he held the door for them, Hud noticed that, while the deputy carried the common .38 revolver, the sheriff's weapon appeared to be a .357 magnum. Power, Hud thought, power.

"Suppose you give us your version of the...incident," Sheriff Stein began, sipping his beer as they crossed the drive behind the officers' black four-by-four.

"Well," began Hud, "since both Kimberly and Gibby here have had so much trouble with vandalism, they asked if I could help out with watching things. I agreed—"

"That right?" Stein asked of both Gibby and Kimberly. They nodded.

"So, I holed up with my cookies and coffee in the shed down there and waited—"

"Report says you had a Browning twelve-gauge. That right?"

"That's right," Hud replied, glancing back. Kimberly trailed the group, pouring her beer on the ground as she walked.

"Why'd you have that with you? Planning to shoot someone?"

As they headed down the slope, Deputy Mertens tripped over a protruding tree root and barely caught himself, dropping his can of beer in the process. Hud turned at the commotion and glanced down at the deputy's brown boots—the largest feet Hud had ever seen. The deputy caught it, smiled in embarrassment, retrieved his nearly empty can, and continued on.

"No," Hud answered, "for personal protection. Turns out the shotgun wasn't enough—should have had five more guys with shotguns."

"Go on," the sheriff commanded, as they reached the little shed near the dock.

Hud told the story quickly and smoothly. Standing once again at the scene, he found every detail etched clearly in his mind. While he went on, he sensed that Gibby was becoming increasingly agitated by the direction the sheriff was taking. Hud tried to calm his friend with warning glances and occasional palms down gestures as he recited the events to the sheriff.

"A knife in your back?" Stein interrupted once more. "How do you know it was a knife? See it? Got any cuts? How do you know it wasn't a ballpoint pen?"

"Look, Sheriff," Hud said, turning to look the little man directly in the eye, "I was up against nearly twenty well-trained Navy SEAL-types in wetsuits. I'll bet you a whole brewery there wasn't a ballpoint pen on one of them. You on?" Hud took a long slug of beer. Then he reached into the shed and pulled out a handful of slashed and tangled duct tape. "This is what they tied me up and gagged me with."

"Hmmm, I'll bet every place in Wasikama County has a roll of this." Stein shoved the sticky wad at his deputy and turned to look out over the dock. "I see all of your boats right where they belong. Are they the boats that got scuttled?"

"Of course they are," Kimberly said. "Gibby and Hud worked their butts off getting them back and pumped out. Take a look. They all have brand new plugs in them. Go on. Take a look."

Tossing his empty can into a nearby garbage can, Stein turned back toward the hill. "Well, I guess we've seen it. Time to head back."

"Wait a minute, Beer!" Gibby elbowed his way between Hud and the sheriff.

Hud could see the fire in Gibby's eyes and the anger on his reddening face. Above it, under the midday sun, his silver hair glowed like an angelic halo clamped to the crown of Satan. Gibby was about to blow. Hud placed a hand on his friend's shoulder and dug his fingertips in— hard. Gibby backed off a step.

"I think everyone here knows what Gibby was going to say," Hud said, looking from Stein to his deputy and back. "Are we right in assuming that you've concluded your investi—"

"Please, Hud," Kimberly cut in, taking his arm as she stepped in front. "Sheriff Stein, would you please take a look out there on the bay? Go on. Take a good, long look."

Stein turned, folded his arms across his slender body, sighed, and stared out past the dock at the tranquil bay. The screech of a bald eagle overhead broke the rhythm of foot-high waves gently lapping at the dock and its covey of boats.

Kimberly stood close, watching him carefully. "Well?"

"It's a nice scene, very attractive," he replied. "Am I looking for something special?"

Hud stepped over for a better angle. The sheriff turned his head to the right, then tilted it upward ever so slightly, and held the position for several seconds. Hud knew he was looking at the large log structure, the Church's headquarters atop and near the far end of the peninsula.

"Yes," Hud said, "they're watching you. But that's not the point."

"Look out at the bay," Kimberly said again, "from the half-way point to the other end. See those eight white marker jugs?"

"Oh...oh...uh huh, I do see them now. And those...mark the spots you got scuttled?" Stein turned to Gibby. "Boy, you did work your butts off, didn't you?" He wheeled and started deliberately up the hill, Deputy Mertens tagging behind, followed by a sullen, discouraged trio.

When they reached the patrol vehicle, the deputy jumped in behind the wheel, and Sheriff Stein climbed into the right seat. Kimberly, Gibby, and Hud stood nearby in a semicircle, waiting for any sign of encouragement. Mertens started the engine, but Stein motioned for him to wait. He scanned the group for a moment.

"You're wondering," he began, "why I didn't listen to your story, pull my weapon, and go charging up the peninsula like Teddy Roosevelt? Well...listen up and I'll tell you why. One...I've been sheriff of this county for fifteen years, and a deputy for twenty years before that. You don't tell *me* how to do my job. Remember that. And two...I responded to a call from the Church just before coming here. They had vandals last night, too."

Hud felt the bottom drop out. He had assumed this particular episode ended with the scuttling. The Bible Bashers hadn't stopped there. He doubted they ever stopped short. With each action, they probably planned a cover-up or a counter move.

"Only there's some differences in the two incidents," Stein went on. "Yours, I'd call something on the heavy end of pranks. Now theirs? Their vandals broke into their chapel, tipped their piano over, and spray-painted a message on their walls. Maybe I don't need to tell you what the message was...but I will. It said, GET OUT OF OUR NEIGHBOR-HOOD, CHRISTIANS. Now *that*, Folks, is a hate crime, and the people of our county and state are very sensitive about hate crimes."

"But—" Hud began.

"Another difference in the incidents? No positive ID in either case, but *you*," he said, pointing at Hud, "saw fifteen to twenty unidentifiable Navy

SEALS in wetsuits. *They* saw two men whose descriptions come very close to a fit on..." he pointed a hand, middle two fingers folded, with the index and little fingers spread to point at Hud and Gibby, "...you two." He motioned to his deputy, and the black vehicle lurched out of the drive, leaving the trio with nothing gained but a cloud of dust.

"Damn!" Kimberly spouted, fanning the dust from her face with one hand. "I think he's working for *them*."

"Maybe...maybe not," Hud said, "That's exactly what those Church people want you to think. Remember, all of this crap they're pulling is meant to accomplish *one* thing—get you so discouraged you'll sell out. Now, I don't have any trouble understanding their actions...but their goals? Can one of you explain to me just why they want your property so badly? That peninsula covers over a square mile. Why do they need to add your land to it?"

Gibby shrugged. "Kimberly, you care to answer that? I can't. I can see anybody *wanting* your property or mine—prime locations, both of them. But them Bible Bashers don't need our land. They've got more'n they need now."

"I don't know, Gibby, just don't know. The things they've done say they *really* want us out. But it makes no sense—like a bad dream. Then, I think about how Stein just treated us and I really start to lose hope. If there were *no* law out here it would be one thing. But with what law we have backing *them*, we're almost helpless."

"Okay," said Hud, "we're all deflated by the Beer Stein show. But at least we know now that we can't count on him. To me that says we have to get organized and change our approach to the problem. So far, we've been waiting, with some watching, for the next dirty deed. They're up there planning...and we're sitting down here waiting. We're giving them every advantage. The only one we've taken from them is the bug, and they'll catch on to that pretty soon."

"So?" Gibby looked intently at Hud as he asked the simple question. But his eyes took on a different glint. The anger seemed to have been replaced by curiosity and perhaps intensity.

"So, after we go into the lodge room and feed our adversaries another cock-and-bull story to keep them away tonight, I'm heading back to the cottage to make some phone calls. We're up against a bigger and stronger pack of rats than we thought. And since the sheriff won't help us, we need to look elsewhere."

Chapter 14

Hud popped up at five o'clock. It was opening day, the busiest of the season for fishing resorts. Despite the early rising, he had managed over ten hours of sleep, and he felt good. He followed his wake-up splashes of cold water with dutiful attention to his daily calisthenics. Occasionally, he interrupted his rhythmic counting to recall pieces of the "radio drama," as Sarah had called the planning for that evening's resort security. He hoped the elaborate pretense, staged for the benefit of the Church "listeners," had worked.

Within range of the bug, Hud and Gibby once again had discussed their plans for additional guards about the two properties for the night. But this time they had argued about the deployment, changing their minds so often they themselves weren't sure what the final plan entailed. The microphone sent a clear message, however, that there would be six armed men well-hidden about the properties. He hoped the Bashers had bought it. He'd know shortly.

After a quick breakfast, he hurried along the dark pathway to the resort. As he stepped through the last of the bushes, he heard voices from Cottage Four to his left. Instinctively, he stopped and moved back into the brushy tunnel. About the time he reached a secure position and began to crouch, an embarrassing thought ran through his mind.

Wow, he thought, how paranoid! I'm so jumpy I hide in the woods at the sound of a human voice. The screened door of Cottage Four slammed and the voices resumed. Hud leaned forward and caught a glimpse of several men standing amid a pile of gear just outside their door. Well, he reasoned, better not step out right now. Might startle them.

"Do we really need this much junk with us?" asked a whiny male voice.

"You gonna catch fish without a pole?" came the answer.

Feel sorry for them, Hud thought. Dragging a rookie around can be bad enough, but having a whiner who's that lazy...glad he's not my problem. Hud couldn't get a good look at the men because their Suburban was parked between his position and the cottage.

"I think Bernie's got a point," said another voice. "Just 'cause we got two boats...doesn't mean we got to *fill* 'em."

"Oh, come on, Rimmy. Not you, too," interrupted another. "You got to at least *look* like a fisherman."

Two others interrupted the conversation simultaneously, and with several voices competing, Hud lost track. In moments, the group had moved around the corner and headed down to the dock. Hud emerged from his hiding place feeling rather silly but glad he wasn't a member of that party. He had long considered himself an excellent fisherman, always ready to share his expertise with beginners, but not with *unwilling* beginners. A spark of self-pity sizzled through him as he was reminded that it was opening day, and he wouldn't be out there.

He heard signs of life from all directions as he angled between the two rows of cottages. With each cottage filled to capacity, it looked like a good opener for Kimberly. Already, there were two parties down on the dock, loading their gear into their boats. He hesitated at the yellow gas pump where a red, six-gallon outboard gas tank sat on the concrete apron.

"Oh, Hud!" Kimberly called from the lodge room door. "Would you fill that tank for Cottage Two? He says he's already put the oil in it."

"Everything okay?" he called back. She gave him the high sign and disappeared inside.

Hud attacked the simple job eagerly, recognizing the old feeling that came with it, the need to be needed. It was Ellie who had first defined it for him, who helped him to quickly ascertain the extent of, or lack of, the same quality in others. The good feeling seemed particularly strong, and it kept him pumped up through the next three hours as he hustled back and forth between the gas pump and the bait house.

While pumping gas he could see Gibby down at the launching ramp, collecting the fees and directing the steady flow of nonguests who chose to launch their boats at Black Rock Resort. Some were area residents, locals, while others had driven north for just one day of fishing. The circular drive around the main building was never without cars. Some of the occupants went into the lodge room for fishing licenses, beverages, and snacks, while others approached Hud for gasoline or bait.

He remembered Gibby's admonition to faithfully wash his hands between gasoline duties and bait sales. Old timers knew that a drop of petroleum contamination could render the customer's bait useless. As Gibby so often said, "No self-respecting walleye is gonna bite on bait that stinks of gas...don't matter if it's chubs, shiners, nightcrawlers, or leeches."

"How d'you know that's a dozen?" asked one customer, an Indian from the nearby reservation, as he suspiciously eyed the nearly two-dozen chubs Hud had netted and carelessly sloshed into his bucket. "You didn't even count 'em."

Hud smiled, winked, and said, "Tell you what. *You* count, and for every chub you find over the dozen you're paying for, you give me a buck."

"Uh, uh, no bet." The man lighted his Marlboro, then smiled and eyed Hud through puffy slits. "You're all right. You know, that chicken shit bastard down at the Ellis place counts 'em one-by-one-by-one. But at least he sells us beer. How come *she* quit sellin' beer?" he asked, with a nod toward the lodge room.

"Don't know," said Hud. "Could be, she's got more than one person can keep up with, and things that weren't necessary had to go."

"Beer not necessary?" He shrugged, turned, and shuffled out toward his old, rusted Chevy Caprice.

By midmorning, the rush had been accommodated. All of the fishermen who believed in morning fishing were out there doing their thing. At Sarah's call, Hud and Gibby ambled toward the lodge room. As they passed through, Hud eyed the round, chrome-legged spy, aware of the current of tension it created. But he felt instant relaxation as he rounded the corner into the secure kitchen for coffee and a well-deserved break. He was surprised at how good that old "county dump" kitchen chair felt. He reached for one of Sarah's warm apple turnovers, took a bite and rolled his eyes for her benefit.

"Now, Hudson Bryant, you're an unappreciative phony," she said. "They're even more delicious than the last ones you had...and *that* time you kissed my hand."

"Wow!" said Kimberly as she burst in from the lodge room. "*This*— is neat! They just keep coming and coming...pop, snacks, lures, maps, film, licenses...plus all your gas, bait, and launching fees. I hope," she nodded toward the peninsula, "*they're* listening. Finally...after all the problems...I'm finally in business!"

Gibby shot a serious glance at Hud, then looked up at her. "Ahh, Kimberly," he began, "I don't want to be a wet blanket. But you know, after today—"

"It isn't going to be like this," she finished for him, sobering as she spoke. "I know, Gibby, but after six months of back-breaking work, unpredictable expenses, and the Church of the Devil...*this is fun!*" She poured herself a mug of coffee and joined them at the table, where they drifted into a lighthearted exchange of anecdotes drawn from the busy morning's experiences. The enthusiastic discussion slowed only when Sarah started the plate of turnovers around a second time.

"Your man due in pretty soon?" Gibby asked Hud.

"About an hour," Hud said, glancing at his watch. "He said last night he planned to fly from Minneapolis into the Falls and then rent a car."

"You didn't tell me, Hud," Kimberly said. "Some old friend coming up for a visit?"

"Not exactly. Really a friend of an old friend...but he comes very highly recommended."

"Recommended? As a fisherman? An airplane mechanic? A septic tank cleaner?" Kimberly's expression grew serious. Her eyes focused on Hud while she waited.

"He's a...security man, considered by my friend to be the best in the Twin Cities," Hud replied and then hurriedly added, "and in addition to his knowledge of state-of-the-art electronics, he did two tours on foot in Viet Nam. There isn't a booby trap he can't spot...or construct. I'm really excited about it. I think he might be just what we've needed to level the playing field."

"Sounds wonderful," Kimberly said. "Maybe he can think in *their* language—wait a minute! If he's so successful in the Cities, why on earth would he be interested in coming way up here to the boonies to help *us?*"

Hud thought quickly. "I asked him that. He said he gets bored hooking up alarm systems in business buildings. This sounded like an interesting—"

"Wait a minute!" Kimberly cut in. "You just arranged all this last night? And he's so interested he'll be here in a matter of *minutes?*"

"Just got lucky," Hud said. "He was looking for something different to do this weekend."

"Uh, uh, Hudson Bryant. No-o-o-o you don't!" The soft lines in Kimberly's face suddenly became rigid, clear definitions of anger. Her right index finger pointed at Hud like a razor-sharp rapier. "You're out of line—making business decisions for *me!*"

Gibby sat motionless, except for the pulsating in one cheek. His eyes were fixed upon some nondescript point on the ceiling. Sarah sat straight, her customary poise seemingly frozen in disbelief.

Hud felt a mixture of fear, guilt, and simmering anger. He was afraid of the outcome of the sudden confrontation, ashamed of his deception, and aware of the flame that grew within him whenever someone shouted at him. For the moment, the fear seized control. He felt as if he had just dropped a priceless piece of crystal to the floor and was afraid to look at the results.

"Friends!" she said, her volume escalating rapidly. "Friends, you said last night. Why, you're just like all the other men. You lie, cheat, do anything to deceive the poor, ignorant woman. No—you're worse. You come in here throwing your money around, thinking you can buy anything you want! Well *I'm* not for sale, Mr. Bryant. Tell me the truth…if you have any idea what truth is. How much you paying this—expert? Five hundred? Six hundred? Seven?"

Hud felt the boiling deep within himself creeping upward, edging dangerously close to that point where he simply didn't give a damn about what *anyone* thought or said. He stood, looked directly into Kimberly's eyes, and managing a soft but firm voice said, "Three—"

"Three? Three?" she cut in. Her eyes took on new fire. "God's gift to security is coming way up here in the sticks for three hundred bucks? He must *really* be good."

Hud's anger met his fear halfway. The result of the mixture was a smoldering fire of determination. I've knocked myself out, he thought, damned near got killed…for *this*? To put up with a control complex? "Three *thousand*," he said, "plus expenses and equipment purchased. That's for three days and two nights of analysis and consultation. Dirt cheap. The real problems are…" his voice softened, "you need help and can't admit it…and you can't tell your friends from your enemies." He picked up his cup, drained it, plunked it down hard on the tabletop, and walked out seething. "Get me out of here," he mumbled as he descended the outside steps to the driveway. He was determined to stop for nothing until he reached his cottage. "Don't think that's the one, Ellie. Think I'd better do my fishing out on the lake."

Chapter 15

Damn it, Hud fumed, as he stomped down the drive toward the path. Seems like, the more I give, the more she wants to fight me. A no-win situation. He liked her independence, her give-it-hell spirit, but he wondered if she had any concept of cooperation, teamwork. The shadows of the tunnel-like path through the central woods provided a background in harmony with his mood. At least, he thought, this path goes somewhere. That one's a dead end.

By the time he stepped into the clearing at Gibby's, however, Hud had admitted to himself that beneath the anger lay a painful, open wound. It was Kimberly's rejection that had cut deeply. He had to stop the bleeding.

Two workmen who had replaced his broken window were leaving as Hud reached the cottage. He offered to sign the work order, but they waved him off, piled into the van, and left. He walked back to his bedroom and inspected the installation. Then he stood for a moment gazing out at Black Rock Bay. He was glad to have the plywood gone and the view restored. The angle of his cottage directed his line of sight directly at the immense, dark rock which jutted up defiantly from the blue, rippling waters at the mouth of the bay. He had always loved the panorama, framed by the outline of his favorite window. At the bottom of the picture sat the two boats on their lifts. He raised his gaze. At the top of the picture, the thick candlelike tufts of the red pines blocked his view. But he could envision clearly the large cedar log structure that housed the leaders of the mysterious church. With two alterations, thought Hud, that's the most beautiful scene in the world. Just replace the Bashers with the Kimberly I thought I'd found, and....

"Hud? Are you there, Hud?"

Turning, he started slowly for the door. Kimberly? It sounded nothing like the voice he had just escaped, but it did sound like—

"Hud, can I come in...and...talk?"

"Come on—" he stopped short. Idiot, he thought, you're not going to subject yourself to more of— "in," he heard himself say. He met her at the sturdy, homemade pine table in the tiny kitchen. From the meek voice that had drawn his involuntary response, he wondered if she'd been crying. But while the subdued figure that stood beyond the table showed no signs of hostility, he saw no tears either. He did see the beautiful, slender face, the dimples, the swishing golden pony tail, and the soft blue eyes that had stopped him in his tracks the first time they met. The sweatshirt of the day was light blue, but it fit the same. "Have a seat?" He motioned to one of two chairs, opened the nearby refrigerator, snatched two Cokes, and joined her at the table. He wondered why he was doing these things. Who was making these decisions?

"Hud, I came to apologize," Kimberly said.

"*Your* idea?"

"Come on, Hud, give me a break," she said.

"Sorry. I guess I haven't quite cooled off. Gibby get on your case?" he asked, popping the top on his Coke and taking a swig.

"I didn't really need any—getting on my case. I'd have come to see you anyway. But no, it was Sarah." Kimberly smiled impishly.

"Sarah? You're kidding."

"No." Kimberly's voice softened and dropped. She stared at the table-top as she went on, "She kind of gave me hell…said it's about time I quit blaming every man in Wasikama County for what my ex did to me."

"She's right," Hud said, trying to visualize the prim and proper Sarah Gunderson giving Kimberly hell.

"And she said I'd better back off on my Wonder Woman power play, that up here in this environment everybody needs help from others. But I'm not ready to buy into that one. How can I hope to make this resort a success by myself—if I don't believe I can do it?" She looked up from the tabletop directly at Hud.

"Kimberly," he said, "you're incredibly strong physically…for a woman with such a…delicate…physique. You lift and move things too heavy for a woman wrestler. But even a strong *man* is going to need help with some jobs here. Besides, you've got the Bible Bashers to contend with. Now, you can lean on Gibby and me…or you can hire somebody."

"That's not it, Hud, not it at all." She frowned at him. "I got angry, no—pissed—because you made a business decision that wasn't yours to make…because you took it upon yourself to throw three thousand bucks or more into this thing without even consulting me. Just turn it around and look at it." Her eyes watched Hud as she tipped the can and drank from it.

Hud felt sheepish. "You're…right. I got carried away—didn't stop to think about it like that. Want me to cancel him out?"

"Half-an-hour ago, I'd have said yes. But, Gibby's right. We're hope-lessly outnumbered. Your man might even things up some. Gibby called your idea a stroke of Bryant genius…I agree. But," she hesitated, "I don't know when I can pay you back…maybe not until after the season." Her voice choked slightly. "Maybe not even *then*."

"Feel better if we put it on paper?" Hud asked.

"Definitely."

"You write it up. I don't have a computer or typewriter here. But remember, half the cost is Gibby's." He looked into her eyes, absorbing the warmth he saw there. A sensation of weightless exhilaration bubbled through him, not unlike that feeling he had each time his plane lifted from the runway and soared upward into the sky. There was something about Kimberly's honesty, her up-front candor that reminded him—no, he thought, don't do that. This is Kimberly…Kimberly Farber. Don't start comparing.

She reached across the table and took his hand. "Are we okay…Friend?"

"Okay, Friend," he replied, squeezing her strong, slender hand.

"Good. Now, I've got to get back," she said, jumping up from the table. "It's possible your man is there by now, too." She eased through the doorway. "You be over soon?"

"Be right there," he replied.

As Hud approached the lodge twenty minutes later, a burly man with medium brown hair and a full beard emerged from the lodge room and lightly jounced down the steps to meet him. Dressed in boots, jeans, and a plaid flannel shirt, he reminded Hud of Paul Bunyan. Could this be—

"T.C. Wolf," the man said in a hushed, raspy voice, extending a powerful hand to Hud. He appeared to be pushing fifty, about the right age for a Viet Nam veteran. His face was expressionless and his eyes mere slits that said nothing.

"Hudson Bryant. Glad you could make it—"

Wolf put a finger to his lips, took Hud by the arm, and led him quickly along the driveway toward the garage/workshop behind the lodge building. Bewildered, Hud accompanied the man. They covered the hundred-foot span in silence, though Hud glanced over at the stranger several times. He had expected…what? A smallish wimp in a pin-striped blue suit? When they reached a dark green four-wheel-drive Explorer that sat nuzzled up against the garage door, Wolf motioned Hud around to the passenger side.

"Sorry about that," Wolf said, when both doors had slammed shut. "But you didn't want those church dudes to know about me. At this point, I have to assume they have every inch of the two properties bugged. Is that fancy log building up on the point their HQ?"

"What? Oh, yeah."

"Ever been up there?"

"No. Gibby used to know the peninsula well, but he hasn't been up there since the Bashers moved in and built the place up." Hud paused. "Excuse me, but what do I call you…T.C.?"

"Wolf." As the strange newcomer talked, he twisted one way and then another, as though memorizing every detail of the property surrounding them. "My mother called me T.C., said it stood for Trouble Cometh. Okay. Here's how we begin. You tell me everything you can about what's happened here, what they've done, and all that. Oh, and when we're done here, can you get me a plat map showing the properties involved?"

"I'm sure Gibby has one. He could relate all the problems better than I, but I'll try," Hud said. He rattled quickly through the events that he could recall, the harassment and broken windows, the slaughter of Herman, concluding with the scuttling of the boats.

"What's in there?" Wolf pointed to the garage door before them.

"Garage on the left side. Kimberly keeps her four-wheel-drive there. Workshop and storage on the right side." Hud was puzzled by the question.

"Soon as we're done here, move the vehicle out so I can park in there. They can't see my car here behind the shed from up there, but if they should come driving in…."

"But where are you going to sleep? I figured you'd stay in my cottage and want your car nearby," Hud said. "I've only got one bed, but I'm willing to sleep on the couch."

"Sleep right here," Wolf replied, "and eat here, too." He motioned to a large cooler in the rear cargo area. "From her garage, I can come and go—they'll never see me. After I've debugged the properties, *you* won't see much of me either."

"But don't we need to talk things over?" Hud asked, slightly irritated by the stranger's take-charge manner.

"We'll talk things over—after I've looked things over. I'll submit my plan...and anticipated expenses...probably tomorrow night. Now, a couple of other options I'll lay on you. They'll cost, but you ought to consider them. One, if you'd like to know more about your opposition, I can go up for a visit. Obviously, I can't make promises on what I'll learn, but I can promise it'll be worth an extra five hundred."

Hud looked at Wolf incredulously. "You've got to be kidding. You don't want to be seen...but you'll go up and visit them?"

"Tonight," came the hoarse reply. He nodded toward the woods on their right.

"So they catch you. Then where are we?"

"They won't catch me," he said. "Think about it. Number two? I have a buddy in Minneapolis, a PI—damned good one. We did two tours in Nam together. For a couple thou, he could find out a lot about this organization. Think about that, too. Let me know by four o'clock. Now," he continued, opening his door to get out, "I want a look at the garage."

Hud followed the cue. He got out, opened the garage door, and led the way inside past Kimberly's old Chevy pick-up. He was about to mention the light switch when Wolf once again motioned for silence. So Hud dropped in behind him and followed as Wolf flipped on the lights and began a slow tour of the aged building. He looked at everything, seemingly missing nothing. His eyes darted over every detail, each tool, each stack of odd-sized scraps of wood, loops of rope and steel cable. Finally, he stepped between two old toilet stools to the electric service box, popped open the enclosure, and stood for some time as though studying the cobwebs inside it.

As the exploration came to an end and Wolf headed back toward the door, Hud realized that the powerful-looking man, who must weigh two hundred pounds and stand close to six feet tall, made no sounds as he moved—no audible footsteps, no bumping against objects in the terribly crowded collection, not even the brushing, swishing sounds of clothing. Emerging from the garage, Wolf led the way into the nearby woods in the direction of the church property. As Hud crunched his way over the ground cover of small branches, twigs, and leaves, he became conscious of Wolf's occasional glances over his shoulder. Finally, the security expert motioned for Hud to stop and wait where he stood. In seconds, Wolf had disappeared among the trees and bushes up ahead.

Hud stood as quietly as he could, aware of the mounting tension the strange experience provoked. *What in the hell is this guy up to? Does he really know what he's here for?* Then Hud recalled the words of the business acquaintance in St Paul who had recommended Wolf. "You'll find him rather strange, no…*weird* is a better word. But he's good." Hud stood for several minutes contemplating his situation while listening vainly for any sign of Wolf's whereabouts. *I sure hope he's good,* he thought. *He certainly is weird.* After nearly fifteen minutes, Hud was losing patience and was about to stride on into the woods to search out the strange man.

Suddenly—a muscular hand clamped over Hud's mouth and a powerful force pulled him over backwards. Before he could react he found himself flat on his back, looking at the upside-down face of T.C. Wolf against the backdrop of a gigantic oak tree.

"What the—" Once again Hud found himself being shushed by the sign language of the stranger.

Hud took the hand that was offered and staggered to his feet. "What did you do that for?" he asked in a whisper.

"Two things," Wolf replied softly, "a little preliminary recon…." While the eyes remained impossible to read, a hint of a grin crossed the weathered face. "And a little marketing. You lacked confidence in me."

Chapter 16

Hud stepped out of his cottage Sunday morning into the gray of dawn. A gentle northwest breeze waved the branches of the red pines, spreading their captivating fragrance over the Gundersons' north woods Shangri-la. Nothing could send him off to a morning of fishing in better spirits than the pines. As he lugged his gear down the slope through the trees, he could touch the grooved, rough skin of their trunks, listen to the brushing sounds of their arms in the breeze, see the billions of rich green needles, and absorb the unique smell. Not bad, he thought smiling, four senses out of five. What can light me up better than that? A vision of Kimberly, the golden highlights of her swishing pony tail accentuated by the sun, flashed into his mind.

"Okay, okay," he said to himself, "it's still a terrific experience."

In minutes, he stowed his gear, lowered the boat into the water, started the powerful engine, and backed off the lift. As he idled slowly over to the resort dock, he remembered that things would be different today. He usually fished with Gibby...and Herman. No more Herman. Hud knew he'd miss the big galoot, sitting up in the bow, his enormous ears flapping in the wind, barking in victory with each walleye caught and retreating in disdain at the smell of the protective film on each northern pike.

And Gibby…good, old Gibby had enthusiastically volunteered to help Kimberly so Hud could get out fishing. Then, to help alleviate the guilt he knew Hud would feel for going fishing without him, Gibby had followed up with a five-dollar bet that Hud couldn't fill his limit of walleyes. Maybe it's for the best, Hud thought. After all that's happened in three days, I really could use some quiet time to myself.

He eased the new boat into an empty stall alongside the resort dock and tied up. Before he could grab his minnow bucket and head up the hill for bait, Gibby lumbered out on the dock, a bucket in one hand and a margarine container in the other.

"Here you go," he said, "shiners and the best pick of the leeches. You gonna head for the slot on the back side of Big Totem Island?" He looked out at the light choppy waves in the bay. "Be nice back there out of the wind."

"Oh, I'll get up to Totem sooner or later," Hud said. "You know that. But I thought I'd try the windy side of Berry Island…and maybe Cookie Island on the way up there. You want to raise your bet?"

"Come on, now. I ain't no fool. If I was fishing against you, I'd raise it quick enough. But, next to me, you're the best fisherman on this corner of the lake. I ain't throwing good money after bad." Gibby's devilish eyes glinted. The humor crinkles at the corners deepened, then suddenly disappeared. "You do like I told you? You put Sarah's four-ten in your boat?"

Hud opened the hatch to the storage compartment along the left side of the boat. The small shotgun was there along with a plastic bag full of extra shells.

"I think you're a little paranoid," Hud said with a laugh, "but I did like Daddy said. But when it comes right down to it, I don't know how much good that little peashooter would do."

"Up close, it'll do plenty. And from fifty yards, who's to tell it's not a rifle. Besides, I ain't giving you my twelve gauge. You lose those."

Hud flushed at the barb, but he smiled. "I still think you're wrong," he said. "Out on the lake in plain sight, those Bashers aren't going to do anything."

"What you just said *should* be right, but you're forgetting some things," Gibby said. That's a big lake out there, twenty thousand acres, and it's got more'n fifty islands in it. Most the time you're out there…ain't another boat in sight. And another thing…them church guys *want* to own this," he went on, gesturing from the resort to his property. "But they think they *already* own the lake. By the way, is that Wolfman still around? Ain't seen nothing of him."

"Oh, he's around all right," Hud replied. "Better check your pockets."

Gibby looked quizzical. "Okay, now git." He untied Hud's line and pushed the boat away from the dock.

Hud eased slowly out into the bay to put distance between himself and the cottages before opening up the big engine. He glanced at his watch, nearly five-thirty. The sun was about to peek over the treeline behind him. Smoothly, he pushed the throttle forward and eased the boat up on plane. As he headed for the gap between Black Rock and the peninsula, he looked up at the log structure. He didn't expect to see anyone in the window at this time of day, but he suspected he was being watched.

At twenty knots, he aimed for the center of the thirty-yard opening between the tip of the peninsula and the rock. Curious, he thought as he looked up at the jagged tip of Black Rock. It really isn't black…more dark gray. But compared to the many other large rocks in the lake, it looked black. Once clear of the bay, he turned right and, following a northeast heading, he paralleled the blunt end of the peninsula for some time, scrutinizing the land for anything, anything that might tell him something about these people.

He knew that around the next point and some distance down the peninsula's northeast shoreline there was an inlet that the group used as their private harbor. There was no real reason to head that way. Indeed, it would be out of his way. But when Hud reached the point, he did a ninety-degree turn to the right, almost involuntarily, as if some remote force had turned his boat. He scooted along, parallel to the shoreline and about a quarter of a mile out, the aluminum hull gently slapping against the small waves. While his best judgment suggested a left turn away from the camp, Hud found himself continuing on. Come on, Hud, he thought. Don't provoke them unless there's something to be gained by it. At this moment, you don't know of anything to be gained.

He had nearly convinced himself to make the turn when he reached the small harbor. His curiosity won out. He recalled the configuration of the harbor the previous year, a couple of small bench-seat fishing boats tied to a tiny dock and an aluminum canoe lying upside down on the beach. Staring off to the right, he was startled by what he saw. On the shore stood a large, new metal storage building. A sturdy, new eight-foot-wide dock extended out approximately a hundred feet from the building. At one side of the dock floated a midnight blue cigarette-type boat, perhaps twenty-two feet long, the style of high-speed runabout so popular on the coast but rarely seen in Minnesota lake country. Fast, Hud thought, maybe sixty knots or better. Instinctively, he slowed for a better look.

What he saw floating opposite the sleek speedboat surprised him even more—a light green Cessna 182 floatplane. Two men were unloading cardboard boxes from the plane and stacking them on the dock. One of them looked Hud's way, then turned back to his partner. The second man stepped around the boxes to join the first, blocking Hud's view of the boxes. They stood there, apparently talking, with their backs to Hud.

He quickly scanned the beach. It was barren—no canoes. No canoes? There should be eight or ten canoes, he thought, probably dark green ones. They must be locked up in that building. The sudden sequence of surprises made him uneasy. He pushed the throttle ahead and began a left turn to head out into the lake. As he turned, he looked back and noticed two large, cube-shaped concrete blocks that sat on the opposing points, as though guarding the mouth of the harbor. He wondered, as he set his course for Berry Island, what the Bashers planned to build on the concrete blocks. Light towers to mark their harbor, perhaps? A retractable security net?

As he cruised to the northeast, the wind-blown spray in his face, he was reminded of more important matters. Remember where you are, he told himself, and keep your eyes on the road. Lake Wasikama, for all the beauty of its myriad rocky islands trailing endlessly in the sky blue waters, stood apart from other lakes for its capricious character, its inherent dangers. The paradise could quickly turn into a wind-driven bully, a gigantic cauldron of four- and five-foot waves. And the glacier-carved lake had become nature's rock garden. Huge boulders lurked everywhere. Some protruded above the surface; some lay just beneath the surface and were marked by white buoys; and others lay beneath the surface—unmarked. The lower units, the shafts and propellers, of innumerable engines had been damaged for unknowing or careless boaters. And more than a few boats had suffered Titanic gashes.

Several times Hud had bucked his way home riding roller coaster waves, blinded by wind-driven rain, wondering with each dip into a swell if it was the one with a rock in it. He had fished the lake steadily for two seasons before feeling comfortable without the lake contour map in one hand.

The sun had risen by the time he approached little Berry Island. The sight of Berry and the islands off to his left struck him once again as awesome. The forests of pines and birches that grew out of cracks in the rocks stood proudly, gleaming in the low angle of the rising sun's rays.

He eased the throttle back to idle when a hundred yards off the windward northwest shore of the small island. After turning his depth finder on, he slipped up to the bow of the boat and lowered the powerful elec-

tric trolling motor into position. Shutting down the Evinrude and using
the electric tilt to raise its shaft out of the water, he gathered his small
tackle bag, fish net, bait, and fishing rod to take his place on the swivel
seat up in the bow.

Many fishermen, particularly novices, shunned the fishing spot
because of the rock-strewn lake bottom whose snags gobbled up lures
and bait and because the northwest wind constantly pushed the boat
toward the dangerous shoreline. But to Hud, the very conditions that
haunted others made the spot one of his favorites. By using a simple
leadhead jig hooked upward through the shiner's forehead, and by moving his bait in a more vertical fashion, up and down near the bottom, he
often caught walleyes here while others spent their time breaking their
lines and rerigging.

He had run two zig zag passes parallel to the shoreline at depths of
fourteen to twenty feet when the familiar *tug-tug–tug-tug* brought him
to full alert. Turning the bow into the wind, he played out line through
his fingertips, feeling the actions of his prey as he did so. Judgment time,
he thought, locking the reel in gear. Right…about…now! He pulled the
rod tip up sharply to set the hook.

"Got him!" he said aloud as he began reeling in. The first violent reactions at the other end of the line suggested he'd tangled with a hefty
northern pike, rather than a walleye. But then, his adversary headed for
the bottom and he knew. Twice, the fish outpulled the drag setting on
his reel, taking line even while Hud reeled in. Amazing, he thought,
aware of the adrenalin the simple act had triggered. The first one always
does this to me. Then, the fish seemed to tire, and he quickly worked it
to the surface. Holding his rod tip high in the air with his right hand, he
grabbed the net in his left hand and carefully scooped the golden brown
fish into the boat. As he removed the struggling walleye from the net,
Hud knew he'd not be taking it home. He guessed its weight to be over
four pounds, but more importantly, it measured out to twenty-one

inches. Recently-adopted state regulations prohibited keeping walleyes between seventeen and twenty-five inches in length.

"Ah, Baby," he said, holding the solid victim up to the sun for one last admiring look. Then, he leaned over the gunwale and gently placed the walleye in the water. It shook itself twice and disappeared into the depths. He checked his distance from the rocks and proceeded to bait up again.

As he tossed his baited jig over the side, the sound of a distant engine caught his attention. Tracing the sound back to the mainland, he scanned the shores for a moment before he located its source. It was the green Cessna 182 taking off into the northwest wind. He watched it with a pilot's interest, and only when the craft became airborne did he succumb to his curiosity. Where did it come from? What was it doing there at the Bashers' camp? Where is it going now?

Hud fished the shoreline of Berry Island for two more hours. Then he moved north to Cookie Island, and finally to the deep slot between Big Totem Island and the mainland. It was nearly noon when he eased his sixth keeper walleye, between twelve and seventeen inches, into the live well, filling his limit. He chuckled to himself. Gotcha, Gibby, he thought. Too bad I couldn't get you to up the ante. He pulled up the trolling motor and stowed everything for the trip home. Then he sat lazily drifting for a moment, only a few feet from the shore of the island, watching a bald eagle return to its six-foot nest of sticks at the peak of an old, dead tree nearby.

Suddenly, the roar of a powerful inboard-outboard engine broke into his reverie. He swiveled in time to see the sleek, blue boat from the church camp come skidding around a nearby point and head directly toward him. The craft approached with incredible speed from his right side at a forty-five degree angle. Hud sat there, momentarily stunned. What are they going to do? Crash into me? He glanced at the rocks close by.

"Oh, no," he groaned. He reached quickly for the ignition key. The engine caught, then died. It caught again—just as the powerful boat slewed past on his right. He jammed the throttle forward and turned the wheel away from the island, but it was too late.

The intruders' wake caught his boat like a tsunami and raised it several feet. Then, like a twig in a waterslide, the Lund slid down and to the left. The jolt when it hit the shoreline rocks threw Hud to the deck. For a moment, there came a horrible clattering as the propeller of the roaring engine came down hard on the rocks. Abruptly the vibrations stopped and the engine revved up almost to a screaming pitch. Hud righted himself and lurched across the seat to turn the ignition off.

When he looked out, the attackers had done a sharp turn and were headed toward him once again. He scrambled for the storage compartment, grabbed the small shotgun, and stood, bracing himself the best he could in the tilted boat. Flipping the safety off, he took aim at the approaching speedboat.

"Damn it," he said aloud, "what do I do now? Shoot at the boat or the people? Don't think I can hurt the boat with *this* thing." At fifty yards, he could make out four men in the boat. The law, he thought, is this self-defense? Guess so. But they've got witnesses. I don't—and I'm out of time. He aimed the weapon at the cockpit and held it there. Twenty-five yards out, the blue leviathan suddenly swerved into a sharp turn and raced away, disappearing around the northwest tip of Big Totem Island.

As Hud lowered the weapon, he felt himself tremble. Could he have pulled the trigger? He wasn't certain. It all happened so fast. But now he felt the anger rising, swelling within him. *Now* he'd shoot, but *now* was too late. He looked at the diminutive four-ten in his hands as his rage bubbled to the top. Catching himself about to throw Sarah's favorite weapon over the side, he reset the safety, and leaned it against a gunwale. It took several long, deep breaths before he felt his control returning.

"That's it, you Bastards," he said, looking off in the direction they took. "You caught me by surprise and kicked my ass twice— but no more."

He felt like a boxer who'd been decked for a nine-count in each of the first two rounds. *Now* I'm ready to fight back? he thought. How? Come on, Bryant. First thing—check the damage. Second—find a way to get this mess home. Raising the engine, he went to the stern to examine it. Pointless, he thought. You know what you're going to find. All three blades of the aluminum propeller were badly mangled. It was apparent that all three blades had come into contact with the rock before the emergency clutch had released. That meant possible damage to the gears as well. Either way, the powerful engine had become a mute passenger.

He stood to assess his situation. The water had calmed and the boat seemed to float normally. If it's leaking, the automatic electric bilge pump will kick in, he thought. So far, I don't hear it. Using his emergency paddle, he moved the boat ahead to a large, flat-sided boulder that stood about gunwale height. Once there, he put rubber bumpers over the left side and tossed both the bow and stern anchors up on shore to hold the boat. Then, one by one, he released the six walleyes. With his thermos of coffee, his remaining cookies, and the four-ten in hand, he climbed out on the rock and sat down. He poured a cup of coffee and bit into a cookie.

Okay, he thought, I'm five miles from home. I'm a decent guy, but not so good I can walk it. What's left in the battery won't take me halfway. I could use what's left to get me around to the open lake—more likely to find help, maybe a tow, there. But then I wouldn't be where Gibby would expect to find me. He checked his watch—half past twelve. When *would* Gibby become concerned enough to take action? Probably after dark. That's over nine hours. Hud decided to use the electric and try to make the two miles to the front side of Cookie Island. From there he might be able to flag someone down. With the decision made, he loaded up and started out.

As the trolling motor hummed quietly, he sipped his coffee and retraced the events of the morning, a morning that had gone from heaven to hell in ten seconds. For the first time, he asked himself how it had happened, how they had stumbled upon him in such an isolated place.

"Stumbled? Stumbled?" he asked aloud. "*I'm* the idiot who stumbled. I do that stupid parade bit past their harbor…let them know I'm out here all alone…and then show them where to find me. And then I crank up the engine. If it hadn't been winding up at full rpm when we hit the rocks, it might be running now. Guess I'm not very good at war games. Naive, to say the least…but I'm catching on."

He regretted having declined T.C. Wolf's offer to snoop around the Bashers' camp during the night. He hadn't wanted to cross Kimberly again after resolving Saturday's conflict. But now, things had changed. They simply *had* to get out of this defensive rut in which they were always being forced to react. Hud decided he'd send Wolf in…*and* hire the Minneapolis detective.

After two hours of bucking the wind with the electric motor, he rounded a familiar point on the homeward side of Cookie Island. The nearly inaudible trolling motor told him the battery was all but dead. He'd go no farther. Wading ashore, he pulled the boat to ground on a beach and sat down on a flat boulder to wait. At the moment, there wasn't a boat in sight. When he recognized the peninsula three miles distant, he returned to the boat for the small shotgun.

Chapter 17

Three hours on this beach, Hud thought, and here I sit. Sleep in the boat tonight? He was hot, sweaty, and gritty, and he could feel his patience evaporating like sprinkles of rain on a scorched sidewalk. He had fished the shoreline of Cookie Island many times when the boats were so thick they needed a traffic controller. But today...they all seemed to be attracted to other parts of the lake.

Two hours earlier, he had spotted a runabout headed southwest—the direction he needed to go. Jumping up and waving frantically, he had caught the attention of one occupant. The man offered a friendly wave and turned his head away. Hud knew then the feeling of the movie castaways who fail to attract the attention of anyone aboard the passing ship or the airplane overhead.

He retreated once again into the trees for shade. But the sun was starting down, and it glared at him from an ever lower angle. Because the branches of many trees in the rocky environment had sprouted five to six feet above ground, the sun easily penetrated beneath them. The only real shade was found so deep in the trees he couldn't see the lake adequately. So he compromised by standing partially shaded behind the trunk of a large, scraggly pine.

During the early portion of his vigil, he had examined the strange Wasikama adventure over and over, from Gibby's phone call to his own lakeside perch on the flat rock. No question about it, he thought, I've underestimated these Bible Bashers. This ridiculous conflict has gone from harassment to vandalism to violence. Sure, nobody's been hurt yet, but it's coming, no doubt about it. The next time I'm in a spot like I was today…I'll shoot…at something. Can't take chances anymore. These guys are serious.

But why is this happening? Why? Why is a little more property so damned important to that church? And why does this little church carry on like a miniature army? Hud found no answers to his questions, but he felt his determination feeding on his fatigue and discomfort. He vowed he wouldn't go down again in round three.

Waving at a swarm of mosquitoes that had invaded his meager shade, he escaped back to the rock on the beach. Mistakes? He had made a couple of doozies today, but his biggest mistake had been taking the Bashers too lightly, trying to deal with the conflict on a part-time basis. I guess I expected them to do *their* thing when it's convenient for *me*, he mused. Their attacks on us are becoming more and more open, yet we can't attack them…or we'll be the *bad* guys. He picked up a stick and began scratching aimlessly in the sand as he pondered.

Hud found himself wondering if he was in over his head. Perhaps Gibby, Sarah, and Kimberly…even he himself had blindly assumed that Hudson Bryant III could simply step in and make things right. But the Bashers were cunning. They had a plan, and they knew what they needed to do to win. He'd been striking out on all three counts. And when he bungled the confrontation at the dock, he marked himself as a prime target. Get rid of him, and they were back to dealing only with Gibby and Kimberly.

But how could he help Gibby and Kimberly? Thanks to the wiliness of the church leaders, Sheriff Beer Stein apparently had placed the burden of suspicion on Hud. Outright aggressiveness against the Bashers would be self-defeating. It would be like physically attacking a business competitor. Business, he thought, yeah...I did all right in *that* competitive arena. How? Simple. Through various means, I found out what a threatening competitor had going and then devised some way to counter the advantage.

The thought crystallized the problem in Hud's mind. We've been kept so busy defending ourselves we haven't formed any plan of our own. We need to find out who these church guys really are, why they're so militant, and why they want Black Rock Bay so badly. *Then* we find a way to end this thing...or win if it comes down to either-or. People *that* bad have to be vulnerable somewhere, have to have some weak links in the chain, have to have left a trail of some kind. He felt a surge of energy within. Yes, he'd set T.C. Wolf and his detective friend loose. They just might find the dangling end of the rope that he could grab onto.

"Looks like you got big problems there," came a voice from the lake.

Hud looked up. Two young men in a sixteen foot boat were drift fishing, letting the wind carry them along their course, directly out from where Hud sat. He'd been so engrossed in the puzzle he hadn't seen them round the point on his right. The boat was a standard resort boat painted an ugly maroon with the yellow lettering WHITE PINES RESORT on the side. Hud's needs directed his eyes immediately to the stern of the boat. What kind of engine? It was a Johnson twenty-five horse engine, the older boxy style from the 'seventies. But it could do the job...if *they* would.

"I'd sure hate to interrupt your fishing, Guys, but I really need some help," he said as he stood. "I've been on this rock for three hours, and I've got to get back before dark."

"You been fishing...or *hunting?*" the man near the engine asked.

"What?"

"What's the gun for?"

Hud glanced to his left. The four-ten leaned against another rock. Oh, brilliant, Hud, brilliant, he thought. You sit here trying to hitch-hike with a weapon out in plain sight. Think fast. "Oh, that," he said, hesitating. "Well...there used to be a family of bears on this island and they weren't very friendly. Since I'm stranded here...with nowhere to go...."

The two men looked at each other and exchanged words too soft for Hud to hear. "Where do you need to go?" asked the spokesman.

"Black Rock Bay," Hud replied. "Tell you what," he continued, fumbling quickly through his wallet as he spoke, "I got twenty bucks here if you'll take me home...forty if you'll tow the boat home."

Minutes later, Hud had turned his Lund about, tied his boat to theirs using a Y-shaped harness and tow rope he carried for emergencies, and climbed aboard his boat. The young man turned the throttle wide open and the strange coupling mushed ahead. After fifty yards, the two boats had settled into the best angle they would find. Hud found he could reduce the resistance his boat set up by moving his weight to the bow. But, with Friday's towing experience fresh in his mind, he didn't like the way the Johnson was laboring. He pointed at the engine and motioned for the driver to back off a little. The driver did so, smiled, and held up a can of beer. With Hud's nod, the man tossed it back. Hud managed to catch the errant throw. He popped the top and settled back for the ride. Gauging their speed, he knew it would take an hour.

When they finally rounded the point, Hud looked up at the Bashers' cedar structure, and as he expected there was a man standing at the window. He waved. There was no response. When close to the resort dock, he pulled himself alongside his benefactors, disconnected the tow rope and thanked them, adding an extra ten to the payoff. With a cheery wave, they headed out.

Hud paddled his boat to the side of the dock nearest the launching ramp. He tied up, and when he climbed out onto the dock, he breathed a huge sigh. Good to be home, he thought. Guess I'd better find Gibby, get the trailer over here, and load the boat on for another trip to town. That dealer is making a mint off me this year.

Hud had started up the hill for the lodge room, his shoes squishing with every step, when he heard Gibby call from off to his right.

"Hud! Hud! Over here...at Number Five!" Just as Hud spotted his friend, Gibby turned and stepped from the deck back into the cottage.

Hud turned and headed for the cottage. It wasn't unlike Gibby to make friends with the resort guests. They'll probably meet me with a beer, he thought. Gibby's told them about his fantastic friend, all the way from California. Then I have to go through the old routine, "I had a friend who moved to California. Where 'bouts do *you* live? Maybe you know him." Oh, well, he mused, guess it's better than what I just went through. But he was tired and hungry. He moved slowly up the four steps to the deck, then stopped, curious about the wet deck boards and the sound of water dripping to the ground beneath. Gibby must have hosed the deck down.

"Come on in," came Gibby's voice as Hud reached for the door.

Preparing an excuse for a quick exit to keep the party brief, Hud stopped short at the kitchen scene that met him. Mixed with the layer of water that covered the floor, he saw broken glass, shards of broken porcelain that had once been dishes, coffee grounds, and an assortment of garbage, from beer cans to bacon grease. The beautiful, light-toned knotty pine walls were blotched and stained. The curtain rods had been pulled off the walls, and the naugahyde chair cushions had been slashed. Gibby stood alone in the room, in the middle of the mess, carefully sweeping the broken glass and porcelain through the water into a pile. Hud stood there frozen, trying to make some kind of sense out of the catastrophe before him.

"Soon's I get this crap out of the way, you start lugging the wooden furniture out on the deck before it soaks up any more water," Gibby ordered. "I'll help you with the couch and mattresses."

"But what—"

"Ain't got time to talk now. Gotta save this stuff—much as we can."

"Kimberly back there?" Hud asked, motioning to the bedrooms.

"Next door…Number Four, the three-bedroom. Trashed that one, too," Gibby said. "Sarah's looking after the lodge. She wanted to help here, but…. Gotta get this glass picked up somehow so we can start on the water with the wet-vac."

Hud started for the first bedroom. He could see the water mark two inches up on the baseboard. Sloshing his way across the commercial carpeting, he picked up the nightstand and a lamp and made his way to the deck outside. By the time he placed the two objects, he felt the fire burning inside, and his movements became quick, determined, almost frenzied. As they worked, his short questions to Gibby brought terse replies. This had been no fight among the occupants—this was a total trash job. And they had added the water, the most destructive of their acts, by cutting the water feed tube to the toilet tank. When Gibby had shoveled most of the glass and porcelain into a plastic bucket, he helped Hud carry the box springs and mattresses, then the bed frames outside.

"Okay," Gibby said, "furniture's out. I'm ready to vacuum. Go next door and get the furniture out for Kimberly. Then, after I get the water and the small trash up, we'll rip out all the carpet and toss it outside. After that, we'll mop 'em dry and set fans."

That's Gibby, thought Hud as he headed next door. When there's a crisis, and he knows what to do, he's a real take-charge guy. Funny, those directions sounded like orders, but I don't feel any resentment. He's right…and I know it. Now, with the Bashers, he doesn't measure up the same. I guess the turf war falls to me.

Numbness changed to anger, then to a heavy sadness when he stepped into the kitchen of Number Four. There sat Kimberly, hunched over with her face in her hands, on a kitchen chair beside a pile of broken glass and porcelain. A broom balanced vertically between her knees, resting against one shoulder. Her bowed back shook violently as she sobbed.

Ohhh, poor Kimberly, he thought. What can I do— But before he could complete the thought, he found himself gently grasping her elbows from behind, raising her from the chair, and turning her around. The flood of tears all but obscured her blue eyes. He wrapped his arms around her, pulling her to him, aware that the broom was caught between them, but unwilling to let go. Once more, he tried to find comforting words, then abandoned the effort and simply hugged her. Despite the convulsive sobbing, he could feel the strength in her tall, slender body.

Damn, thought Hud. They did everything but set off a bomb. Not spontaneous vandalism. Too organized, too thorough. This smacks of the Bashers. Then he recalled the conversation he had overheard early Saturday morning near Cottage Four and things began to click. What was it they had said? "Do we really need this much junk with us?" the whiny voice had asked. Another had said, "….got two boats, doesn't mean we got to fill them." And a third voice added, "You got to at least *look* like a fisherman…." It all makes sense now, he thought. Where was my brain back then? He knew he'd have a tough time with this batch of guilt. But, not much point in telling Kimberly, at least not right now.

He lowered his head and felt her soft hair against his cheek. He knew then that he'd do anything in his power, give anything he had to help Kimberly. There was no way he could deny this lovely creature, this strong-willed queen who had been knocked from the throne that circumstances had forced her to accept. He vowed to respect her feelings, but somehow he would earn her trust.

"Going to be all right," he said, tightening his embrace. "We'll get past this. You can count on it."

She responded only by sobbing harder, that involuntary cry of a child who has just reached the comfort of a parent. Finally, after what seemed like minutes to Hud, her bursts of misery slowed. She pushed back a little from Hud and looked up at him, her tears still streaming down her face.

"I—I don't know how much more I can take." Kimberly hesitated, trying to blink back her tears. "Those...church bums...did this...on my first day in business." She drew a deep breath and slowly exhaled. "Some of the other tricks...they did to the *resort*. But this...this...those so-called Christians...they did this to *me*."

"I wish I could say you're wrong," Hud said softly, "but there's no doubt—"

"I had a chance," she cut in, "even with what the Bashers had done before, I had a chance to make it here. But this...this just about wipes me out." Her words came faster and faster as though racing the convulsions for mastery. "I put four thousand, every nickel I could afford into Number Four," she went on, gesturing to the interior of the cottage, "all new floor coverings, new furniture, new refrigerator, new microwave, new toaster, new dishes. Now I have to do it again, only now I have to do Number Five along with it. And I'll have to cancel out the reservations for both units for—who knows how many weeks."

"Kimberly, look on the bright side. The new refrigerator is—"

"Not to mention the obvious...both parties skipped without paying. And I had just called my ex this morning to see why he's two months behind on the alimony he promised. That was the only part of his dumping me that seemed honorable. Now he says he's run into...complications. There won't be any more money, at least not this year. If I have to hire a lawyer to try to get it, that's more money spent, money I don't have." She paused and looked intently into Hud's eyes. "Hud, I've spent six months trying to figure out where I went wrong. Is this a payback for something?"

"Absolutely not," he replied. "That's nonsense...but the fact that you asked is very important to me. Now, the refrigerator is okay. That little bit of water didn't hurt it."

"Except," she began, breaking away from Hud and tracking through the water to the new appliance. She groped behind the white fixture, came out with its power cord, and held it up for Hud to see. The plug had been snipped off. "They did this to every electrical appliance and lamp in both units."

He studied Kimberly. He liked one thing he saw. Once past the violent sobbing, she seemed to have flipped to the opposite extreme, rattling on like a machine gun. But at least, she had regained some control and her thinking seemed rational.

"Kimberly, when did you discover all this?" he asked.

"Your man Wolf found it early this morning. He was sneaking through the cottages looking for bugs while the guests were out. When he found this one, he turned the water off. Then, when he saw both vehicles were gone, he ran next door and found the same thing."

"Call the sheriff? Take any pictures?"

"They said the vandals would be several counties down the road by that time. But Will Mertens said he'd run the license plates and the names they gave and see what he came up with. Sarah got her camera and shot up a roll." Kimberly stopped abruptly, as though she suddenly recognized her transition from uncontrollable crying to nonstop chattering.

Hud smiled and nodded his approval. "Now," he said, "I think I've earned a hug, one without the crying. Trust me?" He stepped toward her, his arms out. Somehow, though Kimberly seemed neither anxious nor unwilling, Hud found her in his arms, her own around him. While he struggled against his instincts, the current that flowed from her body through his told him what he needed to know. He brushed a light kiss on her forehead, then pushed her away and held her at arms length for a moment. He thought he saw the confirmation in her eyes, but he cautioned himself. It could be only gratitude, he thought.

"Now," he said, pushing her away gently, "if we don't get our butts in gear, Gibby'll be all over us. We can talk while we work."

Kimberly nodded, grabbed her broom, and attacked the pile of glass. Hud began carrying furniture out and stacking it on the deck. It seemed like there was less furniture and it had become lighter. With a combined burst of energy, they soon had the cottage ready for Gibby's vacuum. As they worked, Hud related his own experience.

"Wow," she said softly, "You seem to have made it into our club, haven't you?"

"I guess I'm marked," he replied.

"You don't seem bothered by it. You know…you don't have to be in this war," she said, as they stood together on the deck, resting against the railing.

"I do now," he said. "Do you mind if I ask Wolf to stick around? We've a lot of work to do this week. Kind of have him do some scouting and watch our backsides?"

"I…we…we already asked him," Kimberly said. "He said he can give us a few days—at his regular rate. One look at this mess…and we knew, with all four of us working *here* the Gunderson place is *really* exposed—wide open."

Chapter 18

Father Jeranko and Brother Vance traced their way carefully down a barely visible path through the woods. The trail, one of many that led from the level land atop the peninsula down to the lakeshore, followed an incline so steep it was almost a crawler, rather than a walker. Neither man spoke. They saluted as they passed a young sentry who was dressed in camouflage fatigues and equipped with a knife sheathed to his belt, a hand radio, and a heavy oak staff two inches thick and five feet long. They approached the shoreline at a point midway between the tip of the peninsula and the resort. Here the slope flattened out just above the lake level. They could see the waters of Black Rock Bay, yet remain hidden from outsiders.

"So this is it? Explain your plan," said Jeranko. He wore a khaki uniform that bore no insignia or symbol of rank, identical to that of his long-time associate.

"Plan A, farther out toward the tip, calls for the two-plane hangar to be built," Brother Vance began. "But here, you notice, there's an indentation, almost a small cove. If we follow Plan B, we'll cut the cove deeper into the land. Then we'll build a pair of matching ramps for the aircraft's floats. The ramps will each be four feet wide and extend from shore into the water at a gentle incline. Alongside each will be a narrow dock for a walkway. The ramps will be framed of steel, with rollers like the old-fashioned washing machine rollers. On shore, between the ramps, we'll mount a powerful winch. We simply turn the plane around and winch it in backwards." He glanced at Jeranko to measure the reaction, then smiled deep within. His superior's slow, deliberate nodding translated to an A-plus.

"Still too exposed, though," Jeranko said.

"That's the beauty of this plan," Vance replied. "The Plan A hangar will always be just that, an ugly building in plain sight on the shoreline. That's why our petition for a variance is hung up in committee. But here, we transplant some sizeable trees and bushes to the pointed outcroppings on each side. Rather than *removing* any of the green, we've *added* to it, and we're only visible for a range of forty degrees, straight out in front. If necessary, we can cover that...while we unload." He led the way a little closer to the shore.

Jeranko turned and eyed the hill behind them. "But the hill is much steeper here," he observed.

"That's one of the two negatives of Plan B."

Jeranko looked directly at Vance. His perpetual smile cracked a little wider. "But you're anxiously waiting to tell me your ingenious solution."

"I'm sure you've already figured it out," Vance said. "Our computer parts and our...other goods aren't heavy. We have plenty of manpower. We build a zig-zag goat path up the hill. I've designed a lightweight cart on bicycle wheels." He checked for the nod again.

"Ironic," said Jeranko, "to move the, ah, gold of the twenty-first century around...we do it the old-fashioned way. It's good. Simple, but good. If we add the bigger DeHaviland Beaver to our air force, have you allowed for that?"

"That's why each ramp is four feet wide."

Jeranko simply nodded again. "Can you get the variance for Plan B—quickly?"

"With our two supporters on the board and the beauty of this plan, I guarantee it," said Brother Vance. "Three days—max."

Jeranko stood motionless for some time, as though staring out at the bay. Vance quietly watched him, confident that he knew exactly what his leader was thinking.

"We've got two shipments a week coming in now," Jeranko said. "Soon they'll be daily. We've got to get the floatplane into the bay here. Too many days when it's too rough to land on the big lake. What's your time frame?"

He's buying it, Vance thought. Now I'll give him the clincher. "One week," he said, a touch heavier on the triumphal tone than he'd intended. "Three days to get the variance. Then we'll have separate crews specializing on each segment but working simultaneously. To do the digging on the shoreline, the transplanting, the ramps, the winch, the carts, the path...four more days."

"Do it." Father Jeranko turned abruptly and started up the hill. Brother Vance followed out of habit. As they topped the demanding incline and headed toward the cedar structure, Vance understood the silence that had been demanded tacitly by his leader. Father Jeranko was thinking, always thinking. Sometimes it bothered Brother Vance, but he salved his irritation with the confidence that what came of Father's thinking was seldom short of brilliance.

"Now," said Jeranko, as they settled into the familiar meeting room, "we need to review a number of other things. First, since you have need of our local officials these days, are they happy with our...arrangement?"

"A little problem with one," Vance said, "but he was reminded of exactly how his world turns, and he fell back into line. In fact, he handled one episode this weekend extremely well."

"Good. And Saturday night at the resort?"

"Couldn't have gone better," Vance replied. "In lost rent and damages, the little lady fell another ten to twelve thousand behind. And the fishermen had the dirty plates off and were back in Minneapolis long before the unfortunate scene was even discovered."

Father Jeranko nodded. "Any way they can be traced?"

"None. And what's really beautiful...." Vance went on. "This morning, Farber called her ex-husband and learned there'll be no money coming from him."

"Our cost?"

"Tried for thirty percent...had to go forty," Vance said. "But at forty percent, he won't renege. Who else pays you forty percent for keeping your money?"

"Next thing...Corporal...what was his name?" Jeranko asked.

"David, Corporal David."

"What can you tell me about him? Is he as good as he seems?" Jeranko's hard gaze focused on Vance. He knew it well. It said, "Quick answers now—don't stall and choose your words."

"Nothing," Vance replied, choosing not to toy with his superior. "We have Sergeant Cameron roaming Loring Park, questioning the derelicts to see if anyone knows him. Can't see any other place to start." Vance hesitated. "Can you?"

"Certainly," Jeranko said with finality. "Right here. Start here and work back."

"Yes, Sir."

"Now, this Bryant fellow...what's *he* made of?"

"I'm...I'm not sure yet," Vance replied. "I don't *think* he's any threat. Our people wiped him out again today in our second confrontation. The best he seems able to do each time is ride past down below in his boat and wave at us. That would suggest he's a survivor, but we have no sign that he's an effective combatant."

"But," Jeranko returned quickly, "Let's not *assume*. He arrived when, last Thursday?"

Brother Vance nodded, wondering where the question would lead.

"And you've kept heavy pressure on him ever since," Jeranko said, reaching into the file drawer of his desk for a manila folder. "It could be, the more we provoke him, the tougher he'll get. We have a lot happening in the next few days. Let's back off and let Mr. Bryant cool down. According to this file you've put together, he has a couple of businesses in Southern California. Let's let him do some fishing, and then, if the troubles seem to be past, he might go on home."

"But—"

"Ever the warrior, aren't you, my old friend?" Jeranko smiled. "You hate to start a fight and then run. But in this case, *you're* not running. You're only giving *him* a chance to run. Can you handle that?"

"Of...course, Sir." Brother Vance knew he could handle that. He could handle *anything*. But, he didn't like it. He remembered the strength he'd seen in Bryant's face when they met at the resort. He and Brother Mark had caught Bryant completely by surprise, overwhelmed him. But, while Bryant had been off balance, he hadn't caved in. There was strength there. He was sure of it, and he'd long been convinced that aggressiveness was the answer to strength. And, with Farber's friends helping her repair the damage, it would be the perfect time to hit Gundersons again. This might be one of those rare times when he should bend his orders just a little. He'd have to think about that.

"Good," said Jeranko. "If I'm right, he'll be out of your hair. If I'm wrong...you'll still get your chance to take him out." He plunked the file back into the drawer, leaned back in his massive chair and, with as serious a face as Vance had ever seen on his mentor, he looked directly at Brother Vance. Even the habitual smile had evaporated. "Now, something else...."

Oh, oh, thought Vance. That's the look he gives a condemned man. His face heated up slightly. Tension gripped his upper body. What could the problem be? He had performed well—wonderfully in fact. But that wasn't what those steely eyes were saying. Is it Farber...and Gunderson…the fact that he hadn't gotten them out? Don't—don't let it show, he told himself. He's powerful, but so are you. So be powerful. He looked back at his leader. Their eyes met, and Vance mustered all of the strength he had to hold his focus and not back down.

"I have big news for you, Brother," Jeranko said. "On Tuesday, slightly more than forty-eight hours from now, the Thirteen Colonies of America will commence with Phase One. You've known, of course, that something was coming. And since you yourself dispatched our demolitions teams to Albuquerque, you've had some concept of what's coming."

Vance tried to control his body language, releasing his pent up sigh as slowly as he could. Movement, that's it, he thought. It might be expected with news of such importance. He rose from his chair and walked to the window overlooking Black Rock Bay.

"So…" Vance said, with all the gravity he could muster, "the time has come."

• • •

"Hey, Sergeant Evans!" David called as he stepped out of the mess hall after the Sunday evening meal. The short, husky man stopped and looked back. David broke into a trot to catch up with his leader of Fisher Troop. "Where you heading?"

"Taking a little hike down to the main gate and back," Evans replied. "Got to walk off that big meal." His tone suggested he might accept company.

"Sounds like a good idea. Can I tag along?" David asked. He caught up with his sergeant and together they strode off down the crushed rock road. The acceptance warmed David. He recognized his own craving for social contact, even in its lightest form. And there was no one at the camp he respected more, no, *liked* more than the ex-Marine who had become his mentor. They walked in silence for the first hundred yards between the two rows of large barracks buildings, three structures on each side of the road.

"You get lonely?" the sergeant asked, as much a statement as a question.

"That's the one thing I still have trouble with," David replied. "Nobody talks—at least not about themselves, their background, or their dreams. Meant to be that way? Or did it just happen?"

"Meant to be that way," came the reply, but there was no follow-up. The rhythmic crunch of their boots on the crushed rock seemed amplified in the silence.

Finally, David renewed the conversation, "Care to tell me why?"

"The good of the whole," Evans said. After several seconds, he went on, "Our mission depends on the dedication of every man to the good of the whole. If we someday find ourselves in combat, we can't have a single soldier jeopardizing the mission by deviating from the objective to help a friend. That's standard military attitude, although the traditional armies don't put the same stress on it that we do."

"That seems rather short sighted to me," David said. "If you were in trouble, or wounded or something, and I took a minute to save you, I'd be doing the Minutemen a service—rescuing one of our best soldiers so he can serve again."

Sergeant Evans looked over and smiled. "Thank you. You have my permission to rescue me when it seems necessary."

"You mean that?"

"No, but I admit the thought made me feel good." Evans grinned at David, turned his head and trudged on down the road.

"Can I ask you a question—about yourself?" David asked. Though he got no response, he continued. "Except for Father Jeranko and you, everyone here uses only first names."

"My first name is Evan," the sergeant replied quickly. "My sergeant here in primary action training tacked the S on. He'd never heard of an Evan. It stuck."

"Wow," said David, in mock excitement. "Now I know *two* things about you. You're an ex-Marine, and your first name is Evan."

Sergeant Evans laughed. "I'm not really so secretive. In fact, the thing I miss most from my eight years in the Marines is the comraderie. But even I have to be careful about what I say—who I say it to."

"Big brother?"

After a hesitation, the sergeant answered, "Something like that."

They rounded a bend, leaving the camp clearing behind, and started down the long, sloping road with thick woods on both sides. Maybe, David thought, I've finally found a friend here, a real human being. Gently, careful not to push too hard, he pursued the line of conversation, surprised at the trust the sergeant gradually demonstrated.

He learned that the sergeant hailed originally from Rochester, Minnesota, and had been discharged from the Marines when his drug addiction was exposed. After spending a year in oblivion, he had been found by the church. They had helped him past the ugly wall of rehab, given him reason to fight on, and handed him goals that he could latch onto.

"God was there all the time," Evans concluded. "But I was so gassed I couldn't see it."

They came to a heavy steel gate across the road. Two sentries in fatigues stood with their oak staffs, their backs to the gate. David knew that inside the nearby shed the guards had their automatic weapons stashed.

"Sergeant Evans and Corporal David," the sergeant said to the sentry who stepped forward, a clipboard in his hand. "Just walking to the outside gate and back." The sentry scanned the list on his board, placed a checkmark beside each name, and motioned for his cohort to open the gate.

As they struck out again, David sensed that it was trade-off time, so he volunteered his story of a broken marriage, a wife who dumped him for another man. "Probably seems kind of silly to you," he said, "going off the deep end just because of a woman…but I really loved her. It just about killed me."

"Doesn't seem silly at all. What was her name?"

"Julie—" David replied, catching himself too late. Was that the name he'd given Brother Theodore when the spiritual leader had rescued him from Loring Park? He had long since forgotten the name he'd offered at that time, but he was certain he'd not given Julie's name. That, he thought, was your first real mistake, David. But then, he rationalized, the chance of Sergeant Evans and Brother Theodore comparing conversations was one in a million.

When they reached the outer gate, a simple farm-style pipe frame and wire assembly, they stopped for a moment. Off to one side, partially concealed in the brush stood the sentry, dressed in ordinary blue jeans and a white T-shirt. Sergeant Evans waved at the young man. They turned and started back toward camp, continuing their cautious sharing until they checked back through the heavily guarded inner gate.

David waited, carefully weighing his next question, until they had rounded the uphill bend in the road and were out of earshot of the guards. Better do it now, he told himself. You've set it up. He's responding. Never be a better time. Still, he hesitated.

"Do I hear wheels turning?" the sergeant asked.

"Yeah…I guess you do," David said. "It just struck me. You've been with the church about four years, you said. There was a guy I knew once…he was a grad student when I was a freshman in college. I heard he'd gone off the deep end…then joined some church like ours. Never saw him again. Name was Daniel…Dan…Engebritson—no it was Engstrom. Dan Engstrom, that's it. Ever know him?"

Evans stopped suddenly and turned to face David. "Yeah, I knew him…not well, but I knew who he was. He was in Company A."

David felt the chill of excitement rush through his body. It wasn't the answer he'd expected, and he knew that at least some of what he felt had to show in his face. Control it! his mind shouted. Could he conceal his feelings? He had to. And he sensed from Evans' reaction that he had perhaps only one more question allowed.

"Can you beat that?" David said, trying to effect a smile of amusement. "Goes to show what a small world this is. You said he *was* in Company A?" David studied the sergeant's face. The friendly smile of recent minutes had faded into a look of concern. The sergeant was trying to read David, too.

"Was," he replied, "I heard he committed suicide…about three, four months ago."

The words slammed into David like an overloaded truck. He knew he couldn't conceal the feelings that reverberated through him. Dan…dead? My brother…dead? Suicide? No way. He'd have done it when he was on drugs. Hold on, David. Don't let it show.

"Sorry," said Evans. "Obviously, you were closer to him than you let on."

"No…no closer," he said. "Just that, since my parents went, I've had some trouble dealing with death."

"See the reason for our hard-nosed attitude on personal relationships?" Evans smiled.

Chapter 19

Weird, thought Hud, just plain weird. After the turbulent, taxing events of Sunday, he knew he should have been awake all night, stewing over the problems with the Bible Bashers. But he had drifted pleasantly through the clouds of deep sleep, awakening with a vitality that propelled him from his bed to face the day.

He crunched his Monday morning cereal vigorously, sipping black coffee between bites, and staring out the kitchen window at the huge oak tree at the center of the circular drive. In the darkness, with the mercury vapor yardlight behind the tree, the oak's silhouette offered a plethora of strange shapes that stirred his imagination. Some of the more ominous outlines reminded him of Sunday's experiences, the fishing, the combat, the exhausting hitch-hike home, all capped by the hasty cleanup after the trashers.

Do we call them the Basher Trashers? he thought, a slight smile twisting his lips. Or the Trasher Bashers? He read his humor as a good sign. Despite two major defeats the previous day, and with them the unquestionable fact that he was caught up in a turf war of serious proportions, he could still find at least a smile in the situation. From there, his mind segued to the fierce determination in Ellie's eyes that accompanied her pet cliche, "Time to make things happen." *That* he would do.

Sunday, "the longest day," as he had thought of it at bedtime, hadn't ended with the massive cleanup at the resort. He had called both managers of his Orange County businesses. Everything was going well at Hudson Financial Services, and he had established a verbal agreement with Robert for his buyout of Hudson Professional Services. But for the paperwork, it was all set. Double good, he thought, for Robert and for me.

Immediately following the phone calls, he had been surprised once more by the appearance of T.C. Wolf. Hud had stepped into the kitchen to lock up and turn off the lights. There sat the mysterious man, relaxing at the kitchen table with a Coke from Hud's refrigerator. Wolf had exchanged his Paul Bunyan garb for black clothing topped by a navy blue stocking cap. He had blacked his face, leaving ominous white ovals around his expressionless eyes. After a one-word apology for his surreptitious invasion, Wolf explained that he'd found no way to knock at a door without making noise. Then, he'd gone immediately into the purpose for his visit.

"Going in tonight. Needed to check some things with you," Wolf said, his face as expressionless as in their first meeting.

"Okay," said Hud, subduing his astonishment as he took the opposite chair, "shoot."

"Your questions are: Why do these guys want this property? How many are there? How militant are they? That right?"

"Yeah…for starters."

"See you tomorrow morning—early." Wolf gulped the remainder of his Coke, belched loudly, flipped off the lights, and evaporated into the night.

As Hud cleaned up his breakfast dishes, he wondered just how and when the quiet stranger would reappear. Amazing, he thought, the guy's big, incredibly strong, but he moves about like a cat. No, more like a ghost. Hud hurried through his shower and dressed for his trip to town.

Then, he sat at the table, making his shopping list. It would soon be dawn. The first thing he'd need to do…hook Kimberly's old pickup to the boat trailer and load his boat. His thoughts drifted. What will it be like, to spend a whole day away from the lake with Kimberly? Guess we'll both be pretty bus—

A subtle movement caught Hud's eye, and when he looked up, there stood T.C. Wolf, still dressed as he was the evening before, but with dirt smudges all but covering his front side.

Startled, Hud said, "Sure glad I don't value my privacy. Coffee?"

"No time, be light soon," Wolf said, taking the other chair. He glanced at the window. "Got to be out of here in five minutes. Interesting night."

"Just a minute," Hud said. "Let me get something to write on."

"Forget it," said Wolf, "you can't write fast enough. Just listen up."

"Okay." Hud tensed, swallowed, and tried to focus on every syllable.

"Your estimate of manpower up there is way off," Wolf began. "You thought twenty to twenty-five of them? Twenty-two guards around the perimeter—at hundred yard intervals about half-way up the hill on all sides. Then one outer gate guard and two more at the inner gate. Guards all have what I call chopsticks—long, heavy clubs—knives, and walkies. They're well trained…but no experience. In Nam, they'd all be dead their first night on watch. Didn't find any booby traps. They're confident their guards can keep everybody out."

"But twenty, twenty-five? That fits my estimate," Hud said.

"That's just one shift of guards," Wolf went on with his curt, expressionless narrative. "In all, about two hundred men."

Hud gasped, but before he could say anything, the burly security man went on. "Buildings? That big, lavish HQ, large mess hall, another big building—probably a gym and training facility—six barracks units, several storage buildings, and a couple of other things I haven't figured out yet. Have to check them out in daytime when they're being used."

"You're—you're kidding!" Hud exclaimed. "You're telling me—"

"And a bulldozer, other heavy equipment, five buses—all marked Number Four, and a few more goodies." He paused and looked at Hud, his slits opening wide, exposing dark brown eyes. "This is no little cult. These are serious dudes. But they're also serious about their religion. Chapel holds about a hundred...they sing damned good."

Incredulous, Hud stared at Wolf. He had no concrete reason to disbelieve his associate, yet what he had just heard was....He sat, momentarily stunned. Finally his thoughts cleared. If Wolf was right, they were up against an army, a *real* army. And he had thought they were outnumbered five to one? More like fifty to one. How could the Bashers conceal an operation that big from everyone on this corner of the lake?

"You don't believe me," Wolf said calmly.

"I—I've got to see this," Hud said, "Take me in?"

"I said they were inexperienced. Didn't say they were stupid. You'd be in jail by dawn ...*if* you're lucky. Now, want my advice on how to handle this or not?" The eyes within the white ovals narrowed back to slits.

"I...yeah...guess so," said Hud as he tried to stifle the hollow feeling in his gut.

"Details later," Wolf began. "You got no chance in a war with these dudes. Right now, we do two things....First, we fix up our perimeter to protect against their raiding—buy us time. Then, with a swarm of bees that big...you don't stand around swatting at them. Neutralize 'em with a dose of smoke and get the leader—in this case, leaders. To do that, we got to know what the hell they're doing up there. You understand?"

"Yeah," muttered Hud. "Think so."

"Okay. Looks like you got a shopping list there." Wolf handed Hud a slip of paper. "Get this stuff, too."

Hud looked at the list:

4 doz. steel fence posts
6 spools of barbed wire
500 ft. 16-gauge outdoor electric wiring

fixtures and bulbs for a doz. outdoor floodlights
100 ft. 1/2-inch nylon rope (darkest color poss.)
50 ft. 1/2-inch hemp rope (darkest poss.)
1 large spool of green monofilament–fishing lineheavy
4 30-amp circuit breakers
1 doz. little handbells (loudest possible)
6 bear traps with chains
2 doz. 2" x 2" x 4' stakes
2 doz. signs–DANGER! KEEP OUT!

Scanning the list a second time, Hud made sense of some of the items...but others?

Before he could ask for an explanation, Wolf said, "Just get 'em. I'll get the rest of what I need over in the Falls today." With that, he stood, gave Hud a small wave, and disappeared.

Left trying to deal with an overload of curiosity whipped by a whirlwind of confusion, Hud sat there for several minutes. Finally, he regained control, pocketed the list along with his own, donned his light nylon jacket, and headed for the Gundersons' house. He checked his wallet for his credit cards. With Kimberly's list and his own, he'd probably max out on one of his cards.

After briefing Gibby on Wolf's report, he made for the resort. One party was making its way down to the dock as Hud passed. He waved, then studied them carefully as he walked. A little paranoid since the trashings, he thought. The evening before, he had made a point of rechecking all vehicle license plates for Kimberly. The examination proved only that the numbers they had given her upon registration agreed with those on their vehicles.

The sun was nearly up by the time he had loaded his boat onto its trailer. He gunned the old Chevy and headed up the inclined ramp toward the lodge room, stopping near the gas pump, where he got out and methodically checked the turn signal and brake lights on the trailer.

Satisfied that everything was in order, he looked up to see Kimberly come bouncing down the steps. Along with her customary blue jeans, she wore a pink resort sweatshirt with a matching long-visored cap that also sported the resort logo. Her golden pony tail dangled through the cap's opening in back.

"You all ready?" she asked, reaching quickly for the driver's door. "I'll drive."

Hud glanced back at the long trailer unit, hesitated, then shrugged and walked around to the passenger side. Though the issue was small, he knew it was important to Kimberly, especially important today. She gunned what she affectionately called her "mean machine" out the rear drive and headed down the county road toward U.S. 53, which would take them the forty miles into Mallard.

They drove in silence for some time, until Hud's eyes caught a familiar shape up ahead in the right-side ditch.

"Deer right!" he said crisply.

"Got him," Kimberly said, focusing on the deer while braking smoothly. The full-sized doe turned and bounded back into the woods, flashing its white tail as it disappeared.

"Good ice breaker," Hud said.

"What?"

He repeated the phrase and added, "At least we've got some conversation going now. I was beginning to think it would be a long, quiet, awkward day."

"That's pretty good…awkward," she said. "I…think that's how I feel…after coming unglued the way I did yesterday, all my blubbering, feel kind of—exposed." She hesitated. "No…helpless, scared, and indebted. And now I'm headed for town to add big bucks to the debt. Doesn't make me very comfortable."

"Doesn't make me comfortable, either."

Kimberly jerked her foot from the accelerator and reached for the brake pedal. "It doesn't?" she asked. "You afraid you won't get paid back?"

"Not it at all," he said. "Put your foot back where it belongs." She hesitated briefly, then accelerated to regain the lost speed. He continued, "It's…I'd like us to get to know each other without this kind of baggage lighting up the tilt sign every other day."

"But—"

"Now," he cut in, "there are two ways we can handle the problem…if you're interested in handling the problem." He looked over at her. She waited, nodding almost imperceptibly. He studied her profile, the straight forehead beneath the bill of her cap, the delicate turned-up nose, and the small but firm chin. Except for her pale lipstick, she wore no makeup, but her smooth, tan skin glowed. "Two ways we can deal with that," he went on. "One, you set your fears aside and trust that I'll never use it to pressure you in any way…or two, ask Gibby and Sarah to carry these expenses for a while. I think they can afford it and would do it. Then, you wouldn't owe me a damned dime. Frankly, except for the burden that places on the Gundersons, I'd prefer to go that way." Hud wondered where the words had come from, but since they were out he was glad.

"No," she said, her eyes fixed on the road ahead, "there's a third option. You get your boat fixed, go fishing…for however long you're staying…and leave my problems to *me*."

"Sorry, Kimberly, that's not an option," he said. "I'm staying—indefinitely. I'm in this thing now, whether I want to be or not. And I don't know how much good I can do, but you need all the help you can get. We're *not* going to lose your resort." He glanced back to check the boat, then turned again to study her face before forcing his gaze back to the road ahead. The silence set in again, and Hud patiently waited it out. She needed time to think. Damn, thought Hud, I wish I knew how to handle this. I could tell her about Wolf's recon excursion last night. I could tell her I'm falling in love with her. He knew that either approach might help them past this...or blow up in his face.

Ten miles later, Kimberly broke the silence. "I—I really don't want to chase you back to California, Hud...but I can't handle what we're doing today either, paying *my* bills with *your* money. You know, with all that's happened, it seems like it's been a long time. But I've only known you a few days. A few days, Hud. And I just got kicked in the butt by a man I'd known for ten years, been married to for nine. Can you understand that?"

Hud glanced over at her again. A tear slowly wound its way down beside her nose. The dimple in her cheek was as shallow as he'd ever seen it. Had she not been guiding the tandem vehicles down the highway at fifty-five miles an hour, he'd have moved over, taken her in his arms, and kissed her softly...or violently...he wasn't sure which. Really ironic, he thought. All those women the last two years...couldn't wait to get their hands on his wallet, and now, when he wanted to get close to Kimberly, he couldn't—his wallet was in the way.

"Okay," he said finally, "you got through to me. I'm sorry." He felt heavy as he searched for a fresh approach. The blur of the trees flashing past his window seemed perfectly timed with the blur in his mind. Finally, he hit on another option. It wasn't a strong one, but it was worth a try. "Kimberly," he said, "let's replace option one. What if you borrowed the money to cover all this, plus some for a cushion, from your bank?"

"Ha," she said, "Heileman wouldn't give me five bucks. I'm already in to the limit and beyond in *his* mind."

"But, if *I* secure the loan, he'll jump at it," Hud countered. "That way, your first obligation is to the bank. There's no doubt in my mind that you'll pay it off. So I'm not *giving* you anything. I'm simply lending you my credit rating."

She seemed deep in thought as they passed the Tall Pines Motel, nearly hidden in the pines on the left, and then the Super G Station on the right. Kimberly slowed to the new speed limit. Suddenly, out of the tall forests appeared the town of Mallard. The community of ten thousand always struck Hud as a picture clipped from a promotional brochure, with its neat one- and two-story business buildings and its symmetrical city blocks whose streets were lined with large oak and elm trees. The well-kept houses, painted in white or pastels, all sat well back from the streets on large, manicured lawns and showed a distinctive pride of ownership, but for the pickup truck and trailered boat found in most of the driveways.

As she turned off the highway onto the driveway that led to the boat dealership, Kimberly shifted down, pulled into the parking area, and stopped. With another shift of gears, she backed the long trailer around a group of cars, deftly counter-steering as she backed, turning the truck wheels in the opposite direction she intended the trailer to go. When the rear of the boat was perfectly aligned with the large, open garage door, she stopped.

"You unhitch and get them set up," she said with a slight smile. "I need time to think."

Fifteen minutes later, Hud climbed back into the cab. "All set," he announced. "They think the gears are okay, new prop and bearings should do it. I told them to throw in spares of both. We can pick it up just before five today. Save another trip, and besides, we might need it. It's faster than anything the Bashers have—except the cigarette boat, of course."

"Okay, Mr. Bryant," Kimberly said cheerily as she headed the decrepit pickup out to the highway, "you ready for another breakfast? We can compare lists and get all this shopping organized so we don't have to backtrack." She paused. "I buy."

Minutes later, they were served their coffee in a booth at Hornberger's, a delightful little restaurant, known throughout the region for good food and wholesome, attractive, blond Scandinavian waitresses.

Certainly a sudden change, Hud thought. Kimberly's smiled almost nonstop since we left the boatyard.

"Excuse me," Hud said, smiling across the table at her, "but has something happened that I should know about?"

"Your idea," she said with a smile. "I like the second option, *if* Gibby and Sarah can and are willing to carry me. If they can't carry all of it, I like your idea of the bank loan." She reached across and took his hand. "I could live with that...if you're still willing to sign for me." Her eyes, fixed on his, confirmed the words she spoke.

Hud felt his grin extend from ear to ear. He tried to control it, but it seemed to have been fixed by some exterior force. "Good judgment," he said, placing his other hand over hers. Then he marveled that he could respond to the best news since his arrival with but two words, for inside him, feelings skittered about like Mexican jumping beans. He saw Kimberly study their joined hands for a moment. Then, she gently extracted hers.

"Okay, Hud," she said, her face growing serious again, "we've set aside a big problem for us both. But I have to tell you...I need time to finish healing and to figure out where I'm going. Don't push me. Okay?"

"Anything else?" their young waitress asked as she set a house special breakfast before each of them. They looked at each other and laughed. The waitress aimed a coy smile at Hud. He glanced across at Kimberly, who smiled and nodded knowingly, her eyes following the shapely girl back to the kitchen.

"No push," he said, "I promise." Then he added, "Been there."

"Okay, eat up," she said. "We've got a lot of ground to cover today."

They visited what seemed to Hud like half of the businesses in Mallard that day. Kimberly ordered the replacement carpeting. Then she located and purchased two sets of economy dishes and glasses. In a quick stop at the Chamber of Commerce office, she reminded them that she still had a few openings in June. She told Hud afterward that she knew they'd send no business her way. They favored the resorts within ten miles of town because those guests visited town more often and spent more money there. But at least for her first year, she had paid dues to the chamber, and on every trip to town she reminded them of the fact.

After a quick lunch, they began chipping away at Hud's two lists. First, they hit the smaller shops for the specialty items. Then they headed out to the east side of town to the large home supplies and hardware store. With each of the strange items on the list Wolf had sent along, Kimberly asked about its purpose, and each time Hud shrugged an "I don't know" reply. They backed the pickup against the rear loading dock where a young man loaded the heavier bulk items for them.

"You know," Kimberly said, as they watched the steel fence posts and barbed wire being loaded, "that stuff kind of gives me the willies."

"Me, too," agreed Hud, "because I have the feeling I might be the guy who's going to put it all up. By the way, do you have a post driver?"

"Don't know. What's it look like?"

"If you have to ask, we'd better get one," he said, walking back into the store to rent a driver.

After stopping at a supermarket to stock up on groceries, most of which were for resale to the resort guests, they made for the boatyard. By five o'clock, they were on their way back to the lake.

To Hud's surprise, Kimberly had asked him to drive home. She gave no reason, simply asked. To him, the seemingly insignificant gesture put a glorious cap on the busiest and most wonderful day he'd experienced in a long, long time. Throughout their hustling in and out of the stores in Mallard, there had been a running dialogue, sometimes pertaining to their mission, sometimes relating to themselves and their past lives.

Kimberly's revelation that she had been an interior decorator in Minneapolis before buying the resort with her exhusband surprised Hud. He wasn't sure why. Perhaps, her willingness to tackle such physical endeavors at the resort, coupled with her assertive personality, had led him to picture her as a physical trainer or therapist...or possibly a businesswoman in a position of power. In California or Colorado he'd have pegged her as a ski instructor.

As he wiggled about and finally settled into the worn, dumpy driver's seat for the trip back, he managed to forget about the long trailer unit he towed and enjoy the bond that seemed to be developing between them. It was the first time they'd had a chance to talk about things other than the growing problems with the church group.

"So many people have tried what we did," she said, "made a wild move to escape the big city rat race. Most probably fail because they don't know what they're getting into. The romantic appeal of a resort...or a bed and breakfast...or sometimes even a sheep ranch seduces them, washes away any common sense."

"That what happened to you and...."

"Matt," she said. "Not really. I'd been coming up to resorts with my family for years. I knew about the hard work and the tight profit margin. And I explained it all to Matt."

"But he didn't believe you?" Hud asked, slowing the old pickup to allow a heavily loaded logging truck to pass.

"Wish I could say yes." Kimberly paused and looked out her window as they passed Little Moose Lake, the clusters of white birches along its shore glistening in the late afternoon sun. "No...he faked enthusiasm for the idea and supposedly quit his job. We bought the resort and made the move. Then—surprise! His company asked him to come back. He convinced me that we'd be off to a much better start with the money he could make through the winter months. But...that was all part of his plan."

"His plan?"

"Yep," she said, sounding to Hud like an angry cowgirl. "Turns out, he'd never quit his job—only took a two-month leave. Got me up here, saddled with the resort, and went back to Minneapolis, free as a breeze, to play girlie games."

"I'm sorry—maybe you'd rather not talk about it," Hud said.

"It's all right—think it helps," she said. "Except for Gibby and Sarah, and phone talks with my mother, I haven't had much conversation with anyone for several months—oh, oh."

"What's the matter?" asked Hud.

"Keep an eye on the green school bus coming toward us," she said. "That's the Basher bus."

Hud watched the forest green bus approach. As it roared past, he noticed two things. It had a number four painted in black near the driver's window, and there were no passengers. He recalled what Wolf had said that morning, something about five buses...all numbered the same. It made no more sense now than it had early that morning.

"Start slowing," Kimberly said, "our turn is right around this bend."

Hud shifted down, made the turn, and began to gain speed again as they headed north on the blacktop county road.

"I call this the roller coaster," Kimberly said lightheartedly. She pointed ahead. "With any kind of a load on, you have to get all you can going down one side so you can make it up the other."

As they topped the first hill and started down the other side, Hud looked ahead and saw them gaining rapidly on another vehicle, a green schoolbus.

"Another one?" he asked.

"Back off, Hud," Kimberly said. "Don't get too close. Those guys'll do anything."

But as the lumbering bus began struggling with the next uphill stretch, Hud found himself closing too quickly behind it. On the left rear corner of the bus, there was a black number four.

"Hud, that can't be!" Kimberly said. It's the same bus, going *our* way, and now it's loaded with people," "Back off, Hud, before they spot us."

Hud shifted down and dropped back. But when the Basher bus topped the hill and should have begun to accelerate, it continued to slow and finally stopped.

"Too late," he said. "This might be Round Three."

"Over on this side…guys getting off," Kimberly said. "What should we do?"

Hud peeked around the bus. The road ahead was clear. With a quick check in his mirror, he slammed the gearshift into low, pressed hard on the gas pedal, and snapped the clutch out. Despite its heavy load, the old mean machine responded. Hud turned out to pass the bus only to find a group of muscular, young skinheads in camouflage trousers and white T-shirts forming a line across the highway near the front of the bus.

He slipped the gears into second, pushed the pedal to the floor, and leaned on the horn. The Bashers seemed determined to hold their ground. They waved and gestured wildly.

"Get down, Kimberly, down!" Hud shouted. "I can't stop now!"

"Go for it, Hud!" she shouted, sitting upright and waving a fist at the Bashers.

The line of white shirts and angry faces seemed to grow larger and larger. Hud knew he should slam on the brakes, but somehow, he couldn't. At the precise moment he knew he'd have to hit some of them, they parted like magic, leaving his path clear. But as he roared through the narrow opening, cans of soda splattered against the windshield and the side windows. *Crack! Crack! Crack-Crack-Crack!* Ugly brown fluid spread across the windshield, whipped into a blinding film by the slipstream.

"You did it, Hud! You did it!" Kimberly shouted.

"I can hardly see where the hell I'm going! Where's the windshield washer on this old thing?"

Kimberly exploded into laughter, a boisterous, exuberant laugh that seemed totally foreign to the Kimberly he knew. "Windshield washer? Windshield washer?"

Chapter 20

"Sheriff Stein," Kimberly said into the phone as Hud entered her small office, "you'd better remember there's an election this fall and the people out here in the boonies aren't very happy with your making laws instead of enforcing them." She slammed the phone down. "That bastard!" she hissed, staring angrily at the wall before her. When she turned to Hud, the anger on her flushed face answered the question he would have asked.

"Let me guess," he said. "The good ol' boy says something about representatives of the church calling him and lodging complaints against us for reckless driving, or attempted manslaughter, or something worse." He laughed.

Kimberly took a deep breath, then exhaled slowly. "You got it. They claimed they were off on the right shoulder changing a flat. You swerved over and tried to hit them." She hesitated. "You don't seem very upset. How did you know the Bashers had called with something like that?"

"Pretty obvious," Hud said, "after the way Stein handled his investigation of the boat episode, all but accusing Gibby and me of smashing the church. He'll handle every confrontation with the Bashers something like this. Bet on it." He put an arm around her shoulders and gave her a quick, light squeeze. "But, look on the bright side. They only complain. They don't file charges. The last thing they want is a battle in court. They wouldn't have total control there. Unpredictable things can happen in a court room. You know, I'm glad we took pictures before we hosed the truck down. Might come in handy."

"Unless we go to court, we have no law on our side?"

"Let's find out," Hud said. "Do us a favor, would you? Give Deputy Mertens a call and ask him to stop in next time he's out in this area—alone."

"Oh, I wouldn't count very much on *him*," said Kimberly. "He's a country bumpkin with an I.Q. of ninety-seven and a half."

"Gibby says Will's really quite sharp…that he puts on that act around the sheriff." Hud added, "For his own protection. Stein fired Deputy Orin, the other good deputy. By the way, Orin's running against Stein this fall. Now, what if Will Mertens is in Orin's corner?"

"I'll make the call," she said quickly. "Before he left for home, Gibby said to tell you, you're invited for dinner. And Hud?"

"Yes?"

"Thanks." She stretched up and kissed him lightly on the cheek. "Thanks for everything you've done. Despite all the hassles and chasing today…it's been a *really* good day for me."

He smiled at her. "Me, too," he said, resisting the tempting old movie cliche, that of putting his hand to his cheek to protect the magic spot.

• • •

"I've done some mapping in the three sections of woods today," T.C. Wolf said, stretching the plat map out on Hud's table. "I'll check the same spots tonight—to see if they're good both night and day."

"And tomorrow, I put up the fences and signs?" Hud asked, sensing that he would be assigned the grunt work.

"Right. Here's a sketch I drew from the plat map." Wolf paused, scratching his bearded chin while he thought. "It shows where to put the barbed wire fences, where to stake down the coils of barbed wire, and where to put the signs. I'll be around, too, but don't talk to me, especially anywhere near the outside boundaries or the lakeshore. With the noise you'll be making, they'll have eyes on you."

Hud nodded. He hoped Gibby would be available to help him. "What kinds of things are you rigging up?" he asked.

"Take you on a tour when it's done," Wolf said. "It'll be heavier at the north end next to their property. That's the way they usually come in. Up there, it'll be four lines of defense, and a fifth we can add in minutes if it looks like they're going to get nasty."

"What's in these boxes?" Hud asked, pointing to the four small boxes Wolf had set on the floor when he entered.

"Cellular phones—one for each of you. I've tested 'em, and they work, at least locally." Wolf paused, pulled a phone and its belt-loop holster from a box to show Hud. "You're all signed up. Now you can keep in touch. Wear 'em in those holsters all the time. Won't do any good if you leave 'em home. And showing 'em sends a message to the bad guys."

"Great," said Hud.

"Tell me," said Wolf, his slits focusing on Hud, "is the broad pretty tough?"

"What?"

"The broad—Ms. Farber—will she stand up under pressure? You know, if things get really sticky?"

"Well," said Hud, hesitating, "despite her looks, she's one feisty woman."

"She might have to be. Alone here, she's your Achilles' heel."

"See what I can do about that," Hud replied. "But I still don't understand something. A year ago, there was practically nothing up on the peninsula. Now, you tell me they've built a military base up there. Gibby heard some construction activity during the fall, winter, and spring. But he said it sounded like a bulldozer doing a little groundwork and a few guys maybe putting up a cabin or an outbuilding."

"They're smart. Most of the buildings are easy pre-fab or pole and steel construction stuff. Fast to put up and relatively quiet." Wolf suddenly rolled up the plat map and wedged it under one arm, flipped off the kitchen light, and left. Although Hud's mind buzzed with the recent input, he soon found the accumulation of fatigue creeping up on him and he headed for bed.

Right after breakfast the next morning, Hud and Gibby donned leather gloves and began their assignment. First, they tackled the north section, the woods that bordered the Bashers' property. Ten yards before reaching the property line, where an eight-foot fence had been erected by the church group, they drove the steel posts into the ground and stretched three strands of barbed wire from the road to the lake, angling the fence down to water level five yards out into the bay. Then, in the demilitarized zone they had established, they posted several of the DANGER! KEEP OUT! signs.

"Good," said Gibby. "No way they can say they weren't warned."

"Probably won't stop them," replied Hud, "but it tells them we're no longer sleeping sheep."

In the thicker brush, a few yards back from their fence, they set about establishing the second line of defense, a double row of looping, coiled barbed wire, similar to that seen in war movies. When they had staked the loops down, they stood back to admire their efforts.

"It doesn't *look* all that intimidating," said Hud. "But to get through that in the dark? I'll leave that to someone else."

They finished off their fencing of the remaining two sides of the wedge-shaped piece of land with two-strand fences set with accompanying signs a few feet into the woods in order to be less than conspicuous to the outside observer or resort guest. Hud looked forward to their noon break. It was hot, and despite the fact that he kept himself in good physical condition, the work demanded moves and strains that were not part of his regular workouts. He allowed Gibby to lead, but the pace set by his older friend proved to be a severe test.

Despite the heavy demands of her guests through the morning, Kimberly had put together sandwiches and lemonade for their lunch. While they ate, they chatted about the "fortress" they were building and speculated on the mysterious defenses T.C. Wolf planned to add. As Hud reluctantly followed Gibby to the door, Kimberly drew him aside.

"I think you deserve more than a couple of lousy sandwiches for all your sweat," she said. "How about I cook for you tonight? A really formal, everything but candlelight dinner?"

"You're on." Hud beamed. It was certainly the perfect conclusion to a hot, tiring day, he thought, and there was no one he'd rather spend the evening with. But her eyes said nothing beyond the dinner invitation.

After lunch, they fenced the middle section between the resort and the Gunderson's property from their pathway to the outer boundary. Hud agreed with Wolf's assumption that the middle section of woods between the pathway and the lake was of little strategic value to the Bashers. And to fence the entire parcel, they'd have had to sacrifice the much-used pathway.

Last, they tackled the portion of woods between Hud's cottage and the national park land on the south shore of the bay. Along the park border, they built the same combination of fence and rolled wire they had used along the church property line. It was the second most logical point of incursion for the Bashers' invasions.

They finished the massive task at six-thirty. As they put their tools away, Hud's movements had slowed to a sluggish pace. His feet seemed to weigh fifty pounds apiece; even his hands felt heavy. But he noticed that Gibby's pace had suffered even more than his own.

"Sometime tomorrow," Hud said, "I think we'll get to see what work of art the master has created."

"Can't even imagine what he's up to," said Gibby, "but he's a sneaky son of a bitch. And with his time in Viet Nam, I'm damned glad he's on *our* side."

Hud left Gibby at his own door and headed home, his thoughts occupied with visions of a refreshing shower. He cursed softly when the locked door reminded him to dig in a pocket for the key. Embarrassing, he thought, to have to lock doors in this part of the country. He knew the act had to rankle old Gibby even more.

After his shower, he slipped into his jockey shorts, set the kitchen timer, and stretched out in his favorite chair for a half-hour nap. It seemed he had barely closed his eyes when the *ding* of the timer popped them open once more. Hurriedly, he donned the only outfit he'd brought with him that offered a step up from his north woods garb: black casual shoes, gray dress slacks, a blue-and-white striped button-down shirt, and a maroon tie with horizontal rows of small, gold loops. Grabbing his flashlight for the return trip, he locked up again and set out.

He had just passed the Gundersons' door when he heard the familiar voice behind him.

"Oh, Hud! Hud!" Sarah called. Then, in a demanding tone, she said, "You get right back here for inspection, Young Man!"

Reluctantly, Hud stopped and turned toward her. Sarah stood, her hands behind her back, surveying Hud. Up and down...up and down. He smiled at the prim, little lady. Certainly, he'd play this game for no one else.

"Okay, Mother," he said, "can I go now?"

"And *that's* what you're taking her? A flashlight?" Sarah's look of indignation bordered on a scowl. "Honestly, Hudson, I don't know how you ever hope to attract a *good* woman."

Hud looked down at his clothes, gave a sweeping gesture and said, "Jeez, I thought I'd done pretty well...for a north woods hillbilly."

Sarah smiled. Then, from behind her, she produced a fresh bouquet of bright yellow daffodils. "Here," she said with a wink, as she thrust them at Hud. "Now be on your way, Hudson Bryant." With a devilish grin, she added, "And have a nice evening."

As he tromped along the familiar path, flowers in one hand and flashlight in the other, he wondered if there was more to Kimberly's dinner invitation than gratitude. He hoped so, at least for a few steps, until her earlier words came back to him, "Don't push me, Hud." No, he thought, I'll not push, Kimberly Farber.

Hud recognized the middle-aged couple from Cottage Three as he stepped into the lodge room. Kimberly was bagging a carton of milk and a loaf of bread for them. The barrel-shaped woman thanked Kimberly, turned and saw Hud with his flowers. She scanned him quickly from bottom to top, flashed a grin at him, and turned to nod a silent message to Kimberly. Taking her husband by the arm, she said, "Come on, Johnny. I think we're in the way here." Johnny, a mousy, little man, grinned up at Hud, glanced back at Kimberly, then rolled his eyes as he followed his wife to the door.

The momentary embarrassment washed quickly away when Hud looked at Kimberly. Her pony tail had been released, and her radiant blond hair lay in soft waves on her shoulders. He saw the warmest smile she'd ever turned his way and marveled at the glow it created deep inside his chest. Stepping behind the counter, he handed her the daffodils.

"Beautiful flowers for a beautiful lady," he said, wondering where the words had come from and momentarily regretting the choice of the word "lady." At her gesture, he followed her through the office and into the kitchen. She wore an attractive calf-length, rust-colored cotton shirt-dress and matching low-heeled shoes. Though the dress fit loosely, the belt around her slender waist reminded Hud that the tall, lean woman inside the dress did not lack for desirable curves.

"Thanks, Hud," she said, as she filled a vase with water, "and thank Sarah for me, will you?" With an impish smile, she looked over her shoulder at him.

"Sure will. She filled my order perfectly," he said with a deliberate cough. For the first time, he managed to turn his gaze from Kimberly. The lighting in the kitchen and the adjoining living room was soft. From her stereo wafted the romantic purity of Mantovani, while from the oven came the smell of delightfully seasoned roast beef. The drapes were pulled to cover the large picture window that overlooked the resort. The old kitchen table was covered by a tablecloth, brilliant white, but a trifle threadbare in places. Two flickering candles, one red and one green, barely held erect by two old, unmatched holders, centered the table which was set for two. When he looked back at Kimberly, she stood, a glass of wine in each hand, watching him. She handed him a glass.

"Please don't laugh, and please don't jump to conclusions," she said with a smirk. "I just felt like tonight I needed a date, an evening away from this runaway treadmill I've been on for eight straight months. That is," she gestured in the direction of the cottages, "if those people out there will leave us alone." She looked at him, as though searching him for disapproval or disappointment. "I...don't have any nice things anymore, but I'm very happy that you'd share this time with me."

"Isn't a place in the world I'd rather—but I think you already know that," he said, sniffing the wine. "I'm not an expert, but my nose tells me it's White Zin." He took a sip. "My favorite. How did you know?"

"Cheated," she said with a deeply dimpled smile. "Asked Sarah. Now, you sit down and relax while I see if the world's worst cook can offer you something edible."

Hud took the chair she had motioned to. "Smells good to me," he said. While Kimberly hustled about the kitchen with her final preparations, Hud thought about how comfortable the old chair had become. In only five days, he found himself sitting in the same chair in her inner world for the third time. The thought warmed him. And the humility that seemed to bubble forth from her warmed him even more. He'd never have guessed that the strong, independent Kimberly Farber he'd first met would ever be guilty of such a virtue. Yes, he thought, this chair does feel good. He sealed the thought with a sip of wine.

"Well...here it is," she said, placing a platter of roast beef, potatoes, carrots, celery, and onions before him. "I hope you like it." She took her seat, hesitated a moment, then slid the platter toward him.

"Thank you," Hud said. As he took the white China platter, he realized that, not only was the aroma familiar, but also the artsy way in which the vegetables were placed in an oval surrounding the meat. He managed to stifle the words, "Oh, and thanks to Sarah, too." But the fact that Kimberly had put such care into the preparations for the evening fueled his spiraling emotions even more.

Their table conversation continued quite naturally from that of the previous day. Regardless of the subject discussed, Hud felt good, because he felt comfortable. He was no longer choosing his words so carefully, and Kimberly seemed relaxed as well. At one point, she brought up the subject of Ellie.

"Perhaps you'd rather not talk about her," she said. "I know you were *very* close."

"No problem...not anymore," he said. "Ellie told me...no...she *insisted* that I rebuild and go on." He hesitated. "I hope you don't think this is sick, but I have the feeling that she's up there watching everything I do. Sometimes a little judgmental—but never jealous."

"To have such a relationship, she must have been an incredible person," said Kimberly, as she got up to begin clearing the table. "But then, I guess you are, too. I hope you realize how lucky you were."

"Uh, huh," replied Hud, thoughtfully. He joined in the cleanup effort. While they worked, he carefully weighed a question before he finally let it out. "Do you think it could happen *twice* in *one* lifetime?"

She jerked her head toward him and looked into his eyes. "I—I don't know," she said. "Coming from where I've been...it hardly seems that anyone could be *that* lucky."

As Kimberly ran hot water into a dishpan, Hud realized there was no dish washer. He grabbed a dishtowel and pitched in, wondering at one point if the chore had ever been as pleasant. After two brief interruptions to assist guests with bait, she poured them each a glass of Kahlua on the rocks and led the way into the living room. She chose one of two tawdry recliner chairs and indicated the other to Hud. Interesting, thought Hud, that old couch is the only other seating in the room, and it's placed against the same wall as the television.

The longer they talked, the easier the conversation flowed. While there was enough in their respective backgrounds to last for days, the discussion seemed to gravitate effortlessly to politics, religion, and philosophy. And nothing Kimberly expressed put the slightest chink in Hud's feelings about her. She seemed to be a free thinker. While she had been active in numerous civic, political, and service organizations, her mind was chained to no single line of thought. Although they stumbled into a couple of disagreements, Hud felt no pressure to change his position. When Kimberly glanced at her watch, Hud realized two hours had passed in what seemed like mere minutes.

"Excuse me, Hud," she said. "It's ten-fifteen." Punching the television remote control, she added, "I need to check the weather for tomorrow, especially with all that furniture sitting out on the decks of Four and Five."

"How did you do in the two cottages today?" he asked.

"All caught up until the floor is dry enough for the carpet people to come out."

"You mean you got all those dishes washed and put—"

"And now for an update on the airport closures, we return to Clifton Salisbury in our New York studios," said the attractive Asian woman, a reporter in Los Angeles. The screen filled instantly with the familiar face and trademark white hair of the well-known network anchor.

The two words, *airport—closures,* caught Hud's attention like powerful magnets. He knew of only rare airport closures, usually the result of severe snowstorms or hurricanes.

"Thank you, Sue Kim," the distinguished Clifton Salisbury said. "Information on the simultaneous disabling of thirteen major airports around the country is coming in rapidly now.

"Those damned Muslims," Kimberly spouted. "They're at it—"

"Sshhh!" Hud cut in.

"....to recap our first report. At exactly ten-fifty-nine, Eastern Daylight Time, the control towers at the affected airports received brief telephone messages warning them that in sixty seconds the power for their VASI—that's the visual approach slope indicators that guide incoming aircraft on their final approach—and their runway lighting would be shut down. Each tower was given the name or names of one or two alternate airports and the assurance that those alternate sites would be unaffected by this action."

"That," said Hud, "doesn't sound like Muslim terrorists to me."

"To the moment," continued Salisbury, "we have no reports of any accidents or injuries, although at least two aircraft, too far into the landing process to abort, experienced rough landings. Apparently, the Air Traffic Control people responded quickly and gained control of the situation, diverting incoming flights to alternate airports. The control towers and the airport terminals themselves have, to this point, remained unaffected by this action, and fortunately, there have been no incidents of panic reported."

"I guess you're right, Hud," Kimberly said. "It isn't the usual terrorist style. But why? Why shut down airports, thirteen of them, even if you do it safely? Makes no sense."

"We have a list now of the thirteen airports that have closed. They are...."

Hud and Kimberly watched intently as Salisbury read the list of names that scrolled slowly upward on the screen.

"Logan International–Boston
J.F.Kennedy International–New York
Baltimore-Washington International–Baltimore
Hartsfield International–Atlanta
Miami International–Miami
Indianapolis International–Indianapolis
O'Hare International–Chicago
Des Moines International–Des Moines
Minneapolis-St. Paul International–Minneapolis
Dallas-Fort Worth International– Dallas
Seattle-Tacoma International–Seattle
Oakland International–Oakland
L.A.X.–Los Angeles."

"Wow," said Hud. "They really spread them around, didn't they?" He reached for his glass of Kahlua and found it empty. "Good thing they skipped Denver. No alternates close."

"I still don't get it." Kimberly gestured hopelessly. "What's the point?"

"Witnesses at several of the sites," continued Salisbury, "have reported seeing what appeared to be small explosions about the fields and approach ways that coincided with the losses of power. Authorities are speculating that small charges, placed in key locations among the circuitry, were detonated by some remote means, knocking out the electricity to the essential lighting and—" He stopped abruptly as a hand slipped a sheet of paper before him. Showing his surprise, a rare loss of the composure for which he was known, Salisbury studied the paper briefly, then looked at the camera and continued.

"I have…been handed a message just received here at SRS network headquarters. Apparently, a group calling themselves The Minutemen of the Thirteen Colonies of America has claimed responsibility for the air-port closures." He paused and looked off-camera, gesturing a question with his hands. Turning again to his audience, he said, "This is highly irregular…with no further explanation available, I have been instructed to read this statement to you.

"The Minutemen of the Thirteen Colonies of America take full responsibility for the disruptions of power at thirteen major U.S. airports this evening. We apologize to those of you who have been inconvenienced and perhaps frightened by our actions. Every possible precaution has been taken to avoid physical injury and serious property damage.

"Our objective? To get your attention through an event par-alleling the symbolic Boston Tea Party effected by our common ancestors. Taxation without representation is no longer accept-able. The typical American works almost half the year—to pay his or her taxes, taxes that disappear in the maze of government bureaucracy. It is time to throw aside the common perspective that we merely rent rooms in this gigantic castle we call a nation. Indeed, we own the castle, and it is our obligation to maintain it intelligently.

"Our corrupt leaders have forgotten the lessons learned so painfully along the way. They unnecessarily complicate the leg-islative process to hide their selfish acts, coming forth with mock honesty only to toss another trinket to their constituencies. Their relationships with the voters focus only upon reelection.

"The events of this evening were not acts of terrorism. We are patriots, good, loyal citizens like yourselves. However, unlike many Americans, we will no longer stand to one side and watch this great society follow the path of the Roman Empire. We are organized. We are strong. And we are counted in numbers that will surprise the average citizen and alarm the corrupt politicians who have held a stranglehold on this once free nation. Our members and supporters stand among you, businessmen and women, professionals, farmers, laborers, as well as the unfortunate. Look to your right and to your left. We are there.

"Have no doubts—the second American revolution is coming. It is as inevitable as was the first. Will it, of necessity, be as violent? You, the American people, hold the answer to the question. You, through the democratic process, can bring about the liberty you crave, or you can abdicate your responsibilities and watch our common dream slide into total subjugation, ultimately disintegrating to chaos. You still have a choice, but you must exercise that choice wisely. It is time.

"In the months to come, you have the responsibility to prepare for the grandest privilege, short of prayer to our God, ever afforded to humanity. We urge you to step forward. Turn deaf ears to the deceitful, arrogant leaders of the two-party system. Look to the independent candidates, those untarnished individuals like yourselves who recognize the odor of decay. Listen to them. And, above all, demand answers to your questions. If a candidate is too busy, or if he or she resorts to magical smoke and mirrors to capitalize on your confusion, turn away and seek another. Blend patience and persistence. You will find the key to the liberty for which our forefathers died."

Clifton Salisbury raised his eyes to the camera and stared for several seconds. Hud thought he saw a silent expression of hope in the deep brown eyes. Then, as though jerked back to reality, the veteran announcer ad libbed his way back to another repetition of the evening's events.

Hud took a deep breath and exhaled. Incredible, he thought, that statement by a bunch of outlaws...and I agreed with every word. He looked at Kimberly. She sat slumped in her chair, her eyes fixed on a spot in the old, worn carpeting.

Suddenly, the ringing telephone broke the spell. Kimberly got up wearily and made for the cabinet island between the living room and the kitchen. She picked up the portable phone from its cradle.

"Black Rock Resort...this is Kimberly."

Hud turned to watch her as she listened to the incoming call. He realized that, during the television report, he had lost track of her beauty for the first time all evening.

"Yes...yes, he's here." Handing Hud the phone, she said, "It's Deputy Mertens—wants to talk to you."

"Hud? Will Mertens here," the very ordinary voice said. "Couple of things. One, we checked out all the Minneapolis suburban addresses given by the trashers—all dead ends, no such addresses. Sorry...but I'll keep my eyes open for anything that might connect with them. Then, I hear you got hassled out on the lake Sunday. That right?"

"Yeah, that's right, Will," Hud replied.

"You didn't report it."

"What's the point?" Hud shot back, immediately aware of a simmering that had fired up within him.

"I—I understand. But I wish you'd at least let *me* know about these things," Mertens said.

"I repeat, what's the point?" Hud's mind focused on the answer he hoped to hear.

Will Mertens lowered his voice to a near whisper. "Some fishermen found a body washed up on the rocks today...right close to where I heard you got swamped. The guy was a male Caucasian...dead two to three months...must have been dropped through the ice...a small cable around his ankles...broke loose from concrete blocks used for an anchor. Probably the wave action did it."

Chapter 21

"Up! Up! Up!" came Sergeant Evans' voice from the doorway of the small room he shared with Sergeant Richard.

David Engstrom covered his eyes with his hands when the barracks lights suddenly clicked on. Already? he thought. I just got to sleep. Must be what—Wednesday morning? He forced himself from the bunk where he had lain awake for most of three nights since the news of Dan's suicide, finally to be rescued by sleep at two or three in the morning. He knew he was dropping deeper and deeper into the eye of the hurricane. With little sleep at night, his lack of strength and mental quickness had to be showing. He hoped that the day would bring no more of the unpredictable tears that had popped into his reddened eyes on two occasions. The "something in my eye" line had been used up.

A few extra splashings of cold well water on his face gave him the artificial lift he needed at the moment, but he knew the specter of fatigue would begin stalking him within the hour. As he dressed for calisthenics, he worked on a mind set. Got to be tough, he told himself, really tough. Got to concentrate hard on everything I do. Got to find out if Dan is really dead. Got to find out why—find out if these guys had something to do with it. He wished he had his Julie for comfort. The familiar welling threatened his eyes. Once again, he thought of sneaking out of camp and finding his way home to her, but he couldn't—he was too close now.

He had to find Dan...alive...or dead. And if I find out he really is dead, David vowed, I'll kill the bastards who caused it...or did it.

Somehow, David mustered the energy to lead Fisher Troop through their morning calisthenics. The large breakfast that followed recharged both his physical and emotional strength somewhat, but as he studied the day's schedule, he knew he was in trouble.

After a morning of hard labor building the pathway down to the new seaplane ramp, his troop was scheduled for a ten-mile run in the afternoon. After that, an hour of hand-to-hand combat, and finally an hour of practice on the range. Confident that he was among the best in physical conditioning, he knew he could gut it out and make it. But he also knew that he'd be among the stragglers, and that in itself would escape no one, particularly the sergeants.

I've worked too hard to blow it now, he thought. He found Sergeant Evans at the tool shed, supervising the equipment check-out. With a discreet motion, he beckoned the sergeant off to one side.

"I hate to ask this," David said, "but you said once that with success come perks."

"I did," Sergeant Evans said, studying David's face as he spoke, "and there's no doubt about your success. What's on your mind?"

"I—I'm dealing with a problem, a tough one, and I'm not getting any sleep, Sergeant. Could you give me the day off...to catch up?"

The short, husky man looked up at him. "All this start with our conversation Sunday?"

"Well...yes, I guess it did."

"It wouldn't have anything to do with the dead guy, would it?" the sergeant asked, his gaze unrelenting.

"Oh, no," David replied quickly. "It's God I'm having trouble with. It kind of came to a head when we talked about obeying orders for the greater good, not stopping for a wounded friend. I'm...." David paused and very deliberately looked around to see that no others could hear. He hoped the move was convincing. "I'm not sure that's what God would want." He continued quickly with added emotion, "You know I want to do well. I'd like to make sergeant. But if I'm going to be a leader, I've got to get this resolved once and for all. I can't take a chance on running into the problem before I know where I stand."

"You've earned it, and you've got it," the sergeant said. "I'll handle your men today. If anybody asks, tell 'em you've got diarrhea," he added with a wink.

"Thanks, Sergeant Evans, thanks. I'll make it up to you." David turned to head for his barracks, but the sergeant's hand on his arm stopped him.

"You need some time with Brother Theodore. You're in luck. He's due in this morning," Sergeant Evans added.

"Oh, good," David said, "I'll see if I can find him."

He hurried back to the barracks and stretched out in his bunk. Brother Theodore, one of the leaders of Colony IV, was *not* someone he should talk with. No way, he thought. Then he set about a series of mind games combined with deep breathing to exorcise the crippling dilemma and find peaceful sleep.

It was eleven-thirty when David awakened. He hurried over to the mess hall, gulped his meal down, and left, grateful that he had avoided his troop and Brother Theodore. But the men would be in and out of the barracks before and after lunch. Not the place to be, he thought. He meandered into the woods and found a huge, isolated boulder above the harbor on the northeast side of the peninsula. Climbing up on the monstrous rock, he could see the harbor and a corner of the new storage building, but with a thick cluster of spruces all but surrounding his chosen spot, he doubted that anyone above or below would notice him.

He sprawled out on the nearly flat top of the boulder and closed his eyes. Despite his granite mattress, he found himself once again wishing for sleep.

The gentle northwest breeze washed the scent of the pines over him, bringing the twist of an ironic smile to his lips. He had found paradise...in *hell*. The thought crystallized in his mind until it matched the great, hard stone beneath him, squeezing out his preoccupation with Dan and the downward spiral of his self-confidence.

That's it, he thought, I *am* in hell, playing games with the devil's disciples. Suddenly, it became clear to David that he had concentrated so completely on successful infiltration that he had wasted valuable time. Had he been so dazzled by the group's political idealism and confused by their religious fervor that he lost his focus on the quest? Had he been so completely overwhelmed by the organization, power, and dedication of the members that he had become overly cautious—perhaps even scared?

After months of carefully blending into the organization, he had finally managed his first question, and the answer had established the link between Dan and the church. Then, with that accomplished, he had let the painful part of the answer reduce him to a bawling baby brother. Dan was here, he thought. I don't *know* that he's dead...and I *certainly* don't know that he committed suicide.

The sun found him through an opening in the green cover of the forest, so David sat up and moved to a shady spot on the huge boulder. From above him on the plateau, he heard voices. He listened, but the words were covered by the rustling of the breezes through the pines. Sparked by the logic that had somehow found its way through his depressing fog, he thought about further questions and potential targets for those questions.

His thoughts were interrupted by the sound of footsteps crunching slowly along the steep hillside, coming his way. He could see no one, but the sounds came closer. Questions rattled through his mind. Who? Why? Will it look strange to be found here alone? Why am I here alone?

Can't use the diarrhea story. Then, recalling the explanation he'd given Sergeant Evans, he relaxed. Stick with the story, he told himself. It makes sense that I'd find a quiet place to think.

"Hello, hello…is that you, Corporal David?"

He recognized one of Brother Theodore's two voices. It was the soft, intimate one, not the rich pulpit voice. "Damn!" he said softly. But his mind changed direction in the time it took to utter the four-letter word, for who knew the individuals in the organization better than Brother Theodore?

"Over here," he called.

A large spruce branch bent David's way, and through the opening came the diminutive chaplain. He wore the usual drab clothing, but the old brown-plaid sport coat was hooked on one finger and draped over his shoulder and down his back. Beads of sweat hung on his forehead beneath the thin, disheveled gray hair. He stopped at the edge of the rock and looked up over his wire-rimmed glasses at David.

"I know I'm an old goat," he said, "but that steep path is too much for me. It's a pathway to hell."

David flinched at the choice of words. "Were you—looking for *me?*" he asked.

"Why…yes, yes, I was," Brother Theodore said. "Am I intruding?"

"Not at all," replied David, "in fact…you're just the person I needed to see. Sergeant Evans talked to you?" He helped the frail, little man up onto the rock.

"Yes, he did," said Brother Theodore, scanning the surrounding area before turning to look directly into David's eyes. "It seems our David Engstrom is dealing with some problems."

"Yeah," David responded, determined to carefully control the direction of the conversation. "Having some trouble with—" Suddenly, icy prickles encased his entire body, pressing their cold fear against every nerve ending. He felt naked, and everything within him stopped, even his breathing. There it was, the one word that could stop him—

Engstrom! He quickly turned away. Part of his mind said, "Deal with it," but the rest of his mind had gone numb. Slowly, he turned back to Brother Theodore. The older man's warm, brown eyes peered at him, magnified by the thick lenses of his crooked glasses. As the shock faded, David tried the only thing he could think of. "You said…Engstrom?"

"Yes, I did, David Robert Engstrom, brother of Daniel Engstrom," the chaplain said in a near whisper. He looked around again, paused, and smiled. "and ex-husband of both Annie and Julie. I talked with your Julie last night on the phone. She gave me a good story on your where-abouts, but she couldn't conceal her emotions. I told her you're fine…and that I'd do everything in my power to keep it that way."

David absorbed the warmth that beamed from Brother Theodore's eyes. Mysteriously, the feelings of panic began to subside. "How…how did you find out?" he asked meekly.

"I'll explain it all, but I'll have to do it quickly," Brother Theodore said. "We might be interrupted at any time. Oh, and keep your voice down. It's all right that we're seen together. I'm supposed to be questioning you…but we don't want anyone else in on this conversation." He looked above, below, and to each side once more. "*You* are under investigation."

"I *am?*" David felt the chill reverberate through him again.

"Sshhh!" The chaplain put a finger to his lips. "You *were* being inves-tigated to determine your fitness for promotion to command—ordered by Father Jeranko himself. Brother Jacob has been snooping around Minneapolis trying to pick up on your background. But I've had a feel-ing about you ever since I found you in Loring Park—the voice, the eyes, the work ethic…and the moral code. It was as though I already knew you. So, I started my own search. And somewhere along the way, it clicked—Dan Engstrom. Once I had a name, it was easy to find your trail. With all your accomplishments in college and high school, you left a trail two miles wide…pictures, news clippings, the works."

"What are you going to do?" David glanced back up the incline. He expected to see a squad of troopers storming down the hill after him.

"I'm going to try to keep you alive." Brother Theodore's eyes blazed with an intensity David had never before seen. "You have to trust me. You have no choice. You are *now* being investigated for a very different reason. Since your error—mentioning Dan's name to Sergeant Evans—you are suspected of treason, you and one other person."

"Sergeant Evans didn't seem to pick up on it at the time. He ratted on me?" David asked. Brother Theodore had him, but that alone did not warrant trust. He needed more.

"So far, only to me. But that could change at any time. That's why I'm talking to you right now. If Evans finds anyone who can tell him anything you've said or done that's the least bit suspicious...you're in Brother Vance's office, and then...."

David stiffened and instinctively did his own survey of their surroundings. "That," he said, "raises my biggest question. What happens to...misfits? You couldn't *always* pick and recruit winners. I know of several in Minneapolis...and a couple up here...who were discharged. What happens to them? We're never told anything except they washed out." He realized that he and Brother Theodore were seldom establishing eye contact as they talked. Both heads turned regularly, and both sets of eyes scanned the surroundings for the slightest movement. He expected the huge boulder beneath them to explode at any moment.

"Your question is exactly the one that finally opened these old eyes," said Brother Theodore. His face suddenly turned angry. Then, just as suddenly, tears formed. He jerked his glasses off, brushed the tears away and continued. "The procedure is, when problems are identified, the individuals are put through sessions here at Black Rock, sessions called...*attitude adjustment.*" He wiped away a straggling tear. "If they fail to make the necessary adjustments, they are discharged and taken back to where they were found. All records of them are destroyed. As far as the Colony is concerned, they never existed."

"It really works that way?"

"I thought so, for seven years—the six we had the old camp down on Rainbow Lake, and the year we've been here—I believed it. In fact, I signed most of the orders sending those individuals for special attention."

David studied the chaplain's face. It seemed to have aged ten years in the last minute. Brother Theodore put his head in his hands and began to sob quietly, turning slowly from side to side. He felt the older man's anguish even though he didn't understand it. But he was sure of one thing. He could trust the man. Brother Theodore was not setting him up. No one could act that well. David put his arm around the man's shoulders.

"You're a *good* man," David said, "and obviously you care about me, about all of us very much. What is it?" He cast another glance up the hill.

Pulling himself together, Brother Theodore said, "We've discharged thirty-seven, and you know what? I've never seen even *one* of them again on the streets, in the parks, or at the shelters. Tell me, David, do you ever hear the big boat go out in the middle of the night?"

"Well…I haven't been here long…but, yes, I've heard it go out once or twice. No mistaking the sound of that big engine. Not another like it on the lake."

"Do you know why they go out at a time like that?"

"No," David replied, then added, "and I sure wasn't going to risk any questions to find out, either."

Suddenly, the older man straightened and turned his water-glazed eyes on David. "Think about it, David. Think about it."

"You mean—"

The answer came as a slow nod. Seconds later, Brother Theodore added, "I can't prove it, but that's what I think. And something else…you wouldn't hear about this because you aren't allowed any news up here…but while I was driving up today, there was a report on the radio about a body washing up on one of the islands. It was clearly a homicide."

"Dan—" A massive lump in his throat choked David's response down to one word.

"Could be...." Brother Theodore put a hand on David's knee. "The authorities are speculating that the...body had been there two to three months. That would put it close to the last time I saw Dan. Worse yet, it's possible...I think even *probable* that our washouts are getting their attitudes adjusted at the bottom of the lake."

David's body went rigid. There it was again. Anger stormed through him. He started up, but the old chaplain caught his arm.

"We don't *know*, David. We don't *know*." Brother Theodore squeezed David's arm. "Obviously, you joined us to find Dan. You lose it now and you'll go down, too."

David took several deep breaths, then sat in silence for some time. "Thanks...you're right...can't blow it now." He thought for a moment. "You said there's someone else on their list. Who is it? We should get together."

"We are together." Brother Theodore sighed, then continued, "I've seen it coming for some time now...grooming Brother Jacob to take my place. That's why I was called up here."

A wave of panic swept through David. "They wouldn't—not *you!*"

"Sshhh!" Brother Theodore paused. "You think they're going to give me a pension and a place on the golf course? Now, enough of this exploratory—"

"Then, come on, Brother!" David jumped up and pulled Brother Theodore to his feet. "Let's get both of us out of here right now. You're the key to bringing down this whole rotten organization."

The little man wheeled, jabbed a finger at David's chest, and glared up him. His fiery, magnified eyes radiated power that David had never seen. "You listen, now. You shut up and *listen* to me." The strength in his powerful whisper stopped David cold. "I *am* the key, but I need your help. When I leave this place, it will probably be for a long, deep swim. That's as it should be. I could never live with the guilt I'm carrying. I've not only done bad things…I've worked against the God I vowed to represent."

"But—"

"Shut up and listen!" The command came again as a whisper, but with the intensity of a hurricane. "Here's what we do. I've put together a packet…names, descriptions, and histories of the discharged…along with everything I can think of that can close the Colony down. I've worked on it for several days now. It's good—powerful—but circumstantial. I'm trying to find answers to a couple more questions…questions about the airplane. That plane stinks of more than engine exhaust. We have to make sure there's enough to get Jeranko and Vance."

David stood there frozen, absorbing every word, void of ideas, opinions, or feelings, as though mesmerized by the gigantic eyes that blazed up at him.

"Your job," said the little man, "is to get this information out. If I can get it to you, you have to get out *tonight*. Might not even have *that* long before they decide on you, so you mustn't show yourself from this moment forward. You know the guard set-up. You figure out how best to get out. The only help between here and the authorities might be the woman at the resort and her neighbors. Above all, stay away from the county sheriff." Brother Theodore paused for a breath, then rattled on, "We'll agree on a place for me to hide the packet. I'll try to have it there tonight…maybe tomorrow night. Doubt I'll be…able to…after that. Now, help me down off this mountain so we can find a place."

Gingerly, David eased the little man down the front side of the boulder. He can't be a hundred-forty pounds, David thought, but there's a ton of spirit there. He slid down to join his newfound comrade.

"There…there," said Brother Theodore, pointing to a horizontal crevice near the bottom of the downhill face of the immense granite object. He straightened, turned to David, and hugged him briefly. "Remember, they might already be looking for you. If it looks like they're going to get you, break for it. Don't wait around for the packet. Okay?"

"Brother Theodore," David began, blinking back tears that suddenly erupted from nowhere, "I'm sure the God you've devoted your life to has already forgiven your mistakes. Come *with* me."

"Have you noticed...that big rock on which we came together...how *white* it is? I like that. Yes, I like that." The frail, little man turned and slouched off, dragging his old, brown-plaid coat on the ground behind him.

Chapter 22

"Watch it!" Wolf hissed.

Hud froze, his weight balanced precariously on one foot. Slowly, he pulled his raised foot back to its starting place and looked to Wolf for an explanation.

"You just about tripped a line there." Wolf pointed to a nearly invisible strand of green monofilament fishing line that stretched just below knee level across the path through the thick brush. The grizzled veteran brushed the raindrops from his forehead and stepped over the line. Hud followed carefully.

"What's it do?" Hud asked.

"Like to demonstrate all this magic—can't," Wolf said softly, nodding toward the nearby church property. "First, the warning signs you put up, then the barbed wire, then this." He bent over and lightly touched the taut strand. "This sets off your little jingle bells, four here and two back at the house...warns Kimberly...and tells *them* we know they're here."

Hud nodded his approval. Even in daylight, he had to focus intently to see the line.

"Of course…on a serious mission, that won't stop 'em. But it tells 'em something." He led the way between two spruces, holding one dripping branch back for Hud. "Now, between here and the workshop, we've got two lines of motion detectors," he said, stopping at a white pine and raising one branch to expose a black plastic device that was wrapped in a plastic bag and banded to the tree trunk. "Four of these across this stretch," Wolf said. "Get 'em in any electronics store. They really squeal…and they're cheap. Here's how you turn 'em off. Okay, that's the third line of defense—the end of the warnings."

Hud shivered. Was it the ominous words from his ever serious guide, or was it his chilling, water-soaked clothing? He peered ahead, studying the trees and bushes, half-expecting to see a gun muzzle pointing at him. "No more trip lines?" he repeated.

Wolf's face twisted subtly, almost reaching a grin. "More sensors," he said. "Four professional jobbies in this area," he went on with a sweeping gesture. "Set one of these off, you get floodlights, sirens, and hidden cameras taking your picture. These are all hooked to the electricity in the workshop. I'll show you the control board I made. Come on."

As they approached the workshop, Hud noticed the single black electric power line that stretched innocently from an oak tree to the north wall of the building where it disappeared through a small hole. Once inside, Wolf led him to the electric service box.

"Added two circuits with thirty-amp breakers, here…and here," Wolf said. "This one's for the stuff you just saw in the north section, and the other's for the sensors and lights covering the shoreline. To shut 'em down, you just switch 'em off right here. 'Course, then you got to go out and reset 'em individually before you turn the power back on."

"What about the dock?" Hud asked, noticing for the first time that the fingers on Wolf's massive hands were as thick as broomsticks.

"Can't point sensors at the dock," Wolf explained. "The wave action and the bobbing boats would set 'em off. But I set up two sensors covering the shoreline. Rigged 'em to extra floodlights. If any of her customers set 'em off late at night or early morning, no damage done. 'Course, you know heavy winds through the trees could cause you some false alarms with any of the sensors." He shrugged. "Can't have everything your way."

"But the boats?" Hud asked.

The Bunyanlike character stroked his beard as he eyed Hud. "Don't think they'll try the boats again. So far, except for busted windows, they've avoided repetition." He paused, as if measuring Hud's acceptance of the explanation. "Now, the trinkets in the woods between the properties and on the other side of your cabin are much like these, all wired into the service box in Gunderson's house. Okay?"

"Yeah…okay," said Hud, aware of the swelling confidence the strange man's preparations had triggered within him.

"The bear traps—"

"Go around the ends of the fences out in the water," Hud cut in. Wolf grinned slightly. "You're catching on. But they're a real liability hazard. Don't put 'em out unless you're pretty sure an invasion is coming. I'll check in with my PI buddy when I get back. Soon's he's got much to report, I'll put him in touch with you. Now, a couple of other things you should know."

Hud, his curiosity piqued, studied the coarse features behind the bushy beard and waited.

"I went in again last night. I was right. They only post their perimeter guards at night. The guards shift fifty yards back and forth on the hour and half-hour. And at the top of the hill, on the far side, I found something kind of strange. I was crawling around over there and I started hearing a faint *whump, whump* noise—like coming from the ground. Had me puzzled 'till I came across a couple of fan-driven ventilation shafts hidden in the bushes. One whiff and I knew. They've got an underground firing range." He opened the rear door of his vehicle and climbed in. "Need some sleep." Without another word, he simply closed the door behind him.

What a strange guy, Hud thought. When he emerged from the old workshop, a bright morning sun had found its way through the rain clouds. The trees and grass glistened with their moist coating, and the air, treated by an invigorating mixture of pine scent and rain, reminded him once again why he loved this country. As he headed across the resort toward Gibby's, several children burst from Cottage One and raced down the hill to the beach, yelling and screaming in their newfound emancipation from the confines of their cottages. Hud stopped for a moment and watched. That, he thought, is what this place was meant to be, not a damned war zone. Suddenly, the youngsters stopped, turned, and began running back up the hill. Their happy sounds had turned in an instant to shrieks of fear.

"Dad! Mom!"

"Bears! Bears!"

"Mommy! Mommy! Mommy!"

Bears, Hud thought, bears? They prowl the property almost every night, testing the garbage cans. But mid-morning visits were rare. He had just started down the hill toward the beach when Kimberly stepped around the lakeside corner of Cottage Five. She held a garbage can lid in one hand and a downspout extension in the other.

"Hud?" she called. "Can you help me here?"

As Hud rounded the corner of the cottage, he saw the problem. A large black bear stood midway between them and the beach, her yearling cub close beside her. "Is that Maggie?" he asked.

"She's acting weird," said Kimberly. "I beat these dumb things together, made as much noise as I ever do to chase her back into the woods, but she just won't budge. Stands there and snarls at me."

Hud relieved Kimberly of her tin weapons. "Let's just back off for a minute and review the rules. One, you're not between her and her cub. He has to be the only one since they only deliver every two years and he's a yearling. Two, has she got anything good to eat that she's protecting?"

"Hud, I followed the rule book on both counts. But she acts like she hasn't read the book. The kids want to come out and play. God knows, their parents have suffered enough, cooped up with them through the rain. Would you give it a try?"

"Well...sure...here goes." Walking slowly but deliberately in a direction to force the black, furry intruder toward Gibby's woods, and holding the garbage can lid out in front like a shield, Hud began banging the galvanized downspout against the lid. "Go, Maggie! Go!" he shouted. Maggie retreated twenty yards, her cub at her side. Then she stopped, rose up on her haunches and snarled. Hud moved forward, shouting and banging louder. Maggie dropped to all four feet and retreated another thirty yards before repeating her rebellion. Her second snarl began and ended with a low, throaty growl, accompanied by a waving of her forelegs as she stretched to her full height of over six feet.

"This isn't good," Hud said over his shoulder to Kimberly. "She's really upset about something. I don't think we'd better push her any more than we have. Let's just hang around and see if she doesn't get bored with our company."

"Hud...Hud?" Kimberly's voice became that of a small girl. "You're right, Hud. Come on over here right away—but don't run, don't run! You coming, Hud?"

As Hud backed away from the bear, he waved the downspout menacingly. The bear lowered its massive body to the normal four-footed posture once again and stood there, watching Hud's slow retreat. When Hud reached the corner of the cottage, Kimberly took his arm and led him part way up the hill. The guests had all come out of the cottages and joined in a line at the top of the hill, like spectators at a sporting event.

"Jeez," said Hud, "a great big crowd like that...and I struck out...embarrassing."

"I'm glad you lost, Hud," she said. "Look up there, way up—the top of the tall birch. See them?"

High up in the birch, at a point where the trunk had narrowed to a four-inch diameter, clung two black, fuzzy balls. The higher of the two appeared to be sitting on the nose of the sibling beneath it.

"Oh, my God," muttered Hud. "The adoption thing—never occurred to me. Charged right in there and broke Rule Number One...both of us." He turned to explain to the resort guests who had edged down the hill for a better look. "The sow has adopted a couple of newborn orphans. It happens sometimes when a mother bear dies. I hope you realize that we just broke the rules...got between a mother and her cubs. We were lucky. Now, let's all move back up the hill, and let's be quiet so she can get them down."

After five minutes, Maggie lumbered over to the foot of the birch tree. She gave a short grunt, and the cubs came scurrying down, the upper one bumping against the head of the slower one all the way down. With one last disdainful glance at her audience, Maggie trotted off into the woods, big brother and the twins scampering along close behind.

That afternoon, Hud perched on a tree stump in the woods between his cottage and the neighboring park. Pressing his field glasses to his eyebrows, he watched the hubbub of activity across the bay. One crew of Bashers, using shovels and improvised scoops, dredged the bottom of the small cove. They dumped the sand and mud onto the two points of land that framed the cove, thus extending them farther out into the bay. Another crew sawed and hammered away on a docklike structure, while a third group, using axes and shovels, carved out a pathway with a series of switchbacks leading to the top of the hill.

While he watched, he replayed the bizarre chain of events, from Gibby's first vandalism up to the moment. Then his mind retraced his earlier conversation with T.C. Wolf. An underground firing range! It explained how an army could practice without alarming the neighbors. It also tells us how serious they really are about their soldier games, he thought. However, if the Bashers were responsible for the body found out on Big Totem, he suspected they'd be lying low for a while, tempering their aggressiveness.

But Hud didn't like what he saw across the bay. That little harbor they were building....They didn't need another harbor for boats. Then why—of course, he thought. It's for that floatplane! Calmer water in the bay for takeoffs and landings, and a hell of a lot more privacy. He recalled the curious stack of boxes he had seen on their dock. Except for his present line of sight, the cove offered protection from such observations. If the Bashers would go to all that work to guarantee safe landing waters day in and day out—and the cover for loading and unloading—that Cessna must be hauling something very important to them.

His pulse quickened. His mind and body came to full alert. He was on to something. He just knew it. Now that T.C. Wolf had given them some security, and with the Bashers lying back a little, this was the time to move, the time to become aggressive. He looked at the western sky. It was clouding up again. Going to be a dark night, he thought. Good. Whipping out his cell phone, he called Gibby.

"Dark, maybe rainy tonight," Hud said. "Think you and I ought to go fishing." Then he added, "Let's use your boat."

At five minutes before six o'clock, Hud settled in his favorite chair with his plate of scrambled eggs, hash browns, and toast. For the first time since his arrival, he picked up the remote and turned on the small television. It seemed like it had been years since the reports on the airport closings and on the body found in Wasikama. Both incidents had repeatedly flipped into his thoughts, but with so much going on, he hadn't had a chance to follow up. He caught the end of the local news. Before the words had begun to register, the image of Sheriff Stein brought Hud to the edge of his chair.

"Is it true, Sheriff Stein, that the murder victim found near Big Totem Island in Lake Wasikama has yet to be identified?" the local peroxide-blonde anchorwoman with twenty years hidden behind her garish makeup asked.

"Not yet identified," Stein replied, throwing his tiny shoulders back and searching for the camera. "We're investigating the rumor that the victim may have been a guest at a resort on Black Rock Bay, but at this time we've not substantiated that."

"What the hell—" Hud choked on his eggs. "Why that rotten— Where'd *that* rumor come from?" Only one resort on the bay, he thought. Might as well have just said it.

"But someone in your department has called the FBI in?" the anchor-woman asked.

"Yes," Stein replied, his eyes seemingly fixed on Hud. "Upon further investigation of the evidence, I directed that the call for assistance, under the stipulations of FBI VICAP, be made."

"Why, that lying bastard," mumbled Hud. "But it tells me more about him."

"Thank you, Sheriff Stein." The woman turned to the camera. "Thank you for joining us. Stay tuned now for the network news here on the Big Eight."

Hud gulped the remainder of his anachronous dinner. The combina-tion of the anchor woman's hideous, painted masque and Stein's self-serving statements had turned the eggs into a vile mush. He took his plate to the kitchen, filled a coffee mug, and returned to his chair.

"….it has now been verified," the handsome, middle-aged James Har-rison said, "that all thirteen airports were sabotaged in similar manner, that is, by using small charges to disrupt electrical service to the visual approach slope indicators and runway lights. All thirteen airports were restored to full capability within hours, and there have been no reports of any injuries. The investigating federal authorities apparently have yet to identify any of the conspirators—despite heavy pressure from con-gressional leaders, as well as leaders of the states affected."

Hud's mind had drifted to a vision of black-clad raiders bellying out onto the fields to set the charges, when James Harrison's tone of voice changed.

"In related news....In what may well be a political first in this country, the major news media have just received an Open Letter to the American People, apparently issued jointly by American Liberation Party senatorial candidates Jed Cruzen and Wayne Hartsill. The open letter levels serious accusations, all of which are purportedly documented, against seven members of the Executive Branch and twelve members of Congress. The document is *far* too extensive...and, at least until some portions can be substantiated, far too *sensitive*...to be read here at this time. However, we have our political analyst, Roger Greenberg, standing by."

Hud watched with only mild interest as the familiar, hawkish face of Greenberg appeared in a split-screen format.

"Roger," continued Harrison, "you've read the document. Is it for *real?* Or is this campaign mud-slinging at an all-time low? Neither of these American Liberation Party candidates stands much chance in the election this fall."

"James...obviously I can't read this one hundred and forty-seven page document, which is full of allegations of voter fraud, illegal campaign contributions, fraudulent, wasteful pork barrel projects, immoral—and in some cases, illegal—sex acts, and perjury and then give you a ruling on each in only two hours. But I can tell you this....this is a well-written listing of specific incidents, each accompanied by what would *appear* to be objective, factual documentation—including photographs. You catch my emphasis on the word *appear.* And I can tell you this....a number of the alleged incidents seem to have been common knowledge within the inner circles of Washington. It is possible that we *are* looking at examples of the Washington honor system at work...you don't tell on me...I won't tell on you. One thing for sure, James....If this document and the two young independent candidates, Cruzen and Hartsill, survive the intensive scrutiny to be faced in the next week, we may have heard the first shot of the second American revolution...and it could be a 'shot heard round the world'."

The popular news anchor shifted pages as the screen returned to single image format, glanced briefly into the camera, then continued. "At a press conference this afternoon, candidates Cruzen and Hartsill made the following statement in defense of their position and their document. I quote:

> To Our Fellow Americans:
>
> First, we must tell you that we have never associated in any way, nor do we anticipate associating in any way, with those who recently disrupted traffic at thirteen major American airports. We learned of the events, as most of you did, through media reports. But we do anticipate a phenomenal effort by the two corrupt major political parties to tie us to those events or fabricate other scenarios designed to discredit us, for that is the way they do business. We are clean and we are unafraid. Our closets hold no skeletons.
>
> Traditionally, our political leaders, when backed against a wall, resort to tried and tested tricks, one of them being: Change the subject. Undoubtedly, you will hear charges against us, charges like mudslingers, liars, communists, traitors.
>
> We ask you, fellow Americans, to be objective. Demand the truth. Our goal is not to cast an ugly, dark stain on America's political system but rather to take the first step in the long, painful process required to clean it up, to reset this gift presented to us by our forefathers back onto its cornerstone called truth. Put simply, let's launder the shirt...even if the dirt is on the inside where we can't all see it.

"In other news," James Harrison continued, "It has been reported that...."

The crunch of wheels on the crushed rock driveway caught Hud's attention. He flipped the television off, stepped to the door, and saw

Deputy Will Mertens walking his way through the mist. When he looked again, Gibby had joined the deputy.

"Cup of coffee?" Hud offered as they plunked down on his two kitchen chairs. Filling their cups with potent, black coffee, Hud thought for a moment, then decided on a direct approach. "Deputy Mertens—"

"Will...everybody calls me Will."

"Good—Will...." Hud saw Gibby smirk. "Will, we don't have time to play word games, to pussyfoot around, so if we're to reach any understanding here...we'll have to trust each other."

The pudgy deputy said nothing. He simply looked at Hud and gestured for him to continue.

"I'm—*we're* wondering just where you fit on the Sheriff Stein thing. We know that Dick Orin's running against him. We know Beer Stein is a lousy sheriff. And we *think* he's probably in with the Bashers. Now you know where we stand. Where does Deputy Mertens line up in all this?"

The deputy sipped his coffee and hesitated, his face betraying no reaction to the toxic left-over liquid. "You have to understand first...I'm in an awkward position. If I declare myself, and Stein wins, I'm out of a job. There aren't many jobs up here. But on the other hand, if I don't commit and Stein wins...it isn't much of a job. Understand one thing though—*I* will decide if and when I stand up with Orin against the sheriff. If I spill my guts to you, and you let something slip, I'm in for unnecessary trouble...could be I'm history."

Gibby was right, Hud thought. Just the way Mertens expresses himself tells me he's been playing the role of the clod. "We understand your position. I guess *we're* interested in two things right now. One, if we need law enforcement out here, do we call Sheriff Stein, you, or the state police? And two, is anyone documenting the truth in our confrontations with the Bashers?"

"On the first question," Will answered, "if it's stuff like the previous incidents, you call the sheriff—*then* call me. Gibby has my phone numbers. If you've got a serious, life-threatening situation, you call me, and then explain later that you couldn't get through to the sheriff." The deputy paused for another sip. "If...anything should happen to me...you call FBI Regional in the Cities."

"Will," Gibby cut in, "are you *serious?*"

The young deputy looked hard over his puffy, red cheeks at Gibby and then Hud. "Every day this stupidity goes on, it becomes more of a possibility. Did you know Stein turned that corpse we pulled off Big Totem over to the county coroner—relying on his autopsy? Can you believe that? That poor guy fit the FBI Violent Crime Apprehension Program criteria in all three categories. Luckily, someone—don't know who, of course—called the Feds. When Stein found out, the shit hit the fan. Only thing he *could* do was claim he was the one who call the Feds in."

"I think," Hud began, then hesitated, "I think you just answered our second question. Am I correct in assuming that someone—you don't know who—is documenting the truth?"

Will Mertens grinned deviously and nodded his head. "It's all down, from broken windows to stolen boats to threats, along with our official response to each."

"Then this person should also know that the Bashers have an underground firing range up there. Don't know yet if they're using automatic weapons. Should know soon. Seems that would interest Alcohol, Tobacco, and Firearms, wouldn't you think?"

The deputy's eyes opened wide and the grin became more pronounced. "That'd be enough to close the bastards down."

"Please don't—not yet," said Hud. "It might hurt them temporarily, but they'd likely pay some fines and be right back at their tricks. Look what they've done so far—*without* using any automatic toys. Let's just save that one for the time being. Add it to that mysterious file."

"Okay," Will said, getting up to leave. "Anything else that mysterious person should know?"

"Yeah, one thing..." Hud said, "not sure just how important it is...but I have a feeling about that floatplane they have flying in and out so often. Did you know they're building a separate little harbor for it...here on the bay?"

"The lakeshore variance was approved a few days ago," Will replied.

"Would you mind telling me how those sons of bitches got the variance approved?" Gibby demanded. "Nobody talked to me about it. The review committee is s'posed to meet with the neighbors. I want it stopped, damn it!"

"Easy, Gib, easy," Hud said. "I think we should add this to the file, how the committee members voted, everything. Meanwhile, with the Cessna on this side, we can keep an eye on it."

"I'll see about getting it added to the file," said Will Mertens, as he reached for the door. He stared for a moment at Gibby, then at Hud. "Why do I get the feeling you two are up to something?"

Hud shrugged and said nothing.

"You'd better be damned careful," the deputy said. "Stein will nail you the first chance he gets."

Chapter 23

At dusk, Gibby's runabout eased out of its lift and headed for Black Rock and the mouth of the bay. The sight of the bearded loner heading out for an evening of solitary fishing was a familiar one to most of the area residents. Gibby, dressed in dark jeans, a navy blue sweater and matching stocking cap, sat alone, hunched down behind the driver's side windshield. With the threat of returning rain, the canvas top was up, but the side and rear panels lay in a heap on the floor behind him.

"Come on, Gibby!" grumbled Hud from beneath the pile of window plastic and canvas. "Either goose this thing and get it up on top or slow down. Those two-foot waves are beating the hell out of me!" He knew Gibby hadn't heard him. He also suspected his old friend of deliberately treating him to a rough ride. Finally, as the boat cleared Black Rock, its crafty driver eased the throttle ahead and put the fiberglass craft up on plane.

Careful not to show himself, Hud raised up on one elbow and looked down toward his feet, scanning his clothing, identical to Gibby's except for Hud's black leather gloves. In a back pocket he carried a waterproof miniature flashlight, and sheathed to his belt was a hunting knife. Gibby had insisted that Hud carry a pistol. Hud had finally compromised on the knife, though he wasn't sure what he'd use it for. His pockets held nothing else. Without his wallet, he felt like a nonperson, but that was the point.

After a five-minute run down the northeast shore of the peninsula, Hud felt the boat slow and finally settle in the water. The large engine shut down. The sudden conversion to silence, an event he had experienced a thousand times, took on new meaning. He found himself focusing on each sound, the gentle lapping of the waves against the hull, the evening call of a loon, and the bumping and scuffing sounds Gibby made as he set the swivel bow seat in place, lowered the electric trolling motor into the water, and set up his fishing rod.

When the subtle, intermittent vibrations of the electric motor carried through the decking, Hud knew the time was close. Thoughts electrified by tension suddenly rang like alarms in his mind. What the hell are we doing? he asked himself. A couple of untrained civilians trying to play commando? This is ridiculous. And this…this *shell game* I dreamed up to sneak ashore? Then he refocused on their goal—to get him ashore as darkness closed in, but before the Bashers posted their guards. He believed it would work. By concentrating on the sounds once more, he drove the demons of fear aside.

Hud felt the boat rock slightly. Gibby cast his lead-head jig and leech toward the rocky shore, and as was his habit when fishing, the old-timer began talking to himself.

"Okay, Old Walleye, come and get it.…There's a good spot, right between them rocks.…Didn't get it there, did you, Gibby? Better cast it a little harder this time. Oh, shit! You old fart! When's the last time you threw one into the trees?"

The trolling motor hummed until the hull bumped lightly against the rocks. Then the boat tipped noticeably as the dark-clad figure grabbed the anchor and stepped out on a large rock. Hooking the anchor securely, he disappeared into the trees. Moments later, a second dark-clad figure slid over the gunwhale and melted into the trees.

"Okay," whispered Hud. "Here goes. Remember, long, slow flashes—I'm okay, ease your way back to get me. Short, quick flashes—I'm in trouble, get here fast as you can. I'll be out there in the water. Don't hit me." He gave Gibby a slap on the shoulder. The older man retrieved his lure from the tree branch, climbed aboard the boat, and trolled on down the shoreline.

When Gibby had moved past the small harbor and was nearly out of sight, Hud began to work his way carefully up the steep hill. Each placement of his black sneakers carried the risk of cracking a branch or dislodging a rock. Thank God everything's so wet, he thought. I'm soaked already, but it's quieter going. Every two or three steps, he paused for a full minute to watch and listen, but the only sounds he heard were his own. His heart pounded, but his senses seemed acutely sharpened by his tension. Angling upward and to his left, he hoped to locate the underground firing range Wolf had discovered. If he could make it to the top in time, he would hide in the bushes near the clearing while the guards took their posts below him on the hillside. He hoped their attention would be focused primarily toward the lake, that they wouldn't suspect his penetration behind their line.

Hud moved slowly up the hill, stopped to listen, then moved again. Darkness had set in and still he found no indications of guards in the area. Just short of the flat, level clearing at the top, he dropped to his belly, wiggled under the low hanging branches of a fir tree, and studied the impressive installation before him. Slightly to his right stood the large cedar log headquarters building that was visible from the bay. Fifty yards to his left, he saw a cluster of large buildings that he'd never seen from the lake. Several of them looked like barracks units; one was obviously the chapel; and the largest building in the cluster betrayed no clues as to its function.

Most of the area was well-lighted, but he noticed that his side of the headquarters building was shadowed from the yard lights by the building itself. Good, he thought, observing three windows that began about five feet above ground level. Might get a chance to learn something there. He slithered out from beneath the fir and, crouching low, picked his way twenty yards to the left. Stopping behind a beaked hazel bush, he listened.

From somewhere to his left came a faint whirring sound. Damn—I've found it, he thought. One of the ventilating fans! A few steps brought him to a cluster of hazel bushes, and there in the center stood a sheet metal tubing with a forward-facing grill. The identity of the shaft was confirmed when he smelled burned gunpowder. He huddled there for some time, congratulating himself on his newfound commando skills while inhaling the sulphuric residue that the shaft emitted into the dank night air. Suddenly, new sounds caught his attention.

Boots on crushed rock! Coming his way! Lying flat, he wedged himself as tightly as he could under the bushes. Six young men, all dressed in camouflage fatigues, approached in double file along the perimeter of the open ground just above him. From each man's belt dangled a large flashlight, and each carried something, an apparatus of some kind, in one hand and a sturdy wooden staff in the other. They talked in low voices as they walked. Hud tensed. He was well-hidden, but what if they spotted him? And what was that thing each man carried? Not a gun, but what?

When the group was but thirty yards from Hud's position beneath the hazel bushes, one man abruptly turned and stepped down over the edge into the brush.

"Private James on post," the man said just as Hud lost sight of him. But Hud could hear him scrunching noisily down the hillside through the underbrush. As the remaining five men walked past Hud's hiding place, the yard lights illuminated the mysterious objects they carried— crossbows, quiet but deadly. He shifted his concentration back to the sounds made by Private James. My closest enemy, Hud thought. Can't lose track of him. A second man dropped out of the formation about seventy-five yards past Hud and lumbered down into the hillside forest while the others continued on toward the tip of the peninsula.

Hud lay quietly for a long time, concentrating on the sounds made by the two sentries. Since they seemed to exercise no caution with their movements, he quickly learned to gauge their locations and distance from him. But when things became quiet, he felt himself tighten up. Okay, he told himself, the one guy's too close. Just move when he moves and freeze when he stops. Then he reminded himself of his objectives— to verify their possession of automatic weapons and to get a look into the headquarters building if possible.

Snaking his way back to the ventilator, Hud listened, but the steady *whoosh* of the fan told him nothing. After several minutes, he was about to abandon the quest when the monotonous sound was suddenly interrupted by a faint but distinct, staccato *B-d-d-d-d-d-p! B-d-d-d-d-p!* He knew immediately he was hearing bursts of varying length from an automatic weapon. So they did have them! *B-d-d-d-p! B-d-d-d-d-d-d-p!* More incredible, Hud thought, a ventilation system that pushes the gunsmoke from the underground chamber and yet muffles the gunfire so effectively.

With his primary goal accomplished, he cautiously moved twenty yards to his right, stopping in line with a lighted window in the headquarters building. He lay there motionless for several minutes, listening for the sentries. Finally, the guard closest to the ventilator crunched his way a short distance through the underbrush, and Hud got a fix on him. Minutes later, the other guard coughed. From the sounds, Hud figured he was midway between the two men and about forty feet above them on the hillside. Still, he waited until he heard from each a second time to confirm his judgment.

He took a deep breath and exhaled slowly. Then he wormed his way through the brush and crawled on his belly across the grass toward the window. Reaching the building, he rolled so that his back was against the wall. Facing the woods, he waited again for sounds from the guards before he risked rising up. He knew the lighted window would outline him vividly so there could be no lengthy observations. Perhaps even two or three short peeks might be pushing his luck. He decided on two, no more than two, no matter what he saw.

After a final check on the guards, he stood slowly until his face was just beside the lower pane. Keeping his face a foot back from the glass, he eased sideways to look in.

The large paneled room was unoccupied. His eyes swept around the room, from the huge desk with luxurious leather chairs on both sides to the fireplace on his right, then the open door on his left. No one there. He ducked quickly and turned his attention to the guards. The same light, occasional stirring noises. He considered trying the other two windows. He considered waiting longer at his present station. No, he thought, pushing my luck as it is. One more peek, and get the hell out of here. His second, even shorter look revealed nothing new, so he dropped to his hands and knees and made for the brush line.

Okay, Hud, he thought. Got half of what you came for. See if you can get out of here. The guards remained equal distance from his hiding place. He thought he must be directly above the harbor, and that meant that somewhere close by there should be a pathway down. It would be faster and quieter if he could find it. He held up his watch to catch a glint of light that shown through the brush. Ten-fifty-five. According to Wolf, the guards would shift right or left on the hour, putting one of them right below him, blocking his escape. He imagined an arrow from a crossbow plunging into his belly.

Planning each footstep, he began winding his way down the hill. He knew he had to hurry now, but he couldn't become careless. He'd moved to his left to get around a large red pine when he stumbled across the pathway. He touched the bulge of the flashlight in his hip pocket, then decided against it. Crouching low as he started down the winding dirt pathway, he discovered that, while it was slippery mud in spots, it was relatively clear of debris. He moved quickly down another thirty or forty feet, then stopped to listen.

Heavy footsteps in the underbrush told him the guards were moving! Coming for him? No, it seemed the guard to his right was moving away. But the other was coming closer, at a level perhaps ten feet above Hud's position on the hillside. Then, a flashlight beam began flitting about through the brush above him. Oh, no, he thought, the guy's looking for the path, too. That means he's coming down. Hud hurried on down the path until the beams of light began to dance on the trees and bushes around him. Quickly, he darted off the path to his right, slipped between two spruces and stopped. Ahead of him, an immense boulder the size of a minivan jutted out from the hillside. Reaching the far end of it, he turned and backed a couple of steps uphill until he was hidden. He'd hole up there until the guard went back up the hill.

Suddenly, an arm hooked around Hud's throat from behind. A hand clamped over his mouth. A vibrant tingling radiated from his scalp down his spinal column. He fell backward onto his attacker only to have his legs clamped in a scissors hold. He flailed the only weapons he had left— his arms.

"I'm a friend," the attacker whispered in Hud's ear. "Don't struggle with me. If that sentry hears us, we're both dead. Trust me. Hold still and we have a chance. Still…very, very still…."

Hud felt the arms and legs that kept him so helplessly trussed begin to relax. The hand left his mouth. In another second, he could bolt free—but it would be right into the Basher guard coming down the path. Maybe, if he caught the guard by surprise, he could make it to the lake.

"He's about to go past," hissed the voice. "Not a sound." The man behind the voice released Hud completely. "Don't move. Don't even breathe."

Hud lay there motionless atop the strange body that had attacked him. How weird, he thought, lying on my back on top of a man's body, a total stranger. Then, his mind clicked back in. Obviously, the man was not a threat—but the guard sure as hell was. He felt the man struggling to breathe beneath him. Then, he felt something else. The stranger had begun to tremble. From his chest down to his feet, the man trembled.

"See his light?" the voice whispered.

"Yes, quite a ways down now."

"Okay," the voice said. "Nothing but whispers. That's Private Jesse. He's gone down to check the harbor. He'll probably smoke a joint and then head back up in about ten minutes. By the time he comes back up, we have to finish our talk, then move down and hide about half-way to the harbor. That way, when he gets back up near the top, we're clear. Okay? Get up quietly."

Hud rose carefully to his feet, then turned and offered his hand to pull the strange assailant up. Dressed in the boots, camouflage fatigues, and cap of the Bashers, he stood several inches shorter than Hud and was a slender, young man. His face had been thoroughly plastered with mud, leaving only his eyes with strange elliptical white outlines that seemed to glow in the dark.

"You—you're the guy at the resort? The one with the shotgun?" the stranger asked.

"The one who *used* to have a shotgun," replied Hud, holding his grip on the man's right hand. "Hud Bryant. You are?"

"David Engstrom. I…led that raid. Sorry. What're you *doing* here?"

"I came to verify—" Hud stopped, realizing this could still be a trap. "No, Son," he said, "I think *you* tell me what *you're* doing here."

"Yessir," David said, motioning for Hud to follow him into the cluster of spruces where they crouched to continue the conversation. "That rock is a sounding board," he added. "Now, you're going to have to listen damned fast to catch even half of what I'm going to tell you. No time for questions or debates. Okay?"

"I've got one question," said Hud. "Why were you so sure I'm a *friendly?*"

"I watched you snooping around the range ventilator and then peeking in the window."

"That says a hell of a lot for my commando skills. You watched me do all that, and I didn't even know you were in the same county." The disappointment Hud felt over his inept performance surprised him. He'd thought he was doing quite well at observing and avoiding.

"Actually," David said, "I was impressed with the way you handled things, right from the trick you used to come ashore. I figured you for a former military man, maybe Special Forces. You hit right on their weakness. They really don't believe anyone will try what you did. Otherwise, you'd have run into sensors, infra-red, the works. Anyway, here's the situation. Can't take time to put it in order. Just going to rattle at you for a couple of minutes. Then we're done."

"Okay," said Hud, "shoot."

"I got myself recruited into the Church of the Rock several months ago…to look for my brother Dan. Never found him, but I know he was here. It's possible that was Dan they fished out of the lake the other day. According to Brother Theodore, our chaplain, could be as many as thirty-seven out there." David Engstrom hesitated, a single tear tracking down the mud-stained face.

"Thirty—seven?" Hud gasped as he repeated the numbers. "Come on, now…thirty-seven…out *there?*"

"That's what Brother Theodore thinks," Dan said, "and in a day or so…thirty-eight."

"Thirty-eight? Who's number thirty-eight?"

The mud-faced young man bit his lower lip, blinked his eyes, and replied, "Brother Theodore." He hung his head and shook it slowly. "Had no idea I was getting into anything like *this*." Suddenly, his head jerked up. He sniffed the air, then stood. "Come on—time to move."

Hud followed the young man out to the path, then downward half the distance to the harbor. There, David led the way ten yards off the path and settled them behind a clump of bushes.

When Hud began to speak, he was shut down quickly by a hand signal, so he bent some branches back and turned his attention to the harbor and dock area just below them. The area was lighted by a single yard light. Tied to one side of the main dock rested the menacing, dark-blue speedboat. The space previously occupied by the Cessna floatplane was empty. To the left of the dock stood the newly constructed storage shed. Private Jesse stood at the end of the dock, smoking. Suddenly, in one motion, the sentry tossed his cigarette into the water, picked up his weapon, and headed toward shore.

Following David's example, Hud stretched out on his belly. The change of position pressed his cool, wet clothing against his abdomen and chest, sending a shiver through him. He listened as the barely audible footsteps climbed the path, softly thumped past their hiding place, and faded on up the hill.

"Okay," whispered Hud, "can we get Brother Theodore out of there?" He nodded toward the headquarters building up above.

"Don't know how," David replied. "They keep exterior and interior sentries on duty 'round the clock." He paused. "Don't even know if he's still alive."

"Then, let's get the hell out of here. You know enough to sink these bastards," Hud said, reaching for his miniature flashlight. "I'll signal Gibby to come and get us."

"No—no!" David reached over to push Hud's light down. "Can't go…at least not yet. Brother Theodore put together a packet of info that will really expose them, names of the missing men, descriptions, dates they disappeared, along with other things about the operation. We agreed on a spot at the base of the big rock up there. Said he'd get it there tonight…tomorrow at the latest. It isn't there yet. I was looking when you dropped in on me. I've *got* to wait."

Hud thought for a moment. Such information would get the attention of *all* of the authorities. Worth waiting for. "Can you do it?" he
asked, looking into the centers of the white ellipses. "Can you avoid getting caught for twenty-four hours, find the packet, and get out?"

"Yeah...I think so. Getting the damned packet is the toughie. You—
you could help some, though," David said, "that is, if you're willing to
take a chance."

"How?"

"Trade clothes with me...and make a big fuss getting out. Make 'em
think it's me. It'll take some pressure off." David hesitated. "Be worse
than ever, of course, if they catch you, or even get a good look at you.
Then they might have you, and they'd sure know *I'm* still around."

Hud thought for a moment. He could feel the silent pleading in the
eyes of his young cohort. But Hud's mind had gone beyond the simple
exchange of clothes. If their ploy worked, it would certainly result in a
quick chase by the speedboat. We could lose that race, he thought. He
saw David Engstrom lower his eyes. Then, too, they'll probably want to
use that boat to take Brother Theodore out to dump him. Just might
throw a glitch in that plan, too.

"It's all right," said David, "I understand. It's asking an awful lot."

"No, no, no. It's a good idea," countered Hud. "But we can't just leave
that chaplain there to be murdered."

David lowered his head for a moment, then looked up at Hud
through watery eyes. "Look...I'm damned good at this stuff...and
you're not so bad, either...but there's no way you and I are going to get
him out."

"Then our first priority should be to get out and get help."

David's eyes glared in defiance. "Are you missing a button or two?
You're going to call the sheriff's office and tell them a church is about to
murder its chaplain? They'll drop everything else and charge this fortress
with all three deputies? Come on...."

"But—"

"I already went through the 'buts' with Brother Theodore," David said, his voice warming once again. "I think he wants it this way. He'll be the final nail in their crucifixion."

Hud sat in silence, trying to reconcile the statement. Finally, he said, "Okay, but there's something else we have to do before I go. And I don't want to swim in your boots, jacket, and cap. All I want is your pants and my own shoes until I get ready to go. Then you take my sweater, jeans, and shoes and leave your heavy stuff on the shore. Makes sense *you* wouldn't want to swim in them."

While they made the exchange, Hud explained the rest of his plan and then asked David about the regular flights by the Cessna floatplane.

"Don't know a lot," David began. "I've heard it flies chips and other components for our little computer factory. They buy them in Seattle, then haul them by truck to somewhere in Montana. Come by plane from there."

Hud hesitated for a moment. "And you think...."

"I think it's probably all true except for one part. I'd guess the parts are stolen."

"Thanks," said Hud. "At least you've put me on track. Come on. Let's go to work."

Hud felt confidence, with overtones of aggressiveness, flowing through him as he followed his newfound friend down the path to the harbor. David knew the terrain, the guards and their habits, and he had been trained in covert activities by the Bashers themselves. Instinctively, he knew when to move and when not to. They huddled under the cover of some brush while they studied the big, sleek powerboat and its location at the dock.

"Like to put that yard light out," whispered David, "but that'd bring them down on us for sure."

"No problem," said Hud. "I'll take it from here. You stay out of sight so they don't know there are two of us. Here." He quickly stripped off the hunting knife in its sheath and handed it to David. "I won't have any need for this. You might."

"Thanks." David quickly slipped the sheath onto his belt. "If…for any reason you're looking for me, I *might* be under the storage shed over there," he said motioning to the nearby building. He looked at Hud for a moment, then reached and clasped his right hand in an upright high-five squeeze.

Hud quickly slipped out of his white T-shirt and his black sneakers and handed them to David. "Remember, you're more important than that packet of papers. Look for you tomorrow night. Now get out of here before I start the fireworks."

David slipped into the sneakers, dropped his fatigue jacket and cap near his boots, and melted into the brush.

Hud moved quickly out to the large, blue boat. For the first time on his mission, he knew exactly what he was to do and in what order. Slipping smoothly into the craft, he moved to the stern, whipped out his flashlight and, pointing toward Weed Bay, gave Gibby the "Come on, slow" signal. Then, straddling the transom at the rear, he bent down low. Reaching one hand into the water, he groped until he located the drain plug. He unlatched the plug and wiggled it free. With a hard jerk, he snapped the plug from its tiny safety chain and dropped it into the water. The first bubbling noise, as the water began flowing into the hull, startled Hud. But when he stood erect, the sounds fell into perspective. The splashing waves easily covered the gurgling sound.

Climbing back into the cockpit, he located a large paddle and then unhooked the bow and stern lines from the dock. Pushing hard against a dock post, he set the heavy boat in motion toward the lake. Quickly, he located the battery compartment. With no tools available, it took considerable twisting before he could finally slip the power cables off the battery posts. Good, he thought. That takes care of the automatic bilge pump. With no way to cut the cables loose and drop them overboard, he'd have to be satisfied with simply disabling the pump, at least for the time being.

As he began to paddle, he knew he was at the most critical stage. Really vulnerable right now, he thought, only five feet from the dock. Until I can get some momentum, it'll be slow going. He pulled hard several strokes on one side, then duplicated the effort on the other. Glancing back at the dock, he expected to see the armed guards rushing out with their crossbows, but all was quiet except for the almost musical gurgling at the stern. He pulled harder and harder on the paddle. The gap increased slowly, ten yards…fifteen yards…twenty yards. Far off to his right he could make out the running lights on Gibby's boat, but they seemed to be stationary. Still no alarm behind him, so he continued to pull hard. He was wet and the night air was chilly, but he felt warm, loose, and confident. The fiberglass monster settled lower and lower in the water. It was taking on water rapidly. And unlike the smaller resort boats, the blue monster lacked sufficient flotation foam to keep it from going all the way down. Only quick action by the Bashers could prevent that.

When the boat had filled halfway, it stubbornly refused his efforts to move it with only the paddle. He stopped paddling and flashed Gibby the "fast" signal. Within a minute, the white wake told him Gibby was up and moving, perhaps a mile away. Deliberately, he bumped the paddle against the gunwhale several times. Shouts came almost immediately from the hilltop. Flashlights darted through the trees like fireflies, all heading for the harbor. Several of the Bashers appeared at the outer end of the dock. While three of them skimmed the water with their powerful lights searching for Hud, two others raised their crossbows.

"Point made," Hud said aloud as he slipped over the far gunwhale and began swimming out into the lake. Though somewhat rusty, he knew he was a strong swimmer. He threw himself into his fastest crawl for twenty yards, then stopped to flash the light toward Gibby. He repeated the process several times. By the time Gibby eased up to him, Hud had put nearly a hundred yards between the settling blue boat and themselves. Gibby dragged him over the rail, tossed a rain suit at him, jumped back into his seat, and jammed the throttle ahead. Hud crawled quickly into the rain suit and took the seat beside Gibby.

"W-w-water's c-c-cold," he said. Although he couldn't stop his teeth from chattering, Hud felt a strange warmth inside. His original plan had worked almost to perfection, and his extemporaneous maneuvers had turned out even better. He leaned over and exuberantly slapped his old friend on the back. "We've got 'em nailed to the wall, Gibby!" Then the shivers began, and with them came a vision of David Engstrom, his muddy face smeared by the cold rain as he hid in the wet brush. Jeez, thought Hud, I wonder when the kid last ate anything.

Chapter 24

Seconds before Gibby's boat scrunched its bow into the sandy beach at the resort, Hud pulled both weapons from the port side storage compartment. The boat had no sooner stopped than Gibby jumped out, carrying the anchor with him. With the weapons in hand, Hud leaped from the bow as Gibby tossed the anchor up on the beach.

"*I'll* take the twelve-gauge," Gibby said with a condescending glance at Hud.

"Let's go," Hud said, handing Gibby his favorite shotgun. "They'll be coming over the fences any minute now looking for their missing soldier."

Passing the old workshop, Gibby took off to circle around to the right side, while Hud angled to the left so they'd have the Bashers between them. In seconds, he had reached his chosen spot behind the fish cleaning house. Should be a good angle, he thought. If they trigger the lights, they'll show up like birthday candles while I sit here in the dark. Perfect place to—off to his left he heard a commotion, followed by the barely audible tinkling of small bells.

"Here they come," he said to himself, glancing over his left shoulder to make sure no one had gotten around behind him. Wolf's set-up was about to be tested. Suddenly, a loud whistling sound pierced the night, soon followed by another, then another. The invaders had set off the second line of warnings, the cheap audio sensors. The rustling noises stopped, and for several moments Hud could hear only the irritating alarms. Good job, Wolf, he thought. Won't wake up the whole county, but they're loud enough. He knew he'd soon learn how serious the Bashers were about their invasion. They'd tested the water and found it hot.

One by one, the alarms stopped. Hud assumed the Bashers were locating the alarms by sound and then smashing them. It wasn't the reaction he'd hoped for, but he accepted it easily. The trinkets had done their job. The sounds of movement in the woods resumed, though softer and at a slower pace. He wondered how many Bashers they were up against. The occasional brushing and crackling noises in the darkness gave him no idea. Unable to estimate numbers, he could only guess location by the nearest sounds, and it seemed to him they were much too close.

Suddenly, the dark, wet woods came alive. Floodlights came on, sirens wailed, and a loud bass voice shouted from a tape recording, "You have ignored our warnings! You are being photographed! Unless you leave the property within ten seconds, we will have to assume you intend to do us bodily harm!"

Ten yards from Hud, a Basher, dressed in the now familiar fatigues, froze momentarily, then dropped to his belly and hid his face in the thick layer of wet leaves. Hud resisted the urge to simply walk over, press his rifle barrel into the young man's back, and take a prisoner. But he remembered Wolf's words, "On the first incursion, induce them to evacuate immediately. Though they're the aggressors and you have rights, pointing a weapon at them could land you unnecessarily in court. If they're stubborn enough to return a second or third time…that's different."

Hud pointed his 30.06 hunting rifle in the air, released the safety, and squeezed the trigger. *Bam!* The young Basher catapulted up from the wet leaves, did a one-eighty turn in mid-air, and hit the ground running for the fence. Hud saw several others, deeper in the woods, jump up and begin running directly away from him toward Gibby's position. *Boom! Boom!* The two profound messages from Gibby's twelve-gauge turned them and sent them scurrying toward the barbed wire and home.

Following a preset plan, Hud moved into the woods until he saw Gibby working his way to meet him. Within sight of each other, they turned and began moving through the brush toward the fences, scanning right and left for any sign of stragglers. When they reached the coiled wire, they saw one last invader struggling in vain to climb the eight-foot chain link fence that the Bashers had erected.

"I guess we'll have to hold him for the Sheriff," Hud said.

"Hud," Gibby replied, "sometimes you're a Goddamned hardnose, you know that? Let's just help the little shit over the fence." With that, he pointed his weapon at the North Star. *Boom!* The slender soldier suddenly found strength, for he scrambled up and over, dropped to the other side, and ran off into the night.

When they were satisfied that none of the invaders had remained behind, Hud shut down the circuit breaker. With flashlights and a ladder, they made the rounds, resetting the sensors and replacing the video tape in the cameras.

"Je—sus!" said Gibby. "That's more damned work than it was chasing them bastards off."

"Worked well, though," replied Hud, as he closed up the old shed. "Really worked well. Come on, let's stop in and report to Kimberly. She's probably sitting in there all freaked out, not knowing what's been happening out here." They headed down the gravel drive toward the lodge room.

"You really think I could sit in there with all this going on out here?" a soft voice said from behind several rows of neatly stacked firewood. Kimberly stepped out into the driveway and joined them. "From what I could see, it really caught them by surprise," she added.

Hud looked down and saw a .38 revolver in her right hand. A questioning glance at Gibby brought a nod of the old timer's head.

"Don't worry," Gibby said. "I showed her how to use it."

"Oh, oh...." Kimberly handed the revolver to Hud and stepped out quickly toward the cottages. The lights had come on in all the occupied units, and people stood outside on their decks looking toward the battle zone. "I've got to calm things down," she said over her shoulder. "I'll be right back and make us some hot chocolate. Go on in and wait for me."

"What you gonna tell 'em?" Gibby asked.

"Don't know. I'll think of something...I hope."

Ten minutes later, she jammed her jacket onto one of the wall-mounted pegs in the office and stomped angrily in to join Hud and Gibby in her kitchen. She jerked a large pan from its hook and slammed it down on the stove top.

"Well?" Gibby asked.

"I...think I'm cracking," she said. "Naturally, they were all upset about all the commotion...and the gunfire. I couldn't tell them you just chased an army of bad guys off the property."

"So?" Gibby persisted.

"Can you believe this?" she said, turning to the two men and gesturing hopelessly. "I told them we're having some trouble with a crazy, old bear that's staked a claim to those woods over there and has been trying to claw its way into the workshop. We tried the alarms to scare him off, but it didn't take, so we had to resort to the gunfire." She covered her face with her hands. "I can't believe it," she said, her voice cracking. "I looked those people right in the eye and told them the dumbest, damned lie I ever told in my life." With a pained look on her face, she rolled her eyes upward and shook her head slowly. "It's come to *this?*"

Hud moved quickly to take her in his arms. "It's my fault," he said, holding her close. "I was so intent on stopping those bastards I never even gave a thought to your guests. I'm sorry, Kimberly." He felt her arms around his midsection. Her head tilted against his chest, so he gently stroked her hair with one hand. "I'm sorry. I'll make it up to you somehow."

"Well…" Gibby spouted, "one thing about it. You won't have to worry 'bout none of your guests nosing around in the woods and getting into the alarms or barbed wire."

She pushed back slightly from Hud and looked sadly at Gibby. "No, they won't be nosing around in the woods. They're all checking out in the morning. The word is out about the body found the other day… then Beer Stein's suggestion on TV that it might have been one of my people…then this fiasco tonight. I might as well start packing. I'm done for the season—and it hasn't even started yet." She buried herself against Hud's chest and began sobbing heavily. "I could have quit. Why didn't I? Could have sold…gotten most of my money out…but I was too stubborn—naive…stupid…and stubborn."

"Now, just a damned minute!" roared Gibby. "That's 'bout enough of that snivlin' bullcrap!"

Hud flinched, turned his head, and glared at his old friend. "Enough of that, Gibby," he snapped. "I think your mouth is way ahead of your brain."

"Kimberly," Gibby went on, ignoring Hud, "you saying you'd sell out to them Bashers and leave me and Sarah holding the bag? You know, we got more'n a little elbow grease invested in this here place of yours. You'd sell out on us? You'd dump on *us?*"

Hud wanted to swat the old timer, but Kimberly stiffened, pushed herself back, and looked up at him. Her eyes seemed to say, "No, Hud…no."

"Come on, now," Gibby persisted. "Answer the question. *Would* you?"

"Gibby," she said, leaving Hud and taking the seat across the table from the silver-bearded older man, "you know I'd never do anything to hurt you and Sarah…but the way it's looking, I won't have any choice. I've got a hefty payment to make this fall. I make it—or lose everything.

And with what that church is doing to my business...I won't even have twenty-five percent of the payment."

"Aw, come on, Girl," Gibby snorted. "You're just starting the season. You're not whipped yet!"

Hud stood at the sink, troubled by the confrontation. They were both right, but he knew Kimberly's assessment of her situation was more realistic. And she didn't have the really bad news yet, the possibility of thirty-seven more bodies out there in the lake. If Brother Theodore was right, that would shut down the lake. Only the long-time customers would show up this season, and Kimberly was too new in the business to have any long-time customers. He looked at her as she sat at the table, her face in her hands. He wanted to pull her up and hold her tight, clutch her to him, but that could backfire. Got to do something, he thought.

"Okay, you guys," he said, joining them at the table. "We can solve this, but not until Kimberly gives us that hot chocolate she promised. I'm still wet clear through."

"Oh, my God," she said, peeking through her fingers. "I forgot how wet you are." She jumped up and started for the refrigerator. "There's that jumpsuit still in the spare room. You go get dried off and get it on. Hang your wet clothes and that rain suit on a peg in the office."

Minutes later, Hud inhaled the aroma of the chocolate as he rejoined them at the table. They sat quietly for some time, sipping from their mugs, each dealing with the problem in some far off way. Finally, Hud fixed his gaze on Gibby and held it there until his old friend felt the attention and looked up.

"Gib," Hud began, "you're right. She *can't* give up. But you have to be more realistic about it. Kimberly knows that either or both of us will put up whatever it takes to keep her resort for her. But she also knows that, even with a great season next year, the low profit margin won't cover next year's annual payment and a payback to us for this year."

"Hell, that's simple," Gibby said. "We don't *loan* her the money—we *give* it...to...her...." His words trailed off when he caught the blue laser beams of defiance that blazed at him from Kimberly's eyes. "Ohhhh...*that's* it, huh?"

"That's it," said Hud, "and if you or I were in her place, we'd feel the same damned way—and you *know* it. Now that you understand the basics, give us your solution, please."

Gibby studied his cup for a moment, raised it, and swirled the remaining chocolate around. "Okay," he said in a chipper voice. "We've got two problems here. One, how can we help Kimberly keep this place and turn it into the best damned resort in the county? Two, if she *should* decide to get out, what then?" He raised his cup and drained it. "Okay, number one...I don't know how to give money to someone who won't take it. Ain't never had any practice at that. But it seems to me, with four of us working on it, we'll come up with a way to help you, Kimberly, without making you feel like a kept woman. Number two? You owe us this one. If you get to the point where you're *sure* you want to let go, Hud and I have first option. We'll match your best offer, or we'll give you what you've got in it plus ten percent for walkin' money, whichever is higher. Okay?"

Hud smiled and nodded agreement.

Kimberly's eyes welled up again. With her lips tightly pursed, she looked first at Gibby, then at Hud, but the only answer she could manage was a subtle nod of her head.

"Okay," said Gibby, "that's that. Now, I want to hear 'bout Hud's commando mission tonight. Damn, I can't remember when I've seen him as excited as he was when I pulled him into the boat! But we ain't had no time to talk."

Hud began by complimenting Gibby on his fishing act, hooking the tree with his lure. Then he went on to tell about the ventilator shaft for the underground firing range. "No doubt about it," he said. "I distinctly heard automatic weapons. That qualifies this mess for both FBI and Alcohol, Tobacco, and Firearms." After explaining that his window peeking had produced nothing, he went on to tell of the episode with David Engstrom. "If he can get to us with that packet from Brother Theodore, it's all but over. With all that documentation and a live witness, the feds will jump at it. They've come out looking like losers on some of these paramilitary encounters, but this one will be a clear-cut winner for them." Though he hadn't planned it, Hud felt comfortable with his failure to mention the prospect of thirty-seven bodies yet to pulled from Lake Wasikama. Kimberly didn't need to hear that...at least not yet. We'll deal with that, he thought, if and when it turns out to be true.

"When should we expect this David guy?" Kimberly asked.

"Anytime in the next thirty hours," Hud replied, "and we can expect the Bashers to be right behind him, so we'd better be ready." He reached for the phone and punched in a number.

"Calling Will Mertens?" Gibby asked.

Hud nodded and waited for the call to go through. "Uh, Will, this is Hud Bryant. Sorry to wake you up, but we've got some new information that's too hot to hold till tomorrow." He repeated his account of the evening's episode, barely catching himself at Brother Theodore's prediction on the body count. Then, after listening to the deputy for a moment, Hud nodded his head. "Yeah, we'll get ready. I'm taking the plane into the Falls for gas. We might need to get this guy out of here as soon as we can." He listened again. "No, she won't have to do that. The few guests that are still here have already told her they're pulling out in the morning."

• • •

At the sound of footsteps slogging down the nearby path, David peeked cautiously around the edge of the huge boulder. The rain had begun again, and sounds were harder to pinpoint, but he thought he could hear two men making their way down to the dock to assist those already working on the big, blue speedboat.

From a lower vantage point, he had watched the troopers quickly swing into action. With one end of a long rope tied around his midsection, a man swam out to the sinking craft. In five minutes, a group of the others had joined hands on the rope, pulled the heavy boat in, and beached it. Replacing the lost plug, they had started up a portable pump, powered by a two-cycle engine, and quickly drained the boat. David had taken advantage of the noisy pump to scurry up the hill to the secluded corner behind the boulder.

He huddled in his muddy den, trying desperately to control his mind. Repeatedly, he pushed thoughts of dry warmth and food aside. He fought the specter of another twenty-four hours in his condition by reminding himself of his purpose. From time to time, he found himself considering his three options: give himself up; try his escape from the peninsula now; or hang on until he had Brother Theodore's packet. Each time he pondered his choices, he searched vainly for a fourth.

Since his exchange with the guy from the resort, he now wore oversized blue jeans, two T-shirts, a navy blue sweater, and a stocking cap, but all were thoroughly drenched. The sneakers, much too big for him, had been tied together by their strings and now dangled around his neck.

His watch told him he had but an hour until dawn. At that point, he'd have to stay where ever he was. He couldn't risk movement during the daylight hours. Originally, he had planned to crawl under the storage building down on the beach where he could dig himself into the sand to hide and be out of the rain. But his brilliant plan of faking his escape, while it seemed to have worked, had resulted in too much activity in the dock area. Still, he held to the hope that, with the speedboat secured, all but one or two guards would return to the hilltop.

He pondered the dilemma one last time and then went into action. Moving cautiously, he searched the area below the boulder yet again for the packet. Finding nothing, he crawled over to the path and began moving slowly down the hill. When he reached the level where he could hear the workers clearly and catch glimpses of movement in the light, he edged off the path to his left. Working his way carefully but steadily, he reached the shadows behind the storage building.

It had been constructed so that its floor was at ground level at the rear where he crouched. The downward slope of the beach beneath the floor level left a wedge-shaped crawl space. David knew that the lake side, as well as the end closest to the dock, had been closed in with a wooden lattice work, but the remaining end, also in the shadows, had yet to be finished. Stretched out on his belly, he lay there for minutes, listening to the voices and sounds of activity. The words he could pick up all related to the job at hand. He heard no mention of his name.

He had a half-hour of darkness remaining. Time to get with it, he thought. He located a three-foot stick of driftwood. Snaking his way around the corner, he crawled backward, feet-first, through the wet sand toward the lake. Using the stick, he carefully smoothed over the trail he left. He backed his way under the twenty-four by twelve-foot building until he reached a spot near the center. Through the two-inch-square openings in the lattice work, he could see the four remaining workers under the yard light. He felt confident that, unless they shined a light in from the open end, they would not spot him. And if they believed he'd already escaped, they had probably called off the search for him.

After a final touch-up on his trail, he began digging. Using the stick and his hands, he dug slowly and carefully, pushing the sand up to form a small dike around the exposed three sides of his trench. At one point, a flurry of new sounds stopped his digging. The four workers had apparently finished their task. They were replaced by a single sentry.

The darkness was fading as David gently rolled into his trench. His physical efforts had warmed him, but he was still wet. Cool, lumpy, and uncomfortable, the trench would need some modifications, but he felt more secure. As he lay there, basking in damp satisfaction over his accomplishment, he heard a faint rustling sound at the open end of the crawl space. A deep chill zapped through his body like a miniature lightning bolt. He held his breath for moments, then exhaled quietly. Ever so slowly, he raised his head and turned for a look into the darker area.

There, but eight feet from him, stood a large skunk. It seemed to be studying him, sniffing the air as if to decide on a course of action. David sank in defeat and wiggled his way deeper into the sand. He felt the cold dampness of his sandy grave pressing in on him as he awaited his fate.

Chapter 25

Satisfied that the logs in the fireplace were igniting, Brother Vance turned and nervously surveyed the meeting room in anticipation of his morning meeting with Father Jeranko. Though he felt the inclination, Vance was not a pacer, so he simply stood at the large window, his arms folded across his chest, and looked out over Black Rock Bay. A thin trail of smoke curled upward from a camper's fire directly across the bay in the national park, but he saw no sign of activity at the docks of the resort or the Gundersons. A closer look revealed something else—no cars parked near the resort cottages.

Good, he thought, some more guests have bailed out on her. The first week of her season, traditionally one of the best, had become a financial disaster for the stubborn young woman. A vision of the beautiful Kimberly Farber popped into his mind. Yes, he'd like to take her. Maybe he would.

He flicked a speck of lint from the lapel of his navy pin-striped suit. He detested the suit. But he somehow knew Father would be wearing gray today, and he had learned years before to anticipate Father's selections and appropriately choose contrasting colors and blends. A noise at the door caught his attention. He turned to see his mentor, clad in a rich, gray silk suit, stride purposefully into the large, paneled office. Vance could tell it would be a fast-paced meeting. He quickly took the seat across from his superior.

Without a greeting, Jeranko stared briefly at his long-time compatriot, then nodded his head curtly—the signal to begin.

"First," began Vance, "the floatplane facility. Should be ready for use by the time the de Havilland arrives tomorrow from Montana. The plane and the van from Minneapolis will both arrive about eleven o'clock."

"Good. Good job, Brother," Jeranko said. "I want the van loaded and on the road within half an hour. The property acquisitions?"

"The property acquisition...." began Vance reluctantly, "no progress to report...but the resort appears to be empty."

"Did you have more of our people booked in there again this week?" asked Jeranko.

"No. Two of her units are still down from the...unfortunate vandalism last week. I think the guests in the others probably got scared out by stories of a body being found and by the commotion last night."

"The body...anything new?" Jeranko asked.

"From what I hear from the sheriff's office, the only chances of an ID on the poor soul would come from a match of dental records or DNA, virtually impossible unless there's some clue as to whom they're looking for," Vance explained.

"Too bad," Jeranko said thoughtfully, "too bad. Dust to dust."

"Sir?"

"Dust to dust," Jeranko said. "It's ironic. Our recruits are nothing but dirt when we find them...and that's what the washouts become. Back to the acquisitions. You *must* get those properties—and soon." The leader's eyes narrowed, and the fixed smile faded slightly. "To dock the aircraft on the bay side, we need that privacy. And unless we establish our R and R program soon and staff those cottages, we'll find our young men sneaking off to town to get what they need."

Vance knew the next line. "And *that*," he said, "we cannot have. I think Ms. Farber must be getting panicky by now. I think it's time…with your approval, of course…to make that fat offer. Given a chance to get out from under the resort—at a profit—I think she'll take it. If she sells to us, Gunderson won't stay there—not with us next door."

"Do it," Jeranko said, the iron smile returning for a brief moment. "Corporal David?"

Corporal David, the two words dreaded by Vance. Inevitable, but nonetheless dreaded. Be careful here, he thought. "He was seen being picked up by Gunderson's boat. He's at the resort…at Gunderson's…or on his way to Minneapolis. The squad we sent after him encountered an impenetrable array of security devices, probably the work of that Bryant. They had to abort." Vance hesitated. Seldom through the years had he been forced to acknowledge outright failure to his leader. But now, in close succession—the property acquisition still unresolved, and the defection of Corporal David. Both, he feared, resulted from the intervention of that Hudson Bryant. He struggled to contain the bolt of anger that flashed through him at the thought.

"What's your read on Corporal David?" asked Jeranko, studying his subordinate.

"We have to consider the possibility that he could be a real threat to us," replied Vance. "But I don't think so."

"Your rationale?"

"We know he used deception to join us so he could search for his missing brother," Vance began. "We know the brother had a history of drugs, alcohol, and depression. And we know that when Corporal David was told of the…suicide, he came apart. Remained that way until he disappeared." Vance paused. "Yes, we have to acknowledge that he could hurt us. He knows of vandalism the group has committed, and he knows of our connection to the Colonies. The latter concerns me the most. But, without corroboration, most authorities would be reluctant to take his allegations against an established church seriously. No, I think he's run on home to mourn his brother, lick his wounds, and get on with his life. Just the same, we'll continue the search here and in Minneapolis. We'll find him."

"Soon," Father Jeranko added sternly, "soon. But the very fact that we're having this discussion suggests that, at the moment, we have a loose end flopping around out there. Remember, we had a similar situation in Viet Nam? We closed that operation just in time. You'd better prepare for a strategic withdrawal, just in case. I have to tell you, I don't share your optimism on this issue. But it's your responsibility to take care of it. Do we understand each other?"

"Yes, Sir," Vance replied. He already had such a close-down plan. Within hours, he could sterilize the installation by hiding weapons, destroying certain records, and evacuating Brother Mark and the sergeants, for they were the key personnel whose knowledge could prove devastating to the colony. But all that wouldn't be necessary. He'd find that little turncoat.

"Now, I'll be flying back to Minneapolis in the Cessna this afternoon," said Jeranko. "Keep in close touch. Use the secure line for anything sensitive."

"Are you...ready to see Brother Theodore?"

"Has he come around?" Jeranko asked.

"Yes," Vance said. "It took longer to get the truth from him than I'd anticipated. Have to give the little man credit. He was tough—held out longer than I thought he would. At first, he threatened us with allegations of illegal weapons, conspiracy, tax evasion, and murder, among other things. He claimed to have left a set of documents that supported his charges with a friend in Minneapolis. If forty-eight hours passed without a check-in call from him, the friend was to give the documents to the authorities. However, after some hours of heavy persuasion by Brother Mark, his resistance collapsed. He admitted he had fabricated the story. He cried like a baby and begged for his life."

"And you're getting it *straight* from him now?"

"Beyond a doubt," Vance replied. "Brother Mark reduced him to the sniveling little whimp he always was. You can see for yourself." He jerked a thumb toward the door behind him.

Father Jeranko reached under the desk and pressed the signal button. Vance stood and turned toward the sound of the outer buzzer.

The door opened immediately and in stepped Brother Mark, half supporting and half dragging a small figure, barely recognizable as Brother Theodore. The mass of bruised flesh that had once been a face looked like an ugly kaleidoscope of red, purple, and black. Blood oozed from splits in his lips and the misshapen lump in the center of the mass. While one eye might have allowed a tiny ray of vision, the other was swollen shut. His right arm dangled like an odd pendulum, as though hinged but otherwise unconnected with his body. At Father Jeranko's motion, Mark dumped his victim like a rag doll into Vance's chair. With the shock of the landing, Brother Theodore managed to open the better eye slightly wider.

"I'm deeply sorry it had to come to this," said Father Jeranko in his most authoritative tone. "But I'm told that you, our trusted chaplain, have put together some kind of...documents? Documents? Papers that could cause us to endure undeserved attention from the authorities? *You*—would do that?"

"No...no...no, no," murmured the diminutive prisoner, somehow raising one hand and flailing it weakly before his devastated face. "Was...'fraid...lied...was...'fraid."

"Oh, and now you are telling us you lied to us? You did not prepare such documents?" Father Jeranko glared at the chaplain. "*Did* you...or did you *not* prepare such documents?"

"No...no...no...no doc...mens. Was...'fraid...lied...'fraid."

Jeranko looked up at Vance, then over at Mark. The leader's eyes seemed to say, "I think you're right. I think he's telling the truth." Turning back to his interrogation, he asked, "Brother Theodore, have you ever talked to anyone about our activities, you know, the things that go on here? Have you ever told anything to Corporal David?"

"No, no...ne...ver...talk...ne...ver." Tears trickled down along both sides of the center lump.

"Good, my friend, good," said Father Jeranko warmly. "I believe you, and I thank you. You have done a wonderful job for our church, wonderful." He opened the desk drawer on his right and reached in. "For all you have done, we owe you the dignity of a peaceful retirement." In one smooth motion, Jeranko brought a blue-black .357 magnum from the drawer and raised it toward Brother Theodore's forehead. *Bam!*

"Deposit him until later," Vance directed Brother Mark. "When we've finished here, send someone to clean up. Then collect that squad of eight that I mentioned for our visit to the resort. Civilian clothes—no fatigues."

An hour later, Brother Vance climbed the steps to the Black Rock Resort lodge room. He paused on the deck for a moment and listened, picking up the barely audible sound of tires moving ever so slowly on the back driveway. Good so far, he thought. Now, if I can keep her away from the windows, we can search the resort and buy it, all at the same time. He felt a swell of optimism ripple through him as he opened the door. The tingling bell reminded him to stick with his planned approach, to be as kind and genuine as possible. He moved across the empty room and took a seat on one of the stools.

"I don't believe this!" said Kimberly Farber as she rounded the corner and jerked to a stop facing Brother Vance. After all you've done to me, you have the nerve—"

"Uh-uh," interrupted Vance, raising his hands in a defensive posture. "I come with my apologies to you...and with *good* news. Please...hear me out."

"My turn to interrupt," the attractive blonde snapped. She reached under the counter, clicked something, then continued, "Now, I have the recorder going. You've got two minutes and you're out of here."

He recognized that his task would not be made any easier by this feisty young woman. "I sincerely apologize for any hardships we've—" he almost said "inadvertently," then thought better of it, "—caused. I don't blame you for your feelings toward me," he continued, "but I ask you to set them aside for a moment to hear my message." He resisted turning on his ministerial smile and tried for all of the sincerity he could muster.

"Meter's running," Ms. Farber said coldly. She stood stiffly behind the cash register, her arms folded defiantly.

"Facts," began Vance. "One, you are having difficulties building your business. Two, we need your property badly for our expansion. Three, we need it very soon. And four, our board has decided to increase our offer considerably—to allow you a handsome profit."

"Meter's still running." Kimberly moved from behind the counter and strolled casually toward the north window that overlooked the back driveway and workshop.

Got to stop her, he thought. Got to keep her behind the counter! "Here, I have a written offer here to show you," he said, pulling a document from his inside coat pocket. He had never been one to panic, but as she approached the window, he felt his scalp tingle. "There are some incentives here, in addition to purchase price, that I'd like you to see." Kimberly Farber moved slowly past the window and turned toward the large front picture window. She showed no alarm. Apparently, she'd seen none of his men out back. But if she looked toward the cottages?

"Come on, what's the figure?" she demanded coldly. "Meter's about run out."

Brother Vance wanted to grab her and pull her away from the windows. But any sign of alarm would only bring a negative reaction. So close, he thought, so close to success. He knew he shouldn't have brought the troops, but they *had* to find Corporal David. Still, he knew he'd blown it. Any second now, she'd spot a trooper and it would be all over. To his surprise, she hesitated for a moment at the large window, then strolled calmly back to her position behind the counter.

Talk about luck, he thought. She still hasn't caught on. "Here, Ms. Farber," he said, "take a look at this. In addition to the new purchase price, which should give you a profit of something over seventy-five thousand dollars, you'll see additional incentives, like separate purchase of certain equipment that would normally be included in the—"

Brother Vance looked up from the document into the barrel of a snub-nosed .38 caliber revolver. A bitter chill ran up his spine, followed by a brief vision of Brother Theodore with the hole in his forehead. Again, he put up his hands defensively.

"Now, Ms. Farber, no need for—"

"Out!" she shouted, waving the weapon before his face. "Right now! Out!"

For an instant, he thought of ducking his head and making a grab for the weapon, but the *click* as she pulled the hammer back canceled the impulse. And when he saw the weapon began to tremble, he stood quickly and hustled toward the door. As he descended the five steps to the driveway, a stubborn portion of his mind suggested there must be *something* he could do. But a cocked revolver pointed at his back— especially in the shaking hands of an angry woman—he could only hope to reach his vehicle alive.

"Stop!" she shouted. "Stand right there. Don't move. Don't turn around."

Crack! At the sound of the shot, Brother Vance expected to feel a hot spot where the bullet entered his back. None. He glanced over his shoulder and saw Kimberly Farber standing above him on the deck with the revolver pointed upward.

"Now," she said, the tremors in her voice matching those in her hand, "get your men off my property. Off in ten seconds or I start shooting your legs and move up!"

Defeat! Total defeat…by an inexperienced woman, he thought. It ripped at his callous fibers of machismo like a chainsaw. But there are times, he thought, and then there are times. He cupped his hands before his mouth and called loudly. Instantly, pairs of his young invaders burst from four of the cottages, saw his predicament, and took off on the run for their van.

"And don't do something stupid," Kimberly Farber said angrily, "like telling the sheriff *I* attacked *you*. We have pictures of your storm troopers, of this whole thing. Meter's run out."

With what dignity he could muster, Brother Vance walked quickly to his Explorer, got in, and drove off. He hoped Father Jeranko had already taken off for Minneapolis. "I'll get you, Bitch," he muttered as he turned onto the county road. "Yes…the next time you see me…."

Chapter 26

"Thanks, Sarah," said Hud, "but if I ate one more of your wonderful pancakes, I'd have to go back to bed. Wouldn't be good for anything more active than that." He looked out through the Gundersons' kitchen window toward the circular drive. The golden beams of the rising sun filtered through the thick forest, giving an eerie luminescence to the wafting tendrils of fog, the evaporating moisture of the previous night's rain. "What a *beautiful* morning for flying," he said. "Got lots to do today. Ready to drive me over to the airstrip, Gibby?"

"You be careful, Hudson," Sarah admonished. "And while you're up in the Falls doing that shopping, I'm going to have a heart-to-heart talk with Kimberly."

"Oh, oh," muttered Gibby, "meddling again."

"Call it what you like," she retorted with mock sternness, "but that girl's got blinders on. It's about time she got some good advice from a *woman.*"

An hour later, after a slow and careful preflight check of the Piper Archer, Hud lowered full flaps and pushed the throttle ahead. Despite the soft runway, the small aircraft lifted off from the camelback, struggled for a moment to remain airborne, then eased up and over the trees.

Hud purposely veered left to stay as far from the peninsula as he could before setting course for International Falls. He marveled at the beauty of the shimmering lake, with its myriad islands of timber and stone, regretting that the trip would last only minutes.

After landing at the Falls and refueling, he rented a car and headed into town for his most unusual shopping venture. By one-thirty, he was back at the airport loading his strange cargo into the Piper. After two wetsuits and scuba gear came a powerful, submersible lantern capable of casting an incredible beam. Then, the two new shotguns, a pump-action sixteen-gauge for Kimberly and a Browning twelve-gauge for himself, identical to that he'd lost. Closing the cargo door, he carefully wedged a vase containing a dozen red roses into an upright position between the seats. Minutes later, the rumbling of the wheels ceased as he climbed out and headed southeast. Hud felt pleased with his shopping, especially with the flowers.

As he once again skirted the Basher camp to prepare for his landing approach, he saw their Cessna floatplane land on the lake side of the peninsula and begin taxiing toward the harbor. Sure would like to catch that plane loaded with stolen goods, he thought. As he entered his downwind leg, he saw a dark green cargo van, with a glass bubble vent in its top, turn off the county road into the camp. It was after Hud had landed and taxied to his tie-down that his mind connected the Basher plane with the van. Once the Archer had been secured, he called Gibby for his ride. Then he strolled out to the gravel road and down a half-mile to where he could stand in the road ditch, hidden by a scrubby pine, and watch the county road. Despite the dark feelings that came with anything connected to the Bashers, he felt good standing there in the fresh breeze with the warm sun shining on him.

When Gibby's vehicle approached, Hud stepped out and waved him on toward the airstrip. He had just repositioned himself when the green van emerged and headed south. Sure enough, he thought, whatever came in on that plane is now in that van, probably headed for Minneapolis. There would be time enough to call Will Mertens when he got back to the resort. He walked back to the plane, transferred his purchases into Gibby's Jeep, and asked his friend to drop him off at Kimberly's.

A heavy feeling swamped Hud as they drove into the resort. Not a single car to be seen, near the cottages, and that meant Kimberly's fine little resort had no customers. He imagined how she must feel, physically worn out and emotionally destroyed. He vowed he'd do everything he could to lighten the day, to get her mind off the Bashers and the threatening predicament they had constructed.

After stowing the diving gear and the new weapons temporarily in a corner of the lodge room, he adjusted the bouquet slightly, moved behind the counter and rapped on the door frame. Hearing no response, he cautiously entered the office and peeked into the kitchen. There sat Kimberly at the old chrome table, her head in her hands, and Gibby's .38 revolver on the table before her. In an instant, the perky Broadway entrance he had planned dissolved in the gloom. He walked slowly over to the table, whisked the revolver away, set the roses before her, and quietly laid the weapon on the nearby counter.

Her head tilted upward slightly. When she saw the flowers, she bolted from the chair, turned toward Hud, and threw her arms around his neck.

"Wow," he said softly. "I've got to do this more often." The sudden clinch confused part of him, yet another part of him warmed to the feeling of her body against his. Her arms clutched his neck. Her cheek reached upward to touch his, her breasts pressed against his chest, and her sleek, firm body molded itself to his. But his immediate excitement dampened quickly into deep, loving concern when he realized how upset she was.

"Oh, Hud," she whimpered, "I almost killed him. I don't even know what stopped me. I almost *killed* him."

For a time, Hud said nothing. He put his arms around her and held her to him. He kissed her lightly on the forehead several times, then took her face in his hands and looked into her red-rimmed blue eyes. He felt compelled to kiss her on the lips, but he resisted, instead drawing her head to his shoulder.

"It's okay," he murmured, "it's okay." As her arms relaxed and eased downward to encircle his waist, he thought, she needs me, she really needs me. And I need this. I've missed being needed so much. Then he felt Kimberly's body begin to relax. "Now, why don't you tell me what happened." He eased her down to her chair, then took what was becoming his regular place at the table.

"Thanks, Hud, for the roses," she said slowly. "That's the nicest thing that's happened to me in...*such* a long time. They're beautiful."

"Just the beginning, Kimberly. Lots more where they came from. Ready to talk?"

"It was...Brother Vance," she began. "He came over with a new sugarcoated offer on the resort. Then, while he's pushing me for a quick sale, I look outside and see his Bashers all over the place. I went back behind the counter, picked up the gun, and told him to get out. I guess he saw I had it cocked, because he retreated right away. When I got him outside, I shot once up in the air and told him he had ten seconds to call his men and get off the property. Boy, did they move!" Kimberly took a deep breath and exhaled a sudden burst. "Then I came unglued. Hud, I remember pulling the hammer back. I remember actually squeezing on the trigger. I—I almost shot him."

"I'm glad you didn't," Hud said. He felt the anger mounting within him. "*My* job."

"No, no, no, Hud! Don't even think like that. That's what's so wrong here. They've got us so stirred up, I almost did *their* kind of thing, almost messed up big time."

Hud thought for a moment. He couldn't imagine the condition he'd have found her in had she actually pulled the trigger. If it comes to that, he thought, if someone has to blow one of those apes away, I should be the one.

"Kimberly, I'm moving in here with you." Her eyes opened wide. "Oh, not into your bedroom…but here in the house. You're their prime target, and you can't watch the resort by yourself. Besides, they think David is hidden here. They're liable to be back."

"But—"

"Good," he interrupted, "that's settled. I'll help you here. Gibby can take my cottage, and Sarah can watch their house." He paused. "No, it's not settled…unless you agree."

"I—agree. I would feel safer. You can use the other bedroom there," she said, nodding toward the spare first floor bedroom, "unless it would be better for you to sleep upstairs."

"Your house, your rules," he said with a smile as he headed for the door. "You decide where I sleep."

Using Kimberly's old mean machine, Hud returned to his cottage and gathered some clothes and personal gear. He took a few minutes to brief Gibby and Sarah on Kimberly's experience and headed back to the resort. Kimberly had just finished making up the single bed in the downstairs spare bedroom when he returned.

A strange, almost juvenile elation swept over him as he hung his clothes in the closet. While he fully intended to honor his pledge not to push Kimberly, the thought of being so close to her, sleeping not twenty feet from her, recaptured long-forgotten feelings that none of his one-nighters in Orange County had aroused. For the first time, he admitted to himself that he was truly in love with Kimberly Farber. This, he thought, could make these next few days frustrating. Going to have to exercise self-control. Can't let this situation go from frustrating to difficult.

"Hud, can you help me with something here in the kitchen?" called Kimberly.

When he joined her there, she handed him a large jar of pickles and motioned to the lid. As Hud gripped the lid and the jar in his strong hands and felt the resistance they offered, he smiled inwardly at the macho urge to make the opening appear to be easy, effortless. The lid popped loose none too soon, for the strain was about to show on his face.

"Pickles?" he asked. "You're not—"

"Just getting ready for dinner," she said with a grin. "Got some nice hamburger out for us to grill. If you'd like a drink, the mixings are up there in that cupboard. You know what? I think I'd like a…can you make a vodka martini?"

"A bartender I'm not, but two martinis I can make." He opened the cupboard and reached for the vodka. "I've been thinking, Kimberly. With this week's guests all gone, why don't you put up the Closed sign, lock up the place, and forget business for a while?"

"Already have," she said. "Locked the cottages and baithouse up while you went for your things."

"Then, too, maybe you should—"

"Call next week's guests and cancel them out?" she cut in. Then more slowly she added, "Already have. I found places for some of them on another lake. Told them my well quit."

Hud turned to face her. She had known exactly what he was about to say.

"Sarah told me about the possibility of all those bodies in the lake," she said. "You didn't mention *that* part. With the prospect of mass murders and a war that could break out any minute, I can't ask guests to come here. I can't even *allow* it. Hud, you've talked with this David. Do you think it's true—about the bodies?"

"I—I guess I'd lay odds on it," he said.

"Then this resort is dead for the season. Only ghouls would want to come here once the word is out." She took the drink Hud offered, reached up and clinked it against his. Her face appeared bright and buoyant, but her eyes showed gloom. "Here's to a long, unpaid vacation."

The dichotomy told Hud that lifting Kimberly's spirits would be no easy task. He imagined how he'd have felt if, during his first year of business, he'd had mysterious, armed militiamen in the hallways encircling his offices, if he'd found an unexplained corpse behind each piece of furniture, if he'd suddenly learned that there would be no revenue for the next year.

He stood there for a moment, looking at the slender, smooth face beneath the golden hair, the face that had become more beautiful to him with each day. All the forces in the universe seemed to be driving him to take her in his arms and kiss her, to make everything right for her. But he saw the risk more clearly now. To do so right now might add yet another problem to her present overload. Her husband had rejected her in the most painful way. He'd reneged financially. Then Brother Vance and his troops stepped in. No wonder she's down on men. Yet, the love that swirled within him demanded some form of release.

He set his drink on the counter, moved to Kimberly. Her blue eyes seemed fixed on him as he came close, but they said nothing. He gently took her face in his hands and kissed her on the forehead as he had earlier. Then he backed away.

"I—I love you, Kimberly," he said. "That's all. I love you. If you get things sorted out to the point where you want to hear the rest of it, just let me know. I'll wait." Reading her face and eyes, he saw a rapid sequence of expressions, what seemed like surprise, then desire, and finally deliberate control. "Now, Ms. Farber, let's get that charcoal going. I'm hungry."

"Hud...I—"

"No need," he cut in, "but I do expect you to cheer me up a little. You owe me that."

Kimberly's face warmed, almost smiled. "I sure do, Hudson Bryant. I sure do." She took his hand lightly. "And I'll enjoy trying, especially since you're not pushing me for P.E."

"That's what you call it?" Hud asked. "Physical education?"

"No, phallic endeavors." Her eyes glinted devilishly.

From that point, the late afternoon and evening flew past for Hud. They shared small talk, jokes, and occasional casual touching. They kidded each other and laughed. It seemed as if they had escaped from an oppressive cloud of overwhelming pressures and were free to follow a clear pathway, to find whatever relationship was destined to be. Occasionally, he saw her looking at him in a new way, as though she were studying him, recognizing him for the first time, and perhaps even liking what she saw.

After the meal, they caught the news on television. Little was said about the airport closures, except that the federal authorities were "conducting a thorough investigation." Two candidates for the U.S. Senate and three candidates for the House had called press conferences to announce their resignations from the two major parties. All five expressed their intentions to search out and join unspecified independent parties. Kimberly switched between the two available local channels for information about the body pulled from Wasikama, but there was nothing more.

"Hud, listen!" Kimberly clicked off the television. "Hear it?"

It took Hud a second to pick up the faint sound of a high-pitched alarm whistle.

"They're back!" he said, bounding from the chair and into the office. He pulled his loaded Browning down from the wall-mounted rack, grabbed a nearby flashlight, and scurried down the steps to the rear entrance.

"Listen up, Kimberly," he said, pausing at the door. "Get your thirty-eight and your flashlight, lock all doors, and turn out all lights. Stay in the dark. That way you can see them but they can't see you. Don't shoot at anyone outside, but if they break in…you'll have to do it. Okay?"

"I—I can do it, Hud," she said. "You be careful—please?"

Hud quietly closed the door behind him and ran past the workshop toward the fish cleaning house, choosing once again to follow the left edge of the woods. He hunkered down as before behind the small structure and listened. Only one alarm so far, but it was one those in the last ring of defense. He wondered how they got past the other bells and sensors. If they decided to come back again after what happened the last time, he thought, and if they've gotten this far undetected...we could be in real trouble, sure as hell outnumbered. The throbbing in his temples echoed the thumping in his chest.

Finally, he picked up a slight rustling noise in the brush ahead of him. Soon, there it was again. It seemed to be moving from his left to his right as the Bashers would to get to the lodge. Crouching low, he moved cautiously into the undercover. He stopped and listened. Strange, it sounded like only one of them. No sounds from anywhere else. He moved again toward the sound, then paused. Close now, he thought, only a few yards. As stealthily as he could, he moved to close the gap.

Sensing that he was as close as he could hope to get, Hud flipped off the safety. Straightening up, he thought, God, I hope he doesn't challenge me. I'll have to shoot. He turned on the flashlight and aimed it along the gun barrel toward the source of the sounds.

A large raccoon reared up and faced the glare of Hud's light. "*H-h-a-a-c-c-k-k!*" it cursed. Then it spun around and scampered off into the woods, leaving Hud with a tingling scalp, a dry mouth, and a pounding heart.

Chapter 27

David lay very still, sniffing the air cautiously before opening his eyes. He had developed the routine through countless awakenings during the long day. Thankful that the odor he picked up was only a mild residual rather than a fresh, strong expulsion, he raised his head and peered over the edge of his sandy trench toward the home of the skunk family in the rear left corner. Two eyes glowed in the semidarkness. As with each previous check, the mother skunk sat protectively, in front of her furry mass of young ones, watching him. Thankful yet again, he settled back down in his damp, lumpy bed of sand. Despite his inability to speak skunk, they had somehow reached an understanding that if he came no closer and made no sudden moves, he would be allowed to stay.

He felt cold, almost to the point of trembling. But the thundering headache and the nausea brought on by his hunger created his biggest problem, for each time he dozed off it was with the fear that he'd groan or moan in his sleep and attract the sentries. But finally, darkness had fallen. He checked his watch. Good—almost midnight. After eighteen hours in his miserable grave, he could finally resume his search for the packet.

He was about to move out when he heard footsteps and voices approaching. He wiggled deeper into the sand. Had they heard him? Were they coming for him? He reduced his breathing to the shallowest level he could. They were right beside the building now. What if he coughed or sneezed? He'd be dead.

"Right here while we get the gear out."

David heard the heavy thunk as something was dropped in the sand just beyond the lattice work. He recognized the voice as that of Sgt. Richard.

"You got the key?"

Sgt. Evans, no doubt about it, he thought.

"I got it. Here, I'll open up."

That was Sgt. Mack. All sergeants? What's going on? His thoughts were interrupted by the sounds of boots scuffling and the thumping of heavy objects on the floor above him. He relaxed a little, buoyed by the realization that the object of their mission was not David Engstrom. He wanted to raise up for a peek, but it might be his last. Amid several grunts, he heard four more objects dropped in the sand outside the door of the building. The door slammed, followed by the recognizable sounds of the large padlock being replaced and snapped shut. When the footsteps and voices faded, David decided to risk a look.

He raised up enough to look over the dike of sand he'd built. What is that, he thought, a body? It was a body, a man's body, and the face was turned his way. Unable to see clearly, he moved for a better look through the openings in the lattice work. A cold, yet powerful eye stared at him. It seemed to say, "Do it. Do your job." Brother Theodore! And centered in the forehead of the puffy face was a dark scab. David shuddered. A bullet hole! They blew him away—execution style! He leaned to one side and vomited bitter juices.

When he saw the three sergeants returning for Brother Theodore, David slid back into his hole. Feeling his stomach about to flip again, he held his breath and bit hard into one arm. It seemed to work.

"That deep slot off the north end of Sweet's Island?" Sgt. Evans asked.

"Yeah," said Sgt. Richard. "He wants this one extra heavy and extra deep."

The sounds once again receded. David ventured another look, raising up in time to see the three men carrying Brother Theodore like a target dummy over toward the big, blue boat. With a coordinated heave, they threw his body in. Then they jumped aboard and prepared to cast off. Though he was tired, cold, and sick, the scene he had witnessed touched a match to a charge deep within him. It was time to move.

With a delicate, little wave at his companion, he eased feet first out of the trench and scriggled backwards on his belly toward the opening, never taking his eyes off the skunk. He was about to disappear into the brush when, on an afterthought, he smoothed out his trail in the sand. If, for some reason, he should need the Skunk Hotel for another day he couldn't risk giving away its location.

David eased into the woods and carefully made his way to his left. Picking up the path, he moved quickly up the hill to the familiar point at which he detoured off toward the giant boulder. Searching in and around the crevice for the packet, he turned up nothing. Dejected, he sat for a moment, his back leaning against the boulder. I'm sure that's where he said he'd put it, David thought. Wait a minute. Suddenly he realized something he'd missed. That's where Brother Theodore would hide the packet under optimum conditions. What if they were after him? What if he didn't have time?

He began retracing the way back to the path, searching five feet on each side of his line. With his nose to the ground, he patted the area with his hands, crawling under the lowest branches of the spruces and even checking the top sides of the thick, needled branches. Halfway back to the path, he spotted it nestled in the needles atop a branch about three feet above the ground. Sealed in a plastic kitchen bag, the eight-by-ten-inch packet was half an inch thick.

Kneeling, he slipped the packet inside his jockey shorts. Well, you've got it, he thought. *That's* the hard part. It would be a slow and dangerous trip across the peninsula to Black Rock Bay and safety, but he knew he could make it. He would work his way out toward the end of the peninsula, cut across beyond the headquarters building and down between the sentries to the bay. Once he reached swimming depth, he'd have it made. If necessary, he could make it under water to Gunderson's, popping up only briefly for air—*if* the water temperature was in the mid-sixties.

David's trip across the peninsula and down to the water took even longer than he anticipated. He inadvertently stepped on twigs that snapped loudly. Twice, sentries moved to investigate the sounds, and he nearly bolted from his cover, exposing himself to the silent but deadly crossbows.

His confidence that the water was his ally eroded quickly as he swam toward the middle of the bay, staying under water as much as he could. The ice-cold water numbed his body and sapped his strength immediately. He struggled to find a rhythm but couldn't. At mid-bay and safely out of the range of their crossbows, he paused briefly to tread water and rest, but even that effort took more energy than it saved. Damn, Engstrom, he thought. This cold water is like a concrete wall...and you haven't eaten anything in a day-and-a-half.

He regrouped his thoughts around a core of determination. The resort was the closest but the most dangerous, because of its proximity to the peninsula. No, despite his near panic, he'd head on across to the Gunderson dock. But since he'd heard no alarm from the guards, he'd stay on the surface, roll over, and try to find his relaxing backstroke. He set out once more. He was tempted to direct his mind to something else, his Julie. But in his condition, he knew he had to concentrate on each stroke to make it the most efficient possible. There weren't many left.

• • •

Hud's dream of Kimberly would have been his nicest in years but for the incessant tapping noise. Angry, he opened his eyes. The shapes and shadows in the strange room confused him, but there was no doubt about the tapping noise. Someone was at the window, tapping on the glass pane. Snatching the flashlight from the nearby nightstand, he turned the beam at the source of the agitation. Gibby! he thought. Then he realized that Gibby was gesturing frantically toward the back door. Hud waved and called Kimberly as he rushed past. Moments later, he flipped on the light in the utility room and unlatched the door.

Gibby's arm reached in, groped for the switch, and turned the light off. Pushing Hud aside, he barged into the darkness.

"C'mon," he said, reaching out and pulling someone else into the room by the coat sleeve. "This here's David," he announced. "He made it—swam across the bay to my place."

The foursome stood awkwardly in the darkness for a moment. Then Kimberly broke the silence.

"Stay right here," she said. "I'll close the lodge room door and pull all the shades and drapes." Moments later, she called, "It's okay. Come on into the kitchen."

As David stripped off Gibby's nylon winter parka, the older man introduced him to Kimberly. Hud's excitement rippled through him. He could never have imagined such a thrill over meeting a near stranger. He simply smiled and stood there for a moment, admiring the slender, young man he'd seen only in darkness. He wore a pair of Gibby's blue jeans, the extra six sizes cinched up by a belt, and a heavy gray sweater over a plaid flannel shirt.

"He made it," Gibby said, as they seated themselves around the old table. "And here it is." He tossed a plastic kitchen bag containing a thick pack of papers onto the table. "It's all there, Hud. Even more'n you'd hoped for. You know he hadn't ate for thirty-six hours? With that there bundle of dynamite and this tough kid here...the Bashers are done—finished."

"Only if we can keep David and those papers out of the Bashers' hands," Hud corrected. "I'll call Deputy Mertens. We'll see about turning the packet over to him. Then I'll fly David to Minneapolis in the morning."

"Deputy Mertens?" David asked. "*Sheriff's* deputy?" He shook his head. "Uh-uh, might as well go back to the camp." Despite their assurances that Mertens was reliable, David Engstrom refused to budge. "And besides, I've got something left to do. If I can hide out somewhere—I can take care of myself," he said, pulling what Hud recognized as Gibby's old military Colt .45 from one of the coat pockets. "I'm not leaving here until I've pulled Brother Theodore out of that lake."

Hud looked into David's blue eyes and recognized fierce determination. But to expect to find the chaplain in that huge lake? "David," he said, "we all appreciate your feelings, your loyalty, but that's a hellish big lake out there. I've even picked up the necessary gear for diving. But I was just hoping to find a body—that's *one body,* that's any *single body*—not a particular one."

"But you don't understand," David protested. "You've got the boats and equipment. I'm an excellent diver." He paused and looked at Kimberly. "Ah, Ms. Farber? Could I have something more to eat, please? Mrs. Gunderson fed me...but I threw it up on the way over."

Kimberly jumped up immediately and began foraging through her kitchen.

"Yes," Hud said to David, "With our equipment and your skills, that's a great sounding combination...but it doesn't shrink the lake any."

"Oh, but it *does*. I know where they dumped Brother Theodore."

Chapter 28

Hud awakened at nine o'clock Friday morning to a strange and quiet house. He lay there for several minutes listening for signs of trouble, then replayed the arrival of David Engstrom five hours earlier. The kid was really something, really gutsy, he thought. Sharing the crawlspace with a family of skunks for eighteen hours? I'm comfortable with wild animals, but I'm not sure I could have done that. That skunk would have let me have it first thing.

And the packet? He marveled once again at the job Brother Theodore had done. Apparently, he had prepared most of the document before leaving Minneapolis, for the carefully written affidavit showed two witnesses to his signature. He provided the names, descriptions, and dates attached to the missing Bashers, along with the names and positions of those in the power structure at the camp, from Father Jeranko down to the eight sergeants. But he doubted that any below the rank of sergeant were guilty of anything beyond vandalism.

Brother Theodore had gone on to list the Minneapolis companies owned by the church, their managing officers, and a senior partner in the law firm that represented the church. His allegations of criminal

activity extended from numerous violations of labor and civil rights
laws to income and property tax evasion, fraud, conspiracy, bribery of
public officials, receiving and selling stolen property, assault and battery, and murder. He pointed to the church's seaplane as a transporter
of stolen computer parts. The shipments were moved by rental truck
from Seattle to a small lake in Montana where they were transferred for
the flight to Minnesota.

His disenchantment with the church organization had grown rapidly
upon learning of the tactics Father Jeranko and Brother Vance were
using to pressure neighbors into selling their property to the church. The
Gundersons' property and the resort were intended to be staffed with
women and used as a comfort camp for the troops. He went on to state
that the Church of the Rock had established itself as Colony IV of the
Thirteen Colonies of America, though he had no reason to believe the
other twelve colonies knew of or would condone the criminal activities
of Colony IV. Then he clearly predicted his own murder and burial in
Lake Wasikama.

Hud lay there for a few minutes, his pulse quickened once again by the
astonishment he and the others had experienced as they poured through
the packet of information. He remembered Kimberly's wide eyes as she
absorbed the magnitude of activities and the intentions of their adversaries. He had taken her hand and said something like, "At least now,
they're on their way down and we're just about out of it. They'll be so
busy trying to cover their butts, they won't have time for us."

He jumped up, straightened his bed, and began his bathroom
chores. By the time he stepped into the kitchen, Kimberly stood at the
counter, her back to him, preparing the coffee maker. Her carefully
combed-out golden hair reached to her shoulders, and the red robe,
cinched around her waist, seemed to accentuate her graceful moves.
Hud wanted to begin every day for the rest of his life like this. On
impulse, he walked to her, put one hand lightly on her waist, and
kissed her quickly on the cheek.

"Thank you," she said with a dimpled smile.

"You okay?" he asked.

"I—haven't the slightest idea anymore what *okay* is," she said. "But I'm hoping the end is in sight. Oh, Will Mertens called and said to stay put. Two FBI agents coming to talk to us."

Hud poured a glass of juice while he waited for his toast. "Then I'd better hurry. Got to buzz over to the general store, use their copy machine on the packet."

"Is that really necessary if they're going to pick it up this morning?"

"Absolutely. At this point, I'm not sure I trust any of them. You know, when it comes right down to it, even Will Mertens could be in the sheriff's pocket—doing a snow job on us."

"You really think—"

"No, but it's possible, he said. "This stuff's too important to give *anyone* the only copy."

"Have you figured out the safest place to keep David?" Kimberly asked.

"Yeah. The upstairs south bedroom," he said. Then he took a bite of toast.

"Isn't that kind of a dead-end trap?" she asked.

"Best we have without making him sleep in the woods again. There's a dormer window on each side of the room. We'll ask Gibby to take the window screens off and rig up a rope inside each window so David can choose the best side and make a quick exit down the roof if he has to. Gibby can put a sliding bolt lock on both doors to slow them down. With Gibby's forty-five and a fifty-yard head start out there, I don't think they've got anyone who can catch *that* kid. Is he still asleep?"

"Not still...*again,*" Kimberly said. "He was up at six-thirty raiding the fridge."

"I'll be back as soon as I can," Hud said, squeezing Kimberly's hand. "Keep your eyes open. If you see trouble coming, yell to David first. Then call Gibby."

As Hud pulled out of the drive in Kimberly's pickup truck, he glanced one last time over his shoulder. He hoped he was doing the right thing. Fifteen minutes later, he arrived at the general store at the intersection of the county road and State Highway 53.

He smiled and declined when the clerk, Evelyn, offered to show him how to operate the copier. As he worked, he had to move awkwardly a number of times to shield his papers from her curiosity. He finished within the hour, folded the fresh copies, and slipped them into a spare plastic bag he'd brought along. He gave Evelyn a friendly smile and a wave and set out for the resort. Along the way, he stopped for a moment to slip the original packet inside his shirt, wedged behind his belt.

When he pulled into the resort, he saw a white Grand Am parked at the workshop, so he pulled up next to the baithouse. He had just slammed the truck door when the loud, husky roar of a large radial aircraft engine startled him. Instinctively, he looked up in time to see a white de Havilland Beaver floatplane skimming the tree tops directly over him. When he heard the engine throttle back, Hud knew it meant a landing, and he took off at a trot for the hilltop above the dock. The pilot dropped the huge floatplane in for a picture-perfect landing, then turned around, taxied to the Bashers' new cove, and cut the engine. A bare-chested young man in shorts waded out to secure a cable to the aircraft, and it was winched backwards into the cove until it disappeared from sight. Wow, Hud thought. Not very fast, but that big ship can carry eight to ten people—or an awful lot of cargo. They're really going big time.

He found the others gathered in the lodge room when he returned. Two well-dressed, but ordinary-looking, middle-aged FBI men insisted that Hud read their identification rather than simply scan it when they were introduced. It surprised him that they didn't look like FBI agents, more like plain businessmen. But their polite though cool manner, as they explained their procedure, didn't surprise him. While Agent Watson questioned Sarah in the living room, Agent Milborn met with Gibby behind closed doors in the office. Then the exchange was made. Hud and Kimberly went next, leaving David till last.

Hud's session went as he'd expected. After giving Agent Watson his personal data, he told his story, everything he could remember from the time of Gibby's first phone call. The agent frequently interrupted with questions. Hud searched for reactions as he went on, but none came. While Watson treated Hud with respect, he displayed the emotions of a robot. Finally, as Hud wound down, the agent asked for the packet. Hud handed him the photocopied set. With a quick riffle through the papers, Watson replaced them in the plastic bag.

"I'm sorry, Mr. Bryant," he said. "These are photo copies."

"That's right," replied Hud.

"I'm afraid I'll need the originals also. They are...inside your shirt? Mr. Engstrom will talk about the papers he retrieved. These are not the papers he retrieved."

Surprised and embarrassed, Hud looked down. The bulge hardly showed. Then the full impact of Watson's statement hit him. Both sets? No way, he thought. He worked the packet out of his shirt, held it to one side, and motioned for an exchange. The man hesitated, then betrayed a hint of a smile as he handed the copies back to Hud.

"I understand," he said. "After what you say you've been through, mistrust is natural." He reached into an inner pocket and handed Hud a business card. "You'll get a receipt."

Hud, Kimberly, Gibby, and Sarah sat around a lodge room table comparing experiences while the two men interviewed David in the kitchen.

"Some nerve," spouted Sarah, "asking me to describe any identifying scars on my body. Some of us old-fashioned people don't like to talk about our mastectomies."

"And that Milborn looked at me like he didn't believe me," Kimberly said, "when I told him I didn't have any scars or markings."

Somehow, thought Hud, it doesn't surprise me that you look *that* good all over.

In an hour, David and the two men rejoined them in the lodge room.

"They want me to go with them," David said. "For my safety, they say. They'll pick up Julie and hide us somewhere. I asked them to pick up Julie, but give me until tomorrow. Do I *have* to go with them?" He looked to Hud for the answer.

Hud thought he read negative answers in both agents' eyes. "No," he said, "I don't think you *have* to go. But you *should* go. Without you, they have a case. With you, they have an open-and-shut case."

"I'm just...*not* going. That's *it*," David said. "Sorry. I went through all of this, came up here to find Dan. He's out there somewhere...but I didn't find him. I'd never sleep another night the rest of my life if I don't at least find Brother Theodore before I leave."

As the agents left, it was agreed that Deputy Mertens would pick up David the following morning and deliver him to them at the International Falls airport.

● ● ●

"Okay," said Hud. "There go the yard lights. Let's get loaded and on our way."

Clad in wetsuits with warm parkas over them, Hud and David slung their air tanks over their shoulders, picked up their fins and lights, and moved swiftly through the darkness down to the dock and Hud's boat. Hud had David sprawl out with the gear on the narrow deck space. Then he covered them with a heavy plastic tarp. After checking the hunting rifle in the side compartment, the pile of small styrofoam markers he'd made especially for the night's task, and the extra coil of nylon rope, he started the big Evinrude and eased away from the resort dock. Once they had cleared the bay, Gibby would turn the yard lights back on.

They reached the open water in minutes. Hud turned on his running lights but held back on the all-clear signal to David. Heading east, they soon passed the Basher harbor. The large, blue boat was gone. They cruised on down the lake side of the peninsula, past the first two clusters of rocky islands. He chopped the throttle, leaned over, and tapped the large bulge under the tarp. David clambered to his feet, folded up the tarp and wedged it into an out-of-the-way corner. Hud pointed to his contour map, clipped to the dash beneath a small light he had rigged.

"We're about here," he said softly. "And here's Sweet's Island, about three miles east."

David nodded and took the seat beside Hud. In no time, the boat was back up on plane and clipping smoothly through the small waves. As they approached the long, dark mass that was Sweet's Island, Hud turned off the running lights and signaled for David to keep his eyes open. The ever present reefs and rocks always threatened, but more than that, there had been no blue Basher boat in their harbor when he passed. At one o'clock in the morning, it meant one of two things. They were out on yet another of their burial missions, or upon hearing Hud's boat start up, they had scrambled out first. He really doubted the second possibility. They'd have to have been waiting for a signal from the bay side in order to clear the harbor before he got there. But, he thought, with the Bashers, you never know.

He eased off on the throttle and flipped the switch for the depth finder. Then he turned ninety degrees to the left and paralleled the shoreline until he reached the north tip of the island. Idling the engine to its slowest, he pressed the tilt button to raise the shaft until the propeller turned just below the surface. Then he angled in toward the rocky shore and stopped the engine as the bow bumped gently against a large rock. Scooting forward, he tossed the bow anchor up among the boulders and pulled the line tight.

"Here," he said softly as he stripped his parka off. "Take this and hang it on a branch where you can find it again."

David looked at him quizzically, then did as he was directed. When he climbed back aboard with the anchor, he pushed them from the rocks. Hud restarted the engine and backed them out into deeper water. Then he leaned over to explain.

"I was planning to dive with you, but we have to change our plans. The Bashers are out there somewhere. One of us has to stay on top. If you come up and I'm not here, you'll be damned glad that parka's hanging there. Now, let's get to work."

David motioned his answer with a thumb-and-forefinger circle and a nod. Hud set the boat slowly on a northerly course, studying the contour map but frequently glancing at the sonar.

"Excuse me, Hud," said David, "but do you really think that screen will show him?"

"Absolutely. If we pass within five feet on either side, he'll almost reach up and grab us. Now, I've got to concentrate on the map and the sonar. You keep a lookout for other boats."

The deep trough that Hud probed extended for about a half-mile to the north and reached eighty feet in depth at its center. From the map, Hud estimated the width of the area to be searched at about a hundred yards. That meant one pass if they were extremely lucky, or as many as thirty passes if they weren't. He wasn't sure they'd find Brother Theodore, but he was sure the sonar would tell him if they did. He started up the middle, the deepest, and with each succeeding pass he widened the search pattern to the two sides. There weren't many fish to be seen in such deep water, but those they passed over showed clearly.

They were headed south on the tenth pass when Hud suddenly jammed the control into reverse to stop the boat. Then he shifted to neutral.

"We've got somebody down there," he said, pointing to the screen. He glanced up and saw the young man swallow hard. While the image on the screen gave the impression of a sunken log floating lazily at sixty feet, Hud knew they'd found a body. The sonar had never shown him anything that resembled this.

He concentrated on holding the boat over the target while David donned his gear. Then, with Hud's powerful new lantern in hand, David gave Hud a thumbs-up sign and rolled backward off the gunwhale. In seconds, Hud picked up what resembled a small dolphin on the screen. It moved slowly from side to side. For a few seconds it moved directly away from the log. Oh, no, thought Hud. Wrong way. Look up at me, David. Then it reversed course and in a couple of minutes, the images merged. Good, he mused. He's got him.

Like a shock of electricity, the thought struck Hud that he'd been too focused on David's search. He looked up and quickly scanned the area, fully expecting to see the Bashers bearing down on him. But he saw no other boats. When he returned to the screen, David had disappeared. Hud moved to the stern and flipped down the small aluminum ladder. Soon, David broke the surface, climbed up part way, and stopped. He slipped his mask up on his forehead.

"It's him...it's awful...." David gagged, swallowed, then found some composure and said, "They used an aluminum cable. My knife won't cut it. Do you have something?"

"Come on up, David," Hud said. "We've done our job. He stays there for the authorities."

"Can't! Can't leave him there—like *that!*"

"Sshhh! Sound carries," Hud warned. "Look, David. He did this to nail those bums, to provide rock-solid evidence that will finish them. If we so much as touch him, it could be claimed that we've tampered with evidence. After all this, David...after his sacrifice...we'll do it *his* way."

"But—"

"Get your ass in this boat so we can get out of here!" Hud snapped. David blinked and reluctantly climbed aboard while Hud readied four of the small markers. He had deliberately made the styrofoam chunks smaller than customary fishermen's markers, only six inches long so that the Bashers might not spot them should they be out this way. Around each marker was wound ninety feet of monofilament line to which was attached a lead weight. Carefully, he threw one as far as he could in each of the four directions so that the target was framed on the north, south, east, and west. Then he eased back to Sweet's Island to retrieve the parka.

"Okay," he said, "we're out of here." When David had stowed his tanks and fins and taken the seat beside him, Hud eased the boat up on plane. He checked the lake again in every direction. So far, so good, he thought. He decided to work his way to the northwest in order to return home from a different direction.

His plan seemed to be working well. Even with speed reduced because of the threatening rocks in the darkness, each minute meant another quarter of a mile traveled away from the burial site. After five minutes, Hud relaxed and turned on his running lights. He was angling to the northwest in the narrow channel between Eagle Nest Island and the mainland, splitting his concentration between the limited view and his map, when he felt David grab his elbow and point back over the stern. Hud tensed. He knew what he'd see before he even turned.

A dark, unlighted hull angled into Hud's wake about half a mile behind.

"Damn!" Hud jammed the throttle ahead. "Get the rifle out, David, but don't use it unless it looks like we're dead meat!"

It seemed the Bashers had reduced the distance by half in the time it took to speak the words. He considered breaking for open water and home, but he knew the move would play to their advantage, their speed. Our advantage, he thought, what do we have? Maneuverability…and I might know the lake better. A glance over his shoulder told him they'd closed to about two hundred yards. He knew the sleek, fast cigarette boats, so common in Orange County marinas, but here, speed became relative. At full throttle, he could make but half the speed of the Bashers. For them, it would be like shooting the proverbial ducks in the barrel.

Crack! Something hit the left windshield, created a blinding spider web pattern in the plexiglass, then fell to the deck. David picked it up for Hud to see. An arrow from a crossbow.

"Get down on the deck, flat!" Hud shouted. "Don't give them *two* targets!" With the rifle in hand, David flopped on the deck facing aft. Hud's next glance measured the distance between the boats at about fifty yards.

Strangely, as if triggered by desperation, his mind began to work. Should he tell David to open fire? With the arrow and the cracked windshield, they had evidence of being attacked. But once the nighttime silence over the lake was shattered, the Bashers might respond with automatic weapons. Find a way to use your advantage, he said to himself. He looked quickly from right to left. They had reached the end of the narrow slot between Eagle Nest Island and the mainland. He could see open water on his left.

Thunk! A second arrow imbedded itself in the back of the left-side seat.

Another look at the map gave him exactly what he needed. A hundred yards ahead on the right lay the opening to Slatterman's Bay. But straight ahead, just past the opening, sat Turtle Rock, Hud's solution. Although The Turtle, as everyone called it, couldn't yet be seen in the darkness, he could visualize it well. It began close to shore with an immense hump that jutted six to eight feet above the water. The hump itself occupied an area equal to that of a sizeable house. But where the outer end of the protrusion disappeared, the rock extended out into the lake, a foot or two beneath the surface like a submerged shelf, for an additional fifty feet.

David rose up and peeked over the transom at their pursuers. "I think that's Brother Mark! He's third in command at the camp. Looks like three of the sergeants with him."

"Stay down, but be ready!" Hud shouted. "Going to try something. If I do it wrong, we'll go ass over teakettle!"

Hud began swerving from side to side as if to spoil their aim. The evasive tactics only served to shorten the gap even more. When the mouth of Slatterman's Bay appeared, he feinted hard to the right, as if to enter it. As he'd expected, the Bashers turned to follow, hoping to trap him in the dead-end bay. When they had fully committed to the right turn,

Hud spun the wheel violently to the left. The small boat responded quickly and headed for the submerged portion of Turtle Rock. Because of their superior speed, the Bashers had to reduce throttle and settle for a long, sweeping turn in order to follow.

As the high-powered boat slewed out of the corrective turn, it accelerated once more and quickly slid up on plane. Hud's last glance told him they were back in the chase and coming up fast off his rear left corner. He concentrated on the massive gray hump that lay ahead and to his right. He studied the distance carefully in order to make his next, most critical move, one he'd never attempt under normal conditions. If he misjudged...but there was no time to think about that.

Another arrow narrowly missed and lodged itself up in the bow.

"Okay...now!" he said aloud. "Hang on, David!" He pressed the button to bring the engine up on tilt, even while it still ran at full speed. The boat seemed to hang suspended for a moment. Then it slowed gradually and settled smoothly a little lower in the water. He hoped the slowing was gradual enough that the Bashers would take a second or two to react. When he heard his propeller break the surface, he cut the throttle.

Hud felt the firm but harmless bump of the keel against the rock below. It told him he had done his part well. He looked back to see the speeding monster as it roared out of the bay. Then it swerved right in a futile attempt to realign with him. It hit the submerged shelf with a loud *Thump!* The bow tilted upward forty-five degrees, and the sleek craft became airborne. Hud marveled as it sailed silently past on his left, ten feet above him. It seemed like the streamlined hull was meant to fly.

For a moment, he feared it flew so naturally it would glide to a graceful landing and his plan would have backfired. But at the peak of its flight, the huge boat suddenly rolled over, stalled, and dropped. It smashed upside-down with a sickening *Crunch* on the flat expanse of hidden rock, crushing its occupants beneath it.

Using his emergency paddles, Hud and David surveyed the area around the split and twisted fiber glass hull, looking for survivors. They shined their powerful lantern in an ever-widening circle and saw nothing but debris. After a half-hour search, they paddled clear of the rock and prepared for the trip back. Hud glanced over at David as he eased the throttle ahead. A couple of tears wound their way down the young man's cheeks.

"You okay?" Hud asked.

"No...problem," David replied. "I'm just wondering if I'm a bad person for feeling so good about the way this turned out."

"Just consider the alternative."

Chapter 29

Brother Vance rolled over yet again. He found what seemed to be a comfortable position, willed his body to relax, and tried once more for sleep. But thoughts of the last days of Saigon had clamped onto his mind. The cold, steely fingers of horrendous memories held firm, squeezing a stream of fear through veins that had seldom known fear. As Exec to Colonel Jeranko, his place on an evacuation helicopter was assured. But escape, the theme of the day, had to be postponed. Before he could leave, he had vital tasks to expedite. For hours, he forced his Jeep slowly through the jammed, chaotic pedestrian traffic, searching out his business connections. From some, he extracted large sums of money owed. Others forced him to settle for partial payment. Several he never found.

"Son of a bitch," he mumbled, rising to a sitting position on the edge of his bed. He checked his watch. Five o'clock. It had been hours since Brother Mark's call from out on the lake. The boat had not returned, and there had been no follow-up calls. "Where in the hell is he?" he asked aloud. He told himself they'd had mechanical problems, but something in him denied that answer. Captured? Impossible, he thought. No one on the lake with the equipment, skill, and strength to capture Brother Mark.

But the mystery pointed up the fact that what had begun as mere challenges had mushroomed into problems and were threatening now to fuse themselves into a gigantic bomb that could soon explode in their faces. Although the present circumstances were unlike those in Saigon, the feeling in his gut was the same. The sheriff they had bought now faced an election he could lose. The properties they needed had become untouchable. A body never to be found had drifted ashore. A dangerous witness hovered somewhere unseen, like a toxic cloud that could descend at any moment. And despite his efforts, he'd been unable to locate and neutralize the cloud. This massive accumulation could lead to the exposure of the camp. That, in turn, could bring down the church and businesses in Minneapolis.

Added to all that, he thought, my trusted lieutenant and three of his sergeants are missing. This could be my final warning. Should I wait to see if they get back? If only I'd purchased that second boat. We can't even mount a search with only canoes.

Suddenly, Brother Vance shifted back to the aggressive mode that had gotten him into and out of trouble most of his life. He'd weighed the negatives. Now it was time to work with positives. Snatching up the bedside phone, he dialed Father Jeranko's secure number.

"I apologize for the early call," Vance said. Quickly, he recited the problems. Then he added his report on Brother Mark and the sergeants. "I'll have preparations for evacuation options completed by midmorning. It's your call, Sir."

"A thorough analysis," said Father Jeranko. "I'll have time to free up additional cash. And I'll stop further shipments from the Coast until this all shakes out. Be sure you have the de Havilland all gassed and ready. You know where to meet me. Now, Brother…things are touch-and-go at the moment, but I'm not ready to pull the plug. However, should you uncover even *one more* major problem, leave a message for me and make your move. Take the sergeants out with you and wait up at Station Two for a few days while we monitor the situation. Stay sharp, but cool, my Old Friend. We've been here before, and we always come out all right."

"Thank you. I—have one adjustment I'd like to make in the plan," said Vance. "It will give us added security for our departure...and it *could* get Corporal David for us." He outlined his proposal briefly, heard his mentor's approval, and hung up the phone.

After a solitary breakfast in the plush executive dining room, Brother Vance called the sergeants in for a meeting. He opened the session and realized at once the magnitude of the gap left by the four missing men, Brother Mark and his three best sergeants. Although his evacuation plan had been assembled with extreme care, it would be difficult to carry out with only the five sergeants available. He assigned the leaderless companies to three of the sergeants. After several minutes spent reviewing his latest set of standing orders, he set up his closing.

"In conclusion, I don't have to remind you that none of us in this room can afford to be apprehended by the authorities," he said. "We've drilled on the procedures for evacuation of our command group. You all know your responsibilities under each code. For now, we're still on Code Yellow. This is your chance to finish preparations. But you must not, I repeat, *must not* do anything to alarm your men while we're under Yellow. If we go Blue, you turn over command to your corporals and brief them on the resistance they are to offer. Explain that you and I may be away for a while on a very important mission, but we will maintain contact with them through the communications center. When I determine Code Red, you slip away and meet me here—armed." Vance paused to survey the small group. "Any questions?" He knew there would be none. "Very well. Dismissed. Oh, Sergeant Jared, stay a minute, will you?"

When the others had left, Brother Vance handed Sergeant Jared a single page of instructions. The sergeant quickly scanned the page, looked up at Brother Vance, and smiled.

"This explains your assignment, who you are, and what you are to accomplish," explained Vance. "Can you handle it?"

"Certainly, Sir," the eager sergeant replied. "When?"

"As soon as you're ready. Use the outer office. Report the outcome at once. Thank you, Sergeant."

Sergeant Jared left, and Brother Vance relaxed in his thick leather chair next to the window. My biggest failure, he thought as he gazed at the opposite shoreline from the park to the Gundersons and finally to the resort. Just wasn't to be. As though flipping a switch, he transferred the failure to his mental recycle bin. He had learned long before to concentrate only on successes, to spend his energy on the future and waste none on the past. The nearby telephone interrupted his thoughts.

"Brother Vance," the familiar voice said, "something's up. Two FBI men nosing around here yesterday, asking my people a lot of questions. And I think they've been out in your neighborhood, too."

"And what did you say to them, Sheriff Stein?" Vance asked calmly.

"Nothing!" Stein's voice rattled on in high-pitched panic. "They brushed me off, wouldn't even talk to me. Talked to about everyone else, though. You know what that means? They're coming down on us. You…me…all of us!"

"Relax, Sheriff," Vance said. He knew he'd have to handle the call very carefully. The sheriff's line could already have a tap on it.

"*Relax?* Is that what *you're* doing?" Stein demanded.

"Brother Stein," Vance said, "often, when we are most upset, it is about nothing, nothing at all. But when everything around you seems to be going sour, it is time for a thorough cleansing. A cleansing of yourself, your soul, and everything around you might be in order. Do you understand? I shall pray for you, Brother Stein, while you attend to your…*cleansing.*"

Brother Vance hung up the phone, stood, and stared once more out the window. But he didn't see the golden rays of the morning sun illuminating the many shades of green in the forests or the blue waters of the bay. He saw millions of people, rich and poor, regal and ragged, clogging the streets that would take him from the worst section of Saigon to the helicopters at the base. He made things work out that time. He had made things work out since. And he would make things work out once more.

Sergeant Jared knocked at the door, then stepped inside. "I'm—I'm sorry, Sir. I think I did a good job…but Bryant didn't buy it."

"Did he believe it was Dick Orin, the candidate for sheriff, calling him?" Vance asked.

"Oh, Bryant thought he was talking to this Orin guy all right," the sergeant said. "He said he'd be glad to meet with me, but not today, and not until the Feds have—he called us 'Bashers,' Sir. He said, 'not until the Feds have those Bashers bottled up tight. 'Til then, we're on full alert, with loaded weapons.'"

Damn it, thought Brother Vance. I really thought he'd bite. "Okay, Sergeant Jared. Good job. On your way out, switch us to Code Blue."

"Yes, Sir. Code Blue." The sergeant wheeled and disappeared through the outer office.

Vance checked his watch. Ten o'clock. Although Code Red was now a certainty, he'd hold off until one-thirty. Meanwhile, he'd have to devise another plan for Bryant. If my enemy is sitting over there with his finger on a hair-pin trigger….Yes, thought Vance, I can use that.

• • •

"Will, this is Hud Bryant."

"Bryant…it's three o'clock," Deputy Mertens snapped over the phone. "Do you ever *sleep* between midnight and six a.m.?"

"You said to call you," Hud replied, bristling a little at the reception. "Okay, okay. What's up?"

"We found Brother Theodore, right where they said they'd drop him," Hud said. "We didn't touch, only put out markers, four small white ones."

"Whew!" said Mertens. "I shouldn't be happy about it, but since he was already dead, I guess I am. That deep slot off the north end of Sweet's?"

"Right. About sixty feet of water." Hud paused. "Then, something else happened that you need to know about."

"Shoot. It's got to be relaxing after what you just told me."

Hud quickly explained the episode with the Basher boat. "I didn't do a thing to them, I swear," he added. "I've got a cracked windshield, three crossbow arrows they shot at us, and a witness. But, for some reason, they just crashed into Turtle Rock going wide open."

"Je—sus!" The line went silent. Then Deputy Mertens came back on, "Je—sus, Bryant, you sure have a knack for getting things done, don't you? Okay, okay…my sleep is over with, probably for the next week. I'll send the boat team and divers right away. Is Engstrom okay?"

"Yeah, he's fine," Hud said.

"Listen," said Mertens, "after what you just told me, we'd better get him out of there. I'll be there at five to pick him up. Are all your alarms still hot?"

"Yeah?"

"Keep them hot. Don't know yet, but I'm guessing we'll be putting up a roadblock some time today. Got to keep all those goons at home until the high-powered fed squads can get here. Oh, thought you'd enjoy this…with the FBI hanging around, Stein's coming unglued."

Hud relayed the input from Will Mertens to David and Kimberly. "Now, Guys, we've got time for an hour's nap before Mertens gets here." He stretched out in one of the old living room recliners. "Go 'way," he said with a curt wave. It seemed he'd barely closed his eyes when he felt a hand on his shoulder.

"Hud…Hud…Will Mertens is here," Kimberly said. He looked up into her warm blue eyes and put his hand on hers for a moment. She smiled down at him. "He's out in the lodge room. I knew you'd want to see David before he goes."

"Oh, yeah—David," Hud said. He lowered the leg extension of the chair and popped up.

Will Mertens and David were seated on stools in the lodge room, chatting over coffee when Hud entered. A sudden rush of emotions blind-sided him when he saw the quiet, slender young man sitting there, wearing Hud's own tan coat. He'd known David less than three days, but he felt he was bidding goodbye to a younger brother.

"Hud, you get *me* up, then *you* go back to sleep!" said Will Mertens with a laugh. "Glad I got *you* up this time. We have to hit the road right away." He set his cup down, stood, and started for the back door.

"Sure you've got everything you need, David?" asked Kimberly. "I've still got more of Sarah's oatmeal cookies you could take with you."

"Thanks, Kimberly, but I'm fine." David stood and smiled at Kimberly for a moment. Then he turned to Hud. "You sure you don't mind losing these clothes? I'll get them back to—"

"Don't give it a thought," Hud cut in. As he reached to shake hands with David, the swirling emotions ballooned and he realized he was close to tears. He hugged David, then gave him a slap on the back and a gentle push toward the back door. As they walked, Hud said, "But I do want you to listen to me…Little Brother. And I'm very serious about this. When they have you and your Julie hidden away for your second honeymoon, you'll undoubtedly spend some time discussing your future together. I want you, both of you, on my team. Don't yet know where or what, but I expect first chance to hire you. Have I got it?"

At Mertens' direction, David climbed into the back seat of the patrol four-by-four. "You've got it!" he said with a broad smile and a high-five gesture. "And thanks for all *your* help."

Hud slammed the door shut, and as Deputy Mertens headed out, David waved one more time. Then he dropped to the floor and disappeared from sight. Hud blinked back tears and turned away from Kimberly.

"Thank you," Kimberly said, taking his arm and turning him back toward her.

"Thank me?" Hud asked. The look in her eyes combined with her satin voice to warm him, but the words confused him.

She stretched up and kissed him lightly on the lips. "Thank you...for showing me something that I wasn't sure was there." She turned and led the way back inside. "Now, I don't know how *you* keep going, but I need some sleep—" She looked back with a mischievous grin. "Note, I said 'sleep.' Should we neuter that telephone?"

"Right," he replied, then paused. "No, I guess we can't do that. Too much going on."

After checking the locks, Hud settled once more in the recliner. He knew he'd sleep, but he also knew that the comfort of a bed might knock him out for a week. The next time he awakened, it was ten o'clock, and Kimberly was calling him to the phone. It was Dick Orin, the candidate for sheriff. He proposed a meeting, but Hud quickly rejected the idea, hung up, and sank back into the recliner.

He fell quickly back into a deep sleep. After some time, he heard a voice, a soft, sensuous, seductive voice. It was Kimberly calling from her bedroom.

"Hud? Hud? Come in here and sleep with me."

He struggled to get up from the chair, but his body felt paralyzed. She called again. Once more he tried and failed. Still, she kept calling. But his body simply would not respond to his commands. Gradually the love that he felt stirring within him faded to frustration. When the caustic ring of the alarm clock drowned out Kimberly's voice, the frustration turned to molten anger. He awakened suddenly and bolted from the chair. Locating the clock by sound, he swiped at the vicious intruder, recognizing, as his fingers closed around it, that he held the telephone.

Only the voice that shouted from the tiny speaker kept him from throwing the device at the opposite wall.

"Hud!" Gibby's voice said. "Hud, are you there? Hud? Hud!"

"Huh? Oh, Gibby?" he managed.

"For Christ's sake, Hud, wake up!" the belligerent voice shouted. "I'm at your place. We got Bashers coming at us from the park side! Must be a bunch of 'em. The alarms are all squealing like hell. I need help!"

Chapter 30

"Lock up!" Hud shouted as he grabbed his shotgun and ran out the back door. "And call Sarah—might be Gibby hasn't had a chance!" He cut hard around the baithouse and headed down the crushed rock drive toward the path through the woods to Gibby's, pushing himself as fast as the heavy, unbalancing weapon would allow.

The alarms grew louder. It seemed the adrenalin ran through him in direct proportion to the volume of the shreaking system. He caught a glimpse of the park shoreline as he ran. The ends of two dark green canoes jutted out slightly from behind a clump of pines, suggesting that he and Gibby faced at least four of the Bashers. Could be more canoes I can't see, he thought as he hurtled into the narrow, shaded pathway to Gibby's. None of the alarms in the center portion of woods between the resort and Gibby's had sounded yet. At least that was a good sign.

Breathing had become a struggle when he broke into the clearing and ran past the Gundersons' house. Sarah stood at the kitchen window with her .410 shotgun. He drew deep within himself for a final burst of speed as he crossed the open yard to his cottage. In one last scan of the whistling and screaming woods, he saw nothing of the enemy. He barged into the kitchen and nearly collided with Gibby.

"Have you seen any of them?" Hud asked breathlessly.

"Yeah, every now and then, one pokes his head up, then disappears," Gibby replied.

"Always same place, same guy?"

"Can't tell. With them tough guy hats they wear, all look the same," Gibby said, "but they're in different places. Hud, them goddamned alarms are driving me crazy."

"Does Sarah know the breaker box?" Hud asked.

"'Course she does."

"Then call her and tell her to shut the two alarm circuits down so we can hear what's going on out there," Hud said. Gibby responded immediately, and within a minute a welcome silence caressed the area.

"Come on, Gib," Hud said. "Now that we've got two of us, let's get outside. I'll go for that big red pine on the lake side, and you take the one right outside the kitchen door. We can see each other, have a better chance to figure out what *they're* up to."

When Gibby had reached the cover of his tree, Hud ducked out and ran around the protected side of the cottage to the big pine. He checked Gibby. His old, bearded friend seemed secure behind the red pine. For several minutes, not a sound or sign of a movement came from the woods. The increasing tension wore at Hud, but he told himself there was no choice but to wait out the Bashers' next move. When he glanced again at Gibby, his older friend was gesturing frantically to an area beneath a giant oak tree.

The limited light under the heavy overcast sky made Hud strain to see what Gibby was pointing at in the brush beneath the large tree. Nothing there. Then he caught a movement, a fleeting glimpse of a head that quickly disappeared. About thirty yards to the right, he saw another for only an instant. No doubt about it. They both wore the caps of the Bashers. Several minutes later, a third Basher, off to the left of the first, raised his head slowly. He seemed to scan the clearing for a few seconds, then he, too, faded into the underbrush. The sightings continued at one- to three- minute intervals.

After fifteen minutes, Hud had seen four different Bashers, but no more. What the hell are they doing? he wondered. This is turning into a case of we're watching you watch us.

He looked over again at Gibby who was pointing alternately to his weapon, then the Bashers, then repeating the pattern. Clearly, he was ready to shoot at the next appearance. Maybe not such a bad idea, thought Hud. They're far enough away that our shotgun patterns will spread out. Not apt to kill anyone, but might sting them good and get them started for home. But before he started shooting at real people, Hud wanted to figure out what their intentions were. He shook a negative sign to Gibby, then fell to guessing at the Bashers' objective.

A deep rumble of thunder interrupted his thoughts. A low, tumbling mass of ominous dark gray clouds approached the bay from the west. The gentle breeze suddenly became a light wind. Oh, oh, Hud thought, that's not good. A jagged, crackling lightning bolt seared its way to earth far to the west. He counted the seconds, waiting for the accompanying thunder. The interval between sight and sound told him the lightning was still ten miles off.

In rapid succession, three heads popped up in still different places, then just as quickly melted back into the cover. Weird, he thought, almost like they're toying with us. On the tail of the next lightning bolt, the explanation slammed home to Hud. "They are—they're just baiting us!" he said aloud. "It's the resort—Kimberly!" He jumped up, charged recklessly over to Gibby's tree, and hurriedly explained his theory.

"Come on, Gib," he said. "Let's push 'em back. I've got to get back to Kimberly!"

"That mean I can shoot 'em?"

"Let's each put a couple into the brush and a couple in the air," Hud said. "Ought to make believers out of them." Gibby followed Hud's example as he chambered a shell. As one, they stood and began walking toward the woods, alternately firing and sliding the pump action as fast as they could. Bam! Click-click. *Bam!* Click-click. *Bam! Bam!* Click-click. Click-click. *Bam! Bam!* When they had each fired four rounds, they stopped and listened. Obviously in retreat, the Bashers crashed noisily through the underbrush, rushing away from Hud and Gibby toward the park.

"Get to the house and call Kimberly," said Hud as he took off on the run. "I'm on my way."

He stretched his strides to the maximum, easing off only slightly when he reached the unstable footing of the path through the woods. Midway to the resort, his legs began to feel rubbery, but he forced himself to keep up the pace. He broke into the open at the resort boundary, and the sight of Kimberly's lodge seemed to pump new strength into his legs. Through the last three hundred yards, he glanced from side to side, down at the dock, and ahead to what he could see of the woods to the north. No sign of Bashers in that area, and no alarms sounding. He hoped that meant he was in time.

As he rounded the baithouse, he groped in a pocket for his key to the back door. But upon reaching the door, he quickly withdrew his hand and flipped off the safety on the shotgun. The heavy wooden door was open. The splintered door jam told the story. Hud quietly ducked inside and up the four steps. He paused to listen, his Browning shotgun ready. Hearing nothing, he darted into the office. He expected a Basher to pop into view firing at him. With limited space for movement and with doorways to be checked out, his cumbersome shotgun felt like a Howitzer cannon.

Hud checked the lodge room, then the kitchen. With each movement deeper into the house, he exercised less and less caution. By the time he'd cleared the living room and both downstairs bedrooms, his frenzied search had become one of reckless abandon. He rushed on, checking the closets, bathroom, upstairs bedrooms and closets, and finally the basement.

Okay, he told himself, slow down, get your breath, and think. Take a good look around. He rechecked the lodge room. Nothing unusual there. The office? No. The kitchen—yes. There beside the toaster lay Kimberly's .38 revolver. A sniff of the barrel and a check of the cylinder told him no shots had been fired. Obviously, Kimberly never got a chance to use it.

"Damned Dummy, Bryant," he mumbled. "They faked you out with one of the oldest, worn out tricks right out of a B-western. And you, Stupid, you fell for it." When he considered what might happen to Kimberly because of his ineptitude, he began to choke up. But then a raging anger swelled within him, and as it grew, it displaced his guilt. Come on, Hud, he thought. Push the emotions aside. You can't stand here and cry *or* swear. You've got to think. Why take Kimberly? Revenge, rape, ransom? The potential of forcing her to sign over the property? All were possibilities, but somehow he didn't believe the reason was among them.

He leaned the gun against the counter and ran a glass of water. Guzzling the cool liquid, he gazed out the window. The clouds had continued to darken, and they had settled even lower over the bay. Then he silently scolded himself for standing there at a time like this, observing the weather like a pilot. But he couldn't resist looking over toward the cove that hid the Basher floatplane.

"That's it!" he said. "A hostage for their getaway." He slammed the glass to the countertop, spilling water over the formica. Grabbing his Browning, he ran for the back door. As he turned toward the bay, he heard the unmistakable, throaty roar of a cold radial aircraft engine starting up. It spit, sputtered, and coughed before finally catching and settling down to a fast idle. No, he thought. No—no—no!

He sprinted over the hill, listening with a pilot's ear to the warm-up of the de Havilland engine. Half running and half stumbling down the hill, he made it to the dock and jumped into the first resort boat. He laid the shotgun across two bench seats, spanning the space between them. As he turned to start the little fifteen horsepower Evinrude outboard, the huge Pratt and Whitney radial engine revved up, its large, three-bladed propeller splatting against the air. A look over his shoulder confirmed his fears. The white monster eased out of the cove.

Hud turned his attention to his tiny blue engine. On the second pull, it started. He scrambled over the bench seats to the bow, unhooked the bungy cord bowline, and turned to start back. On impulse, he grabbed the two-pronged bow anchor and carried it back with him. Anything he could possibly need must be close at hand. He checked the de Havilland Beaver. Surprisingly, it had turned and was taxiing toward the resort. Hud, the pilot, read the move. He's loaded and wants the longest take-off run he can get. Twin lightning bolts, one seconds behind the other, flashed their irregular paths to earth. Closer, he thought.

When he released the stern line and pulled away from the dock, the floatplane had turned to line up for its take-off. Even before completing the turn, the pilot opened the throttle and raised the elevator. Hud knew it was then or never. He twisted the throttle wide open. His little engine seemed mute beneath the roar of the four-hundred-fifty horsepower radial powerplant. But he felt the frequency of the engine vibrations increase, and the light aluminum boat quickly swept up on plane. He angled toward the Beaver's path to shorten the distance. But as he closed in from the left, the propwash, laden with water from the lake surface, caught Hud's bow and pitched it violently to his right. His sixteen-foot boat felt like a tiny kite in a tornado. Sharp needles of water stung his face.

He knew it was too late to try to pass the aircraft and block its take-off from the front. His only chance was to catch the Beaver from behind and off to one side, just out of the worst of the blast. Moving off to the aircraft's right, he found he still had a slight advantage in speed. But it would only hold for seconds. He'd have just one try at the Beaver. The heavy shotgun would be unmanageable with only one hand and much too dangerous with Kimberly in the plane. But it would be ready if he succeeded in stopping them.

Hud gained on the Beaver until he was parallel with its right side pontoon. He marveled at the size of the massive, boatlike structures on which the plane floated. Quickly, he tossed his two-pronged anchor over the top of the float and watched it disappear beneath the surface. Then he dropped back and the yellow nylon anchor rope began to play out. But the snakelike rope caught on the shotgun and, before he could react, whipped it over the gunwhale and into the lake.

He had no chance to save the weapon, no time to mourn its loss, and no idea how he'd manage without it. But the plane had to be stopped. As the floats rose higher in the water, the Beaver gained speed rapidly. The rope grew taut, and Hud dropped back to pull the anchor up. If it caught on the strut connecting the float to the plane's fuselage, he'd have himself a tail-hooked Beaver. If the anchor slipped off....

Suddenly, the anchor surfaced and one of the prongs hooked itself on the strut. Hud throttled down, shifted to reverse, then opened up again. His stern swiveled from side to side unpredictably, but the plane reacted immediately to the additional drag. The giant adversary slowed and tilted to the right. As the opposite float lifted up and out of the water, he feared his maneuver would backfire. If the right wingtip caught the water, the plane would cartwheel and probably land upside down, with Kimberly trapped inside.

The pilot countered the move with his ailerons, however, and the left float settled back into the water. When the engine slowed to an idle, Hud's drag on the right side began to turn the aircraft to the right toward the shore. He seized the opportunity. Quickly slipping his boat between the floats, he ducked under the tail and eased up to the entangled strut. He wrapped the anchor around the strut twice and dropped it back into the water. Got 'em, he thought. No way they can slip loose now. But he felt like an old-time whaler who had just buried his harpoon in an angry leviathan, committing himself to a rough ride, either to victory or to death. Having stopped them, he needed an ace up his sleeve, but what? His shotgun lay at the bottom of the bay. And within seconds, one or more of them would be coming down that short ladder to the float.

Hud looked about for a miracle. Across the bay, the two Basher canoes were headed his way. Sitting there, hunched over under the belly of the large plane, with the wind from the large, idling propeller in his face, he felt he'd really messed things up for Kimberly. To get her away from the Bashers, he needed something, a threat of some kind, from which to negotiate.

Ahead, through the blur of the turning propeller, he saw another bolt of lightning crackling and straining to reach the lake just beyond the bay. That's it! There's my ace, he thought. If I stick the bow of the boat into that prop, they're dead in the water. Even one little ding will knock that baby so far out of balance, it'll shake the engine right off its mounts. Having found the best bargaining chip available, he searched his frantic mind for a follow-up. Only the realization that the Bashers would have to be careful using their weapons so close to the vulnerable airplane and its floats got through his frantic thinking process.

A brown combat boot appeared on the top rung of the ladder. Then its mate followed. He saw camouflage fatigue trouser legs and picked up an oar. The first hand that appeared held an Uzi-like automatic weapon. Hud chose an opening between the rungs of the ladder, balanced himself, and tightened his two-handed grip on the oar. When the Basher's crotch was framed by the ladder opening, Hud rammed the oar handle at his target as hard as he could.

The man grunted in pain and flew backward, flailing his arms as he splashed into the water. His weapon popped loose and disappeared into the bay. Thrashing his way back to the float, the young warrior threw both arms over it and held on, his face a grotesque mask of pain. Hud grabbed the ladder and pulled his boat closer. As the Basher gasped hard for air, Hud leaned across the float, put a hand on the man's head, and pushed him under water. After two repetitions, the pain in his victim's eyes became panic. Hud released his grip and put his face down close to the freckled face of the young Basher.

"Now, you son of a bitch!" he shouted over the noise of the idling engine. "You *listen* and you listen *good!* Can you hear me?"

The man nodded his red crewcut.

"You get up there just as damned fast as you can. You tell them this. Send Kimberly Farber down here, and I let you take off. But if you show any weapons, or hurt her, or try anything I don't like, I stick the bow of my boat in your prop. Got it?" He cuffed the man on the side of the head. "Got it?"

"Y-yeah," the Basher gasped. "Got it."

Hud moved back under the fuselage and eased the boat ahead until the bow came within two feet of the whistling blades. He watched the dripping Basher struggle up onto the float, then scramble up the ladder. Hud sat there grasping a strut to hold the boat where he wanted it. The strange amalgamation of aircraft and boat had gradually turned to where it pointed back toward the resort dock. He tried to predict Brother Vance's reaction. Certainly their leader had to understand that without a propeller his aircraft was useless.

The Bashers in the canoes had passed the midpoint in the bay and were paddling swiftly toward the plane. Then Hud spotted two new elements in the battle. His own Lund raced out from shore toward the Basher canoes. It was Gibby. And trailing slowly in Gibby's wake came the Gundersons' boat with Sarah at the wheel. In a single, close pass, Gibby swamped both canoes, rolling them upside down. Then he cruised out toward the center of the bay and settled, as if to watch and wait. Hud could see a wall of rain out on the main lake, and the flashes in the rumbling clouds overhead made him uneasy. Not the time to be out on the water in anything metal, he thought. He yelled upward for the Bashers to hurry, but he doubted they'd heard him.

He felt the Beaver rock slightly, a sign of movement above. Then, the two most beautiful, white sneakers he could ever hope to see cautiously made their way down the ladder, followed by perfectly filled blue jeans. Sliding the boat back and close to the float, he watched for her hands to appear. He'd been afraid they might be tied, an effort to make his escape more difficult. But Kimberly's hands worked their way down the ladder separately. She stepped aft of the ladder and crouched to see Hud.

"Come on, quick!" he shouted, taking her hand and almost jerking her down into the boat. Her strained face and her silence told him how deep the fear ran. "Get down, just ahead of that seat there, down on the floor, way down." Kimberly scampered over the bench and huddled up in a ball in the bottom of the boat. As Hud reached for his knife to cut the anchor rope, the pilot seemed to anticipate his freedom. The large radial engine revved up to a deafening roar, and the cascade of stinging water needles pelted Hud mercilessly as he slashed at the rope.

When the last strand parted, the powerful propwash flushed the light aluminum boat from between the monster's legs, turning it sideways and nearly rolling it over. Hud twisted the throttle wide open to counteract the force and regain control of the boat. He knew it was time to face the last part of the test—getting away from the Bashers' automatic weapons. They could open the doors and have a wide range of fire to the rear on both sides—not the place to be. But if he could zig-zag and make them miss for a few seconds, the plane's speed would soon take them out of range. He pulled the steering tiller hard to him, putting the boat into a sharp left turn toward the resort.

But as he broke out from behind the aircraft into the danger zone, he saw the door on the left side open part way. A figure wedged himself into the opening and raised a weapon toward the fleeing boat. Unable to hear the automatic weapon firing, Hud was startled to see the surface of the water just behind him erupt in a wide pattern of explosive, puffy pockmarks. He began another sharp cut to his left to get directly behind the Beaver, but before the boat could react, the threatening pattern swept in and enveloped them.

Hud had never been on the receiving end of weapons fire. The deadly barrage set up a cacophony unlike anything he'd ever heard. The shells penetrated the water with a *ploonk*, the thin aluminum hull with a *teetch*, and the heavy wooden transom with a *thud*. Others glanced off the steel engine with a *clink*. But he didn't hear the hammerlike blows to his exposed left shoulder and then to his left thigh. And he didn't hear the tiny engine quit.

The firing stopped. The aircraft doors closed as the plane roared away and headed toward the slot between the peninsula and Black Rock.

"Kimberly!" he shouted, expecting the worst as he turned to her. "You all right?"

"I'm fine," said the soft but commanding voice from close beside his ear. "But you sure aren't. Here," she said, tugging at him, "let's get you off that seat and down in the boat before you fall in the lake. You're really bleeding—bad. I can row us in the rest of the way."

"Wait," said Hud. "Look...at that!" He tried to point, but his arm wouldn't raise up.

The powerful Beaver lifted slowly from the water. But from a perpendicular angle to its left, came a blue and silver Lund boat racing at high speed. The aircraft had gained perhaps three feet of altitude when aluminum met aluminum. The Lund clipped the bottom of the left float, then rolled over and lay there, a strange, rounded shape rocking in the waves.

"Gibby!" Hud shouted. "Gibby!" Kimberly grasped him under the arms as he sank down to the floor of the boat. "What'd you do that for, Gib? You stubborn old Norsky. You didn't have to do that...didn't have to...."

Despite the rain that had begun, Hud felt dark, swirling fog closing in. He strained to focus once more on the de Havilland Beaver. It faltered, then struggled for altitude, dragging a dangling float that clipped the tops of the waves, sending a spray with each contact. Finally breaking free of the lake, it climbed slowly, banking right to miss Black Rock. The left float hung awkwardly, trailing in the slipstream.

"Looks like a pterodactyl with a broken leg," Hud said weakly. "Glad I don't have…to land…that…." The dark fog seemed to wash over him, blurring his vision. As the lumbering aircraft passed Black Rock, he thought he saw the float break loose and fall to the water. Then, through a long tunnel, he heard a distant voice.

"Looks more like a *one-legged* pterodactyl."

Chapter 31

Something within Hud tried to tell him it was a dream. But the terror he felt as he hurtled toward the churning, boiling black clouds ahead could not be denied, for the threatening wall stretched higher and higher. He pulled back on the control, but nothing happened. My God, he thought, as he searched for the upper limits of the awesome monsters. They must go up to forty-thousand feet, and I can't gain any altitude. Never get over the top! He spun the large wheel to turn back, but midway through his turn, the anchor flipped over the side. Damn! he thought. Every time I turn, that thing falls out. He lowered his flaps to slow the craft, then grabbed the yellow nylon rope and pulled. A sharp pain pierced his left shoulder. The anchor wouldn't budge—not an inch—no matter how hard he strained.

He found himself locked into a tight orbit around the taut rope, spinning faster and faster, around and around. With each rotation, he lost altitude. "Cut the rope!" he shouted. "Cut the rope!" He whipped his knife from its sheath and reached to cut the rope. But the knife had no blade. He snatched the radio microphone from its ceiling hook. "Mayday! Mayday!" he called. "Archer-four-seven-four-three-Charlie—Mayday!"

Finally, the ugly, dark clouds began to fade and the sun broke through, but its rays seemed filtered by a thick, white fog. Something grabbed his hand. He flinched, but the adversary gripped tighter. "Let go! Let go!" he shouted. The grip held firm. If only he could see better, he could fight it off. He forced his eyes to open wider.

"Welcome back. You've had a tough trip."

When he looked up at Kimberly's face, he knew the sun had truly come out. She smiled and her blue eyes seemed to reflect something beyond concern. She squeezed his hand again and simply gazed at him. He lay there for a time, absorbing the strange, new magic that was accompanied by a swelling deep within his chest. The feeling was too good to be trusted.

"I—I've had some bad, bad head trips," he said, trying to lift his left hand to point. "Ouch!" The pain in his shoulder felt like a jab by a red-hot spike.

"Uh-uh," she said, grabbing his hand. "Not *that* one."

"Is this—is this another dream?"

"*You* decide," she said, bending over and kissing him.

The kiss was neither a perfunctory peck nor a passionate union, but rather a thrilling infusion of pure love. Hud questioned the feeling only briefly, then let the euphoria envelope him. When Kimberly finally broke away, she hovered over him, stroking his head and maintaining the bond with her eyes. He wanted to reach up and pull her to him. But the pain held one arm down, and the other, he discovered, was encumbered by intravenous tubing. Hud knew he was back in the real world. He rolled his eyes, then looked about the room.

"Falls hospital?" he asked.

She nodded. "You were in deep shock—lost a lot of blood—soaked up most of two bath towels on the way in. Didn't think there was time to wait for an ambulance, so we bundled you into the old, mean machine. You know that pile of junk will still do ninety?"

Hud managed a smile. "We?" he asked.

"Gibby and Sarah," Kimberly replied. "Sarah fished him out of the lake about the time we got to shore."

"Gibby's—Gibby's alive? He's okay? Really?" he asked.

"Oh, he's fine...had a big goose egg on his forehead," she replied. "He said he jumped a little late, and the boat hit him when it went over. Sarah insisted they check him over here. They didn't find anything else."

Hud felt his body relax. Maybe everything will work out all right after all, he thought. He looked at Kimberly. Although her golden hair was neatly pulled back into the customary pony tail and her face appeared fresh and clean, her yellow Black Rock Resort sweatshirt showed smudges of dirt intermingled with large dark-red, nearly black splotches.

"Looks like I finally put my mark on you," Hud said.

"What?" She looked down, then smiled.

"What time is it?" he asked.

"It's Sunday, eleven in the morning."

"You've been here *all night?*" he asked.

"Finally *my* chance to wear the shining armor," she said.

"Are you okay?" he asked.

"I'm filthy," she replied with a gesture to her clothing. "But I'm okay. In fact...I feel better than I have in *years*." Her smile broadened, accentuating her dimples, and her bright blue eyes beamed with an intensity Hud hadn't before seen.

"Yeah...you look good," he said. "What's wrong with *me?*"

"The doctors said you might have some trouble with that left shoulder," she said. "They had to fish a bunch of bone chips out. The bullet in your leg missed everything important. You're going to be fine. They recommended lots of rest, then exercise and fishing...and some therapy for the shoulder. I told them—"

"I'm sorry, Mrs. Bryant," said a middle-aged, matronly nurse as she burst into the room and crowded in to take Hud's temperature. "I think you'd better leave now. He needs his rest."

Hud replied quickly, "She's not—"

"I've been called *much* worse things," Kimberly interrupted, grinning devilishly. "She's right. You need rest, and so do I. Gibby said he'd be up this afternoon, and I'll be back tonight." She bent over and kissed Hud on the lips, gazed into his eyes for a moment, then left.

Hud drifted into sleep, awakened briefly to eat his lunch, and dropped off again. When he opened his eyes, it was three o'clock. He found Gibby sitting across the room in the visitor's chair watching him.

"Just thought I'd buzz up here and…see how you're doing," Gibby said as he approached the bed. "Just wanted you to know I…." The rotund old woodsman stood there for a moment, shifting his weight from one foot to the other, his red, weather beaten face radiating from behind his silver beard. "I…hope you're feeling better. S'pose you're wondering what all's happening back at the war."

The statement startled Hud. No, he thought, I'm not wondering, not wondering at all. In fact, I've hardly thought about it, prefer not to think about it. He realized that nearly every minute since he landed on the tiny airstrip had been focused on that conflict. Today, for the first time, he felt free of it, and he liked that freedom.

"Yeah, what's happening?" he found himself asking.

Gibby took off as if he'd heard the starter's gun at a track meet. "The Basher plane crash-landed on a lake up near the Falls," he began. "According to the news, three was killed and four was taken in by the cops. They're still draggin' for the bodies, but it looks like that goddamned Brother Vance must be one of the dead ones."

"The way to kill the dragon…" Hud said, "cut off its head."

Gibby seemed to ponder the statement for a moment, then give up and rattle on. "The deputies found two of the guys from that there speedboat alive. They was all banged up and huddled up, shivering and shaking when they was found. The FBI's got their heavy duty squads on all the fence lines of the camp. The Bashers shot a few times, but they ain't hit nothing. Will Mertens thinks they'll hold out a few days 'til they figger out their leaders cut and run out on 'em. The news this morning says the Feds think the Bashers was hauling stolen computer stuff and, get this—*drugs*—from Seattle to Minneapolis."

It surprised Hud that the good news seemed to touch no emotions. After all the tension, fears, and fights, he should have been elated. Instead, he found the news interesting, but no more stirring than a report on the garden club. Just sick of it all? he thought, or something much better to think about. Anyway, I'm out of the war now. Time to focus on the future.

"The deputies dragged up seven bodies in Wasikama so far," Gibby went on. "Guess that old chaplain was right. And Wolf called this morning. I asked him if he could look up Kimberly's ex-husband and back him against a wall. You know, maybe shake some money out of him. Maybe even get him to admit he was in cahoots with the Bashers." Gibby grinned. "Wouldn't that be the nuts? I can just see that wimp, with those big paws of Wolf's around his neck, reachin' for his wallet. Oh, and I almost forgot, Dick Orin has called for a grand jury investigation of Stein and two of the county commissioners. Don't matter whole lot, though. Stein's as good as dead in *this* election. That FBI guy, Watson, talked to Kimberly and me. Said he'll have to hear your version, too."

Hud smiled at the rapid fire report, but suddenly he felt tired. How, he wondered, do you tell such a good friend to go away, at least, to stop talking?

"And the best thing—" Gibby stopped. His eyes seemed fixed on Hud's face. "Aw shit, Hud. Here you are, barely back from the dead, and I'm running off at the mouth like a school kid. He moved over to the bedside. "Thanks, Hud, for all you did. I—I'll find a way to pay you back. I'll get out of here and let you sleep."

Through the next two days, Hud awakened for trips to the bathroom, the nurses' ministrations, a check by the doctor, and chats with Kimberly or Gibby and Sarah. In each case, he lasted no more than an hour before dropping off again. His left leg seemed stronger with each toilet trip, but the episodes posed an aggravating challenge. With one weak leg, one arm bound tightly to his body by a sling, and the movements of the other arm hampered by the plastic tubing that, in turn, connected to his "shadow," the tall spindle on casters that held his I.V. bag, things were awkward. He vowed to shed the restrictions as soon as possible. During the brief periods when he lay awake, he concentrated on the future.

• • •

The pilot of the crippled de Havilland Beaver fought desperately to gain altitude through the rain and lightning, but after ten miles of skimming the tree tops, Brother Vance knew they were going down. He ordered Sergeant Donald out of the seat nearest the left rear door, slung his tiny Czechoslovakian Skorpion submachine gun securely onto his back, checked to see that his wallet pocket was buttoned, and strapped himself in.

With one float missing, the overloaded plane caught its left wingtip in the water and flipped, as he knew it would, into a diagonal cartwheel. When the Beaver pancaked onto its back, the jarring, sudden stop wrenched at every joint in his strong body. Without pausing for even a glance at his subordinates, Vance placed a hand below his head to break the short fall to the ceiling of the plane, then released the seatbelt. Scrambling to right himself, he pushed open the door and slipped into the chilling water. He swam the fifty yards to shore and disappeared into the woods before the second survivor even cleared the sinking aircraft.

He struck out on the run south toward Highway 53, crashing through the underbrush, driven by a single thought, to put distance between the crash site and himself. After a few hundred yards, his systematic mind, pushing all pain aside and ignoring fatigue, began setting his goals in order, thereby eliminating that split second of confusion somewhere along the way that could be his downfall.

Vance estimated he'd run three miles when he heard the roar of a semi-truck, accompanied by the sizzle of the eighteen wheels on the rain-drenched pavement. First goal accomplished, he thought. He stopped in a small clearing hidden from the highway by a cluster of fir trees. Removing the Skorpion from his back, he stripped off his dripping-wet black suitcoat and carefully wrapped the weapon in it. Then, with the bundle cradled in his left arm, he made his way out to the highway. He began to feel the effects of the crash and the long run as he raised a hand toward an oncoming pick-up truck. But he focused instead on the north woods spirit of brotherhood, that willingness to help one another, as the vehicle approached. As if on command, it slowed and stopped.

After Vance's brief explanation that his car had broken down several miles back and that he had to catch a plane in twenty minutes, the grizzled, old driver seemed to accept the ensuing silence. He pressed hard on the accelerator, and minutes later he dropped his passenger at the International Falls Airport Terminal.

By the time darkness had begun to mix with the steady rain, Vance had rented a car under an assumed name and driven into town, where he bought two pairs of khaki trousers, along with shirts, socks, sneakers, a nylon jacket, and a duffle bag. He changed into one of the new outfits. As he stepped from the store, the sound of sirens brought him up short. He nodded his head approvingly as a parade of flashing lights passed by. In addition to two sheriff's vehicles, each towing a boat, there was a firetruck and a paramedic van. Good, he thought, they're just starting out to the crash, and here I stand in new, dry clothing. Double good—this is a different county. Those deputies might not even know whose plane it was.

He carefully buried the black suit in a back alley dumpster before checking in at a small, nondescript motel. Later, as he relaxed over his meal in a nearby Thai restaurant, Vance sorted out what he thought of as his second- and third-stage objectives. The thought of his top priority, Hudson Bryant III, burned within him like the blue flame of an acetylene torch. If Father Jeranko had let him take Bryant out earlier, things would have been different. But now, he thought, or at least until I report to Father Jeranko at the cabin in Montana, all decisions are mine. For that matter, so is Hudson Bryant.

For many years, Vance recalled, he had served as Jeranko's front man in high-risk endeavors. Some of them had gone sour because of circumstances beyond their control. But never had they lost an operation because of one man, never. He felt the rhythmic throbbing in his temples increase. In fact, no one man had ever beaten him at anything. Yes, he thought, Bryant will be the ultimate loser, and soon. Then, he'd simply change rental cars and meet Father Jeranko in Montana. They had money. They'd start again.

• • •

"Oh, Mr. Bryant," the elderly information clerk in the blue smock called, as an aide wheeled Hud toward the hospital door. "You had another phone call this morning checking to see how you were. I'm sorry, I didn't get his name. I told him we were discharging you this morning, and he said not to bother putting him through to your room. He'd see you soon."

The thought of the calls warmed Hud almost as much as the bright sunshine when the aide stopped the wheelchair at Kimberly's truck. As he pushed himself gingerly up onto the truck seat with his single crutch, he smiled at his driver. With her long, flowing golden hair, her loose but tantalizing yellow shirt-dress and matching heels, he had never seen her more beautiful. But there sat a perfectly coiffed, magnificently dressed princess on the dirty, stained bench seat that had a broken coil spring protruding through it. Better the vehicle were a pumpkin, Hud thought. Got to do something about this truck.

Kimberly smiled at him. "Come on. Let's go home." She drove out of the parking lot and soon had them headed south out of International Falls on Highway 53.

"David Engstrom called from somewhere out of state," she said. "Couldn't say where. He and Julie are together. They're fine. At the end of our conversation, David asked me if you were serious about that job offer. Were you?"

"Never been more serious," Hud said. "I could tell in ten minutes that David was a real find. And if he and Julie have a good relationship, then she's got to be a winner, too."

"But what would you have them do? Move them to California?"

"Could do that," he replied, "but I'm thinking of something around here."

"Around here?" she asked. "You thinking of staying?"

"Definitely," he said. "I love this country…and I want to marry you."

Her slender face beamed, and she reached for his hand. "I love you, Hud…and I think I'll want to marry you." Then she sobered. "But I'll need time together to decide that. Does that upset you?"

"Not even a little," he said with a grin, "I intend to wipe out that indecision in no time."

"Hud, we've talked about everything else," she said. "My problem of finances has only gotten bigger. With all the bad publicity, there'll be almost no business this year. Probably not much more next year." She glanced over at him. "You know I have a problem with your paying my bills. But if I know you, you didn't spend all of the last two-and-a-half days sleeping. Am I right?"

Hud grinned. "You're right. I do have some ideas."

"And?"

"Really very simple. First, I find a strong Minneapolis attorney. The four of us file one whiz-bang civil suit against the Bashers—right away. We take what few guests we get the next two seasons and spoil the hell out of them. We devise ways to counteract the bad publicity and then hit the winter sports shows. In short, we really focus on the *third* season…because it might take that long to bury the bad rap."

"Wow! You really *weren't* sleeping all that time, were you?" Then, looking puzzled, she said, "I can't disagree with any of your strategy, but there is something you didn't cover…and one step that makes no sense to me."

"Okay," he said, "shoot."

Kimberly eased the old truck around the familiar, long, sweeping curve that headed the two-lane highway southeast. "My old problem is still there, only now it's been compounded," she said. "How do I make payments and survive with little or no revenue for *two years?*"

"Oh, that's simple, too," he replied with a grin. "I figured that out last week. I ante up to match what you paid for the resort, and we become fifty-fifty partners. That's operating capital to make payments, expand, remodel, and survive on. If we get married, it won't matter. All of our assets will go into joint tenancy. Should we, heaven forbid, not marry, we carry on as a partnership, with you as the managing partner."

"You make it sound so easy," she said with a laugh. "What if, heaven forbid, we don't marry, and I decide I want to sell out? We've now invested nearly twice what the resort is worth."

"Oh, that's simple, too," said Hud. "You walk with the revenue from the sale, and I have an incredible tax write-off."

"I—I'll try to live with that," she said. "But what's with the lawsuit against the Bashers?"

"That's the other part of my plan," he said. "One way or another I intend to buy that camp from them."

"You *what?*" She turned quickly to look at him, jerking the wheel as she turned, then too quickly correcting the move.

"I figure," Hud continued, "with all the legal problems they're facing, they'll need to free up cash in a hurry. With our suit hanging over them, we negotiate from strength. Sell to us—we drop the lawsuit."

Kimberly's eyes opened wide. "Hud—what would you want with that whole big camp?"

"Not sure," he replied with a grin, "but you'll never have to worry about bad neighbors again." He paused and glanced over at her. She was focused on her driving, but her relaxed smile told Hud he'd encounter no argument on the subject. "You know," he continued, "that big camp is configured all wrong, and it's too far away to be a good addition to the resort. But we could set up a nonprofit foundation, remodel the camp, and open it up to youth groups, maybe even the aged and the disabled."

"Oh, my God! You're really *serious,* aren't you?"

"Absolutely," he said. "You know, I've had a gaping hole in my life the last few years. I've been lucky, made some money. But unless you're into impressing people or buying power, it just accumulates and really doesn't do anyone much good. I'm *not* into either one."

"I know," she said. "I wouldn't be here if you were."

They rolled on in silence for a few moments. Hud absorbed the strange panorama they had entered, an area of low, flat marsh lands. From the swamp grass and water protruded the skeletons of drowned pine trees, their stark, bony arms seeming to beg too late for help. One of the few ugly sides of nature, it always made Hud feel a little sad. He forced his mind to refocus.

"Of course," he went on, "we'd need a good team of managers. I have a young Minneapolis man and his wife in mind for that."

Kimberly drove on quietly for some time, her smile seemingly frozen, and tears trickling down her cheeks. Finally, she said, "Hudson Wade Bryant III, I'm going to lock you up before someone else spots you."

"Please do. Really neat, don't you think?" he said. "Helping all those people escape their prisons for a couple of weeks each year? I love that, but I have to confess, the irony of this idea makes even my liver smile.

They bashed you all over the place, trying to get the property away from you, and in the end....And, I have to admit, there's a little revenge—"

Hud's pronouncement was cut off by the sudden, horrendous clatter of hail striking the cab and box of the pick-up. Two of the stones somehow crashed in through the rear window and out through the windshield.

"What the—" Despite the clear, blue sky and the bright sunshine, Hud instinctively looked back, expecting to see small, white pellets bouncing about in the truck box. Instead, he saw a black car about thirty yards back. The driver was leaning out his window and pointing something at them. Hud forced his attention from the object to the driver. What he saw drove a cold, leaden lump into his gut.

"Hud!" Kimberly shrieked. "What's happening?"

"It's *Vance*—he's *not* dead!" he shouted. The freezing fear of helplessness encircled him with its tentacles, threatening to extinguish his courage with one mighty constriction. If only we had a gun with us, he thought. If only I were driving. It's got to be Kimberly's show. Will she lose it?

"What'll I do, Hud? What'll I do?"

"Listen to me, Kimberly," he said. "Don't think. Don't talk. Just listen and do what I say. We've got to end this quick. Even driving with one hand and trying to shoot with the other, he'll rip us apart with that automatic. Now, step on it. Get us up to eighty—no—seventy." He looked over briefly. Her lower jaw jutted forward and she had a firm bite on her upper lip. "Get mad, Kimberly, get mad!" he shouted. "Get damned mad!" He looked back again.

Vance reached out again and fired two short bursts that sprayed wildly at the pick-up, punching holes in the tailgate.

"That weapon really kicks. He's having trouble doing it left-handed," Hud said. "Now listen, Kimberly. He's after me, so let's help him. He'll like this because he'll get to shoot right-handed. If we pull this off, we'll get him...and maybe live through it. If we don't...we're dead. Ready?" He reached across with his free arm and patted her thigh.

"R-Ready."

"Remember, don't *think*. Just *do*. I'm going to have you hit him and try to roll him. After you do, I can't help much. It'll be up to you. Okay, nobody coming from the other way. Pull over in the left lane, then weave a little, like you don't know what to do." Hud watched for Vance's reaction.

The Basher leader began to reach out with the weapon again. Then suddenly, he retracted the automatic, swerved to the right, and began to accelerate.

"Good," said Hud. "He's buying it, Kimberly. Now get ready to hit the brakes, but don't skid. Then, off the brakes, turn right, and ram him. Then left and brakes again. I love you."

In the truck's right side mirror, Hud watched the black car gain steadily. He could see Vance shift the vicious weapon to his right hand. Then, with a sudden burst of speed, Vance drew up nearly even with Hud.

"Brakes!" Hud shouted. He pressed his body back hard in the seat.

Kimberly braked hard. The black car shot on past. Hud could see the muzzle flashes, but only two of the deadly bullets penetrated his window, both well in front of him.

"Turn right!"

Kimberly let up on the brakes and turned hard to the right. *Poom!* The truck shuddered as her right front corner caught Vance's rear left fender, turning him broadside before them. They could hear the screech of four tires traveling sideways down the pavement at seventy miles per hour, even over the loud roar of the tired, old engine.

"Left! Brakes!" Hud shouted.

Kimberly corrected to the left. Then, just as she locked the brakes, Vance's car rolled once…then again. On the third tumble, it catapulted high into the air, continuing its lazy roll as if in slow motion. The truck began to skid to its left.

"Back off the brakes! Don't lose it!"

She regained control just as their adversary dropped from ten feet in the air to the concrete, crunching upside-down and reducing the stream-lined auto to a rectangular hulk of crushed steel. Debris shattered the windshield of the pick-up, all but blinding them. The carcass of the black auto continued to bounce down the roadway, as though its course were controlled by huge magnets. Although Kimberly had cut their speed in half, they quickly closed on the bouncing bundle of scrap metal and were but a second from hitting it again.

"Ditch!"

Kimberly jerked the wheel hard to the right. The truck rumbled across the gravel shoulder and became airborne. Hud leaned forward, braced his hands on the dash, and glanced at Kimberly. She sat up tall and straight in her seat. With her pretty little jaw still locked forward, still biting her upper lip, she worked at guiding the old truck long after its fate had been turned over to gravity.

The thundering crash he expected never came—only a gigantic *Whoosh!* as the truck landed in four feet of water. The seatbelts strained at their moorings, bit hard into flesh, but held. Suddenly, it became quiet. Only the weak hissing of the punctured radiator and the ticking of the cooling engine could be heard. Hud looked over at Kimberly. She sat rigid, looking straight ahead, her ghostly white knuckles squeezing the wheel. Water seeped in beneath the doors.

"You okay?" he asked softly.

"Hud," she replied, still facing the millions of translucent crystals that had once been a windshield, "would you consider a partnership in an interior decorating company?"

"I think—it's time to look for another truck."

Epilogue

Hud finished checking the eight resort boats, then stood at the end of the long dock and looked out over the peaceful bay. Gentle, foot-high waves lapped at the end of the dock, struggling vainly to reach the toes of his boots. Because of the northern latitude, darkness was just setting in at ten o'clock. The soft afterglow of the sunset served as his cue to check the grounds, dock, and boats each evening. In a few days the first mosquitoes would hatch, and the pace of his pleasant evening round would become quicker. He heard the clomp of boots on the dock and turned to see David Engstrom approaching.

"Julie and I got back with the lumber from Mallard, cleaned up, and came on over. Kimberly sent me down to get you," David said. "And in two minutes, she'll be sending Julie down to get *both* of us. Sarah has everything for our celebration about ready." The two men stood for several moments in silence before David spoke again. "Hard to believe, isn't it? A year since the colony folded."

"Yeah," Hud replied, "but it's been a good year, right?" He turned to see a tear trickling down the cheek of his slender partner. "Still gets you, huh?"

"Shouldn't. Doesn't most of the time," David said, quickly brushing away the tear. "But, for some reason the evenings like this...when it gets dark, and he's still out there...still out there somewhere."

"Wish I had some magic for you, Partner," Hud said. "All I can say is, he's at peace, no more troubles. Something else. It was his sacrifice—and your search for him—that helped us bring the Bashers down. I wish we could find him so I could tell him that. I never met him, but I think he'd like knowing it."

David looked upward toward the first of the evening stars. "I—I guess he knows. You all done here on the dock?"

"Yeah. We'd better get up there," Hud said.

As they trudged up the hill to the lodge room, they discussed the remodeling project at the new Sunset Hill Camp. In the two months since Hud had taken possession of the peninsula, he had worked with David and Julie under Gibby's supervision to convert one barracks building, as Gibby had said, "from a goddamn rats' nest to a downright friendly recreation center."

"You know, Hud, we'll have the rec center done in a couple of weeks. I—I'd still like to start booking campers in for July and August," David said. "Just small groups, maybe twenty-five...or fifty. A chance to try our wings."

"Love your enthusiasm," Hud said with a laugh, "but I have a little trouble with your guilt."

David stopped Hud and looked into his eyes. "Guilt?"

"Guilt," Hud repeated. "I'm paying you and Julie as managers. So far, you've been working your tails off, but it's been all grunt work, digging in the ground and pounding nails. I think you see all this money going out—none coming in. You feel a little guilty...right?"

David smiled sheepishly. "You can see right through skin and bone. How'd you get so smart?"

"By surrounding myself with good people like you," Hud replied with a grin. "Now, I *won't* back down on certain things. I want the camp done—finished—the wood paneling in all the rooms, the recreation gear tested, and the staff well-trained before we accept one camper on the premises. But—I *do* know of a group of forty inner-city kids that would like to come the first week of August. They'll be wild, damned hard to manage—a real test. Want to tackle it?" Hud turned and continued on up the hill. David followed silently. Hud knew the signs of David's cal-culating mind.

"We can do that!" David blurted out as they reached the steps to the lodge room. "We can handle them. We'll be ready."

"You're on," said Hud. "I'll call Minneapolis in the morning. Now, you go on in. I'll be right there." As David scampered up the steps to the lodge room, Hud turned for one last scan of the resort. Things looked good. Laughter, the language of good times, rode the beams of light from the windows of six of the eight cozy cottages. How wrong I was, he thought. I predicted only two occupancies per week for the sea-son. We've already beat that for the first three weeks, and the rest of the season is filling in quickly. I knew those sport shows would help, but I didn't expect this. He sensed a movement on the steps behind him.

"Great, isn't it?" Kimberly said, standing on the step above and behind Hud. She wrapped her arms around him from behind and rested her chin on his shoulder, her head snuggled against his.

"Yeah, even the pesky bears. I love 'em. But I sure hope those new chains on the lids keep them out of the garbage cans tonight. Really don't like picking up garbage before breakfast every morning…gives me morning sickness."

"I can do the morning clean-up," Kimberly said. "I used to."

"Uh, uh," replied Hud, turning to kiss her cheek. "It's the only sacri-fice I've made for this marriage. Anyway, I fixed the problem…I think."

Tugging at Hud's arm, Kimberly said, "Come on, now. Will and Roberta Mertens are here. It's party time." She took Hud's hand and led him through the lodge room. Her fresh pony tail swished from side to side, its rhythm matching the provocative swaying of her yellow shirt dress as she walked. Hud couldn't imagine her appeal ever fading. He wanted to change direction, to pull her away from the mix of voices in the house, to find privacy for love making or even just talking. But Kim-berly persisted, leading him around the corner and into the kitchen.

A tantalizing blend of spicy smells wafted through the colorful streamers and balloons that decorated the kitchen and living room. The old chrome-legged kitchen table had been extended and covered with one of Sarah's fine white linen tablecloths. On the table, a large floral centerpiece and two tall, yellow candles were surrounded by large plates of marinated shrimp, oysters Rockefeller, stuffed mushrooms, rumaki, and spicy potato skins.

The sounds of an animated discussion came from a cluster of people in the living room. Gibby and the portly Deputy Mertens, both dressed in their newest plaid-flannel shirts, were either arguing calmly or agreeing vociferously. Hud wasn't sure. David, along with Will's pleasant, shy wife Roberta, provided the obligatory audience. Julie Engstrom and Sarah worked at the counter in the kitchen.

"Here you are, Mr. and Mrs. Bryant," Julie said with a smile, her brown eyes flashing, as she turned to Hud and Kimberly with glasses of champagne. She wore a powder blue skirt and a simple, but flattering white cotton blouse. Her medium-length black hair glistened, even in the limited light. "We start with this. Then you can change to what ever you want." More than what she said, the way in which she said things reinforced Hud's perception of the bond that was growing between the Engstroms and themselves. Julie scooted back to the counter.

Hud and Kimberly stood for a while, sipping their champagne and taking in the warm, if unusual scene.

"Don't laugh," Kimberly said. "The streamers were Gibby's idea. When I insisted on having the party here, he couldn't say it, but he immediately locked onto the problem of the God-awful carpeting and furniture. You have to admit, the circus banners do distract."

"Are you embarrassed?" Hud asked. "You know I've wanted to replace all this junk."

"Gibby was afraid I'd be embarrassed. But I'm not, not at all," she said, squeezing his arm. "In fact, I find it kind of neat—amusing. "

Sarah ushered them into the living room, where she made a fuss of refilling the champagne glasses. At her cue, a sequence of ad lib toasts giving thanks and focusing on a brighter future were offered. Will Mertens gave his thanks for the housecleaning in the sheriff's office. David expressed the Engstroms' gratitude for their exciting career opportunity and their "new" family. Gibby heaped layer after layer of praise upon Hud, "Ain't nobody else in the world got a friend like this guy." Hud thanked the entire group for being what they were, "real people."

"Now, Hud," said Sarah, "your darling wife and I have a little bet going on this." She glanced about smugly, then continued, "And for the record, I bet on *you*. The question....What is the significance of the day?"

Hud thought for a moment. "This is June eighth. Two months ago, we got title to the peninsula. About four months ago, David and Julie joined us. Twelve months ago, Brother Vance descended to that other place and the Bashers surrendered." Then he smiled and winked at Kimberly. "Oh, yeah, eight months and seven hours ago, I married the most wonderful woman in the world. He reached out, encircled Kimberly's waist, and pulled her to him. "And despite her lack of faith in me, I have to tell you, the eight-month anniversary far outranks the others."

Amid cheers and asides, Kimberly looked up at Hud and said, "Well done." She stretched up and kissed him. "Have you ever considered politics?"

The group fragmented for a time while filling their plates at the table. Hud loaded up with rumaki, marinated shrimp, and potato skins. Topping off his drink, he found a seat next to Will and attacked the tempting hors d'oeuvres.

"You know, Hud?" the convivial, pot-bellied man said between mouthfuls, "We cleared up this mess on the bay, and we cleared up the dirty politics in the county. But, thanks to the Thirteen colonies—uh, twelve colonies—we've made some headway on the mess in Washington, too. Hey, we got seventeen independents elected to Congress last

November. I hope that's enough to wash away the 'what's the use' attitude of the voters."

"Don't know that that's happened yet," Hud said, "but it's a good start. I still don't hear the politicians squealing on one another, so the unwritten agreement, the no-tell rule still prevails."

"And there's another problem that hasn't been resolved," said David. "They still haven't caught up with Number One, Father Jeranko. Hud, where do *you* think he is?"

"They missed him in northern Montana. My guess is Canada."

"But just the same, things turned out pretty damned good," said Gibby. "Best of all...Hud ends up owning the camp. That there's *real* justice." He turned a serious face to Hud. "You got any customers lined up for the camp yet?"

"As a matter of fact, yes," replied Hud. He glanced at Kimberly. She smirked and turned away. "Thinking about leasing the camp...to a large church group from Minneapolis."